Samuel Pepys and the Stolen Diary

Martin Lee is the author of the Inspector Danilov historical crime thrillers set in Shanghai. This is his first foray into the Restoration in the company of Samuel Pepys as an Investigator. The next book in the series will be published in 2017.

Samuel Pepys and the Stolen Diary

M J Lee

To my incredibly patient wife, Sharon, who managed to survive this recreation of the Restoration, and to my daughter, Eve, who made this book both possible and impossible.

Mr. Pepys and Will Hewer thank you from the bottom of their hearts.

First published by Endeavour Press Ltd in 2016.

Table of Contents

Chapter 1 1
Chapter 2 6
Chapter 3 10
Chapter 4 13
Chapter 5 21
Chapter 6 25
Chapter 7 38
Chapter 8 41
Chapter 9 51
Chapter 10..58
Chapter 11..62
Chapter 12..69
Chapter 13..76
Chapter 14..80
Chapter 15..88
Chapter 16..91
Chapter 17 104
Chapter 18 114
Chapter 19 121
Chapter 20 125
Chapter 21 135
Chapter 22 138
Chapter 23 141
Chapter 24 151
Chapter 25 159

Chapter 26 165
Chapter 27 170
Chapter 28 183
Chapter 29 187
Chapter 30 192
Chapter 31 199
Chapter 32 207
Chapter 33 211
Chapter 34 216
Chapter 35 226
Chapter 36 229
Chapter 37 239
Chapter 38 242
Chapter 39 250
Chapter 40 252
Chapter 41 259
Chapter 42 262
Chapter 43 266
Chapter 44 269
Chapter 45 273
Chapter 46 278
Chapter 47 281
Chapter 48 285
Chapter 49 289
Chapter 50 291
Chapter 51 299
Chapter 52 302

Chapter 53 307
Chapter 54 312
Chapter 55 322
Chapter 56 327
Chapter 57 332
Chapter 58 336
Chapter 59 339
Chapter 60 342
Chapter 61 348
Chapter 62 356
Chapter 63 363

Chapter 1

I waited and listened.

The house creaked and sighed like an old man getting out of bed in the middle of the night to use the pot. The clock in the hall swung the hours. The wind whistled its song through the gaps behind the panelling. To my right, the low, rhythmic sound of snoring.

Somewhere, off in the distance, a dog barked at the moon.

I stood there in the deepest shadows, where the dying glow from the fire hugged the rays of the flickering candle. I stood and listened and waited. In my line of work, being patient can mean the difference between dangling a barmaid off the end of my knee, or dangling at Tyburn off the end of a rope.

I prefer the former.

It was time to move. I padded silently across the hallway to the bottom of the stairs. As I passed the open door to the kitchen, I glanced inside at the maid. She lay sprawled across the table, her head resting on an outstretched arm, snoring gently. A curious spaniel lifted its head from the basket and saw me. I stopped and stood still. Eventually, it grew bored of seeing nothing and lowered its head back down, returning to its dreams of chasing rabbits or rats.

Everybody tells me I'm small for my age but as nobody knows what age I am, I wonder how they are able to hazard this judgement. Being small does give me an advantage in my profession, though. Most windows, chimneys or tight spaces hold no terrors for me. My ability to gain entry to even the most secure place has won me a certain notoriety. 'If you want a job done well, Jack Turner's your man,' they would say. Well, I know I'm good at what I do. A thief for hire, that's what I am. The best in the city, I would say. But then I would, wouldn't I?

My employer this time had given very specific instructions. 'Go up the grand staircase, through the dining room, and ascend to the second floor. On the right, you will see a closet. Bring me a diary that is lying on the table. Mind the third step, it creaks. And mind you steal nothing else, just the book.'

Yes, sir, no sir, three bags full, sir. Teaching me how to do my job. You don't hire a carpenter and then tell him how to turn wood. Well, you don't tell Jack Turner anyway.

I climbed the stairs, avoiding the third step as I had been told. As I reached the dining room, there was an almighty crash of gears and whirring of cogs, followed by the deep throb of a gong reverberating through the house. Well, I near jumped out of my breeches at the sound, I'll tell you. Then the gong sounded again, echoing through the house and off the panelled walls. Three. Four. Five. I stood still and waited. Six. Seven. Eight. Was this never going to bloody end? Nine. Ten. Eleven.

Silence, like waiting for the next shoe to drop.

I half expected the maid to wake up and start cleaning. But she didn't. All I heard was the groans of the house as it swayed in the breeze and the gentle snores of the maid and the dog.

I looked down at my stockinged feet. The big toe poked through on my left foot. I would have to get them darned by Mother Spring after this job. Once I'd been paid, of course.

Got to get a move on, Jack me lad. Time doesn't wait for

thieves.

I climbed the stairs and saw the closet on my right. A shaft of warm light beamed through the milky windows as the moon poked its head from behind the clouds. At least I wouldn't have to light another candle now.

The man's closet was where my employer said it would be. A small room painted in a lively shade of purple. Why would any man choose such a colour? The closet was neat and tidy, an ordered mind this man. A day bed stood in the corner, a table, a globe of the world, two tall candle stands and a bookcase filled the room. The bookcase was fronted with fine glass. Strange, why would anybody shelter their books behind expensive glass?

Then I saw what I had come for. As my employer had said, a book lay open on the table. Next to it was a quill, its point freshly cut and sharpened, the end still blue with dried ink.

I picked the book up. At the top of the page, I recognised a date. 31st May 1669. Yesterday, I think, but one day is much like another to me.

After the date, curious shapes ran across the page. Neat and tidy, just like the room, each shape exactly the same size. I'd never seen writing like it before. Not that I can read a lot mind you, but I'm proud to say that I can sign my own name and read a few words in a ledger. Learnt it myself I did, from Mr Isaac on Half Moon Alley.

No matter. This book had nothing to do with me. I slipped it into the pocket of my coat. A special pocket, perfect for small jobs like this. This was when I should have left the way I came. Those were my employer's instructions. 'Take the book and leave. Do not take anything else, understand?'

But how could I resist the temptation of an empty house

with a sleeping maid and a snoring dog? It was like Eve and the apple to me. There to be taken.

I walked onto the landing again. Still as the plague.

Opposite was a bedroom with a strong aroma of roses and cloves. Whoever she was, this woman enjoyed her fine scents. I'm sure she wouldn't miss a few trinkets. On her dressing table was an oak box with an embroidered cover. Ye gods, these people make it easy for thieves. May as well place a bill outside the front door, advertising the presence of an easy mark.

I opened the box. Inside were a few strings of pearls, some bangles and one nice bauble; a locket surrounded by what looked like diamonds. Probably cut glass, though. You can't trust anybody or anything these days. I held it up to the flickering light of the candle in the sconce on the wall. A pretty little thing. Well, I wouldn't be greedy, already being paid for the job as it were. It should fetch a silver penny or two at Mr Isaac's.

Outside, the wheels of a carriage trundled to a creaking stop across the cobbles of the lane. I crossed over to the window and onto a balcony that looked over the street. Muffled voices and laughter came from the carriage at the end of the yard. The doors began to open.

It was time for me to bid farewell to my woman's closet. I stuffed the locket into the pocket next to the book and hurried downstairs to the dining room. The voices were louder now, approaching the house. The dog ran across the hallway below me and began to scratch and whine at the door, followed by the maid, rushing out to open it for her master.

I took my chance and raced down the stairs and across the hallway to the window where I had entered. I half expected shouts of 'Who are you?' or 'Stop thief.' But there were none.

I climbed through the window and crept away into Seething Lane. A black cat crossed my path as I left the house. More good luck was sure to come Jack Turner's way once I had delivered the book to my employer. Maybe the barmaid at the King's Head would let me play beneath her petticoats? The likelihood would be as sure as the King's touch, once she heard the jingle of coins in my pocket.

Chapter 2

Pepys didn't know how long he had been sitting there in his closet staring at the empty desk. Sometimes, as the candle flickered and the joints of the old house creaked, he imagined that the diary was still there, open at the last entry.

But it wasn't.

The new goose quill still lay on the desk, it's nib scarcely christened. As was the pot of ink bought from Jones the Bookseller earlier that month. But, in between the two, lay a space where the diary should have rested, waiting to receive his day.

He had come back that evening from the theatre with Elizabeth. A boring play, even if the actress in it, Moll Davies, was a pretty sight with even prettier ankles. They had dined quickly on some leftovers before Pepys had said his goodnights and retired to his closet.

He remembered climbing the stairs with his candle, strolling into his room and sitting down at the desk. It had been a good day. A day when the world and everybody in it had behaved well. A day full of compliments and those small favours that make life so enjoyable.

He had kicked off his shoes and wriggled his toes inside their cotton stockings. The toes were stiffer now, a consequence of age and good living. The days of rushing from coffee house to coffee house, drinking in the newest wines and the latest gossip, were behind him. These days, life was more sedate; a short visit to the Navy Board to assess the work of the clerks, a meeting or two, lunch at one of the Inns near the New Exchequer, a visit to the Theatre followed by music with friends.

He remembered reaching across to dip the goose quill in the ink, but the diary wasn't there.

Of course, he had searched the closet in that frantic way that everyone does when they realise that something valuable is missing.

Had it slipped under his table? Had he put it on the bookshelf? Had a servant placed it beneath the covers of his couch for some unknown reason? Had Elizabeth removed it? Had someone put it behind the globe that stood in the corner?

He had searched everywhere. Twice.

And then searched again.

No diary. Not a word of it, anywhere in the room.

Elizabeth would not have touched it. The servants would not dare. Nobody was allowed into his closet. They understood it was his refuge, where his books and his world were ordered and in harmony.

He had questioned them anyway, waking the servants in their truckle beds in the kitchen.

Had anybody seen his book? Had anybody moved it?

They all shook their heads. Jane even having the temerity to ask him, 'Where did you put it, Mr Pepys?' in that Cambridge accent that still clung to her like a stook of corn.

For a moment, he wondered if she had ever read the book but then dismissed the idea as quickly as he had thought of it.

Jane wasn't interested in books. The limit of her world was the four walls of their house. He had always been careful, though, writing every entry in the shorthand he had learnt at Magdalen all those years ago. Jane and the rest of the servants would be unable to read it. And, more importantly, neither would his wife, Elizabeth. He shuddered to think what she would do if she knew the extent of his affairs.

After interviewing the servants, he had rushed across the yard to the Navy Office, stammering an excuse to the drowsy night watchman; 'Left my favourite walking stick in the office'. Beneath the minutes of the Tangier Committee of 1665 and 1666 were the five other diaries for previous years, still nestling in their linen wrapping. At least, they were safe.

But where was the latest diary?

He had sat in his chair facing the empty space for the whole night. Had it been mislaid?

No, he had seen it that morning, lying on the desk as he dressed, the half-finished entry for the 31st May still fresh on the page and in his mind.

A short entry, describing the current state of his finances, his fruitful meeting with the Duke of York, and a pleasant visit to Mrs Mitchell. Shame her mother had been around, he would have enjoyed a kiss from those plump lips. He had stopped writing as his eyes were tired, meaning to finish his entry later.

Where was it?

He had searched once again as dawn came up, fighting its way through the smoke of an early June day in London.

Nothing.

Gradually, he realised that the diary must have been stolen. The realisation came upon him slowly, reluctantly. But it was the only possible reason for its disappearance. How and by whom he did not know, but he was determined to find out. Before its secrets were revealed to the world.

The house had begun to stir. The servants swept the floor with their besoms. Jane bustled around the kitchen, her voice softly singing a hymn from her youth in the Fens. Even the dog joined in the morning activity, scratching annoyingly on his wife's door across the corridor, pleading to be allowed in.

It was then he heard the scream.

Chapter 3

The door to his closet banged open and in the entrance stood a tiny, beautifully formed woman, her pallid face framed by brown ringlets, her lips and chin clenched and the nostrils of her retroussé nose flaring. God how he loved to kiss that nose, feeling its softness against his fleshy lips.

'Where is my locket?' her voice had the slight hint of French musicality from her youth which she had never lost.

Her temper was as French as her ancestry. He expected something to be thrown at his head, a china cup or a potpourri. Something small that she could hold easily in her delicate fingers but still aim at his head.

Instead, she folded her arms across her chest, waiting for his answer. She was still as beautiful as when he had married her twelve years ago. No. She was more beautiful, age giving her face more character and strength.

'What locket is that, my dear?' he said in a voice as calm and collected as he was able.

'Samuel Pepys, you know which locket I mean.'

Pepys opened his arms, hoping to soften her harsh tones with the calming oil of reasonableness. 'You have so many lockets, my dear, I couldn't possibly keep count of all of them.' He smiled at the end of his speech.

The pomander, when it came, narrowly missed his head, slamming into the wall behind him and shattering.

'Don't waste your words, Samuel Pepys, you know exactly which locket I mean.

He loved the way she said his name. Samuel. With the rise at the end and the long, drawn out song of the 'l'.

'You have me at a loss, my dear. Which locket?'

She crushed her arms tighter across her chest. 'The locket that Will gave me for the Christmas of '67.'

'Oh, that locket.' Pepys thought frantically. If he told her his diary was missing too, there would be cries of 'Voleur, voleur', and stamping of tiny feet. The servants would be in an uproar, the neighbours excited and the Constable called to arrest whoever had violated their house. He couldn't risk that. The loss of the diary must be kept secret until he had worked out where it had gone and who had stolen it. 'You should have told me it was that locket you were asking about.'

'Well?' She waited for her answer, her foot tapping on the wooden sill that guarded the entrance to his room.

'That locket? I took it to the jewellers for cleaning.' He didn't know why he said it, except that it was the first thing that popped into his head.

'Why didn't you tell me?' Her voice softened a little.

'It was meant to be a surprise. I know how much you loved it and thought it would be a treat for our anniversary.'

'Which jewellers?'

'The one at the New Exchange. They specialise in cleaning jewellery. They even work for Lady Castlemaine.'

'The King's whore? I want nothing to do with her.'

Pepys heard her say 'nozzing' in the delightful way she always did. A small smile touched the edge of his lips.

Her eyes narrowed suspiciously. 'You are not lying to me?'

Pepys shook his head.

'Samuel Pepys, have you given my locket to that whore?' 'Which whore is that, dear?'

'You know which whore I mean! Deborah Willetts, that viper who crept into our nest and played the cuckoo.'

Pepys smiled again. Elizabeth often mixed her metaphors both charmingly and alarmingly.

She saw the smile. 'Well?' 'Well, what, my dear?'

'Have you given my locket to the whore.' She enunciated each word slowly and painfully. 'If you have, I swear I will leave you, Samuel Pepys. You will never see me again.'

Pepys closed his eyes and leant forward as if bowing to his wife. 'I swear on my honour and all I hold dear, I did not give your locket to Deborah Willetts.'

Her voice softened once more. 'Why am I to believe you?'

'You don't need to believe me, dear. I went with Will to the jewellers. Ask him yourself?'

'I will, Samuel Pepys, I will. And if I find out that you are telling me lies again, we will be finished. I will leave you and never return. Do I make myself clear?'

'As a soul in heaven, my dear.'

Chapter 4

'You got my message, Will. It was a little presumptuous of me, but I'm glad you could come at such short notice.' Samuel Pepys clasped the hand of his friend. 'Do sit down, I've taken the liberty of ordering coffee.'

'Your message was quite short. And the lad who carried it even shorter. 'Urgent we meet. 10 o'clock, Bowman's Coffee House, St. Michael's Alley. Bring money.' With a message like that, who could resist.'

'Accept my apologies. I have been up all night thinking on this problem and only now have come to a course of action. You did bring the money?'

'All I had in the house. Twenty pounds with a few coppers.'

'That should be enough for what I have in mind.'

'And what's that?'

Pepys pulled his bottom lip using the index and forefinger of his right hand. It was an affectation he had adopted when he was thinking, often leading to bruising on the skin beneath the mouth. There was a large bruise beginning to form there now. 'Extraordinary times require extraordinary actions, Will.'

'Extraordinary?'

Before Pepys could answer, they were interrupted by the arrival of a steaming jug of coffee, two cups and a plate of cakes in the French style.

'Here you are, gentlemen, and would you be requiring anyfing else?' The owner of the coffee shop bent over and rubbed his hands in that particularly ingratiating manner adopted by landlords everywhere.

'No, that will be all,' said Pepys without looking up.

'Well, if you need anyfing else, Mr Pepys, sir, John Bowman is at your command, nuffing is too much trouble for Mr Pepys and his esteemed friend.' He nodded at Will Hewer.

'I'm sure you can be of assistance to us, Mr Bowman. We will call you across later if we may.'

'Just say the word and I will do my best to oblige you both.' With that, he bowed from the hips and edged away, an ingratiating smile etched on his lips.

'I remember when we had to beg to get a seat here, Samuel.'

'Times and people have changed, Will. And I see the same has happened to Mr Bowman.'

'What do you mean?'

'He's just lost a significant amount of money. Gambling in the markets, I expect. And he's just sold his house, moving back into his old place nearby. His wife is not at all pleased with him.'

Will turned to look at the proprietor of the coffee shop, who smiled back and rubbed his hands once more. 'How on earth can you know that? He merely asked us to call him if we needed anything.'

'Actually he said if we needed 'anyfing'. The accent is still remarkably strong.

'What accent?'

'If I'm not mistaken he was born just off the Strand, about three minutes walk from here.'

'You know all this from his voice?'

'You can find out a lot if you listen, Will. And observe. Try it sometime.'

Will poured the coffee into the cups. The luscious aroma filled the air between them. 'You haven't called me here so urgently just to give me advice on my sight.'

Pepys put his cup down on the table. 'The book was stolen last night.'

'What book?'

'My diary.'

'Diary?'

'You still have that surprising habit of repeating my last words as a question, Will.'

'Then please explain yourself better, so that I may ask more pertinent questions, with less surprise.'

Pepys looked down for a minute and then decided to confess all. 'I keep a diary of my thoughts and actions, things I see and hear and feel.'

'I know.'

'You know? How? I have only ever told two people about the diary.'

'Really Sam, for an intelligent and organised man, you can be wilfully stupid at times. Everybody knows you keep a diary.'

'Everybody?'

'Myself, your wife, the servants.'

'And I suppose the butcher, baker and candlestick maker are also aware of my inner feelings.'

'True, knowing your servants' proclivity for gossip.'

Pepys closed his eyes as he realised what he had thought a deep secret was known by everyone. 'I have been a wilfully blind man, haven't I, Will?'

'No more than usual, Sam. Look on the bright side, though. I don't think anybody has read your diary, but we are all aware you write one. For heaven's sake man, do you think you can retire to your closet every evening to write God knows what, and people would not be curious?'

'Of course, people would know I was writing. I suppose telling them I was merely copying the sermons from last week at St Olave's didn't wash?'

Will Hewer shook his head. 'Heading each entry with a date didn't help either.'

'At least, it's in a code.'

'Code? It's written in shorthand, Sam. Most Cambridge graduates can read Shelton's system. Even a few who graduated from Oxford may have the capacity.'

Pepys shook his head. 'I have been blind. And maybe a little stupid too.'

'Why?'

'The diary contains words that could be construed as possibly libellous, even treasonable, concerning the character of the king, or lack of character.'

'In these times, that could be dangerous, Sam.'

'Very dangerous.'

'So you think it has been stolen by the King's agents?'

'You will know soon enough once I am taken to the Tower.'

Will laughed. 'Aren't you being a little too dramatic, Sam? Taken to the Tower, indeed.'

'I have enemies, Will. After my defence of the Navy last year in Parliament.'

'I thought you spoke well.'

'So did others. Unfortunately, they would have preferred me to speak badly.'

'You do have a talent for making powerful enemies, Sam.'

Pepys squinted down his long nose. 'The further one rises the more one becomes a target for those with poisonous minds.'

'You have discounted the servants? Perhaps one of them has removed the book.'

'I questioned them this morning. None of them even

entered my closet yesterday. And besides, there was something else stolen. A piece of my wife's jewellery.'

'Just one piece?'

'A diamond locket, the piece you gave her for Christmas in '67. I tried to make her give it back but she set great store on it.'

'My gift…stolen?'

'She doesn't know it's missing yet. I told her that it was being cleaned.'

'Was nothing else missing?'

'Nothing.'

'Strange, just two pieces. Your diary and my gift.'

'I have been thinking on it for the whole night. Here's what I believe happened. Somebody was sent to steal the diary. He thought he would help himself to a little bauble at the same time.'

'What are you going to do?'

'Not me, Will, us. I have a plan.'

'As organised as ever, Sam. Out with it.'

'Be patient, Will. First, we must check the local thieves and their accomplices. Pray, call the landlord to us.'

'Mr Bowman.' Will waved his arm in the air until the owner noticed and came running across.

'Yes, gentlemen, how can I be of assistance?'

'You have lived in the City for many years, I believe, Mr Bowman.'

The landlord nodded his head until it almost fell from his shoulders. 'That is indeed true, Mr Pepys, sir. Born and bred just two minutes' walk from here.'

Pepys nodded at Will.

The landlord continued his speech. 'Was the servant for a merchant and then went into the coffee trade with Mr Rosee, in Cornhill. Luckily, the recent conflagration spared us and here we are, talking to the honourable gentlemen.'

'So you would be acquainted with the criminal fraternity in this neighbourhood?'

The landlord raised his hands in mock horror. 'I don't have nuffing to do wiv no criminals, Mr Pepys, you've got the wrong man, sir, yes you have. I'm an honest trader, me. None of that criminal stuff.'

'But speaking hypothetically, Mr Bowman, and understanding that you would never have any dealings with such gentlemen in your chosen profession as keeper of this august establishment,' Pepys drew breath, 'speaking hypothetically, how would one recover articles that may have been stolen or accidentally mislaid by persons unknown? For example, a piece of jewellery?'

The landlord smiled. 'Well, speaking hypofetical, Mr Pepys, occasionally one hears of goods that have fallen off the back of a cart, or been mislaid if you catch my drift.'

'And where might one find those articles, speaking hypothetically, of course.'

'Speaking hypofetical again, one might find them at Mr Isaac's, just after the sign of the Golden Horn in Half Moon Alley. But that is speaking hypofetical like, and the said Mr Isaac must never be aware that his name had ever been spoken out loud by any landlord or even coffee shop proprietor.'

'Snug's the word, Mr Bowman.'

'Snug's the word indeed, Mr Pepys, could I interest you in more coffee?'

'Thank you no, Mr Bowman, I've drunk enough to wake the dead of St Bart's. Oh, and Mr Bowman, I wouldn't take any more risks in the market, if I were you.'

'You are so right, Mr Pepys. Lost a packet on a ship of

Amber from Russia. Taken by pirates, she was. Had to sell the house and move back with the mother. The wife ain't best pleased, I'll tell you. Never again, Mr Pepys, as God is my judge, not worth the trouble.'

'I do agree, Mr Bowman.'

The landlord withdrew, the ever-present smile painted firmly on his lips.

Will leant across the table. 'How did you know?'

Pepys tapped the side of his nose. 'Just look and you will see, Will. People tell you everything.'

'But how did you know about his losses?'

Pepys waved his hands. 'Look around you, Will, where are the clocks that Mr Bowman was so proud of? Even the tall clock has vanished from the entrance. A coffee shop without clocks is a rare thing.'

'They could have been sent for repair?'

'Where are the rings that used to adorn Mr Bowman's fingers? And didn't you observe that our landlord is noticeably thinner? Now people in is profession only lose weight when they are worrying. What do people worry most about?'

Will shook his head.

'Money, the root of all evil and the cause of all worry.'

'But...how do you know he had moved back home and his wife was unhappy with him?

'Look at his feet, Will. He's still wearing his shoes from home and they are remarkably clean. Nobody could walk a long way through the streets of London without attracting dirt, mud and decadence. Thus, he hasn't come far.'

'And the unhappiness of the wife?'

'Simple. Look at the holes in the elbows of his shirt. His wife no longer cares to take care of him. And which wife would happily move back with her mother-in-law? Understand human nature, Will, and you will go far.'

'I prefer to enjoy life one step at a time.'

'I'm glad you said that, Will. For our next steps, we must pay a visit to Mr Isaac.'

And afterwards, we are summoned to meet the King.'

'We?'

'Yes, Will, the first person plural.'

'The King?'

'Our monarch, by the grace of God, King of England etcetera, etcetera. It will become very tiresome for me to keep defining words for you. So step lively, first our fence, Mr Isaac, and then our monarch, Charles Stuart.'

'Fence?'

'A receiver of stolen goods. One day, someone will compile a dictionary for you.'

With that, Pepys stood up, adjusted his periwig and left the table. He had only gone two steps when he suddenly turned back. 'Oh Will, don't forget to pay Mr Bowman before you leave. He does need the money.'

Chapter 5

'What have you got for me, Jack?'

'See, there you go again, Mr Isaac, nothing but business. No, 'hello, how are you, Jack?' or 'It looks like rain, don't it, Jack?'

'We don't have times for small talk in this humble hestablishment. Business is what we wants and business is what we does. So what do you have for me? Tempt your Uncle Isaac with a little trinket or three.'

Jack reached into the inside of his coat, making sure that Isaac didn't see the book hidden there. He pulled out the locket that he had stolen from the house. Before he could even hand it over, Isaac had snatched it from his grasp.

The old man held the piece up to the light from the single candle in the sconce on the wall. His watery eyes stared hard at it and he began to mutter to himself.

'You should get yourself another candle. The light's not good enough to see this locket.'

'Why would I be wasting money on candles? Candles cost threepence each. That's a lot of money, threepence. Can't go wasting threepence every day, can we?' He held the locket closer to the single candle whose flame began to flicker.

'It's a lovely piece, ain't it? Worth a lot, I reckon.'

The watery eyes turned and stared at Jack. 'You let me do the reckoning, Jack Turner, you concentrate on the stealing, that's what you is good at.'

Jack looked away. He hated Isaac's eyes, the way they chastised him without words. 'So what's it worth then?'

'It's not so good. Silver frame, not gold. The inset's

probably glass, not diamonds. The workmanship, a bit shoddy. Knocked out in Hamsterdam or Brussels by the look of it. They makes 'em by the barrel load over there.'

'Are you sure?' Jack reached out to look at the locket for himself but Isaac ignored his hand.

'I'll give you a ducat for it.'

'Come on, it's worth far more than that. Here, give it back, I'll take it down to old Ma Hennessy over in St Giles. She'll give me a lot for it, she will.'

'Aye, and have you coshed, robbed and left for dead before you walk ten yards after the deal. 'Ow many times do I has to tell you, you can't trust 'em thieves in the Rookeries. Rob you blind, they would. No sense of honour, them lot. Ma Hennessy, the worst of 'em all.' He held the locket up to the light once more. 'Well, cos it's you, Jack, and you're like a son to me, I'll give you two ducats. You can't say fairer than that, can you?'

Jack held out his hand again. 'I was thinking more like five ducats, Mr Isaac. It's a very pretty thing.'

'Pretty? Pretty don't pay the rent, Jack me lad. Pretty don't buy candles. Pretty don't put food on the table or bread in your belly.' He held the locket up to the light once more and shook his head. 'I must be getting soft in my old age.' He spat on his hand and held it out to Jack. 'Four ducats, it is. There, that's my final offer.'

Jack spat on his own hand and grasped the wrinkled fingers. It felt like he was holding a chicken's foot.

'Let me get the geld for you.'

'None of that clipped stuff either. Four ducats, Spanish coins is what I want.'

Isaac took a large iron key from around his neck and opened a wooden box that lay covered beneath his desk. Jack could hear the clink of coins as Isaac delved inside.

'Here they are. The best I could do, Jack.' He handed over four coins. Jack felt the substantial weight of silver in his palm.

'Three of 'ems good but one of 'ems been clipped on the side. I mean you just can't trust anybody these days. Finding coins without a little clipping ain't possible. You know how it is, Jack.'

Jack felt the wonderful heaviness of the coins in his hand. He knew that Isaac had better ones than this. After all, it was him that was doing the clipping. But he could still feel the weight of the diary in his inside pocket. His employer was going to meet him at two o'clock today to pay him five pounds for it. And if he were willing to pay five pounds for it, why not ask for ten? After all, he had the diary and his employer didn't.

He could already taste the smooth ale of the Pelican in his mouth. Even more, he could feel the soft lips of the barmaid who had poured the beer. 'These'll do.'

'Good lad, Jack. Any more where these came from?'

'A lot more. But give it a week or so, then Jack will pay 'em another visit.'

'We've always got a hankerin' for a few coins. If Jack could listen his way to the clink of gold or silver, we would be very grateful, very grateful indeed.'

'I'll bear that in mind, Mr Isaac, but now my whistle needs wetting and my flute needs playing. If you catch my drift.'

Isaac shook his head. 'Jack, Jack, I dunno why you do this. You have such a talent for thieving, you could become rich.'

Jack was already walking out of the shabby shop. 'Me, rich, Mr Isaac? I prefer to spend my money on wine, women and whelks. I just waste the rest.'

But Isaac didn't hear Jack's reply. He was already holding the locket up to the light mumbling to himself. 'A pretty piece, you are, my beauty, a pretty piece to fetch a pretty penny.'

Chapter 6

Pepys boarded the Hackney carriage just as Will emerged from the coffee shop. 'Glad you could make it.' He leaned back and shouted up at the driver. 'Half Moon Alley, if you please.'

The man snuffled in his dreams, one eye popped open. 'What you wanna go there for? Nuffin but fieves and mountebanks there. I could take you to see an 'anging. Lots of people going. Even let you 'ave a good seat, close to the action. Me bruvver's got the best seats, all ready and waitin'.'

'Thank you but no. Half Moon Alley, if you please.'

'Dunno what's 'appenin' to the world. People missin' a good 'anging'. It's not right, is it?' He mumbled to himself before clicking the horse into movement. The horse's head started up from his bag of feed, and he reluctantly trotted forward, leaving his sheltered spot out of the wind.

The Hackney swung around in the narrow street, just missing an ass being milked next to a wall, causing a loud barrage of cursing from the owner of the animal and the woman holding the jug.

Inside the cab, Will's fingers were tapping on the sill of the open window. 'About this summons from the King....'

'Don't worry about that.'

'But if, as you say, the diary contains libellous and treasonable statements concerning his Majesty...'

'I said possibly libellous and treasonable, Will. It's all in the interpretation. Anything can be made to seem different with the correct interpretation.' For the first time, Sam leant away and actually looked at Will. 'Pray tell me, what is your point?'

'Well, if the statements in the diary are possibly libellous and treasonable, wouldn't it be a little dangerous to walk into the lion's den?'

'Ah, I see where you are going with this. But there are a few flaws in your argument. Firstly, the invitation to an audience with the King was received before the diary was stolen. Secondly, the King is hardly likely to invite me to watch him play Pell Mell if he wants to clap me in irons and bundle me away to the Tower. No, I think a visit from a rather burly sergeant-at-arms would be more likely. Finally, and most obviously, one cannot ignore a summons from one's sovereign lord and master.'

'So you are saying...'

'It's hardly likely that he would arrest me during a game of Pell Mell.'

'Good. I suppose that's good then.'

'Yes, I suppose it is.'

'But I'm not ready to meet the King.'

'Yes, you are.'

'I'm not dressed for it.' He smoothed down his blue woollen coat, worn for comfort and warmth rather than style. He pointed to a hole in his stocking.

'Nobody will notice. And anyway, I've seen worse at court. Once, Rochester came dressed as a gorilla. The King simply enquired if he had forgotten to shave that morning.'

'But Rochester is a Lord with 20,000 a year.'

'Rochester is a mad drunken oaf with the wit of a chimney sweep. Stay away from him, Will. He's nothing but trouble.'

'And what about the court?'

'What about the court?'

'The Tracts say it is a den of iniquity and licentiousness.'

'They would, wouldn't they?'

'What do you mean?'

Pepys pulled his bottom lip with his fingers. 'Well, if you wanted to sell more papers, would you write that the Court is a boring, tradition-laden, faddish clique of middle-aged nobodies with nothing between their ears, and even less between their legs? Or would you write that it's a Beelzebub's feast of wanton sexual indiscretion? Which would you find more interesting to read?'

'Probably, the latter.'

'I rest my case.'

Pepys stared out of the window. 'Interesting choice.'

'I'm sorry, I don't follow you.'

'Interesting choice of location for Mr Isaac's house of business.'

'Why?'

'It's outside the Liberties of London. The City authorities have no remit there.'

Will remained silent, waiting for the explanation that was to come.

'The local constables, the bailiffs and the parish have no authority there. Can't arrest anybody or bring them before the local magistrate.'

'Good place for a thief to live.'

The carriage merged with the other traffic from Fenchurch Street and jostled its way through Aldgate. Underneath the arch, the shouts of the hawkers, the bellows of the drivers to 'Give way, give way there,' and the rumble of wheels, animals, and people all formed one mass of sound that made speech impossible. The two friends sat in silence.

Eventually, the Hackney elbowed its way through and

began to pick up speed along the wider road of White Chapel. Within five minutes, the carriage edged passed a cart full of barrels. The stench of herring played a fishy concerto on their nostrils. 'We is here,' came a shout from the driver. "'Alf Moon Alley. That'll be eighteen pence.'

'Pay the man will you, Will.'

Will searched in his purse for a few coins and found only two shillings.

'Aven't got any coins for change. 'Ave to give you some tokens instead. Good ones mind, from 'Arris the Butcher's on Fredneedle Street.' He passed the small tokens back down to Will. 'Are you sure you don't want to go the 'anging. I can wait 'ere for you. Take you to the 'anging later. You wouldn't want to miss it. Me bruvver has got seats right at the front. You can 'ear the last words of the dangler, and, if you're quick, dip your scarf in his blood. Can't beat a drop of 'anged man's blood for curing a cold. Now, you couldn't want a better day out. Not if my name's Jed Fisher.'

Pepys had already crossed the road, weaving his way through a flock of sheep being driven to Leadenhall market.

'No, thank you,' said Will, 'but do wait here for us, we won't be long.'

Will left the driver as he continued to explain the joys of a good hanging. Pepys was already striding down a narrow passageway between the buildings.

Overhead, the sky was a narrow trench of grey light. The alley itself stank of piss, the remains of the ale deposited by the drinkers of the White Swan at the corner.

Pepys stopped before a dingy shop on the left. Above the door, a dusty wooden sign swung slowly in the breeze. 'Isaac and son, traders and victualers.'

'Hurry up, Will. Hell will freeze over unless we make

haste.'

*

'How can I be of assistance to the honourable gentlemen?' The owner ended this sentence with a little chuckle like the cough of a baby strangled at birth.

He was dressed in a long, black woollen coat that draped down to his ankles. Above the coat sat a white face, it's paleness emphasised by the beginnings of a white beard on the chin and in patches of fuzz around the rest of the face. The white hair hung in clumps from beneath a brown hat with a broad brim.

'And to whom do we have the honour of speaking,' said Pepys.

The chuckle again. 'The honour is all mine, sirs. It's not often that we get such fine looking and well-dressed gentlemen in my humble place of trading. The name is Isaac, Jeremy Isaac to give my full name, son of Jeremy Isaac and grandson of Jeremy Isaac. We've been very frugal with the names in the Isaac family and this humble place of trade has been in the family these last hundred years or so, since the time of Good Queen Bess, bless her soul.' He looked all around the shop.

Pepys took it all in too. He was standing in a small path surrounded by goods of all kinds and descriptions. Pots of ink, floor brushes, chamber pots, small tuns of wine, sacks of flour, resin from the Baltic. Everything and anything that could be sold had found a place here. Pepys touched a wooden desk on his left. It was covered with a fine layer of dust as if unmoved since the day the shop had opened.

'You seem to trade in all manner of goods.'

'I dabbles here and there, whatever my customers need or require. I don't have the luxury of specialising like the houses the gentlemen are more likely to frequent in the New Exchange or on Cheapside. Whatever my customers requires is what I provides. Got to keep the customer happy is my motto.'

'I require a bauble for my wife. A locket, set in diamonds or Venetian glass, no more than one inch round.'

'The gentleman is very precise in his requirements. Very precise indeed.' A little chuckle again.

'And the gentleman will pay handsomely for such a bauble. If one matching its description could be found.'

'Handsomely, the gentleman says. How would the gentleman describe 'handsomely' in economic terms?'

'That would depend on the merchandise meeting my exact requirements. My wife has a particularly hankering for such a bauble.'

'One has to keep one's wife content. It's the first rule of husbandry.'

'It's a rule I adhere to. I would rather suffer the slingshots and arrows of outrageous despair than waken the dragon that inhabits the barbed mind of an unhappy wife.'

'The gentleman speaks with wisdom. But if he had such a shrew for a wife, she would require taming.'

'You are an educated man, Mr Isaac. The works of Mr Shakespeare appeal to you.'

'I'm an humble trader, sir, no more, no less.'

'And I am a humbled husband. Hence the need for the jewellery I have described.'

The chuckle again, this time deeper and longer. A pause for thought, accompanied by a long scratching of the chin. 'I may have such a piece for the gentleman and his hesteemed wife. It came in this morning, you understand, sold by a dear, devout friend who is a little down on his luck at this moment.'

'Such is the way of the world.'

'So it is alas.'

'May I see the piece?'

Mr Isaac held up his hands. 'Ah, there I must disappoint the gentleman. The piece has only just come in, I have had no time to happraise or value it, even less to enter it into my ledger.' He pointed at the large book that lay open on top of his desk.

Pepys turned to go. 'Come, Will, we are wasting our time here. This man obviously has nothing of value for us to see.' He adjusted his periwig and turned on his heels.

'But...' stammered Will, following him out of the door.

Mr Isaac rushed from the side of his desk to reach the entrance before Pepys. 'Gentlemen, gentlemen, do not be so hasty. I may not have happraised the piece but I'm sure that if you were to make me an offer, an handsome offer, I would not be able to refuse such gentlemen of quality.'

He took Pepys' arm and led him back to the desk. Taking a cast-iron key from the depths of the long coat, he opened a large chest that lay concealed on the floor, covered by an old mat. Inside the chest, he scrabbled around, muttering to himself the whole time. Finally, he cried, 'here it is.'

He brought Will's gift to Elizabeth out from the box. 'Isn't she a beauty, gentlemen? Most beautiful, most desirous, even though I do say so. I believe it would fetch a pretty penny even from the King himself.'

Pepys reached for the locket stolen from his wife. Mr Isaac let him take it reluctantly. He walked to the only source of light, a single candle burning in an old sconce.

He brought the piece up to the light. It glittered and shone, bringing the radiance of beauty to the dingy shop.

'How much do you want for it?'

Mr Isaac chuckled again. 'It's a very handsome piece, gentlemen. I'm afraid it commands a very handsome price. The gentleman who sold it to me was very particular on this point. 'Mr Isaac,' he said, 'this belonged to my wife's mother, do make sure it goes to a good home, an handsome home.' 'Don't you worries, said I, it will only go to gentlemen of quality.' I was very particular about that. 'Only gentlemen of quality,' I said.'

'How much do you want for it?'

Mr Isaac rubbed his hands together and give his little chuckle. 'How much would the gentleman say it was worth?'

'I asked you for a price, not a debate. Out with it, man, or we'll be off. Will, we're wasting our time.' He made to leave again.

'Gentlemen, Sir Will, stay a while longer. It's just that Mr Isaac is unused to having such gentlemen of quality in his humble place of trade.' He paused, gave a chuckle, and tapped his fingers in the dust on a tun of wine. 'I couldn't ask for less than ten pounds for this hexquisite piece. The gentleman who sold it to me demanded this price. Because it's for you sir, I would only ask that I recover my costs in the transaction. I'm sure you'll agree that is fair.' He held his arms open wide.

Pepys thought a while. 'We'll give you twelve pounds if....'

'If...'

'If you also provide us with the name of the gentleman who sold it to you?'

'Ah, alas, alas, that sirs, is impossible. The gentleman

in question requested anonymity.'

'Thirteen pounds.'

Mr Isaac rubbed his chin. A few hairs fell onto the black wool of his coat. 'Fifteen pounds, sirs, I couldn't ask for less.'

'Fifteen pounds, it is.'

Mr Isaac rubbed his hands. 'Gentlemen, gentlemen, what a wonderful bargain you have made. This piece will turn the barbed maze of your wife's mind into a soft welcoming lawn of comfort.'

'And the name of the seller?'

Mr Isaac rubbed his chin once again. More hair fell onto his coat. He chuckled once more. 'I may have mispake a while ago.'

'Mispake?'

'Mispake on the quality of the gentlemen in question. In truth, he wasn't a gentleman at all but a young man, a small young man.'

'His name?'

'Jack Turner. He told me he found the jewellery on the street. Dropped by some poor, unfortunate lady as she rode by in her carriage. He ran after her but alas the carriage moved too quickly. Jack brought it to me. I specialise in lost property, you see.'

Pepys waved his hand as if all the explanation was of no consequence to him. 'His residence?'

'Of this parish, gentlemen, down the street, past St. Botolph's on the right, at the sign of the Feather you'll find Seven Steps Yard, Jack Turner has his place at the end.' He held out his hand. 'My money.'

'Pay the man, Will.'

*

'That was expensive.'

'But at least we have the locket back. Here, you keep it safe, Will, we can return it to her after we have seen the King. Now is the time to pay a visit to Jack Turner.'

They strode across the street dodging through the sellers of brushes, pots and pans, ink and paper, all yelling their wares and touting for custom.

'Coachman,' shouted Pepys.

The coachman jerked awake from his perch at the front of the carriage. 'Time for the 'anging. Take you there right away.'

'Not at this time, Coachman. We must go to Seven Steps Yard.'

'You really don't want to go there, sirs.'

'Why?'

'It's full of fieves and vagabonds. Makes this place look like 'eaven. I don't know if I want to go there, sir, bless my soul, I don't.'

'Five shillings for the trip.'

'Giddy-up there you lazy nag. We ‘as a journey to attend to for the gentlemen.' He lashed the old horse with the reins.

Pepys and Will Hewer climbed aboard. 'I'm not sure I can afford to be your friend anymore, Sam.' He counted the remaining coins in his purse. 'I hope Mr Turner will be cheaper than the rest. We have just three pounds, six shillings and threepence half- penny left.'

'Do not fret, Will. I'm sure Mr Jack Turner will return the book once we explain its importance. But, if we have to pay him, so be it. Friendship can never be measured in the profit and loss of a ledger book.'

'There speaks someone with pounds of money and

not a pennyworth of sense. I remember a man who used to know to the farthing what he was worth.'

'Ah, so true, Will. These days I pay my bankers to know that figure. Houblon is so much more accurate than I ever was. You should employ him too.'

'If I have anything left after this adventure, I will endeavour to do so, Sam. But have a care with my money, it was obtained with too much difficulty to be despatched with such ease.'

'We is here. The sign of the Feather at Seven Steps Yard,' shouted the Coachman. 'I'll stay ‘ere if you please sirs. The ‘oss dun want to go in there, 'e values 'is hide, 'e does.'

‘That was quick,’ said Will.

‘The ‘oss moves quickly when there’s a few coins to be ‘ad. ‘E knows it means a bag of oats for ‘im. Gots to look after your workers.’

Pepys looked out from the open window. The street was narrow and dark. A gutter ran down the middle but no water flowed there, just a green, foul-smelling slime that looked as though it were alive. Two drabs dressed with the artlessness of their profession leant against the wall of the Inn where a sign painted with the feathers of the Prince of Wales creaked in the absence of any breeze.

'It doesn't look very welcoming,' said Will.

'That doesn't surprise me. Come on, we don't want to keep Mr Turner waiting.' Pepys launched himself out of the coach.

'I'll wait ‘ere for you, sirs, but I won't be waitin’ long, if you catch my drift. ‘Ere is not a place a body waits.' He was holding a thick staff of wood and beating it against his palm, looking around constantly as he did so.

'We won't be long.'

‘Shortly or longly, don't matter to me or the ‘oss. We still gets paid.’

Will looked at the remaining coins in his hand. ’I’ve ascertained that fact already.’

'Ave a care, gentlemen and ‘ave an ‘urry, if you please.

Pepys and Will stepped down from the Hackney. As they did so, the two drabs levered themselves off the walls of the Inn and sauntered across to the cab.

'What have we here then, Lou.'

'Looks like gentlemen.'

'We don't gets many gentlemen here, do we, Lou?'

'I had one here last week. But he had come and gone in five minutes. Hardly touched the sides.' She let out a rich guffaw of a laugh. 'Either of you gentlemen want to pluck a girl's bow,' she shouted, playing with the tie at her waist. 'We could make excellent music together, couldn't we, Sarah?'

'That we could. And for you fine gentlemen, two for the price of one, just for today mind. We wouldn't be wanting to set a precedent, would we, Lou?'

Then she stopped and looked carefully, 'Mr Pepys, is it you, sir? Do you remember me?'

Pepys smiled. 'It's Sarah, the barmaid, isn't it? You're not at the Old Cock anymore?'

'Well, yes and no, sir. The landlord said I used to drink more than I served, and spill more than I drank. So I left his employ six months ago. But still at the old cock, if you gets my meaning, sir.’ She gave Pepys an outrageous wink.

‘I have missed your company, Sarah,’ he laughed.

'I bet you have, Mr Pepys. A proper little octopus, you were. More hands than a crew of sailors.' She looked around her. 'But what are you doing in this neck of London. Not your usual stomping ground, is it?'

'We're looking for a man by the name of Jack Turner.'

'Little Jack? He lives over there.' She pointed to a broken-down house with dirty windows and holes in the roof, leaning into its neighbour for support. 'Saw him about ten minutes ago. With another man, another gentleman, heading towards his house. Looked like him and Jack were doing a spot of business.'

'Business?'

'Jack's a tea-leaf, Mr Pepys. A good one, mind. Steals to order does our Jack. None of that street thieving for him, he's gone up in the world. You orders. He thieves. Very good he is at it too. And generous when he's flush.'

'Thank you, Sarah. I'll bid you good day.' Here's sixpence for your trouble.' Pepys raised his hat and walked towards Jack Turner's hovel, followed by Will.

'It's been a day for the nobs, aint it, Lou? Maybe, we is going up in the world.'

'Not us, Sarah. The only way we're going up is to spend more time lying down. Come on, I heard there's a new ship from Barbadoe at the Black Bull. Maybe, we can get a few sailors to board us.'

'With their cutlasses in their hands, I hope.'

Chapter 7

Pepys and Will stood in front of Jack Turner's hovel. It was one of the meanest dwellings in a city full of mean homes. Unfortunately, the fire had spared it, choosing instead to feast on a better class of residence. It leant heavily to the right, like a drunk looking for support. There were just two rooms, one sitting above the other. The door showed signs of being recently painted, sometime in the last century or two. Water from the tiles dripped onto the street even though it had not rained for two days, and plaster formed flakes like dandruff all round the base.

'Perhaps we should call the constable?'

'And tell him what Will?. That we are looking for a diary, stolen by a Mr Jack Turner. We have no proof that he was the thief other than the word of Mr Isaac, whom I'm sure would deny he had ever met us. The constable would arrest us for wasting his time.'

'So what do you propose we do?'

'Speak to him, directly.' Pepys knocked on the door. There was no answer. He knocked again, this time harder. As he did so, the door swung open. 'For a thief, he doesn't seem to care about his own security,' said Will. Pepys stepped through the open door. 'Hello, Mr Turner,' he shouted.

The bare room echoed his words back to him. He stepped further into the house and shouted up the rickety stairs in front of him. 'Mr Turner? Mr Turner?'

Still no answer. Pepys began to climb the stairs. 'Do you think that's wise?

'Sarah said that he came back with a gentlemen. Perhaps, they are up here.' He climbed up, each stair creaking under his weight. Will followed him reluctantly.

The landing sloped down towards a closed door, following the lean of the house. Pepys shouted again and steadying himself against the wall, pushed open the door.

Jack Turner was sat in the only chair in the room, lounging back as if he were drunk. His eyes were open and the tip of his tongue showed between his teeth. A red stain covered his chest, the blood dripping onto the floor and pooling around the legs of the chair. Already, it was beginning to flow, like the rest of the house, towards the far corner.

A slim pearl-handled knife stuck out from the side of his throat.

Will Hewer entered the room and immediately flinched at the sight of the body.

Pepys took out a lace handkerchief and covered his mouth. 'I fear Jack Turner will thieve no more.'

Will's hand started to shake. 'What are we going to do?'

'Well, looking around here, I do not see the diary.'

'There's a dead man in the middle of the room and all you can think of is your damned book.'

'There's not a lot we can do for him at the moment. As you pointed out, he is dead.'

'Very dead.'

Pepys walked towards the body. 'That's interesting.'

He knelt down by the side of the chair carefully avoiding the blood. He uncurled Jack Turner's fingers and held up a silver button about the size of a crown piece with a device engraved in the centre. 'This must have belonged to the killer.'

'Our young man must have ripped it off in the struggle.'

But Pepys was staring out of the open window. He placed his finger in front of his lips and glanced around the room. 'Don't you realise, Will, there was only one way into Jack Turner's house,' he whispered. 'Sarah said that he had come in here with a gentleman. We saw nobody leave.'

Before Will could answer, a tile slid off the roof and smashed onto the cobbled streets below.

Chapter 8

Above their heads, a strange sound echoed through the rafters. A mixture of the soft pad of a leather sole and the hard tap of something wooden. It tapped and slid itself over to the far end of the room and then it stopped.

Will rushed to the single window. A green glazed tile lay shattered into pieces in the gutter. He leant out and strained his neck back towards the roof. A figure dressed in black disappeared behind the lop-sided chimney stack.

Without thinking, he levered himself up and stood on the edge of the window sill to see the man. Holding on to the eave, he leant out. Someone was crawling on all fours along the ridge line of the house next door. Will saw him reach the gable end and peer over the side.

'Hey, you, stop there,' shouted Will as loudly and authoritatively as he could.

The man looked back over his shoulder and smiled. Grey hair flowing in the breeze, a grizzled chin, cold eyes. Will would remember the face for as long as he lived.

Then, the man stood up at the end of the gable and leapt into the air, vanishing from view.

Will pulled himself up and over the roof edge onto the slime-dampened tiles. He looked down at the alley below. The ground below seemed a long way off. The shattered tile still lay there, smashed into green pieces on the cobblestones.

He turned back to the roof. The chimney lay up ahead, leaning crazily to the right. He launched his body over the edge of the roof, pulling himself up with the tips of his fingers. He crept up the tiles slowly, feeling the wet moss, bird droppings and damp lichen between his fingers, wishing that he hadn't worn his blue woollen coat and breeches to meet Sam that morning.

The wind whistled through the age-worn bricks of the chimney. He looked down once more. The ground seemed further away now but the shattered remains of the tile still lay there. That could happen to his body, he thought. Just one slip and he would be flung down to earth and smashed against the stone cobbles.

A shudder ran down his spine and his leg began to tremble. He pressed his body deeper into the slimy tiles. What am I doing? He decided to go back down to Sam. He shuffled his body sideways, but as he did so, his leg caught on one of the tiles. It came free and slid slowly down the roof, and over the edge.

Will held his breath. Two seconds later, there was a loud crunch as it shattered into a thousand green pieces.

The only way was up. He took a deep breath and gripped the hard edge of the tiles with his fingertips. He inched his way up slowly, pushing off with his new shoes against the roof. Gradually, the chimney loomed closer, cutting off the rays of the watery sun.

He reached up and grasped the safety of the chimney like a child seizing his mother's breast. It was still warm. Across the roofs of London, he could see the ruins of Saint Paul's still standing out sharply against the skyline, its remaining blackened stones pointing like a bony finger upwards to the heavens. Beyond St Paul's lay the rest of the city, largely rebuilt now, the new tiles glistening through the coal haze in the early summer light.

Reluctantly he levered himself up using the chimney as support. He could see even more of London now, all the way to the red brick of White Hall. The King was there, waiting to meet him. Well, not exactly waiting for him, but there nonetheless, and Will was to meet him that afternoon in the company of Pepys. His mother, bless her departed soul, would be so proud of him.

He looked down at his dirt-smeared jacket. The blue wool had turned a dirty brown from the moss, bird shit and soot of the roof. Not the best attire for meeting one's monarch. He would go home and change. He was sure he had time.

A blast of wind rocked the chimney. Have to get down from here first, though. In front of him, the gable of the roof sloped down to where it met the wall of the next house. He took another deep breath and, fixing that point in his gaze, rushed crab-like along the raised gable. He reached the safety of the other wall and stopped.

There was a noise from the ground below, like a heavy piece of cargo landing on a ship.

He stepped up onto the other roof and placed his feet carefully on either side of the decorated gable.

One step. Two steps. He tried a third and his foot straddled a lump of vivid-green moss and slipped out from under him. His body jerked forwards and downwards, one foot jerking to the right. He grabbed the raised gable and felt his body wobble, deciding if it was going to fall on the left or the right. He shifted his weight backwards, sitting down heavily on the decorated point of the roof.

A sharp stabbing pain shot up his spine. He dragged his right foot back under him and onto the gable, regaining his footing and his balance.

A close run thing, he thought, got to concentrate. The pain was less now; a dull ache rather than a hot poker.

He stood up once more and held his arms to his side like a performer in one of the shows at Vauxhall. He wished he hadn't worn shoes, though. Those performers always worked in bare feet. Too late now.

He took another step forward. Then another. And another. His legs wobbled shakily while his arms flapped up and down like a fledgling discovering how to fly. His momentum was carrying him forward towards the edge of the gable but if he stopped walking, he would be unable to keep his balance.

He carried on going forward, each step bringing him closer to the end. He slid his foot against a decorated tile in the shape of a rabbit and stood still. For a moment, all was well as he concentrated on retaining his balance. Then, he made the mistake of looking down. His feet began to slip from under him again as the soles of his shoes could find no grip on the moss-covered tiles. His arms flailed against the air, desperately trying to hold himself upright. His hips jerked and his arms followed, wheeling crazily behind him.

Then he fell forward.

As he fell, he thought this was not the way he was supposed to die. He wanted the warm white sheets of a comfortable bed, relatives weeping beside him, doctors shaking their heads, a vicar reading a passage from the Bible. Then music. The rising song of a heavenly choir, two angels on either side, trumpets softly blowing, as he ascended to meet his maker.

But no. Here he was falling to the hard cobblestones of a shit-covered London street after chasing a man across a slimy roof.

This was all Pepys' fault. If he survived this, he was going to kill the man, best friend or not.

His body hit wooden boards knocking the wind out of his lungs. He reached out and felt the rough grain of the wood beneath his fingers. His head lifted and he opened his eyes. He was on a wooden scaffold five feet beneath the roof. A man was holding a trowel covered in lime, ready to apply it to the wall.

'Good morning,' said Will.

'Mornin',' answered the man.

'If I could be so bold as to ask, how do I get down from here?'

'The same way as everyone gets down.'

'And that is...'

'You gets your leg over the side and you climbs down. Like him.'

Will lifted his head higher and saw a man limping round the corner of an alley.

'He came the same way you did. 'Cept he landed standing up. You should try it next time.'

'There won't be a next time,' said Will, lowering his body over the edge of the wooden platform.

'That's what the last one said.'

But Will didn't hear these words, he was already climbing down the scaffold, using the cross bars to go from one level to another. He reached street level and planted his shoes firmly in the muck. Never had he been so glad to stand in the mud of London. He felt like kneeling down and kissing the ground at his feet but saw a cat scurry into a hole, chased by a rat, and thought better of it.

He ran down the alley and came out in front of the house.

'What are you doing, Will?' The shout came from above. Sam's head was leaning out of the window.

'I'm going after him.'

He raced across the street and turned the corner into another narrow alley. The stench hit him like the charge of a bull. It seemed that this alley was where all the waste that flowed out from the sewers of London for the last 1000 years had found its home. The man was at the end now, nearly sixty yards away. He was moving quickly but seemed to be limping. Perhaps, he had hurt himself in his descent from the roof?

Will redoubled his efforts, his shoes sliding through muck and filth and shit and slime. On the left, two men were standing outside a tavern smoking their pipes and supping from three tankards, oblivious to the stench that surrounded them.

He ran on. The man turned left at the end of the alley. Will tried to increase his pace but the faster he ran, the slower he seemed to go, as his shoes slipped and slid on the shit. He was tempted to shout 'Stop that man' and create a hue and cry but in this area, he doubted whether anybody would come to his aid. More likely, they would stop and rob him.

He reached the end of the alley. The man had crossed the street and was running past the apple and quince sellers, their wares laid out on mats in front of them. A performing dog did a quick somersault as the man ran past it. A paper seller, holding the latest copy of the London Register, quickly jumped to the side as he realised the man had no desire to purchase a copy. A vendor of brushes and brooms was pushed out of the way, landing in a heap of reeds and rushes.

Will recovered his breath and started to run again. He too ran past the apple and quince sellers, and the dog once more did a somersault. But the paper seller made no attempt to sell him a copy.

'What's all the hurry about? Not another fire?' shouted the broom seller.

Will did not hear the words shouted after him. He ran faster down the street, his breath now shallow and laboured. He turned a corner and ran into something hard. His feet left the ground and he found himself falling in slow motion to land flat on his back.

The man stood there, with what looked like a leg in his hands.

Will scrambled for breath, his chest rising up and down as it tried to fill itself with air. The man stood over him with the leg, still with its boot attached, raised like a cudgel.

He closed his eyes waiting for the blow to come crushing down on his face and head.

It never came. Instead, he heard the man mutter to himself, 'That's better, don't often use the leg but it does come in handy at a pinch.' He fixed the wooden leg to the end of a stump with two straps.

Will heard the man step closer to him and, once again, there was the peculiar sound of a hard tap and a soft slide on the cobblestones.

The man bent down next to him, 'Who are you my little dandycock?' His purse was taken out of the pocket along with Elizabeth's locket.

'No matter, these will pay me for my trouble.' He held up the locket where it glittered in the afternoon light. 'A pretty little thing.'

In his head, Will was screaming, 'Don't take the locket. Take the money but not the locket.' He opened his eyes and shouted. But nothing came out. It was as if his whole body were paralysed with fear.

He tried again. Nothing.

The man stood up, threw the purse onto Will's chest 'I'll leave you the tokens. They ain't worth much anyway.'

Then, he limped away, one leg slightly trailing after the other.

Got to get up. Got to go after him. Elizabeth's locket... Will slowly lifted his head from the dirt of the cobblestones. His breathing was easier now, the shock of the attack wearing off.

The man walked down Gravel Lane and into a tavern on the corner. Got to go after him.

Will staggered to his feet, a stabbing pain lanced through his chest. Got to go after him.

He lurched forwards, stumbling on a large pat of horse manure. Flies buzzed around his head.

Got to go after him.

He was becoming steadier with every second, The Tavern was in front of him.

Now I've got him.

He lurched through the door and stopped. At least twenty drinkers and smokers, some with their tankards raised to their lips, also stopped and looked at him.

He rested his hands on his thighs to get his breath back. 'A man,' he said through heaves of breath, 'came in here...did you see him?'

Half of the congregation of the tavern nodded their heads and half shook them. Will pressed on. 'Which way did he go?'

Some men pointed to the side, some to the back, and even more to the door which Will had just come through. One even had the temerity to point upwards towards the kippered ceiling.

Will knew this wasn't the sort of establishment where he was going to receive any help from public-spirited citizens. He chose to go through the back door, reasoning that if he were running from somebody, that's what he would do.

He dodged the drinkers and pushed open the door at the rear. A yard surrounded by a high wall, with two wooden barrels, a pile of fish heads and a rat playing with a dead cat. But no sign of any man.

He had got his breath back now. The shock of being struck across the chest had finally worn off.

He turned back and went into the tavern again.

One drinker, bearded and besmocked, sucked on his pipe and blew a cloud of weevil smelling smoke to the tanned rafters. He shook his head, rattling his pipe on his teeth. Hiding his hand from the others, he pointed to the door at the side.

'Thank you,' said Will and charged for the door. He opened it and stepped out. Hounds Ditch lay before him, lined on either side of the street with shops, hawkers and travelling salesmen. To the left, he could see the towers of St Botolph's, untouched by the Great Fire. To his right, the street stretched up the densely packed lanes of Bishopsgate.

He couldn't see the man anywhere. He had vanished into the crowd as quickly as a bishop ravishes a young boy.

He returned to the tavern. 'A pint of your best ale.'

The tavern keeper poured the beer from a large jug. 'Twopence,' he said, holding the drink back until he received the money.

Will dug in his purse but only found the tokens and a few coppers. The barkeeper looked at the tokens strangely and bit down on one with his large yellow teeth. He handed them back. 'Dun take no tokens from that butcher. He's in Clink now for selling rotten meat.'

Will searched again and found sixpence.

'That's better. Good stuff, coined at the Tower down the

street. Bit clipped, but she'll serve.'

Will drank it down in a single draught. Running was thirsty work. And running after murderers even thirstier. Time to go back to Pepys and tell him that the man had escaped.

But first another pint of this delicious ale.

Chapter 9

Fifteen minutes later, after two wrong turns and three pints of ale, Will found himself standing in front of Jack Turner's hovel once more.

Sam's head popped out of the upstairs window. 'I see you didn't apprehend the villain?'

'He ran faster than me.'

'Only to be expected. I believe snails run faster than you. Come up the stairs. While you have been sporting yourself around London, I have been investigating Mr Turner more thoroughly.'

'Shouldn't we call the constable?'

'I've already done that. But he will arrive in his own sweet time.'

Jack Turner was still sitting in his chair, his legs splayed out in front of him. The blood had now flowed down to the corner of the room where it washed up against the wall as if trying to escape from the scene of the crime. The knife now lay in Pepys' hands.

'See here, Will, not your common or garden knife.'

Will pointed at Jack Turner sprawled out in his chair. 'Did you take that out of his neck,' he stammered.

'Yes, of course, where else would I take it from? But look at it.' He held the knife up for Will to see. 'Five inches of the finest Toledo steel, pearl handled and beautifully tooled. A gentleman's blade, Will, not that of a common or garden robber or assassin.'

'Can we go downstairs? Looking at him sitting there is...'

'I didn't know you were so squeamish, Will. If it pleases you, we shall descend.'

Will dashed to the door and took the stairs two at a time. Pepys followed him at a more leisurely pace.

'Tell me about the man you chased?'

'Medium height, long grey hair, dressed in black.'

'That covers half the population of London that's not female. Anything else?'

Will thought for a moment. 'He spoke well.'

'You had a conversation with him?'

'Not really. He hit me with a leg…'

'Hit you with a leg?'

'I think it was a wooden leg.'

'I presume it was his own leg. I don't suppose he borrowed it from a passing cripple?'

Will thought for a moment. 'No, it was definitely his own leg.'

'That explains the noise we heard on the roof. I thought it sounded too hard for a shoe. It wouldn't surprise me if our killer lost his leg in the recent war.'

'He's an ex-soldier?'

'Probably, Will, but for which side, that is the question.'

'I also heard him say some words as he stood over me.'

'What did he say?'

'I think he wanted to know who I was, called me a 'Dandycock'.'

Pepys laughed. 'Not a bad description of you, Will, if a little presumptuous for a man who's just attacked you with a wooden leg.'

Will looked down at his shoes and ripped stockings. 'I have a confession, Sam.'

'You're not turning Catholic?'

'The locket. Elizabeth's locket. He stole it.'

Pepys strode over to the window. 'That could be awkward, Will, Elizabeth can be a difficult woman when's she’s upset.’

‘I’ll tell her. It’s all my fault. I shouldn’t have gone charging after that man like a hare after a late March.’

Pepys pulled his bottom lip. The bruise was getting larger and clearer. He turned back to look into the room and see his friend. ’No, you did the right thing, Will.’

'Do you still have the button?'

Pepys opened his hand. The silver button lay against his palm. 'The device proves that the killer was an aristocrat.'

'No, it doesn't, Will.'

'But, I thought...'

'It simply proves that we found a button in the hand of a man who's been murdered. No more, no less. And anyway, these buttons are often sewn on the livery of a servant, not only on the clothes of the master. No, we have to try harder. But it will help if we know whose device this is.

'Should be relatively easy to find out.'

‘Good, we can perform that task together. But first, we meet our sovereign lord and master, King Charles.’

Will looked down at his torn and dirty suit. The hole in his stocking was now bigger. ‘I’d forgotten about that.’

'Hallllooo, Constable Halfbeak here.' A booming voice bellowed from outside the door.

Pepys placed the knife in his pocket.

The door swung open and the entrance was immediately swallowed up by a round body dressed in bright orange. The body turned sideways and edged through.

'What have we here, then?' The voice boomed again as if shouting to someone across a parade ground.

‘A murder, upstairs.’

The constable looked at them through his beady eyes. ‘Well, gentlemen lead the way, we won’t get back to our dinners by standing here and making words.’

Pepys and Will climbed the stairs again, followed by the heavy tread of the constable. Pepys opened the door and pointed to the dead body.

The constable pulled a large sheet that served as a handkerchief from his pocket and mopped his brow. Before he had finished, sweat drops had already formed on his forehead again. 'Little Jack Turner?' He clomped into the room. 'I don't suppose this was suicide?'

Pepys shook his head.

'Jack wasn't the type to kill himself. Liked life too much did little Jack. And liked other people's lives even more,' said the constable staring at the dead body. Then, for the first time, he seemed to notice the two men standing in the room. 'And you are?'

Pepys stepped forward over the outstretched leg of Jack Turner. 'Pepys is the name. Samuel Pepys of the Navy Office. And this is Will Hewer, my clerk and friend.' Will nodded at the fat man in front of him.

'Your business, here?' The voice had changed, becoming harsher, more strident.

'We had an appointment with Mr Turner to purchase some effects of mine that he had found in the street.'

'Yes, little Jack made a habit of finding things in the street.' The constable rubbed his bulbous nose and waddled forward to examine the corpse of Jack Turner. 'Lot of blood. Stab to the neck. One blow. Whoever did it, knew how to kill.’

‘I agree completely, Constable. A soldier, or an ex-soldier, I believe.’

‘Probably. But where’s the murder weapon?’

‘Pepys reached into his pocket and produced the blade. ‘You just happened to have it on your person?’

‘Actually, I pulled it from his neck.’ Pepys pointed to the prostrate Jack. ‘I wanted to take a closer look at it.’

‘And?’

‘And I did. As you can see, Toledo steel, mother of pearl handle. Not a normal blade for a soldier.’

Constable Halfbeak squinted at Sam. ‘You seem to be very observant for a man who works at the Navy Board.’

‘We are a watchful crew there, both in our duties and our religion.’

The constable stepped back, careful to avoid the stream of blood that flowed towards the corner of the room. 'Right, I'll get the Parish attendants to come and bury him. I suppose he doesn't have any money.' He reached forward and shook the purse that lay at Jack's waist. 'Empty, as usual. It'll be a pauper's burial for him.'

'No relatives?' asked Pepys.

'None that I know of. Who would mourn a tea-leaf like little Jack?'

‘That's it?' said Will.

'That's it. Can't do any more 'cept bury the little bugger. Now, gents, anything else I can do for you?'

'No, thank you, Constable...?'

'Halfbeak. Constable Halfbeak of the parish of St. Botolph's, gents, at your service.' He attempted to bow, but his vast waist meant he merely nodded his head and shifted his leg slightly forward. 'Could I invite you to join me in a spot of dinner? The Bear does an excellent Mutton pie on a Wednesday.'

'Thank you, but no, we have an appointment with his Majesty. Let us go, Will.'

‘His Majesty? Wish him well from me, sirs. And if you

see your way to mentioning the name of John Halfbeak, Constable of the parish, to his Majesty, I would be forever in your debt.' The Constable attempted a bow again but succeeded only in nodding his head once more.

'I'll be glad to mention your name, Constable Halfbeak, such an efficient servant of the parish deserves recognition.'

'I thank you kindly, Mr Pepys. If there's anything that you need, do let me know. John Halfbeak knows a few able people in a manner of speaking.'

'Thank you, Constable, but now we must leave.'

'I'll join you in departing, gentlemen. A murder always leaves me peckish.'

'That's it? We're just going to leave him here?'

'Yes, that's it, Will. The good constable will handle it from now.'

'That I will, gentlemen. The Parish attendants will be here before little Jack has had time to go cold. And he'll be in his grave by this evening, as the moon decides it's time to have a look over the earth.'

'I congratulate you on your alacrity, Constable Halfbeak.'

'I runs a tight ship, Mr Pepys, as you might say in the Navy.'

'We might say it, but we rarely do it, Constable. Will, let us depart. The constable has work to do.'

'Actually, the constable has eating to do. The attendants have work to do. It's the way of the world.'

'It is indeed, Constable Halfbeak, and long may it remain so.'

'A man after my own heart, Mr Pepys. Bless my soul, we must have dinner together soon.'

*

‘I fought you were never comin.” Mr Fisher was still holding the cudgel in his hand. ‘The ‘oss were right scared. Hairs on his mane have turned grey, they have. And you do know we've missed the 'anging. He'll have danced his way to hell by now and the crowd'll 'ave gone for their victuals.' The coachman put his hat back on his head. 'I suppose you don't want some victuals?'

'You suppose correctly, Coachman. First, we must go to White Hall, followed afterwards by my home at Seething Lane, if you will.’

‘Got another 'anging tomorrow. Don’t suppose I can interest you in a ringside seat?'

'Your brother has a few I believe,' said Will.

'Rights you are, sir. Always keeps a few seats at the front for guests does me bruvver. Never misses an 'anging, he don't. Likes to see 'em dance. Well, don't we all?'

‘White Hall, if you please. A shilling it is if you get us there before one.'

'Rights you are, sir. White Hall comin’ up sharpish. Get along there, you lazy nag. Can't keep the gentlemen waiting.’

Chapter 10

On their journey to White Hall, they rattled across the breadth of the City. Ludgate Hill was a hive of activity. The rhythm of nails being driven into wood, the rasp of saws, the shouts of workmen, the rumbling of heavily laden carts and the smells of tar and pitch, all dedicated to the rebuilding of the city after its devastation during the Great Fire.

'It's remarkable how quickly life returns to normal.'

'Not for Jack Turner.'

'True, Will. But for the rest of them, see how quickly people forget the fear and devastation of that night.'

'No point in staring back into the past, better to get on with life is what I say.'

'How remarkably pragmatic of you, Will. But if we don't learn from the past, aren't we condemned to repeat its mistakes? I mean look outside.' Pepys pointed to the new houses on either side of the street. 'Built on exactly the same lines as before, and perhaps now even closer together. I grant you, there may be a little more use of brick, but if another fire should start in a bakery, then I hazard London would face yet another conflagration.'

'People get on with their lives and the devil take the future. It's the only way that anybody can live. Only God knows what the future holds.'

'Ah, the future. Ours seems to be concerned with a visit to the Court. A word of advice, Will. Only speak when spoken to. And if the King says anything, laugh.'

'Is that all?'

'And don't talk about his mistresses to anybody.'

'I read they hold great power over him.'

Pepys sighed and stopped staring out of the window. ‘The King has three mistresses as far as I am aware. Lady Castlemaine has been one for a number of years and has borne him five children. But she is not in favour at the moment. Another pregnancy seems to have swelled both her greed and her belly. He has recently taken up with two actresses. There is Moll Davis, a pretty thing but not a lot of brains. The other is Nell Gwynn, the 'Protestant whore' as she calls herself.'

'I saw her at Dukes in ‘The Maiden Queen’. Dressed as a gallant she was, and splendid in the role.'

'The King does seem to have a predilection for that sort of thing. Oh, and I forgot the latest. Louise De Kerouailles. French, a bit of a strumpet, but dangerous. Avoid her like you would avoid the clap.'

'That's four.’

'That's for... what?'

'Four mistresses.'

'It changes daily. And I don't keep count.'

'Neither does the King, it seems.'

They continued in silence for the rest of the trip. Pepys stared out of the window of the cab as the noise of rebuilding and construction gave way to the more typical sounds of commerce and strife as they rattled towards White Hall.

He missed the action and activity of his early years at the Navy Board when the King had just returned and London was alive with possibility. A new King for a new age, fighting the dour dullness of the Lord Protector’s time.

There were still times when the old energy returned. Last year, when he defended the Navy in parliament, standing up to the bullies baying for his blood. And, through dint of hard work and oratory, silencing them and the braying hordes at their back.

And there were the affairs that kept him feeling young and desired.

Ah, Debs Willett, how he missed her small breasts and pretty mouth. But he had been discovered by Elizabeth and forced to disown and dismiss the young girl. It had cost him dearly, not least in disbursements at St Olave's.

But for a short while he had been alive and in love.

Now he felt alive again. The diary was missing but he was active once more. His mind and his body racing to discover who had had stolen it and murdered Jack Turner.

As if conjured up by his thoughts, he thought he saw Debs Willetts strolling along the Strand arm in arm with a young vicar.

It can't be her.

He blinked his eyes and leant out of the window of the coach.

'What is it, Sam?'

But there she was, laughing gaily, her head thrown back revealing the soft throat he had loved so much. And next to her, a tall young man dressed in the solemn black of a Preacher, but without a hint of solemnity on his face.

He shook his head once again. Was he dreaming?

No, there she was.

Will leant forward and touched his arm. 'Leave her, Sam. Nothing good can come of opening old wounds.'

He was tempted to order the cabby to stop but Will's touch on his arm stopped him. He was right. Nothing good could come from seeing her again. And besides, there were more important matters to resolve right now.

He sat back against the hard horsehair seat and pulled the blind down, plunging them into semi-darkness.

‘It’s for the best, Sam.’

Pepys closed his eyes. Will was right. It was time for thought not for distractions. There had been too many of them in his life.

Chapter 11

'We're comin' to the Cross, gentlemen. You want the Parade or the Square?'

Pepys woke with a start from his thoughts. 'The Square, I think, cabbie. We can walk to Pell Mell from there.'

'The Square it is, sirs. No 'angings 'ere though. More's the pity.'

'Do I look well?' Will took out a handkerchief, wet it with his tongue, and rubbed the stains on his coat and breeches. He then turned his stockings around so that the tears lay against the backs of his calves.

'As well as ever, Will.'

'What's that supposed to mean?'

'What it's always meant. You are as well as can be expected given the circumstances.'

'What circumstances?'

'Well, given that you possess the world's worst tailor, you have just chased a man across the roofs and through the streets of London, and you have a periwig that looked as though it were constructed by a murder of crows. Those circumstances.'

'Thank you, Samuel Pepys. You really know how to make a man feel comfortable just before he is about to meet his Lord and Sovereign.'

'St. James' Square. Delivered safe and sound. That'll be eighteen pence, gentlemen plus the shilling that the gentlemen promised.'

Pepys alighted from the Hackney, smoothed his clothes, adjusted his periwig so that the curls sat squarely on his shoulders, and strode off in the direction of the Pell Mell.

‘Well, Mr Fisher, thank you for arriving on time. We are off to see the King.'

'Oh, ‘im. ‘Ad ‘im in the back of me ‘ackney once. Didn't leave a tip. Shall I wait or not?'

‘Please do. We'll be back shortly.’

‘Long or short…’

Will looked at the coins in his hand, ‘I know, I know, doesn’t matter how long because you still get paid.’

‘And the ‘oss. He likes his oats does the ‘oss. Oats costs money.’

But the last speech fell on nobody's ears but the horse, as Will Hewer was already rushing after the striding Pepys.

*

'Sam, tell me truthfully, how do I look?’

Pepys stepped back and stared at this friend's clothes. He took out a handkerchief, wet it and wiped a spot of bird shit his friend had missed. ‘You look as though you have come to pay court to a wealthy lady, Will.'

'Is that good?'

'As good as it is going to get.'

'But do I look as though I belong at court?'

'Nobody looks as though they belong at court, not even the King. But, trust me, Will, you will do. Now, look smart, we're nearly there.'

They had walked across St James' Park to the other side, next to the Pell Mell court, before being accosted by three guards.

'Mr Samuel Pepys to see the King.'

'Ah, Pepys, the King has been expecting you.' The voice came from a tall thin man, with a sharp, beak-like nose and a permanent sneer etched into his thin lips that infected every sentence he spoke. Across the bridge of the nose, a square black patch only added to the severity of his face. 'You're late.'

'Good morning, my Lord Arlington. We were unavoidably detained.'

The sneer again. 'You have made a habit of being late, Mr Pepys. Let's hope you won't become the late Mr. Pepys.' A little cackle came from the thin lips. 'Let us approach the King.'

Pepys followed Lord Arlington and Will followed Pepys, staying as close to his side as was possible.

All three of them strode across the marble-chipped courtyard, their feet crunching and sliding on the white stone.

They walked past two more guards, who saluted them, and stepped out into an open lawn at least ten furlongs long. Pepys could see the King was at the end, surrounded by courtiers dressed in the glorious colours and fashions of the day. He was standing over a round wooden ball with a large hammer in his hands. He swung the hammer and the ball trundled towards a metal hoop set into the lawn. A polite smattering of applause came from the assembled courtiers. The King took the applause with a casual wave of bejewelled fingers.

'It looks like you are in luck again, Pepys. The King seems to be winning.' ‘Thank you, Lord Arlington, but luck has nothing to do with it.’

The King bent once more over the ball. He looked up, assessed the correct angle, and with a measured swing of the mallet, the ball flew through the hoop at the end. Again, a round of applause, this time louder.

Arlington took this moment to stride forward. Pepys strode after him, with Will striding after Pepys. They passed the assembled courtiers and approached the King as he wiped his face with a cloth.

‘Damn hot work, Pell Mell, even on a cold day. Yes, Arlington.'

'Your Majesty, may I present the late Mr Pepys.’

Pepys bowed in the correct manner, with his right leg thrust forward and his arm swinging down as he bent from the hips. 'I am sorry to be late, your Majesty. Unavoidably detained.'

'Not in the Tower, I hope. I don't remember signing the warrant.' There was laughter from the courtiers.

'Very witty, your Majesty.' Pepys stepped back and said, 'May I present my clerk at the Admiralty, Mr William Hewer.'

Will took the opportunity to bow in exactly the same manner as Pepys. Unfortunately, as he did so, his periwig slipped from his head onto the lawn, revealing his close cropped hair and a large bald spot in the middle of his crown.

'It seems we have a monk amongst us,' said the King. 'You are?'

'Hewer, your Majesty.' Will attempted his bow again, this time holding on to his periwig with his hand. He noticed the buckle of his shoe had a large dollop of bird shit lodged in it. He rose and quickly wiped the back of his shoe on his stocking.

“'You were, your Majesty?’ If I were ‘Your Majesty’, what pray am I now?’ asked the King.

There was a single titter from the assembled courtiers. They all stared at Rochester who had his hand clamped over his mouth, eyes pretending to be shocked.

Will shuffled uncomfortably from one leg to another, trying to hide both his nerves and the hole in his stockings. 'You're still your Majesty, your Majesty,' he finally blurted out, bowing again to give himself something to do.

'That's very good. I would hate to be somebody else. The family would abhor that, especially brother James.' The King gestured towards a tall, elegant man standing to one side. More titters from the courtiers arrayed against the edge of the Pell Mell court. 'And from which family are you?'

Will looked across at the courtiers. They were all staring at him. 'I'm a Hewer, your Majesty.'

'And what do you make, Hewer?'

A frown appeared between Will's eyes. 'Nothing, your Majesty.'

'Nothing?' said the King in mock outrage, 'and yet you have the temerity to call yourself a Hewer?'

Pepys intervened. 'I think, your Majesty, that Mr Hewer here is more of a vessel for your Majesty's witticisms.'

'Oh, a ewer, Hewer? Thank you for the information, Mr Pepys. I will drink to your health, Master Ewer.' He reached out his hand to the left. A servant came forward with a glass and another with a jug of wine. The King took the glass and raised it to his lips. 'To you sir, may your cup forever runneth over.'

Pepys nudged Will in the ribs and he immediately began another low bow, holding onto his periwig with his hand.

The King placed the empty cup back on the tray. 'Enough of the frivolities, gentlemen. Another game awaits. My Lord Buckingham, I believe it is your turn to challenge me.'

A small man stepped forward. His coat was made of the finest blue silk, etched with gold along the seams and with bright silver buttons down one side. His periwig was parted in the middle and its dark curly locks extended on either side of his shoulders and down his back. He bowed and the wig stayed exactly where it was. 'I believe it is my game, your Majesty. Shall we have a little wager on the side?'

'On the side of the angels or the devil, Buckingham?'

'On the side of both, your Majesty. Twenty pounds to the winner.'

'Ah, the angels will be on my side, Buckingham, divine right of kings, don't you know? Let us begin.'

Arlington coughed loud enough for the King to stop walking towards the end of the Pell Mell court. 'Your Majesty, the orders for Mr Pepys.'

'Ah yes, Pepys, I knew there was some reason you were here today. My minister tells me…' here he pointed to Arlington with his mallet, '… there have been rumours of plots in the Navy. That is your purview is it not?'

'It is your Majesty, but I concern myself with supplies, contracts, etcetera. The things that others find far too tedious to bother with.'

'That's of no consequence. You did well last year in Parliament. Questions are being asked again. Look into it for me, will you? Arlington has all the details.' He waved again with the mallet towards the minister.

Pepys bowed down. 'As you command, your Majesty.'

But his Majesty was already walking toward the start of the game. 'Buckingham, I do hope you have the money that you are going to pay me. I feel it is my day today on the court. The gods are smiling down on me.'

Slowly, Pepys rose from his bow. Other than the quip about the Tower, the King had mentioned nothing about the diary. If he didn't have it, who did?

'Come with me, Pepys. We have a lot to talk about.' The plump, smiling face of Arlington was leaning over him, the black patch across his nose shining in the sunlight. 'You'd better bring Hewer, or Ewer, whatever his name is.' Another smile crossed the lips. 'I have taken the liberty of asking Sir Joseph Williamson to join us.' He strode off across the Parade towards White Hall.

Pepys stared after him. Will took the opportunity to lean over and whisper loudly in his ear. 'Williamson, isn't he...?'

'The head of the Secret Service. Now, we may discover who has the diaries. Come on, time to find out what the hell is going on.'

With that he hurried after the loping Lord Arlington into the Palace of White Hall.

Chapter 12

After an age of climbing rickety stairs, descending narrow staircases and climbing once again, they reached a large, barely furnished room; walls of empty shelves, a simple wooden desk, a large clock ticking loudly, two chairs and, in the corner, Sir Joseph Williamson himself, standing and staring out of the window. He made no acknowledgement when they entered.

'Sit down, Mr Pepys and...' Lord Arlington waved his arm to indicate the two chairs and his inability to remember Will's name.

'It's Hewer, spelt with an 'H'.'

'Ah yes, the man who works with his hands. We have something here that may prove workable for you both.'

'Shall we cease the pleasantries?' Williamson had turned round so that Pepys could now see his face. The light coming in from the window seemed to accentuate the sharpness of his cheekbones and the point of his chin. But, most of all, the light caught his eyes; piercing blue like the sharpest Toledo steel, only twice as cutting.

Arlington sat down behind the desk. 'Please explain what we require of Mr Pepys and his, er, companion, Sir Joseph.'

Williamson made a short bow like an executioner checking the neck of his victim to see that it was in the right position. 'The King's life is in danger. Now, you may believe that the King is always in danger. It is one of the hazards of being a King. However, this time, it is not only the life of the monarch that is under threat but the very existence of the monarchy itself.'

He spoke these words in a soft whisper. Pepys had to lean forward to hear them clearly.

'We are assailed by plots. The King's father, Charles, was executed by the regicides. We have tracked most of them down and...,' here he paused and blew on the ends of his wrinkled fingers, 'removed the threat. A few still exist though, in Holland and in Switzerland, planning and plotting as they always do. The Catholics, and there are still many, not least here at court, are still working for the return of the Pope to these shores. They pray and plot and scheme from their priest holes and their secret churches.'

'And cause fires,' interrupted Arlington.

Sir Joseph sniffed loudly and carried on. 'The Irish, as ever, are revolting. And here, I make no comment on their appearance, even though it is well known that they are a slovenly race. Rather, despite being severely chastised by the late Lord Protector, the next generation is in the process of taking up arms once again.'

'A lot of plotters against the King,' said Pepys. 'I'm surprised his Majesty has time to play Pell Mell with all these plots.'

Sir Joseph ignored him. 'And there are still, of course, the Anabaptists, the Quakers, The Presbyterians, The Fifth Monarchists, the Behmenists, the Philadelphians, the Muggletonians and the Ranters. There's even a group who call themselves Adamites, who celebrate the glory of Christ by dancing around naked. I believe that they will find many friends at Court these days.' Once again, he blew on the ends of his wrinkled fingers. 'All these diverse sects are committed, in one way or another, to the removal of the present King.'

'I don't see what this has to do with myself and my friend, Will Hewer.'

'Be patient, Pepys. Sir Joseph is giving you the background to your task.'

'Let me make myself clear, Mr Pepys.'

Here his pink tongue slipped out between the lips like a lizard testing the air. For a moment, Pepys imagined that it was forked.

'I don't like you or your kind, who think because they have been educated at a poxy Cambridge college, they are better than the rest of the world.'

'The 'poxy Cambridge college' that you are referring to was Magdalen, which despite the pronunciation of its name, was a place of delight for me.'

'Mr Pepys, your happiness, or the lack thereof, is of no consequence to me. I am a professional. I protect the Monarchy, the institution, not the person. And I do so without fear of favour nor advancement. In short, I will do whatever it takes to ensure that the institution is protected from miscreants, plotters, malefactors, delinquents and reprobates. Do I make myself clear, Mr Pepys?'

'As mud, Sir Joseph. But why involve me in your planning and plotting and subterfuges?'

'Despite our advice to the contrary, The King has commanded you investigate this particular scheme, Pepys. He seems to have an inflated estimation of your abilities. So be it. Pray continue, Sir Joseph.'

Pepys was aware of the clock ticking on the wall behind him, its mechanism deafening in the silence of the room. He thought about his diary. Did they have it?

They had not mentioned anything so far. But they may be keeping this news for the end of the interview.

Sir Joseph's tongue slid out from between his lips once again, tasting the air. 'The King has commanded it.' He said this in a voice so low that Pepys could hardly hear. Then, he gave a start as if waking from a reverie. 'This is your mission. You are to go to Chatham and investigate the mood of the Navy. We have heard rumours of Dutch spies working amongst the crews, stirring up trouble and fomenting unrest.'

'Pay them and there wouldn't be any unrest.'

'The management of His Majesty's economy is not in my portfolio, Mr Pepys. Merely the management of his safety.'

'Pay them properly with coin and they would be as loyal as any Englishman.'

'As loyal as those Englishmen who fought for the Dutch against us last year, helping to capture the Royal Charles?'

'When faced with the choice of feeding one's family or starving as a patriot, which would you choose, Lord Arlington?'

Arlington looked at Sir Joseph Williamson. Pepys was aware that something had passed between them. An agreement or an acknowledgement, he wasn't sure.

Arlington ignored his question. It was Sir Joseph who continued, again with the appearance of the tongue between his lips before he spoke. 'The King has commanded that you investigate the state of Chatham dockyard and any disaffection there, reporting back to him, and to us.' He indicated himself and Arlington. 'Are you willing to accept the commission or...' Here, he paused and blew on his fingers once more, 'do we need to find other means of persuading you?'

Pepys understood the threat that came from behind those blue eyes. Did they have the diary? Or was the threat something else? A weakness that even he didn't know about? Or were they threatening him with the Tower? With torture? He realised that he had no option other than to accept. 'Persuasion is not necessary, Sir Joseph, if the King commands me, so be it.'

A smile flickered across the face of the Head of the Secret Service. He had a smile like that of a hyena who has just discovered the corpse of a decaying cow lying in a field.

It was Lord Arlington who spoke. 'You will depart for Chatham tomorrow, reporting back to us by the 9th.'

'But that is only seven days...'

'The time is pressing, Pepys. Our intelligence suggests that the attempt on the King's life and the mutiny in the Navy will take place before the 12th.'

'The anniversary of the Dutch raid on Chatham two years ago?'

'You remember it well, Pepys.'

'Who could forget that day, my lord?'

'True, a sad day. A day of infamy.'

Pepys thought for a moment. 'Before I accept the commission, I have two conditions.'

'You are in no position to ask for conditions, Mr Pepys,' said Sir Joseph, suddenly turning back from the window to stare at Pepys with his blue eyes.

'Nonetheless, Sir Joseph, I will make them. First, I am to be accompanied by my clerk, Will Hewer, to Chatham.'

'Me? Why do you involve me in all this?'

'I need your help, Will. Seven days is too short a time. It will take us that long to work out what is happening. Can I count on you?'

'Of course, if you need my help. I will accompany you.'

'It's very touching, friendship, isn't it? Almost enough to make one believe in the essential goodness of humanity once again.'

Lord Arlington smiled from his perch behind the desk.

'Most touching, Sir Joseph.' He turned back to Pepys. 'And your second condition?'

'That I report my findings directly to the King. It is on his command that I have undertaken this commission after all.'

Lord Arlington and Sir Joseph Williamson looked across at each other. Once again, Pepys was aware that a message had passed between them without any words being spoken. It was Arlington who replied. 'Agreed, Pepys, you may present your findings to the King in Council. We and the other members of the Cabal will also be present to hear your conclusions.'

Arlington opened a drawer in the desk and pulled out a letter which he placed on the desk. 'Here is your letter of commission, Pepys, signed by the King. It provides all the usual encouragements to assist the bearer in any way possible.'

'So, you already knew I would accept?'

'Of course, Pepys, why else would we bring you here and brief you?' Arlington scratched the black plaster on his nose and pulled another letter from his desk. 'Here is an introduction to the Commissioner of Chatham Dockyard, Lord Turton. He has already been informed of your arrival.'

'Everyone seems to know my movements except me.'

'Not everyone, Pepys.' He scratched his nose once again and looked at Sir Joseph, who continued to stare out of the window. He pushed the papers across the desk. 'You will also be contacted by one of our agents in Chatham. I presume you have no objections to working with a woman?'

'A woman? You use women in your work?'

'As you may have gathered, Mr Pepys,' Sir Joseph

spoke without removing his eyes from gazing out of the window, 'we use everybody and anybody in the cause of the King.'

Arlington stood up. 'We will see you here at noon on the 9th of June, Pepys, to read and hear your report. Do not miss the appointment.'

Pepys got to his feet and adjusted his periwig. 'Until the 9th, gentlemen.'

'Oh, just one more thing, Mr Pepys.' Sir Joseph's tongue slipped out between his lips once again, 'do be careful what you write, won't you?'

Chapter 13

'Sam, what did he mean?'

'Shush, Will, the walls have ears.' Pepys looked around him as he walked down the corridor. 'We'll talk later, not here, not now.'

As if on cue, a group of men in deep discussion came around the corner. Pepys recognised one of them from the rounded stoop of his walk and the sharp rap of his cane as it echoed down the corridor. If there was one person he didn't want to meet now, it was Anthony Ashley Cooper.

He pushed Will into an alcove to allow the men to pass.

'What the…'

Pepys placed his finger across his mouth, quieting Will.

The men walked past them without looking up, lost in their discussions.

When they had gone by, Pepys' shoulders relaxed. 'Thank God, they didn't see us, Will.'

'Ah, Mr Pepys, I thought it was you. I do hope you are enjoying this alcove.'

Pepys raised his head and stared at the man in front of him. The legs were short and stocky. An ebony cane added a black third leg in contrast to the white stockings of the other two. Black trousers cut in the modern fashion were enveloped by a black coat, the light reflecting off the silver buttons. A frill of soft linen led to a ginger beard and a hooked nose, framed by an even more ginger periwig. Pepys' eyes focused on the wart that lay to the side of the mouth. A single, long ginger hair extended from the wart and began to curl back on itself. The mouth opened and began to speak again.

'It has been a long time since we last saw each other, hasn't it? Last summer, I believe, during the parliamentary enquiry on the debacle that is the King's Navy. You acquitted yourself well, Mr Pepys, dissembling falsehoods seem to be your speciality.'

Pepys recovered himself enough to hear the challenge in the last statement. 'I do not know what you mean, Mr Cooper. I merely presented the facts of the situation. It was all written down in black and white.'

'But words, and indeed facts, can be twisted to suit any argument, can they not? Your performance in Parliament was exemplary, you were meant for the Theatre, Mr Pepys, not government service.'

'I am happy to play my part in government, my lord. I enjoy the theatre but I'm afraid it does not suit my personality. Too much pretending to be what one isn't.'

'You should go to see Dryden’s new play at Duke’s tonight. There's a role in it that would be perfect for you.'

'A role on the stage? I'm afraid I'm no Mrs Barry, Mr Betterton or even Nell Gwynn. The limelight is not for me. I prefer to work in the background. To be one of the props, if you like.'

Cooper reached up to touch the wart at the side of his mouth. To Pepys, the hand looked nothing less than a claw cleaning the beak of an eagle.

'The background, do you say? Perhaps, your trip to Chatham will change that situation. Give you a more starring role?'

Pepys shook his head. How did he know about the investigation?

As if hearing Pepys' thoughts, Cooper replied. 'Nothing is secret in White Hall, Mr Pepys. At least, not for long. Did you enjoy your journey to the dockyards? And a word in your ear, Mr Pepys,' Cooper gestured for Sam to move closer. As he did so, Pepys caught a whiff of breath that could sink a thousand ships. He jerked back and turned his ear towards Cooper. 'Make sure it's the Catholics who are behind it all, won't you, Mr Pepys. We wouldn't want people to think that you harboured leanings in favour of the return of the Papists, would we?'

Pepys jerked his head away. 'We wouldn't want people to think that at all, Mr Cooper. I thank you for your advice.'

Cooper waved his claw-like hand and began to move away, stopping after just three taps of the cane. 'Do enjoy the Theatre tonight, Mr Pepys, you may find it all very illuminating even though you don't enjoy the limelight.'

The cane began tapping down the corridor as Cooper hobbled away.

'Who was that?'

'That was a man you don't want to meet, Will.'

'But having just met him, wouldn't it be better to know who he was in order to avoid him in the future?'

'I will tell you over dinner, Will. This morning's events have left me ravenous. A lobster at the Castle on the Strand should serve to fill the gap.' Pepys shivered and looked all round him. 'Let's be off. This place is haunted by ghouls, most of whom are still living.'

With that, he launched himself down the corridor in the opposite direction from Anthony Ashley Cooper.

'Our coach is that way, across the park.'

'Good, let us enjoy the walk. Remove the cobwebs from the mind and stimulate the stomach. And more importantly, clear our noses of the stench of the court.' He paused and cupped his hand to his ear. 'Do you hear that?'

Will stopped and listened. All he could hear was the

wind whistling down the corridor and far off, a woman screaming. He wasn't certain whether it was in anger, fear, or pleasure.

'The woman?'

'No, the lobster calling our name. Let's be off.'

Chapter 14

'Four lobster and a pint of sack.' Pepys smiled at the serving woman. 'What else do you recommend?'

'Well, my dear, the oysters are fresh in from Colchester this morning. Still swimming they were when they came up the Strand.'

'A dozen of those, if you please.' Another smile and a long stare at the body of the woman as she walked to the kitchen. 'She must be new. Haven't seen her here before.'

There was an exasperated grunt from Will. 'Sam, if you could keep your mind on the matter in hand.'

Pepys held up his hands in mock surrender. 'Mens reus but not actus reus, Will. He that cannot appreciate the beauty of the feminine form is condemned to a life of ugliness.'

'And he that appreciates the feminine form while he is already married is condemned to a life of cold stares and even colder beds. Don’t you remember the trouble you had over Deborah Willett only last year?'

'Guilty as charged, Will, but not guilty since then. I have turned over a new leaf, but occasionally my eyes betray me, as they are wont to do. Luckily, neither the courts, nor Elizabeth, have found cause to condemn people for guilty eyes. At least, not yet.

'Those who are seen to be guilty, are guilty.'

Pepys tilted his head. 'You have a very Puritan view of guilt, Will. Did three years at Cambridge teach you nothing of the law?'

'It taught me that we are in a pickle, a stew, a mess. That's what it taught me.'

'Ah, I see your point. Let me sum up our position.'

Will nodded his head once again.

'The diary has been stolen. It contains certain unfortunate references to the proclivities of his majesty, and of the court. But nobody has actually told us they have it, yet. The thief is dead, stabbed in the neck, by an unknown man. And the locket is lost again, stolen by the same man.'

Will blushed. 'Please don't remind me. What will I say to Elizabeth?'

'You will tell her the truth, Will. That the locket is being polished at the jewellers.'

'I'm not very good at dissembling, Sam.'

'Just pretend you are on the stage, Will. An actor saying his lines.'

'Easy for you to say, not so easy for me to do.'

Pepys grasped his friends arm. 'But you must, Will, if we are to do our duty and discover who is behind all this.' He let go of the arm. 'Drink your wine, it's delicious.'

Will ignored the glass in front of him. 'And this duty also involves the investigation of plots against the King in the Navy?'

'That is our assignment. The difficulty is in our report a week from now.'

'Why?'

'Well, if the plot exists...'

'Of course, it exists. Lord Arlington and Sir Joseph told us it exists.'

'Plots have always existed, Will. They are a very useful method of keeping the population quiet with the threat, or perceived threat, of an outside force damaging their life and liberty.'

'So the plot doesn't exist?'

'I didn't say that. It may exist and it may not. We will discover the truth in Chatham. No, the problem remains what do we say in our report.'

'I don't understand.'

'People don't want to hear the truth, Will, they want to discover support for their existing beliefs.'

The serving woman placed a bowl of oysters down on the table. ‘Here you are, gents. A dozen of Colchester's best. Be careful with the knives. Sharp they are. We had a gentlemen cut himself last week as he was opening one. Near bled to death, he did. Took me half an hour to clean up the blood. Enjoy.'

Will picked up his knife and looked at it. 'I think there's still blood on this.'

But Pepys was already wedging his knife into the hinge of the shell and levering off the top half. He quickly cut away the muscle holding the flesh and swallowed the oyster whole.

'Heaven, I think, Will, is a fresh oyster washed down by a pint of sack. These are the manna of the gods.'

Will was still holding his knife.

'Do tuck in or there will be none left.'

'You were saying...'

Pepys stopped for a moment as he inserted the knife into another oyster. 'What was I saying? Ah, yes, beliefs. The King wants to believe that his Navy is loyal to a man, despite the fact that he refuses to pay, feed, or clothe them.'

'So they can't be plotting against him.'

'Yes, the belief in divine right often gets in the way of the truth. A trait that seems to run in the Stuart line. His father suffered exactly the same affliction.'

'And lost his head because of it.'

Pepys leant forward and whispered, 'Indeed, Will, I

was there at the execution of Charles, but let's not talk about that here.' He slurped down another oyster. 'Are you going to eat any of these? Or shall I finish them all?'

Will began to open his oyster, taking extreme care with the knife. 'So he wants you to report that all is well in Chatham.'

'Exactly, Will. He wants me to report that all is well because I have already discovered and removed any miscreants who were plotting against him. Hence, all is now well.'

'So, we not only have to discover who is plotting but remove them too.'

'In a nutshell, Will. Talking of shells, you are falling rapidly behind.' A pile of oyster shells lay on the table in front of Pepys. Will was still opening his first.

'But what does Sir Joseph want?'

'That is a good question. Will. Put simply, they want me to fail.'

'That's simple enough. But how can you fail?'

'By not discovering a plot. By discovering a plot and doing nothing about it. By discovering the wrong plot.'

'That sounds awfully complicated.'

'Bureaucracies have a habit of complicating the simple, Will. And bureaucracies attached to the Court complicate the already complicated.'

'What about Mr Cooper? What does he want?'

Pepys swallowed another oyster. 'And don't forget, Lord Arlington, Lord Buckingham, the King's mistresses and the rest of the court.'

'Not forgetting them, what do they want?

'Ah, that we have yet to discover.'

'I'm sorry, I don't understand.'

'Really, Will, you are going to have to eat and think at

the same time. Shall we order another dozen? I seem to have finished these.'

Will nodded his head.

Pepys waved his hand at the serving woman. She came rushing over. 'What can I do you for, gents?'

'Another dozen of the Colchester and another pint of sack.'

'Certainly, sirs. Before or after the lobster?'

'At the same time, I think. My friend has some catching up to do.'

She looked at Will still holding his first oyster. 'Do you want me to shuck them for you, sir?'

'That would be most agreeable. My friend may then be even able to enjoy a few.'

Will banged down his glass on the table. 'Sam, I do wish you would take this more seriously. It all seems a game to you.'

Pepys placed his own glass next to the pile of shucked oysters. For a moment, he was silent before he answered. 'I do take these events gravely, Will. And I use that word with all its shades of meaning. But we will not survive and solve them by running around like an actor who has forgotten his lines. Only three things will serve us in the coming week.' He took another sip of Sack from his glass.

'And they are?'

Pepys counted on the fingers of his right hand. 'Our organisation. Our intelligence. And our ability to make our masters believe that we are indispensable to their plans.'

'Not so easy.'

'Not easy at all, Will, but if it were easy, it wouldn't be a challenge, would it?' Pepys raised his glass. 'Now, drink up, there's a good fellow. In the next week, we have to find the missing diary, go to Chatham, discover who is plotting in the Navy and stop them from doing whatever it is they want to do.'

Will's head dropped onto the table. 'All in a week?'

'All in a week.'

'Where do we start?'

'Well, we could start with these delicious lobsters brought by the even more delicious...what is your name, dear?'

'Here we are, gents. Your shucked oysters and fresh lobster.' She placed a steaming plate of crustaceans in the centre of the table. 'It's Mary, sir. But don't you be taking my name in vain. It's the only one I have.'

'Thank you, Mary. A name that smells as sweet as a rose, fair sprung in June ...'

'I think you mean 'that which we call a rose, by any other name, would smell as sweet'.'

'You are well acquainted with the theatre, Mary.'

'I used to sell oranges there, sir. Didn't like Shakespeare. Too soppy for me. Much preferred Webster. I likes a bit of blood and guts with me oranges.'

'I'm afraid I don't share your view, Mary.'

'Sam, Sam. Can we get back to the matter at hand?'

'Thank you, sir. I'll leave you to your food and your friend.'

'Thank you, Mary.' He turned to Will. 'She really does have the most excellent smile.'

'Sam, what are we to do after the lobsters?'

'First, we are to go home to Seething Lane for a quick change of clothes and to fetch Elizabeth.'

'We change our clothes after seeing the king?'

'We didn't have time before, Will.'

'And after Seething Lane?'

'To the theatre. Didn't you hear Mr Cooper? He seems

to be awfully keen that we attend this evening. I wonder why?'

'What is playing?'

'Dryden's latest, Tyrannic Love. I'm sure it will be as melodramatic as all his attempts at the stage.'

'That's a harsh judgement, Sam. I enjoyed Maiden Love.'

'You would enjoy a Punch and Judy show, as long as it had a stage.'

Will threw down his fork. 'The diary has been a stolen, a man murdered, myself attacked in the street, and you think the best thing we can do with our time is to visit the theatre?'

'No, the best thing we could do with our time is to visit Sir William Coventry, and that we will do tomorrow morning.'

'Why him?'

'He is the one man who should be able to unravel some of this Gordian knot of conspiracy for us, and suggest who was behind the theft of the diary. These Lobster are excellent, Will, you should try one. Mistress Mary has done us proud.'

'One final question.'

'Ask away, Will. When your curiosity is sated, we may start on your hunger.'

'You still think it's important to get your book back?'

'It is key, Will, to my future and that of Elizabeth.'

'It is so important?'

'Indeed it is. Now eat up, we mustn't be late for the theatre.'

Will picked up his fork once more, stabbing the two tines into the soft body of a lobster.

'Oh, and one more thing...'

Will leaned forward. 'What's that?'
'Don't forget to pay the bill on your way out.'

Chapter 15

Pepys stepped into the hallway of his house on Seething Lane to find the dog yapping around his ankles. He gave it a quick kick, hoping that Elizabeth wouldn't notice. The dog yelped and retreated back to its basket in the kitchen.

The noise brought his wife out of her room. 'You're late,' she shouted from upstairs. 'I'm sorry, dear, affairs of state.'

'Are you sure it wasn't a new affair of yours, Samuel?' Her head popped over the wooden balustrade of the staircase. 'I'm sorry I didn't see you there, Mr Hewer.'

'Good afternoon, Mrs Pepys. I hope you are keeping well?'

'As well as can be expected given the affairs of my husband.' She stared meaningfully at Pepys.

He sighed, handing his hat to Jane. 'My dear, I have told you many times that was an unfortunate aberration due to the pressures of work and the close proximity of the party concerned. There is no need for you to be jealous anymore. Will is able to vouch for me.'

Will edged his way further into the hall.

'At least there is one honest man that I know.' She ran down the stairs and curtsied prettily in front of Will.

'A pleasure to see you, Mrs Pepys.'

'And you too, Will, but why the formality? Has Samuel been working you so hard you forget our friendship?'

'No... no, it's just...'

She stepped forward and examined his legs. 'Your stockings are blackened and torn. What has Samuel been doing to you?'

'Nothing, I fell over a wall. Nothing really.'

'You must let Jane wash your feet and borrow a new pair of Samuel's stockings. Please fetch them, Jane.'

'New stockings? I only washed them yesterday. Those'll be good enough.'

Elizabeth's face grew stern. 'Please fetch some clean stockings for Mr Hewer.'

'You must get yourself ready too, my dear, Mr Dryden has his new play tonight at Dukes.'

'I won't be long. I would have liked to have worn my locket tonight.'

Will looked at Sam Pepys, who immediately stepped forward. 'You need to change too dear, give Will time to put on new stockings.'

'Where is my locket, Will?'

Pepys nudged Will gently on the arm. 'Hm, yes, the locket. Still being cleaned, I think. We'll get it when it's ready.'

Elizabeth looked at him with her round eyes. 'Are you sure it's being cleaned, Mr Hewer?'

Will stared down at his shoes, noticing that the lump of chicken shit was still embedded in the buckle. When he looked up, Elizabeth was still staring at him. He could feel his face going bright red. 'Of course, Elizabeth, we took it to the jewellers in the Old Exchequer, where I bought it. They'll make it look as good as new.'

'But Samuel said that you took it to a jewellers in the New Exchange?'

'Did he?' stammered Will.

'Yes, he did.'

'Come along, dear, better get yourself ready, we'll be late.' Pepys put his arm around her chivvying her upstairs.

Elizabeth shrugged off the arm. 'Well, Mr Hewer, which is it?'

Will blushed. 'Of course, I forgot. We took it the New Exchange first but they were too busy. The King and his mistresses, you know. So then I took it back to where I bought it.' Will smiled an inane grin and tapped his foot on the wooden floor.

The only reply he received was a 'Hmm' and the swish of her dress as she climbed the stairs. Halfway up, she stopped and turned, 'I hope for your sake, Samuel Pepys, this has nothing to do with that harlot. I can't bring myself to say her name in this house. I know something is going on, and I will find out what it is. If she is involved, I will leave you, Samuel. Do I make myself plain?'

She turned once more and stomped up the stairs, her shoes beating a tattoo on the old wood. The third step from the top gave a loud squeak as she stepped on it. 'And how my times have I asked you to fix this stair?'

Chapter 16

As soon as they entered the Dukes Theatre, the noise hit them. In the auditorium, people were standing up and shouting across to their friends up in the boxes, oranges were being sold and thrown, wine was being drunk. On their right, a monkey ran chattering down the aisle chased by his owner. 'Percy, come back here, this minute.'

The stage was brightly lit by the wax candles arrayed in sconces at the front, while above them, two immense Candelabra poured out their light over both the actors and the audience.

They were approached by a young man whom Pepys had never seen before.

'Ere you are sir, I saved these seats for you and your party.' He pointed to three seats on the end of the sixth row. 'A good position to see the stage and 'ear the actors.'

The man was a bum warmer, saving seats for patrons who couldn't be bothered to get there at noon to reserve the best ones. Not a bad job if you could get the work, thought Pepys.

'Just sixpence each, sir. Best seats in the 'ouse. Perfect for your 'onour and 'is lady.' The man held his hand out, palm upwards. Pepys delved into his purse and gave the man his money. With one shilling and sixpence to enter, this was proving to be an expensive night.

'I see you brought some money,' said Will.

'I hope he has enough for oranges. Look isn't that Lady Castlemaine?' Elizabeth pointed to a box that lay to the left of the stage above one of the doors where the actors made their entrance.

'Where?'

'Up there.'

His wife was right. There she was. The King's mistress was looking slightly plump due to her pregnancy but still caused Pepys' heart to leap. He had admired her from afar for so long. It was rumoured that she had been supplanted in the King's affections by other, younger women, but Pepys refused to believe she could ever be rejected in such a demeaning manner. Her skin was as white as powdered snow with two beauty marks pasted just below her rosy cheeks; a small butterfly and a single star. She raised her vizard to cover her face as though she was aware that Pepys was staring at her, and leant into her companion to whisper in his ear.

Out of the corner of his eye, Pepys caught somebody waving at him. It was Cooper, still dressed in his bright green suit. He pointed to the stage and mouthed some words that Pepys couldn't hear in the hubbub.

The bell rang for the beginning of the play. Will and Pepys took their seats with Elizabeth in between them. The better to protect her from the wandering hands and eyes of the other members of the audience.

A group of fops muscled their way down to the front where their seats had been guarded by two burly footmen. Pepys recognised Lord Rochester from this morning in St James' Park.

One of them tripped on a basket that someone had placed in the aisle. He fell onto an old man, knocking his periwig off and revealing a head as bald as a boiled egg. The man and his companions pushed the fop to the ground.

For a moment, Pepys thought that a fight was about to break out between the two groups. But just as fists were being raised, a blast of trumpets issued from the musicians beneath the stage and the curtain rose at the back.

All eyes turned towards it and the hubbub died a little. Pepys recognised Kynaston, dressed as a Roman, striding down to the front, over the green baize that covered the wooden boards. He struck a pose, with his left hand gripping the shoulder of his toga, and his right arm raised and ready to begin his declamation.

'Percy, got you, you little fucker.' This interruption was followed by a stream of loud chatter from the outraged monkey and a loud shush from the rest of the audience.

Kynaston settled himself and struck his pose again.

'Self love which never rightly understood,
Makes poets still conclude the plays are good.
And malice, in all critics, reigns so high,
That small errors, they whole plays decry;
So that to see this fondness, and that spite
You'd think that none but Madmen judge or write.

Pepys leant forward to hear the lines. It was the latest epic from Dryden, whose recent appointment as Poet Laureate ensured a fair audience. He hoped that it wouldn't be too smutty. He hated it when the theatre descended into sexual innuendo. They should save that for the mummers on the streets or the Punch and Judy shows from Italy. But with Nell Gwynn in the cast, he wasn't hopeful.

The prologue finished, Kynaston retired from the stage and the first act began. From stage left, a crowd of actors emerged and assembled in the middle, surrounding Mohun as Maximin.

From his seat on the sixth row, Pepys could see their thick white face paint and kohl-rimmed eyes.

Mohun separated himself from the pack, grabbed the fold of his toga with his right hand, raised his left arm and paused before beginning his speech;

Thus far my arms have with success been crowned,
And found no stop, or vanquished what they found.
The German lakes my legions have o'erpast,
With all the bars which art or nature cast:
My foes, in watery fastnesses inclosed,
I fought alone, to their whole war exposed;

In the pause while Mohun took breath, a loud fart ripped through the audience, causing a roar of laughter.

'Robert, you've just farted in A Minor,' shouted one of the fops.

'A minor? Where is he? I could do with a little boy right now.'

Ignoring the interruption, Mohun raised his arm once more and began to declaim in a voice that resonated all the way to the back of the theatre;

Did first the depth of trembling marshes sound,
And fixed my eagles in unfaithful ground;
By force submitted to the Roman sway
Fierce nations, and unknowing to obey;
And now, for my reward, ungrateful Rome,
For which I fought abroad, rebels at home.

More bombast. thought Pepys. This was going to be a long three hours if the writing continued in such a vein. Elizabeth and Will seemed to be entranced, though, staring at the stage, fixated on the actors and their words.

The rest of the first act continued much like the

opening scene with the actors strutting about the stage, striking poses and stumbling over their lines. It was only when Nell Gwynn came on that Pepys perked up. She was supposed to be the latest infatuation of the King and he could see why. Big eyes, small breasts and a winning smile were combined with no little acting talent. Nell moved like she had been born to live on the stage. It was as if a light focussed only on her as, dressed in a translucent white shift, she spoke her lines and glided effortlessly from scene to scene.

At the end of the first act, he only had eyes for her, and her alone. The others, Mohun and Kynaston, vanished, becoming mere vessels for lines. She spoke and he listened to her voice as if it were just for him.

Then she was walking off stage, the last words were said and the attendants began to change the scenery.

A few people stood up and stretched. Others left their seats, bored already by Dryden's never-ending couplets. The women dropped their vizards, the better to see and be seen. Lady Castlemaine leant over to gossip with a man in the next box.

Orange sellers moved through the theatre selling their wares. One approached Pepys.

'Ere, don't I know you. Didn't pay for your oranges last time you was 'ere.'

'Madam, I think you must be mistaken.' He turned back to face Elizabeth and Will but felt a tap on his shoulder.

'Nah, it's you, ain't it? I'd recognise that mangy mane anywhere. Where's my bleedin' money?'

'I think you are mistaken, my dear lady. I have never bought oranges from you.'

The audience in the surrounding seats pricked up their

ears, hoping that a new, more exciting play would take place right in front of them.

The woman's voice rose. ‘Don't you my lady me, I want me money for me oranges. You eats 'em, you pays. Oranges don’t grow on trees.'

Pepys thought for a moment. 'But they do, dear lady, they do.'

The woman's head went back in a howl of anger. The audience leant forward. 'There you go agin, dear lady this, dear lady that. I's wants me money.'

Pepys was aware that the audience was now staring at them. He felt a dig in his ribs from Elizabeth and heard an urgent whisper. 'Pay her, everyone's looking.'

The woman looked ready to explode.

'I'd like to buy some more oranges today if I may?' He blurted out.

'How many you want?'

The audience began to go back to its gossip, the prospect of an entertainment vanishing with Pepys' offer.

'Give me a dozen.'

'A dozen for the gentleman, it is. Very generhous, my dear sir, very generhous indeed.' She handed over the contents of her basket.

Pepys collected the small oranges in his hands giving half to Will.

'That'll be seven shillings.' She put out her hand.

'Seven shillings? For oranges?'

'Four Shillings for today and three Shillings from before. That makes seven Shillings if my 'rithmetic be right.'

Pepys recognised when he was beaten. 'Pay her please, Will.'

Will placed the oranges in his lap and delved deep into

his purse.

The orange seller's hand closed around the money she was given. 'Fank you gents. A pleasure doing business wiv you.' She walked down the aisle, shouting, 'Oranges, gets your oranges here.'

At that moment, the trumpets rang out for the second act. Pepys bit into one of the oranges, skin and all. His face screwed up. It was as sour as the play. He threw it on the floor with all the other rubbish.

The actors prattled on but Pepys wasn't listening. Somewhere in London his diary was being read by someone at this very moment. It's secrets, his innermost thoughts, revealed to the reader. Part of him wished he had never written it. But the other half knew he was glad he did. It always gave him pleasure to read the words again, reliving the fleeting passages of his life once more. In his diary, he was the lead actor, the star, the Latin tag of his own life. All others revolved around him and his desires.

The action on the stage continued as Maximus fell in love with St. Catherine and was torn between his duty and desire. There was no conflict in Pepys' mind. Duty always came first. Duty always had to come first.

He was woken from his reveries by loud shouts that weren't coming from the stage. Two men were grappling with each other in front of him. Pepys recognised the fop and the older man from before. It seemed the argument had erupted once again. The actors on the stage stopped and turned toward the audience, more intent on watching the developing fight than speaking their lines.

'Take that, sir.' The fop threw a feeble punch that only succeeded in throwing himself off balance.

The older man took advantage and landed a kick right between the breeches. The fop doubled over and squealed like a young girl experiencing the joys of orgasm for the first time. He collapsed amongst the orange peel, spit, and dirty rushes of the theatre floor.

His friends drew their swords.

The rasp of steel was matched by the friends of the older man. Both sets faced each other over the prostrate body of the fop, who groaned and rolled about in the shit, holding onto his swelling and swollen member.

Nell Gwynn walked to the front of the apron, close to the sconces. She leant out and held her hand above her eyes as if staring into the far distance. 'Gentlemen, gentlemen. If you want to fight, please come on stage. We poor actors can save ourselves the trouble.'

The audience roared with laughter and the two groups looked at each other.

'I suggest you put away your pricks.' She gestured to the swords they held in their hands, 'and look to your friend's prick. He sounds like he has just been gelded.'

The audience laughed again.

'Is there a doctor in the house to can save this poor man's manhood?'

'You could doctor it yourself, Nell,' a wag shouted from one of the boxes.

'Ah, but if I did that, he would enjoy another death. A little death.'

The audience roared with laughter and two attendants came in to help the injured man to his feet. He limped out of the theatre, followed by his friends.

'Now, where were we?'

'On the stage, I believe.' The same wag shouted.

The play began again. Nell and Hart continued their scene as if nothing untoward had happened. Pepys heard the musicians tune their instruments and then the first strains of a beautiful air rang out throughout the theatre. On stage, St. Catherine was dreaming that she was in paradise. On hearing the music, Pepys knew he was already there.

'Mr Purcell has surpassed himself,' he whispered

'Shush,' was his wife's only response.

Pepys closed his eyes and Purcell's music washed over him. He gathered in the lusciousness of the strings. He swam in the calm waters of the bassoons. He cleansed himself in the beauty of the voice. What did it matter if the diary was missing? If only life could only be like this all the time. But then the music ended and he was back in the theatre with its stench of smoke, orange peel, dried sweat and the wax of the candles.

The play continued on the stage. St. Catherine, droned on. Maximus strutted and preened. Only Valeria in the pretty shape of Nell held his attention. Even the angel, Ameriel, descending from on high with a flaming sword to smite the wheel of life, only relieved the tedium for a short while.

'That was very prettily done,' said Will.

'Shush,' said his wife staring at the stage or at the naked body of the Angel, Pepys wasn't certain which.

Maximin was left on stage;

How hard it is this beauty to forget!
My stormy rage has only shook my will:
She crept down lower, but she sticks there still.
Fool that I am to struggle thus with love!

For a moment, Pepys was taken back to his time with Deb Willett. He too had suffered the pangs of love as he watched from afar, driven ever closer by his desire.

He had touched her lips and her bosom, drawn like a moth to the innocence that was her flame.

But then Elizabeth had found out and he was forced to denounce and renounce his love. He knew now it was nothing but an infatuation, a disease that had infected his heart with all the virulence of a pox affecting the balls.

On stage, people were dying with such a speed that Pepys found it difficult to keep up. He wished it had all happened earlier and faster. He let out a huge yawn.

'Shush,' scolded his wife with tears in her eyes as she stared at the stage.

'Make haste,' shouted Maximin.

'I only wish you would,' said Pepys.

'Shush,' said his wife.

There followed an orgy of death that could only happen in ancient Rome and the theatres of London. Maximin died. Placidus died. Even Valeria in the lovely shape of Nell died. Porphyries remained to say the last words over the body of Nell and he left by the stage door on the right.

'Thank God, that's over,' said Pepys.

'Shush,' said his wife.

Only Nell was left lying on the stage. He could see her small bosom rising and falling with each breath even though she was supposed to be dead. Two attendants came on the stage to carry her off. But as they started to lift her, she rose and said;

'Hold; are you mad?
You damn'd confounded dog!
I am to rise, and speak the epilogue.'

The audience laughed. Pepys saw Lady Castlemaine throw her head back and guffaw, nearly falling off her chair. Luckily, her companion had his arm around her shoulders to stop her from tipping backwards.

On stage, Nell stood up and, in her voice with its London twang, began to speak;

'I come, kind gentlemen, strange news to tell ye;
I am the ghost of poor departed Nelly.
Sweet ladies, be not frighted; I'll be civil,
I'm what I was, a little harmless devil.'

Pepys wasn't sure if this was the real Nell Gwynn speaking or the poet Dryden making play with her.

She continued to speak her lines from the heart;

'To tell you true, I walk, because I die
Out of my calling, in a tragedy.
O poet, damn'd dull poet, who could prove
So senseless, to make Nelly die for love!'

Were they lines or was she improvising the poet's words on stage? Pepys still couldn't be certain. But then, she walked to the front of the apron that jutted out into the auditorium. She stopped for a moment, gazed over the audience before finally fixing her eyes on Samuel Pepys himself. She spoke again;

'For the writer's pen is his phallus,
The blue ink his seed,
And though he's impotent,
He's prolific indeed.
He scribes each night,
A daily nocturnal rite,
His words will be his death,

Strung by the neck till out of breath.'

Pepys held his breath. The words from the stage were for him. He was sure they were for him. She was looking straight at him. Nell Gwynn was staring at him. He was sure she gave a small nod as she finished her line. A nod that was just for Pepys telling him that she had spoken the message for his ears, and his ears only.

He looked across at Elizabeth and Will. They were both enraptured by Nell's performance, standing at the front of the apron, her translucent white shift shimmering in the candlelight.

The words, they were just for him!

She turned now and looked up at one of the boxes. Dryden was sitting there with his friends, a playful smile dancing across his face.

Nell spoke again;

'As for my epitaph when I am gone,
I'll trust no poet, but will write my own:-
Here Nelly lies, who, though she lived a slattern,
Yet died a princess, acting in St Catharine.'

He stayed rooted in his seat as the audience rose to its feet, roared its approval and applauded the actors. He stayed still even as Nell came out and took her bows. He didn't move, even as his wife poked him in the ribs.

'Samuel, time to go.'

He mumbled some answer. Had he really heard those words on the stage? Were they really aimed at him?

Elizabeth touched him gently on the shoulder. 'Samuel, I don't think I have ever seen you so affected by a play. Has St. Catherine impressed you so much?'

'I'm well, my dear. A little tired, I think. Shall we go home and have our supper?'

'If you want, Samuel, but we have nought but yesterday's leftovers.'

'Good, good.'

'Fine play, if a mite too long,' said Will.

Out of the corner of his eye, Pepys saw Cooper with a smirk on his face. The man cupped his hands around his mouth and shouted down from his box, 'I do hope you enjoyed the play, Mr Pepys.'

Chapter 17

The following morning was fine and bright, a pleasant June day when the sun fought the yellow haze of the city, breaking through to shine its light on all the citizens assembled beneath its rays. If he hadn't been so troubled in mind and spirit by the events at the Dukes Theatre the night before, it would have been a morning when Pepys would have rejoiced in the glory that was the world.

He ate a hearty breakfast of collops of bacon, and a slice of hare pye left over from two days ago. Will, as ever, was on time arriving before the clock in the hall had struck the seventh hour.

'Let us walk to Tower Stairs. On such a morning as this, our legs should see the light of day.'

They went out through the front door of the house and turned left along Seething Lane. The Crown was already open and several workmen, still wearing the button hats and clothes of their trade, had stepped outside to enjoy their ale in the sunlight. One of them raised a glass. 'Morning, Mr Pepys.'

'Who's he?' asked Will.

'I haven't any idea.'

'But he seems to know you well enough.'

'Fame has both its advantages and its curses, Will. Notoriety has only the latter.'

There was a snort from Will. 'You mean to say you are famous now? Really, Sam, your vanity knows no bounds.'

Pepys laughed. 'Thank you for pricking my balloon of pomposity, Will. The words are welcome, if not welcoming.'

'It's my occupation, Sam. Clerk to the Admiralty. Pricker of pomposity to Samuel Pepys.'

They both laughed.

'You really didn't know him?'

'Never met the man before in my life.'

'Most indigent workman I ever saw, drinking ale this early in the morning. It's almost as if he was waiting to greet you, Sam.'

They turned the corner at All Hallows to walk down Tower Street, past the hawkers laying their wares out on the street. The Tower itself loomed at the end, its dirty white stone stained with the rust and lichen and the coal dust of London. As they walked closer, they could hear the howls of the animals in the King's menagerie, all calling for their food on this bright morning.

'It must be feeding time,' said Pepys.

The high pitched squeals of the monkeys, the barks of the deer, and the deep-throated grunts of the camels were silenced by a long, open-mouthed roar of a Lion.

'Somebody is hungry,' said Will.

They turned right just before the Tower and walked down the path to Tower Stairs. They passed two other workmen standing on the street corner.

'Let us hurry to our wherry, Will. I feel we are being watched.'

They hurried down the stairs. A wooden boat waited for them, manned by an old bearded Waterman and his young son, both dressed as soberly as their vessel. Pepys and Will clambered down the stairs and into the rocking boat.

'Welcome aboard the Godspeed, gentlemen. If you would have a care there.' The bearded waterman directed them to sit towards the end of the wherry on a plank that stretched across the boat. No cushions or blankets were provided for their comfort.

'You could have picked a more luxurious mode of transport, Sam.'

'I didn't want to draw attention to ourselves. Our mission is supposed to be secret.'

'But everybody already knows, Sam. You said so yourself.'

'Ah, but we must keep up appearances, Will. Appearances are everything.'

'The tide is with us, gentlemen. With the aid of the Almighty, we will be in Gravesend before the afternoon. Praisegod, let us depart.'

'Before we go there, we must pay a call, if you please, boatman, to Temple Stairs.'

The boatman shook his head. 'We'll have to pull against the tide.'

'Can't be helped. Please let us depart.'

'You heard the gentleman, Praisegod, Temple Stairs.'

The younger boatman pushed away from the stairs and leapt aboard the boat, as his father pulled on the oars.

'Why are we going there?'

'Have you forgotten, Will? We must visit Sir William Coventry before out departure for Chatham.'

'He's the man who knows everything?'

'The one and the same, Will. Despite his recent incarceration in the Tower, he still holds immense power in the country and the army, and even more knowledge.'

'Knowledge is power.'

'No, Will. Knowledge is knowledge. The application of knowledge is power. Never forget that. It is only in action that power is seen. Until then, it is just potential.'

'We are in a very philosophic mood.'

‘I have been awake most of the night, Will. I believe we may finally have discovered a plan of action. Hopefully, Sir William will confirm it.’

As they left the pier, Pepys looked back at the stairs. The two workmen they had passed had come down to the water's edge and were watching the boat as it pulled away.

*

They were shown into a large, comfortable room with a circular desk at its centre. In the middle of the desk sat Sir William Coventry, reading a pile of papers. He held up a hand as they entered and carried on reading the paper he was holding, a deep frown spreading across his forehead.

Pepys stood in the middle of the room, waiting for the command to sit. On his left, a large clock ticked remorselessly, counting out his life with each monotonous click. A fire roared in the grate overheated the room, giving it a stuffy, wood-smoked smell. Next to him, Will was wiping his shoes on the back of his stockings, fidgeting constantly. Pepys touched his arm to get him to stop.

Sir William reached the bottom of the page. He picked up a quill from the pot on the desk in front of him and quickly scrawled something across the paper. Pepys presumed it was his signature because he then produced a large silver pot, dousing the letter in a fine talc. The pleasant aroma of lemon verbena drifted up to Pepys’ nose from the page. Finally, Coventry melted some wax and sealed the letter.

He looked up. ‘Pepys, I'm so happy to see you again. Sit, sit.’ He gestured to two chairs in front of the round desk.

Pepys recognised the warm, welcoming smile of the man he knew so well and sat down. Will remained standing behind him.

'I'd get up to give you a hug but being in the middle here makes it rather difficult.'

Sir William gestured to the wood that completely surrounded him.

'I've often wondered how you manage to get into the middle? Do you scramble underneath like a terrier down a hole?'

'Nothing so adventurous, Pepys. There's a hinged entrance somewhere beneath all the papers. But once I'm in, it's far too much trouble to get out. As you can see, being in the centre here means that everything is arrayed around me.' Sir William spun slowly around on his stool to demonstrate the ease of dealing with a multitude of documents.

'An ingenious design, Sir William.' Pepys gripped his bottom lip between his index and fore fingers. 'Is this the famous desk?'

'The one Buckingham made appalling jests about in his play?'

Pepys nodded.

'It is.' Sir William's face changed instantly. The welcoming smile replaced by a tautness about the lips and a fire in the eyes. 'Damn the man. He provoked me and I reacted like a blind dunce at a country fair. Sir Cautious Trouble-All that's what he called me. And what's more, he had the gall to remove the scene from the play when I complained to the king.'

Pepys could see him growing redder and redder, the unfairness of the situation still playing on his mind. He sought to smooth Sir William's troubles. 'At least, you are home now.'

'Aye, having spent eighteen days in the Tower,' he spoke through gritted teeth. Then he seemed to calm himself and his voice went quiet. 'Shouldn't have challenged him to a duel, though. Lost the King's confidence. Never get it back now. Look at Clarendon and what happened to him.'

'Don't worry, Sir William, the King has a short memory and forgives easily. Remember how he forgave Milord Buckingham before.'

'Thank you for your kind words, Pepys, but I fear they are not the kind that I want to hear. It will be impossible for me to have any relationship with the King again.'

'Never say never, Sir William. Look how he forgave those who fought against his father in the Civil War.'

'And went after those who signed his father's death warrant with a wrath that was biblical in its vehemence. Even digging up old Cromwell's head and placing it on a spike above London Bridge. No, sir, the man will not forgive easily unless he has need of me again. If he feels the Kingdom is under threat, he will call for my talents. Until then, I will enjoy the wilderness as a marooned man. Enough of our King Charles, you asked to see me, Pepys?'

'I did, Sir William. Let me introduce my assistant before I describe the reason for my visit.' Pepys gestured for his friend to step forward. 'Will Hewer, clerk at the Navy Board.'

Will bowed deeply.

'I remember you well, Mr Hewer. An elegant hand, if memory serves, a bit of a dandycock but good with figures.'

A broad smile crossed Will's face. 'Thank you, Sir William, it is always gratifying when one's efforts are noticed.'

'A little cautious in your recommendations, though. Be blunt, be more direct. Nobody has time for circumlocutions anymore. It's the modern world. Time is short and it flies by like a wing'd chariot.'

The smile was not broad now. 'Thank you for your advice, Sir William, I will keep it in mind.'

'It's advice you should take too, Pepys. You have visited me for a reason. I won't know what it is until you state it.'

'It's a rather delicate, matter, Sir William.'

'Aren't they all?'

'I have been tasked by the King to go to…'

'To go to Chatham to investigate the dockyard and report back to him on the 9th of June.'

Pepys' mouth opened and his jaw dropped to his chest. 'How do you know?'

'Everybody knows.' Sir William sat back on his stool. 'You must remember, Pepys, the court has no secrets and the greatest source of indiscretion is the King himself. In fact, gossip is the King's bedfellow every night, along with his various mistresses.'

'Mr Cooper has already let me know his feelings on my role.'

'You would like me to explain the various agendas of the members of the Cabal to you?'

'If you would be so kind, Sir William, I am just a humble servant of the King's at the Navy Board.'

'You underestimate yourself, sir. I know the King places great trust in you. You served him well last year during the Navy debates in the Commons.'

‘I simply did my job, sir.’

‘You did it well. And now you must do it again.’ He leant forward, his stool creaking with his weight as he did so. ‘They all have agendas, Pepys.’

‘All, sir?’

‘All. Let’s start with Mr Cooper, he would like you to find another Catholic conspiracy.’

‘Why, sir?’

'Ah, there's the rub, Pepys. A combination of ambition and religion, I believe. Ambition for power and the faith to make it all happen. Blaming the Catholics plays well with the Commons and Mr Cooper has his followers in that rabid institution.’

‘And the others?’

‘Buckingham would like you to blame the Dutch for everything, the better to force the King into an alliance with the French. Lord Arlington on the other hand, would prefer you to blame the French, forcing the King into an alliance against them.’

‘I can’t blame both of them.’

‘That is true, Pepys.’

‘Caught between Scylla and Charybdis.’

‘Unfortunately, there are other rocks you must navigate.’

Pepys raised his eyebrows.

‘Sir Joseph Williamson would like you to blame the regicides.’

‘I thought they were all dead?’

’Some were caught and hanged. Others fled to the Continent and plot the return of the Commonwealth once again. Sir Joseph holds power through the immense system of spies and turncoats that he operates. Obviously that organisation can only be maintained if a threat to state existed, perceived or real.' He stared directly at Will. 'You must trust nobody. You never know who is working for you or against you.'

'It sounds like a nest of vipers, Sir William.'

'It is, Pepys, and at its centre is the King Cobra himself, playing each one off against each other till he tires of them.'

'So what does the King want?'

Sir William sat back and the stool creaked again. 'Ah, if we knew that, Pepys, we would be Kings ourselves. But I suspect that the one thing he wants is peace. To enjoy himself, play his games and fiddle with his mistresses, while England burns.'

'So what am I to do?'

'Your job, sir, nothing but your job.' He picked up a document from his desk. 'And now, if you will excuse me, I need to plough through my correspondence. It is not a field that will till itself.'

'Just one more thing, Sir William, you remember I told you about my diary?'

'I remember it well. I write one too.'

'Well, I'm sorry to have to tell you, it's been stolen.'

'That is bad news. But I'm sure you'll start another one.'

'You don't understand, Sir William, I have been indiscreet in the diary. If someone were to publish its contents, I would be in danger of finding myself in the Tower, losing my life and my wife.'

'That is dreadful news.'

'I was indiscreet about his Majesty and some of his ministers...'

'Not wise, Pepys, in this political climate. Take it from me, the Tower is not the place to spend too much time. Cold, draughty place. It could be the death of you.'

'That's what worries me, Sir William.'

'Have you heard from the thief? Just buy the diary back from him.'

'I have heard nothing yet. We visited the thief yesterday.'

'Good. You bought it off him?'

'No, Sir William, he was dead and the diary missing.'

'That is unfortunate for both yourself and the thief.' Sir William stared into the fire burning brightly in the corner. 'Well, if the thief has been stabbed and your diary missing once more, I think you will have to wait to be contacted. There's nothing much you can do till then.'

'Thank you for your advice, Sir William, that is what I have decided to do.'

Coventry waved his hand at the stack of papers in front of him. 'And now if you will excuse me, Pepys...'

Pepys stood up. 'Of course, Sir William, thank you for your time and patience.'

The man behind the desk simply waved his hand in dismissal.

Pepys and Will walked across the rugs, past the ticking clock and opened the door to the salon.

'Pepys...'

Pepys turned back, "Yes, Sir William.'

'Trust nobody.'

Chapter 18

They boarded the wherry in silence, Pepys thinking over Sir William's words.

'Where to now, gentlemen?' asked the wherryman.

Pepys awoke from his reverie with a start. 'To Gravesend. Make all haste, if you please.'

The wherryman stared out into the oily depths of the river. 'Aye, we'll be quick, tides still running. Not as strong as this morning, though. Praisegod, cast off, look lively there.'

'Yes, father.'

He untied the rope, throwing it into the rear of the boat. He jumped in after it and leant out to push the wherry away from all the other boats that crowded round the pier waiting for custom.

There were a few shouts of 'Have a care, there,' and 'Don't scrape my paint' but soon the young man had the wherry out into the middle of the channel.

The old man pulled on the oars, his forearms knotted after years of rowing against and with the tide.

They moved quickly over the water, the tide and the man's strength taking hold of the boat and propelling it up the river towards their destination.

The vessel was making good speed past the wharves of the river. On either side, Pepys could see a hive of activity: animal skins being laid out to dry in the morning sun, bales of wool stacked like fluffy dominoes against the wall of a warehouse, a team of men pulling a ship onto a dry dock, it's gleaming barnacle encrusted hull slowly being wrenched from the grip of the river. And all around him the sounds, smells and sights of the greatest and busiest river on earth. It never failed to fill his heart with joy.

'Traitor's Gate.' Will pointed to the small landing stage which was dominated by the forbidding stone walls of the Tower. 'I hope we never have to enter there.'

'So do I, Will. So do I.' Pepys turned back to the Wherryman, 'Your wherry is not as gaily painted as the rest.'

The man pulled on his oars rhythmically, never seeming to be out of breath. After three long strokes, he answered. 'The Lord cannot abide gaiety. If he meant for wood to come in reds and greens, he would have made it so.'

'Ah,' said Will. 'The fleece of the wool you wear is white. And yet you have dyed it black.'

'Black is not a colour, It is the raiment of the righteous. The Lord approves of sobriety in everything. We must always be ready to receive him when he comes.'

'Dressed in black?'

'Dressed in black.'

'It seems our boatman is one of the more devout Puritan's on the river, Will. We should leave him to his Lord while the rest of us enjoy our life on earth, and on the river.'

'Aye, enjoy it while you may, sir. For the kingdom of the Lord is nigh. King Jesus is upon us.' The young boatman had spoken for the first time.

'And when will that be?' asked Will.

'Soon. The Lord will come soon. Sodom and Gomorrah will perish. Evil-painted whores, prattling fops, unbelievers, misbelievers, Catholics and all heathen papists will be swept away on a tide of righteousness. Goodness and Godliness will prevail.'

The strident blue eyes of the younger man stared at Pepys.

'Hold there, Praisegod. Now is not the time.'

The man's eyes scanned the river and he muttered, 'Yes, father.'

'Forgive him, gentlemen. The power of the Lord is fearsome strong within him. Sometimes, he does not know when to hold his tongue.'

'You called him Praisegod?'

'It's his name. Given to him by Preacher Lawson on his baptism three years ago. His birth name was William. We both prefer Praisegod.'

'As we all would,' said Will.

The elder boatman looked at him for a minute and carried on rowing.

They lapsed into silence, skimming past the docks at Wapping, the kilns at Lime-house, and past Cuckold's Point at Rotherhithe with its orchards and gardens. It was a fresh June day, bright blue of sky and with just a whisper of breeze coming down the river bringing, with it a tang of salt.

Pepys sat upright on his wooden seat staring out at the shore as it raced past on either side. Will remained silent, occasionally shifting his position, looking for a scrap of comfort on the bare boards.

The old Wherryman rowed with a rhythmic grace, the prow gliding over the river as neatly as a scythe harvests corn.

The time passed quickly as the sun reached its zenith. They were near Greenwich now. The hill and the naval dockyards were on their right just slightly ahead. For a moment, the boat rocked as it crossed the outflow of the Ravensbourne. A young boy waved to them from the shore. Will waved back. Pepys did not move. The boy shouted something but the breeze along the river took the boy's words away and floated them back toward the smoke-laden streets of London.

Now was the time. The young boatman was in the rear of the boat on the rudder. His father pulled the oars steadily. If he spoke quietly, neither of them would hear.

'Come and sit by me, Will. I would speak with you in private.'

Will moved to sit with Sam in the prow of the wherry.

'I have a favour to ask of you.'

'Ask away.'

'When we get to Gravesend, I want you to go straight back to London.'

'What?'

'Take another boat back to London this afternoon.'

'Why? We're going to Chatham...'

'I have been thinking on this, Will. You would serve our cause better if you were in London. I have asked Balty to meet us at the Ship in Gravesend. He will accompany me to Chatham.'

'Balty? Your brother-in-law?'

'Keep your voice down.' Pepys looked at the two boatmen. The elder was still pulling on the oars while the younger held the tiller and stared out into the river.

Will moved closer. 'But the man's an idiot and a braggart. You can't stand him.'

'True on both counts. But, at the moment, I need him. The Commissioner in Chatham is expecting two men. Balty can be you for a few days if you don't mind.'

'Why would I mind a jackass taking my identity?'

'He also has more of a common touch than you do, Will. I want him to go into the Inns and Taverns where the sailors congregate. He will get them to tell him far more than you ever could.'

'If you can keep him sober and if he can remember what they told him the next morning.'

'You criticise Balty too severely, Will. He is not the ideal investigator but, in these small matters, he can be trusted to do his duty. And besides, I need you in London.'

'Why?'

'It strikes me the theft of the diary, the murder of Jack Turner and the plots against the King are all related. I don't know how, yet, nor do I know why. But, I need you to talk to three people while I am away. The first is a herald at the Court of Arms. Find out whose device is on the silver button we found in Jack Turner's hand.'

'That is easy enough to do.'

'Next I want you to pay a call on Mr Dryden.'

Will leant back and pointed to himself, 'You want me to call on the Poet Laureate? And what reason on earth would I have for doing that?'

'I don't know, Will. Find a reason. He was at Cambridge, too. Use that as a reason. Flatter him. All writers love to be flattered. And, if that fails, talk to him about a commission. Writers are always short of money.'

'When I get to meet him, what shall I ask?'

'Ask him about Tyrannic Love. What was his inspiration? Why does he prefer rhyming couplets? The usual idiotic questions. What I really want to know is, why he wrote Nell's epilogue? Who put him up to it?'

'I don't know if he'll tell me, but I can but ask.'

'Good man. Finally, I want you to go and see Nell Gwynn.'

'What?'

Both boatmen looked at Will as he raised his voice.

Pepys smiled at both of them. The elder continued to row and the younger turned back to stare out across the marshes on either side of the river.

Will leant closer to Pepys. 'What? You want me to go to see the King's mistress?'

Pepys nodded.

'On my own?'

Pepys nodded again.

'In the name of heaven, why?'

'I need you to find out how she knew to look at me when she spoke her epilogue. Somebody told her to do so.'

'Aren't you making a rather large presumption here? How can you be sure the words were meant for you? They could have been Dryden talking about himself. Or Nell Gwynn could have made them up on the spur of the moment. That's what actresses do all the time.'

'I've thought about it long through the night, Will. I know the words were aimed at me.'

'So you want me to ask the King's mistress, why she was looking at one particular man, called Samuel Pepys, last night?'

'Yes.'

'What if she won't tell me? What if she hasn't got a clue what I mean? What if she throws me out of her house on my neck?' Will thought for a moment, 'what if she tells the King?'

'I rather think the King has better things to do with Nell Gwynn that talk about you, Will.'

'That's probably true.'

'You can but ask Will. And I trust you to do it with your usual charming, self-effacing manner.' Pepys looked Will straight in the eye. 'I need you to do this for me.'

Will nodded.

'Good, that's settled. I've arranged for a boat to take you back to London on the evening tide. Balty will meet us in Gravesend. He will take your place and we will ride to Chatham. Meanwhile, let us sit back and enjoy the rest of the journey. Essex on one side and Kent on the other, a blue-skyed day and the Thames flowing softly beneath us. Who could ask for more, Will?'

'I could think of many things,' said Will beneath his breath.

Chapter 19

Balty was waiting for them at the Ship. 'I got your message, brother, and came down immediately.' He wrapped both of them in a bear hug. 'It's good to see you both again.'

He was a huge man, dressed in the latest fashions. His wig curled well past his shoulders while his coat and breeches, in fashionable light blue, stretched over a bulky frame that betrayed his love for food and drink.

'Landlord, three pints of ale for our weary travellers.' His voice boomed out across the inn.

'Coming straight away, sir, And would you like some more venison pie?'

'Of course. Where would dinner be without venison pie?' He leant into Pepys. 'I hope you don't mind, Brother, I ordered a few snacks while I was waiting. Travelling makes me hungry. Now sit, and tell me what brings you to Gravesend, the most aptly named town in the country. I've heard tell it's the dead centre of England. Gravesend, dead centre, get it?' He boomed out another laugh and clapped Pepys on the shoulder with a hand the size of a bear's paw.

Pepys smiled and sat down, clearing away two plates and one trencher filled with scraps from in front of him. The Landlord arrived with three tankards of ale and three more plates of venison pie. Balty immediately raised his tankard in a toast. 'To Samuel, my sister's wonderful husband. My patron and protector.' Without waiting for either of them to drink, he took an immense draught from the tankard, finishing with a loud 'ah' and a wipe of the mouth. 'Waiting is thirsty work, 'pon my word.'

'Balty, I'm glad you could make it. We have work to do.'

'And what would that be, Brother?' asked Balty between mouthfuls of pie. 'Do try the expensive pie, gents, it's very deer. It's very deer, get it?' He laughed again, spluttering bits of pie onto the table.

Will had remained quiet through all of this. 'You really want to go to Chatham with him?'

Balty's ears picked up. 'We're going to Chatham? I like Chatham. Good food there. Better ale, though.'

Pepys ignored Will. 'Yes, we are going to Chatham. We need to look into the dockyard.'

Balty thumped his chest, again throwing more pie from his spoon. 'I'm your man. I'm good at looking into things.' He leant forward once more and whispered to Pepys. 'Is this a paid looking into?'

'You will be paid for your trouble, Balty.'

'Right-oh, I'm your man.' He thought for a moment. 'Trouble?'

'Here's what I want you to do. Just go round the alehouses of the town, where the sailors and the dockworkers drink. Keep your ears open, and tell me what they say.'

'Keep my ears open? Balty's good at keeping his ears open. Better at going round taverns and alehouses, though. When do we start?'

'We ride to Chatham as soon as you are finished eating.'

Balty eyed the empty plate in front of him. 'One more should do it. Don't want to start on an empty stomach, do we?'

'Are you sure you can afford this?' said Will.

'I can't not afford it. We have to know what's happening in Chatham, and Balty's the man to do it. Aren't you Balty?'

Balty just nodded his head as he tucked into Will's plate

of venison pie.

'And besides, you are needed in London, Will. I'll meet you at the Swan in Greenwich four days from now. I hope your investigations go well. We need to find the diary, before anybody else.'

'You still have no idea who has it?'

'Not yet, but we must discover it. Quickly.'

Pepys looked over at Balty, scraping the plate clean with his spoon. The red face of the man with its bulbous nose appeared over the top of the plate, followed by an even larger red tongue.

'One more for the road?'

Pepys nodded.

'Landlord, two more plates of venison pie and three more tankards of ale, if you please,' Balty shouted across the Inn. Then he said in a much quieter voice to Pepys. 'Don't worry, I'll finish them if you can't.'

Pepys turned back to Will. 'To answer your question honestly, I still don't know. It could be the King or Sir Joseph or Lord Arlington or Cooper.'

'Or somebody else?'

'Or somebody else,' agreed Pepys, 'all I know is that nobody has contacted me yet. There was the message given to me by Nell Gwynn at the theatre last night, but nobody has said that they have the diary.'

'I would have thought that if somebody had it, they would have told you by now.'

'I agree, Will. Why has nobody contacted me?'

The plates of food and ale arrived.

'Don't stand on ceremony, gentlemen, get stuck in, as the actress said to the King.'

Again, Balty's laugh boomed across the Inn.

'Why has nobody contacted me?' said Pepys out loud.

'How about some mulberries before we go,' said Balty, 'and a dish of syllabub. Protects the arse against saddle sore does syllabub, well-known fact that.'

Chapter 20

Finally, they were ready to leave the Ship. Balty had brought his horse from the stable and Pepys had hired a flea-bitten nag from the Landlord.

'Make sure youse looks after her, sir, she is prime is Daisy. Don't get menny like her in Kent. Or Essex. Or even parts of Sussex.'

'I'll bring her back three days hence,' said Pepys from his position seated on the back of the nag.

'And she likes an apple or two for her supper, but can't abide carrots.'

'Shall I give her a feather pillow of an evening?'

'That won't be necesry, sir, she don't sleep much, don't Daisy. More of a wakin' hoss is our Daisy.'

Pepys dug his heels into her sides and, reluctantly, she began to walk away from the Inn. Pepys looked back and saw Will waving him off. For some reason, a wave of sadness washed over him as if it were the last time he would ever see his friend again. 'Pull yourself together,' he said aloud.

'That's what the headless chicken said,' shouted Balty.

Sam sighed and wondered how he was going to survive three days with this man. Balthazar-but everyone called him Balty-was his wife's brother. He had been a burden to Pepys since his marriage, always seeking favours and money. Three years ago, Pepys had finally found him a job as a muster master on board the good ship Henry, which suited him like a linen shirt. It was free and easy, requiring little work except the counting of men and the spending of money. Something that even Balty could do with ease. But once again, Balty was ashore and without employment, causing Elizabeth, and, therefore, Pepys, much worry.

'Sam, I wonder if you could lend me some money. I seem to be a little short this month.'

A large grin appeared on Balty's face and an even larger hand was thrust towards Pepys.

'Later, Balty, when we get to Chatham.'

The grin got wider. 'Right-o. Good idea. Might spend it all if it lands in the pockets now. Money doesn't seem to stay in my pockets for long. Always think there's a hole, but haven't found one yet.'

The last sentence ended in a roar of a laugh, like a lion coughing up a chicken bone.

They plodded up to Watling Street, passing fields of grazing sheep, sleeping cows and long lines of orchards, with trees planted in such a regimented fashion they could be soldiers on parade. The sun lit everything in a harsh light that was only interrupted by the passing grey shadows of the clouds. Balty was singing of course, as he loved to do.

'Twas down in the meadows where the violets are blue,
I saw pretty Polly a-milking her cow,
The song that she sung made all the grove ring,
Oh, my Billy's gone from me to serve the king,
Oh, I would that the wars were well over,
Crying, I would that the wars were well over'

Even the skylarks and the corncrakes surrendered their territory to this new, strange breed of songster. Up above, a kestrel hovered, it's wings beating to keep it in position above a possible prey shuffling through the grass below. Strange, thought Pepys, one thousand five hundred years ago, an ancestor of that Kestrel had hovered over a Roman centurion as he marched down the same road. Now, his offspring hovers over me. Five hundred years from now his children will fly over other travellers on this ridge. 'The rain it raineth every day,' he said aloud.

Balty looked up in the sky. 'Nah, doesn't look like it. Won't be no rain, yet awhile. Could do with some, though. All this singing gives a man a thirst.'

They continued to plod on, finally reaching Strood in the late afternoon, passing through that shabby little town till they reached the bridge over the river. There, two men approached them

'Good afternoon, Mr Pepys, I believe.'

Pepys nodded. The man in front of him was thin and poorly dressed, rubbing his greasy hands together as if desperately trying to wash them of some sticky substance.

'My humble name is Fridley, with a 'd'. Welcome to Rochester. I'm afraid the commissioner is indisposed at the present time, preparing for the visit of an Italian Duke. I have your barge ready on the other side of the bridge to take you into Chatham if you would be so kind as to come this way.'

They trotted slowly after the two men, the hooves of the horses clattering the stone of the bridge. At either side, an iron parapet jutted out from the walls, giving them shelter from the late rays of the sun as it slowly began to set.

On their left, across the Medway, the tower of Rochester Castle and its neighbouring Cathedral loomed over the river.

'I believe Julius Caesar first built the fortifications here,' said Pepys.

'That is what the local people say, sir.'

'You don't seem so sure, Mr Fridley with a 'd'.'

'The local people are very proud of their town, Mr Pepys, perhaps too proud.'

'I'm sure that if Caesar were here, he would have come, seen and conquered even the pride of the local people.'

'After crossing the Rubicon, sir.' said Fridley with a sniff.

'No, I believe it would have been after crossing the Medway.'

They reached the end of the bridge. Mr Fridley began to descend the stairs to the river.

'Our horses?'

'Tripp, my assistant, will look after them until you return. You will be spending three days with us, am I correct?'

'That is so, Mr Fridley.' Pepys and Balty got down from their horses, which were led away by Tripp. Pepys was almost sorry to see Daisy go. She had been a quiet, peaceful companion, unlike Balty.

'Good, sometimes the instructions we receive are not so precise,' said Fridley over his shoulder as he led them down the stairs to their barge. 'Luckily, the tide is out at the moment. It's quite a force when it starts to rush in. Many drunken sailors have lost their lives in its wet embrace. We would not be able to make our way up the river when it is in full flow.'

Four sailors waited on either side of a short gangplank. As Pepys and Balty walked past, they doffed their caps, putting them back on the second Pepys and Balty passed. They stepped aboard and sat down at the end on the red velvet cushions placed on a banquette at the rear.

'The barge will take us to Hill House, where a room has been prepared for yourself and your assistant.' He looked at Balty, who was scratching his rear.

'What? Riding always makes my arse sore.'

Fridley sniffed. 'As I was saying, your rooms and supper have been prepared for you. The Commissioner would like to invite you to breakfast tomorrow morning, at your convenience, Mr Pepys.'

The men had climbed aboard, fixed their oars and started to pull out into the river. Around them, countless ships lay at anchor, sheltering in the lee of the town. The barge slid silently over the water, only the rhythmic splashes of the oars disturbing the calm of the late summer's evening. Pepys loved moments like this when the days of summer lingered on like guests at a party.

The houses on either side came right down to the river, sometimes extending over it as if dipping their toes in the water. Most of them seemed new. Some people in this town were doing very well from the money that had poured into it after the depredations of the Dutch.

He looked back at the strong stone arches at the bridge they had left behind. On his right, two men were raising a fish trap from between one of the arches. Four large salmon seemed to be caught in its net. The fisherman unhooked the gills of the salmon and slammed its head down against the iron parapet of the bridge. The fish stopped moving and he lay it next to its companions. A trail of blood dripped down the iron and onto the white stone of the bridge, where it congealed, turning black in the sun of the late summer evening.

'Can I be of any help, Mr Pepys?' asked Fridley.

'I'm sorry, I missed what you were saying.'

'Can I be of any help? Our instructions from London were very clear. We were to afford any assistance that Mr Pepys required. Unfortunately, they were not at all precise on the reasons for your visit.'

So that's what he was after, thought Pepys, fishing for information. He considered keeping this man, and whoever had primed him to ask the question, dangling in their ignorance. But, maybe it was time to set the rooster amongst the hens. 'The King has ordered me to investigate the situation at Chatham. He has heard rumours that all is not how it should be.'

The man's mouth opened, 'Rumours, Mr Pepys, what sort of rumours may I ask?'

'No, you may not. I am not at liberty to say. However, please arrange a tour of the Dockyard, magazines and other buildings tomorrow. I wish to see their state of readiness.'

'I'm not sure the Commissioner...'

'Make it so, Mr Fridley.'

'As your Lordship commands.'

'As the King commands, Mr Fridley. As the King commands.'

The rest of their journey up the Medway to Hill House passed in silence with Fridley pointedly staring out into the river.

Hill House was as Pepys remembered it from his last visit; eminently comfortable with the convenience of being situated close to the dockyards and the Commissioner's house. He was quickly introduced to his rooms by Fridley.

'What time shall I return tomorrow morning, Mr Pepys?'

'Early, I like to start work early. Shall we say seven o'clock?'

'Certainly, sir, however...'

'However?'

'The Commissioner seldom rises before nine, so...'

'So I would be kept waiting for him.'

'I'm afraid that would be the case, Mr Pepys.'

'Nonetheless, we will start at seven, Fridley. With or without the Commissioner.'

'But Mr Pepys...'

'I am tired now, Fridley, please leave me.'

Fridley placed his hat back on his head. 'Of course, Mr Pepys. I hope you sleep well.' He bowed and departed.

When he had gone, Pepys turned to Balty. 'It's time for you to patronise the Taverns and Inns of this town, Balty. Find out what you can.'

'Actually, Sam, it's time for me to get changed. I must metamorphose like the swan, but in reverse, from a beauty into an ugly duckling.'

'I'm sorry, Balty, I don't understand.'

'This costume,' he pointed down to his sky blue suit and breeches, 'will not serve in the hostelries of Chatham. Something more homespun is required.'

'Why didn't you say that in the first place?' Pepys muttered under his breath.

Balty left the room and returned five minutes later wearing a simple shirt and leather waistcoat, brown sailor's trousers and leather boots. His wig had been removed but his head was now covered with a simple felt cap. 'Voila,' he bowed, 'I give you Balty, a sailor who has just returned from a long voyage to the Americas, Virginia to be precise. There he saw many strange things, not least of which was the sight of people enjoying the freedoms of their chosen religion.'

Pepys stepped back and admired the transformation, 'You do like dressing up, Balty, but it will do, it will serve.'

'Such a man returning from Virginia would have

money to throw around. People talk more after a few drinks, and they talk even more after more drinks. It is sad but it is the way of the world.' He held out his hand.

Pepys dug into his purse and pulled out two sovereigns.

'That will do admirably.'

'Do try not to spend it all, Balty.'

'I will try but I wouldn't want to spoil the milk for a ha'porth of cream.'

'I haven't a clue what that means but do come back with news of what is happening here. I must be forewarned before I see the Commissioner tomorrow.'

'But I thought he doesn't get up before nine?'

'Tomorrow, he will be up and here at seven, you mark my words. Our Commissioner may be lazy but he's not a fool.'

'I'd better get going. The beer will be getting warm and the wenches warmer. Wouldn't like either of them to go cold. Not good for the arse, cold beer.'

'And cold wenches?'

'They're not good for the heart.' He pounded the centre of his chest with a clenched fist.

Pepys sniffed. 'Wake me when you return, I would talk with you.'

With a wave of his workman's cap, Balty was gone.

Pepys was left alone in the house. He crossed over to the sideboard and poured himself a glass of wine. Time to sit and think for a while. To organise all that had happened and find the patterns. There were always patterns. All he had to do was recognise and organise them. The course of action would then be self-evident.

A knock came on the door and a servant entered. 'This came for you, sir.' The man held a note in his right hand.

Who would be sending him messages? His mission

was supposed to be a secret even if it seemed most of London knew exactly where he was and what he was doing. 'Thank you,' he said taking the note from the man, 'who delivered this?'

'I don't know, sir. It was lying on the hall table. As it was addressed to you, I thought I should bring it as soon as possible.'

The servant still stood there. Was the man waiting for a tip?

'Will there be an answer, sir?'

'I will know when I have read it. You may leave me now.'

'Yes, sir. Just pull the cord if you need me,' he pointed to a silk tasselled rope that hung from the ceiling, 'Mr Fridley says you are to be accorded any service that you may or may not require.'

'Thank you, Mr…?'

'Billingham, sir. Like the port only with a 'B', not a 'G'.'

'Thank you, Billingham. I will call you if I need you.'

The man took the hint and departed. Pepys looked at the note in his hand. On the cover was written his name and nothing else.

He unfolded the note. There were eight lines written on it in an elegant hand.

'Your pen is your phallus,
The blue ink is seed,
And though you're impotent,
You're prolific indeed.
I now have your diary,
It's words are quite bold
Your end could be fiery

So do as you are told.

Pepys read it through twice and then once more to check that he understood it. The threat was clear. Finally, the thief of the diary had contacted him. What's more, they used the same words as Nell Gwynn had done in her speech in the theatre.

He hadn't been mistaken, she had been speaking to him. If only he could contact Will and tell him. He considered calling back Billingham and giving him an urgent message for Will in London, but he knew if he did it would be opened and read. Will would have to manage on his own for the next three days.

He read the note once more. The thief had apparently decoded the contents and knew exactly what Pepys had written. But what was the last line? 'Do as you are told'. What in God's name did that mean? What was he going to be asked to do?

Pepys sat down on the end of his bed. He didn't like being blackmailed by anybody.

There was a sense of helplessness, an ability to do nothing that annoyed him. He had always believed in action. Do it. Sort it out. Make it happen. Now, he would have to be patient, not an emotion that suited him at all.

He had set the wheels in motion with Will and Balty. The thief had sent his first note. Tomorrow, he would see, hear and feel for himself the mood of the Navy and its dockyard.

He had never done as he was told. And he wasn't going to start now.

Chapter 21

He was woken by the sound of singing:

'There was a maiden fair,
Whose luscious dark brown hair,
Hung down in locks over her eyes,
She would enjoy my sweet surprise.
With a hey noddy, nuncle, no
A hey noddy, nuncle, so.'

He rose, pulled on his purple housecoat and strode out into the hallway. Balty was there, being supported by Billingham and two servants.

'We found him at the back door, sir,' one of the servants blurted out.

'Drunk, I believe.' Billingham sneered.

'With a hey noddy, nuncle hey.' Balty carried on slurring his song.

'Bring him inside and lay him down on my couch,' ordered Pepys.

Balty carried on singing as the servants carried him through the doorway and stumbled into the room. He pushed them away and tried to stand on his own feet. 'I'm all right, jus a few glasses, sat's all.' He swayed there for a moment, his eyes desperately trying to focus on the world around him. Then his right foot lost its tenuous link with the floor and he fell to the right. Luckily, one of the servants caught him and, aided by the other, they carried him to the couch.

'Leave me. I will look after him.'

'Yes, Mr Pepys.'

The two servants left the room followed by Billingham. Balty was already snoring loudly on the couch. Pepys shook his shoulders. No reaction except the snoring became far more musical.

Pepys shook the man's shoulders again, lifting the heavy, inert body off the couch and letting it fall back.

Balty's eyes flickered open as he tried to work out where he was and how he had got there. Eventually, his eyes focussed on Pepys. 'Hello, Sam,' he mumbled.

Pepys caught a waft of beer-soaked breath. There was an edge of pickled egg there. Not a pleasant smell. He gave Balty a glass of wine. 'Here, this will help.'

Balty swallowed the wine down in one gulp and held his glass out for more. Pepys poured him another. For a moment, the shock of the wine revived Balty and he seemed almost sober.

'Well?' asked Pepys.

'Quite well, thank you, Sam. Had a few drinks with some sailor friends off the Royal Sovereign.'

'I can see that. Tell me what you discovered.'

Pepys watched as Balty's eyes swivelled from side to side, attempting to organise his thoughts. He took another swallow of the wine. It seemed to help.

'Not a happy ship. Men haven't been paid for three months. Dockyard bleeding the ship dry. Talk of friends in Holland, manning Dutch ships and proud to do so. One showed me a pamphlet about the King. Does he really have three nipples?'

Pepys ignored the question. He encouraged him to take another swallow of wine.

'Anything else?'

'Meetings. Men from different ships and the dockyards. Some sort of plan. Happening soon. A vicar at the heart.' Balty pounded his chest and immediately began to cough.

'Drink more, Balty.'

'King Jesus was going to punish them all unless they acted,' that's what one of them said. 'King Jesus was going to punish them all.'

'King Jesus?'

Balty's eyes began to close. Pepys knew he had got all he could out of his brother-in-law. Tomorrow, he would remember more. For now, he let Balty sleep on his couch as he paced the room waiting for the dawn that would soon come.

What would he do next?

Chapter 22

The trip back to London had been relatively uneventful, save for an unfortunate disagreement with the boatman on the expense for the boat. Will had bargained the man down from his first outrageous price to something far more reasonable. The man didn't take kindly to taking or leaving Will's offer, however, and had left him at Tower steps muttering and calling into question the marriage of his parents.

For Will such name calling mattered little when weighed against the clink of coin in his pocket. That night, he enjoyed a very creditable loin of beef at the Nag's Head with the savings he had made on the trip.

Over his second helping of beef, he wondered how he had got himself so involved with Samuel Pepys. True he had once been Sam's clerk and indeed, it was Sam who had introduced him into the service of Naval Administration, becoming both a mentor and a protector. But he had moved on since those early days back in '62. He had proven himself in his service and now stood on his own two feet in the Navy. But still the old ties remained. He guessed they would always be there. Himself and Sam joined at the hip like the twins born in Essex last year: impossible to separate.

He drank the last of his wine and ate the final chunk of beef, laying his fork down next to his trencher. Unlike Sam, he didn't enjoy the social side of Navy life. He much preferred his books and his ledgers. Look at him here, eating alone and enjoying every minute of it. And unlike Sam, he didn't enjoy the company of women. He found them too trifling, too wearying, too absorbing of the little time he had to spare.

He laughed to himself. Of all the women he had met, he only held one of them in sincere esteem; Elizabeth, Sam's wife.

It was strange that the wife of his best friend should be his one true love. But God always played such tricks on the hearts of men. He knew the love would always be platonic, though, he had no desire whatsoever to see it consummated.

He thought about ordering another slice of beef but decided that he had eaten enough. One should always leave the table with room in your stomach his father had told him. A philosophy he had kept all his life.

One should not be prey to the blandishments of excess. It led to problems in life. Moderation in everything was the key.

He wished Sam would be more moderate, particularly when it came to women. Last year he had to act as a chaperone when Elizabeth found out about Sam's affair with Deborah Willett. An awful time, consoling Elizabeth and controlling Sam.

His friend's infidelities always troubled him. Strange word, he thought, infidelity. Like an infidel, a non-believer. A non-believer in the institution of marriage, or maybe more, a non-believer in love.

Will knew he believed in love. He just wasn't very good at expressing it. Better to stay with his books and his work at the Navy Board. Safer, much safer than the treacherous harbours of love.

He shook his head, wondering why he had wasted so much time thinking on these matters.

He felt the silver button safely hidden in his purse. Tomorrow he would go to the College of Heralds and find out to whom it belonged.

For now, though, another glass of wine and perhaps another small slice of the Nag's Head's fine beef.

Moderation was fine, in moderation.

Chapter 23

'Good morning, Commissioner, it is a surprise to see you on such a bright and joyous morning.'

Pepys bowed and the Commissioner stepped into the receiving room at Hill House, followed by two clerks and the ubiquitous Fridley.

'And good morning to you, Mr Pepys. As it was such a wonderful morning, I decided to visit you early. I do hope I haven't incommoded you?'

'Not at all, Commissioner. But I was given to understand that you didn't rise this early.'

'I wonder where you got that idea, Mr Pepys,' the Commissioner glanced across at Fridley, who had suddenly discovered that there was a stain on the floor and was intent on rubbing it out with his foot. 'I believe that the early bird gets the worm, does he not? So, let us repair to my house, where my housekeeper has a splendid breakfast waiting for us.'

'Lead on, Commissioner. I believe a good breakfast is always the precursor to an excellent day.'

'Indeed it is, Mr Pepys. A man after my own heart.' He turned towards his clerks. Fridley stopped rubbing at the stain he had found. 'Fridley, pray tell Mrs Welch that we are on our way.'

'Certainly, Commissioner.'

'After you, Mr Pepys.' The Commissioner bowed to let Pepys past. They both walked down the path from Hill House to the Commissioner's residence at the side of the Dockyard with views across the Medway. 'I'm afraid the house is old and needs some repairs. Commissioner Pett neglected it so.'

'And how is the former Commissioner?'

'I'm afraid I do not know. I believe he has retired to Suffolk.'

'After Parliament's report, I'm surprised he wasn't retired to the Tower.'

The Commissioner remained silent. Pepys decided to probe some more. 'I believe he was blamed unjustly for the disaster at Chatham in'67.'

'That is a belief not widely held,' the Commissioner answered.

'Marvell seems to disagree with you.'

'Ah, Mr Marvell's poem. Well written, I'll give you, but his criticism of the Navy Board and the King was well short of the mark.'

'But some of his barbs hit home. And most were true.'

'But that was two years ago. A lot has changed in two years. I will show you many of the changes today when we visit the yards and the new forts.'

Pepys noted that Commissioner had changed the subject adroitly. Perhaps, the man was a better politician than he had first thought. Pepys decided to play the King's card. 'I look forward to that, Commissioner, and reporting back to the King on everything I see.'

The Commissioner was silent for a moment before he recovered his composure. 'We have arrived. Please enjoy my humble home, Mr Pepys.' A valet waited at the door and led them to an elegant room, decorated in a very vivid primrose yellow. They sat down at the table and immediately the dishes began to arrive; Green Geese, Welsh Haslet, a fricassee of ortolans, lamprey pie, venison pasty, a tray of plump French oysters, a trio of custards, and finally a collation of cold meats in the Italian style.

'You have done us proud Commissioner. A remarkable spread of dishes.'

'As I said, Mr Pepys, a man who starts his day well, finishes it even better.'

'So true, Commissioner.'

'A glass of wine?'

'A small one to help the digestion.'

The valet stepped forward and poured a large glass for Pepys.

'It's from Aquitaine, a claret I believe.'

Pepys sipped from his glass. A delicate wine. The valet stepped forward and placed another glass filled with orange liquid in it at Pepys' elbow.

'Do try the orange juice as well, the oranges came from Spain.'

Pepys put down his wine and picked up his glass of orange. He had tried it before but found it far too sour for his taste. This was different, though. Sweet and refreshing, with a touch of tartness to wake up the palate.

'One of the advantages of living in a port. One can enjoy the best the world has to offer.'

'You certainly seem to be taking advantage of your position, Commissioner.' Pepys let the double meaning of his last speech lie between them like a steaming cow turd at a wedding.

The Commissioner pretended to ignore his words. 'Do try the venison pasty, from Ireland, you know. Wasted on the Irish though.'

They continued eating and drinking for the next hour until Pepys finally pushed away his plate, 'I can eat no more. You have overwhelmed me, sir.'

'A dish of tea, before we start our inspection. From China, just arrived yesterday.'

Pepys shook his head. 'It's time we began, Commissioner.'

'Of course, Mr Pepys, we will not adjourn our inspection any longer. Let me lead the way. Fridley here will take notes for you.'

Fridley stepped out from a door at the side of the room. He was a little too quick for Pepys, as if he had been listening to the conversation all the time.

He got up from the table and pulled his coat across his stomach. 'After you, Commissioner.'

*

'The Ropery has been repaired and is now in full working order.' The Commissioner stepped into a long, low warehouse followed by Pepys and the retinue of clerks. Inside a few men were lounging about, leaning against a barrel of rope, stacked like an immense bobbin of cotton on its side. The rest of the warehouse was quiet with motes of dust hanging in the air.

'There doesn't seem to be much work going on,' said Pepys.

The Commissioner looked nonplussed, mumbling, 'Er, the men will be here or hereabouts. At another warehouse, perhaps,' he finally answered.

'I sent them to paint the dry dock, milord, to prepare the area for the arrival of the Italian Duke on the sixth.' One of the clerks, the one with the large boil on the end of his nose, spoke and then immediately looked down at his feet.

'Please address me as Mr Pepys. I am not a 'milord'. How many men did you send to paint the dry dock?'

'I believe it was three, Mr Pepys.'

Pepys harrumphed, turned and left the place. He was nearly halfway through his inspection of the dockyards and he was not a happy man. The whole of Chatham dockyard seemed to empty of people and activity while the workers he did see were idle and listless. Over the whole place lay a torpor of inaction and laziness. Something was not right here.

'Please bring me the full complement of the dockyard.'

Fridley came running after Pepys. 'I don't know if we can find it that quickly, sir. It may take a few days.'

'Find it and bring it to me. I wish to know how many men are employed in the dockyard.'

'Of course, I will find the figures for you, sir. It will just take time to collate them from all the heads of the departments. I'm sure you understand.'

Pepys pinched his lower lip with the thumb and index finger of his right hand. This was becoming tiresome. 'If you find any delay, remind the heads of the departments, if they want to keep their heads, they should work quickly. Where to next?'

'The Ordnance Magazine, sir.'

'Lead on, Fridley.'

The Commissioner came waddling up. 'Shall we partake of a dish of tea and some cakes first? All this walking gives a man a thirst, does it not?'

'I think the Ordnance Store first, Commissioner. The cakes and tea can wait.'

Pepys strode off through the dockyard followed by a train of clerks and officials like the pied piper leading his troop of errant children. He was quickly caught up by Fridley.

'This way, sir.' He indicated to his right.

'What's over there?' Pepys pointed to a warehouse in

front of him, across an open square. For once, this area seemed to be a hive of activity with men moving in and out, loading wooden boxes onto carts.

'Just another warehouse, sir. For storage.'

'I perceived that, Fridley. For the storage of what?'

'Goods and other accoutrements of the Navy, sir. There is so much we have to store.' Pepys stepped towards the warehouse. Fridley stepped in front of him, 'This way, sir. The head of Ordnance is waiting for us. Master Daly is not a man we should keep waiting.' Once again, he gestured towards his right and walked in that direction.

Reluctantly, Pepys followed him, looking over his shoulder at the one hive of activity in the whole dockyard.

They walked past two quiet warehouses before turning left to a large, stone-built magazine. Standing in front of the great oak doors was a short man, whose feet were planted firmly in the ground in exactly the same manner as a portrait of good King Henry that Pepys had seen at court.

As Pepys approached, the stance softened to a bow.

'May I introduce Master Daly, Sir, the Master of Ordnance.'

The bow was held for a second longer that it should have been. Pepys sensed that there was an insolence, a reproof in it. The man stood erect and looked him in the eye. 'Welcome to the Ordnance, Sir. Is there anything, in particular, you would like to see?'

'Nothing, in particular, Master Daly, simply show me your operations.'

'As you wish. Follow me. But be careful, there is molten metal in here. An Ordnance is not a place for a casual stroll.'

Pepys ignored the remark. 'Lead the way, Master Daly.'

The doors opened and Master Daly stepped into a world full of smoke and dust and noise. In one corner, a blacksmith hammered a long shaft of metal, sparks flying with every strike of the hammer. In the centre, a group of men were carrying a large earthenware bowl using two sets of tongs. From the bowl, a warm orange glow and black smoke fumed. The men lifted the bowl and turned it over. A long stream of molten fire poured into a trough, producing even more black smoke. Around the rest of the Ordnance men hammered, water hissed, and foremen bellowed orders.

'You are busy, Master Daly.'

'There is much to be done, sir. Arms do not make themselves.'

'But they do make the man, don't they?'

Daly glanced at Pepys from under the row of his hat. 'They do indeed, Mr Pepys.

'You know your Virgil.'

'I find reading in the evening a welcome respite from the labours of the day. And you, Mr Pepys?'

'A Cambridge education, I'm afraid, Mr Daly. And where did you learn your trade?'

'In Kent, sir, at Tunbridge to be exact. Then I joined Master Pett after my apprenticeship.'

'You've been here a long time, Mr Daly, and seen many changes.'

'Perhaps, too long, Mr Pepys, and seen not enough.'

The Commissioner stood at the entrance to the foundry. 'Will you not join us, Commissioner?'

'Thank you but no, Mr Pepys, the heat is not good for my chest.'

'Well, we'll leave you behind then. Lead the way, Master Daly.'

Daly walked under a large arch and then they were in another area about three times as big as the first. Here, there were twice as many men, who were stripped down to the waist. The heat was intense. It came from a large open oven in the far wall. Even from where he was standing, Pepys could feel the waves of hot air raise the hairs on his forearms. A trickle of sweat ran down his back and pooled at the top of his breeches. He took off his hat and wiped his forehead with a handkerchief.

'As hot as hell, Master Daly.'

'I wouldn't know, sir, never having been to hell. Shall we approach the fire?' Pepys nodded.

Master Daly walked past a gang of men pouring hot metal into a mould. On top of the mould was a small hole with a pouring funnel. The hot metal flowed into the funnel and vanished with a gush of steam. The arm of one of the pourers jerked and a few drops of metal leapt out from the funnel and up into the air. The man who was supervising the operation gave a jump backwards and the hot metal landed between his feet, hissed on the earthen floor and instantly began to harden.

'Well done, Mr Rigby. Well danced that man,' shouted Master Daly.

Mr Rigby raised his hat to Master Daly as the rest of gang finished pouring into the mould.

'You have to be nimble on your feet in a foundry, Mr Pepys, otherwise you don't have feet to be nimble on.'

'Most of your men still seem to have their limbs, Master Daly.'

'Aye, and those that don't, we find work for elsewhere. I look after my men, and they look after me,'

'An admirable sentiment, Master Daly.'

They were close to the fire, now. A stoker was just

raking the coals while another prepared to shovel some more onto its glowing embers.

'We never let the fire go out. Too much trouble trying to get it started again. Even when the Dutch were coming up the Medway, my men remained behind and tended the fire.'

'I'm glad to hear that some people care about his Majesty's dockyards.' Pepys looked back at the rotund figure of the Commissioner silhouetted in the doorway. 'I would have words with you, Master Daly, if I may. But not here, the heat would roast the arse off Beelzebub himself.'

'I will be attending the dinner on the Sovereign tonight. We can talk then.'

'That would be most opportune.' Pepys turned to leave but as he did so, he saw something swinging towards him. He heard a shout and then the breath was forced out of his chest as something hit him squarely in the back. He landed heavily on the damp ground of the earthen floor, his face scraping across the years of coal dust, metal filings and dirt. Above him, in slow motion, he saw a large wooden block hit the stone of the wall and shatter, showering him with lumps of wood. This was followed by the thump of a large iron chain landing just inches from his head. He opened his eyes and saw the ridges and imperfections etched onto the surface of the chain.

A weight was lifted off his body. Master Daly was kneeling above him, smiling. 'I told you a foundry was a dangerous place, Mr Pepys.' He held out his hand to help Pepys up.

Pepys took it and stood up gingerly. Fridley came rushing up and began to brush Pepys' clothes, removing splinters of wood and dirt from his breeches.

Pepys picked up his periwig from the floor, wiped more splinters from it and placed it back on his head. 'I thank you, Master Daly.' The wreckage of the wooden block lay against the wall not a yard from his feet. Even nearer, a heavy iron chain lay coiled like a snake ready to strike. 'That was a damn close thing.'

Pepys looked towards the roof where a rope hung down. It still swung silently, back and forth. On the opposite wall, a set of steps led up to a gangway that ran the length of the building. The gangway was empty. How had the block and tackle come free if there was nobody there to untie it? And why had it happened at that particular moment? Nobody seemed to have seen anything. Or, if they had, they weren't saying. A frisson of fear ran down Pepys' spine. He was certain he needed to be more careful now. Something was going on in this dockyard and somebody was trying to make sure he didn't find out what it was.

Master Daly interrupted his thoughts. 'As I said, a foundry is no place for visitors.'

Pepys gestured to Fridley to stop brushing his clothes. It was important he didn't show any fear at this time. 'Perhaps now would be a good time to take some tea.'

Chapter 24

'Excuse me, there's nothing here.'

'Right, you are, sir.' The man looked where Will was pointing. He shifted his weight against his crutch. One leg was missing just above the knee, the empty trouser leg sewn back to cover his arse. 'Nothing there at all.'

Will was standing outside of Derby Court, just south of St. Pauls. He knew this was where the College of Heralds should be. It had always been here since the old Queen's day. God rest her soul.

'Burnt it was, during the Fire. Bloody Catholics.' The man spat on the ground at Will's feet.

'But there's nothing here.' Will pointed to the wasteland of earth and a few mounds of tussock grass.

'Well observed, sir. It was all taken away; stone and wood and all the rest. Can't waste good stone.'

'Taken? Where?'

'How would I know? Just the local watchman, me. They pays me to watch the land. I watches it. It doesn't move and anyway, who would steal land? Particularly, when there's nothing on it. But I ain't complaining. Good jobs is hard to come by for an old veteran. And good jobs where one just sits and watches is even harder to come by if you gets my drift.'

'All the records were burnt in the fire?'

'I don't think so. The Heralds were out like flies round shit that night, shifting and moving stuff. You should have seen them, nursing their books and bits of paper like a bitch and her puppies. Took 'em down the river, they did, just before the fire got here. Didn't save St Pauls, but saved their bits of paper instead. That's the nobs for you, ain't it?'

'Where did they go?'

'I can't rightly 'member, sir. Me wound, see, ' he pointed to his missing leg, 'fects my memry shocking it does.'

Suddenly the man had remembered his role as the wounded soldier. The hand not holding the crutch suddenly appeared in front of Will. He dug into his purse and found a sixpence.

The man looked down at it, 'the whereabouts still escapes me, sir. I'll 'ave to see the pothecary about this memry. Shocking expensive pothecaries. They'd bleed a man dry when they not taking his blood, if you catch my drift.'

Will dug deeper into his pocket and produced another sixpence. 'There. I'm sure your memory has been sufficiently medicined.'

The man took both coins, biting them between two large rotten teeth, before placing them into a small hole on the top of his crutch.

'I do believe they went down to the Palace of Whitehall, sir.'

'Where in the Palace?'

'Don't rightly know, sir, as I'm not in the habit of visiting Palaces. Went there once, to get the King's touch for me leg. Didn't help, though. Legs don't grow back once they been removed by a surgeon, do they? Not even with the King's touch.'

'Well, I shall be off to the palace, then.'

'So you should, and if you see the King, let him know that Old Jem's leg sends its regards.'

'I'll do that if I see him. Goodbye…?'

'I'm known as Old Jem but me real name's Thomas. Dunno how I came to be Old Jem. It sort of came and stuck to me.'

Will waved goodbye and walked towards Puddle Wharf to take a boat to the Palace. Helping Sam was costing him a pretty penny. He'd put it all down in his ledger to keep a record. There would have to be a reckoning with Sam when he returned from Chatham.

The stairs were packed with people, all fighting for a place on a boat. Will managed to ally himself with a Captain of the Guard and two of his men. Together, they shared the cost of one of the wherries. Well, at least they divided the cost with Will paying half and the Captain the rest.

Will took the opportunity to question the Captain on the location of the College of Heralds.

'Are they the men who wear them old tabards?'

Will nodded.

'Walk in front of the King when he visits Parliament?'

Will nodded again.

'Dunno where they are. 'Ere Tom, you know where the College of Heralds is?

Funny geezers, wearing red tabards and silk stockings?'

Will could see the cogs and springs of Tom's mind working as he tried to figure out the meaning of the question and if he knew the answer.

'In Scotland Yard, I fink. Had to carry a lot of ol' chests, didn't I? During the fire it were. Didn't get paid nutting for it, never.'

Will thanked the soldiers and gave them a shilling to drink his health. This was starting to prove costly.

When they arrived at the Palace, the soldiers directed him up the stairs and through the gate, past the chapel on the left and the Great Hall. He continued on his own, walking past the pantry and across the courtyard to the Jewel House. Here they had told him to turn right and keep walking until he hit Scotland Yard. The College of Heralds was in one of the buildings.

Nobody challenged him as he walked through the palace. In fact, everybody seemed to be so intent on going on their business, he was almost invisible. Servants were carrying food. Soldiers with heavy halberds marched down the corridors. Civil Servants practised being civil and servile. Courtiers lounged about doing nothing, waiting for the call to attend the King.

Will walked across Scotland Yard and looked at the range of buildings in front of him. Which one of them held the College? An old man in a bright red tabard with the lions of the King emblazoned on his chest came out from the door on the left. In his arms, he carried four vellum scrolls.

'The College of Heralds?'

'In there, for the moment.' He pointed back towards the door he had exited.

'I'm looking for help to find a crest.'

'Don't you mean a device?'

'I suppose I do.'

'Well, go inside and ask. Somebody will help you, I'm sure.' The old man walked away leaving Will standing on his own.

Will approached the door and peered inside. Against one wall was a massive armoire filled with books, its sheer size dominating the room. He could see nobody. 'Hellooo,' he shouted.

Louder, he thought, must shout louder. 'Hellllooooooo.'

'How can I help you?'

He jumped. The voice came from behind him. He turned and was faced by a burly man dressed in black, his face buried in the shadows.

'I'm looking for one of the Heralds. I want to find out who this crest belongs to.'

'You mean, device. Which Lord has this device?'

'I suppose I do.'

'You need a Herald of Arms. Ashmole's your man, he's the Windsor. Up the stairs on the right. I would be wary of disturbing him, though...'

'Why?'

'Shall we say, he's a little eccentric.'

Will ascended the stairs and knocked on the door on the right. A loud 'enter' resonated from inside. He pushed the door open and walked in. The office was large, much larger than he expected. Three of the walls held bookcases while in front of the fourth, the far wall, a small man sat at a large desk scribbling away. Beside his right arm, an immense globe depicting the world in all its glory stood on a brass stand. His desk was covered in papers, dividers, set squares, quills and ink.

'My Lord, I am sorry to disturb you.'

The man looked up from his writing. He had short curly hair that was receding at the front to show a vast expanse of wrinkle-free forehead. Below the forehead, Will was struck by the intensity and sleepiness of the eyes. An apparent contradiction, he recognised, but they were both alive and half asleep at the same time.

'And so am I. The History of the Garter will not write itself, young man.'

'I am aware of that but the Herald said you were the man to see.'

'The man to see about what?'

'About finding who owns a crest...a device,' he corrected himself quickly.

'I am your man, but can't you see I'm busy?'

'I'm sure it won't take up too much of your time. And I would be happy to make it worth your while.' As soon as the words came out of Will's mouth, he regretted them. More cost. Would the expense never cease?

'I do not need your money but the building fund does. As you can see, we need a new College.'

'I visited the old one this morning.'

‘Nothing left, such a shame. A beautiful building.’

'So I believe.'

Ashmole got up from behind his desk and held out his hand. Will shook it. As he did so, he felt a strange stroking of the palm. Ashmole must be one of the new Freemason's he had heard so much about, with their strange handshakes and even stranger rites.

'I see you are not a practitioner.'

'No.'

'That will be two pounds then.'

Will raised his eyebrows. 'Two pounds?'

'For the building fund.'

Will delved deep into his purse. He refused to think of the mounting costs but, in not thinking of them, thought of them even more. In his mind, a ledger page with Sam’s name at the top was filled with yet another figure.

Mr Ashmole took the money. 'Now, where is this device you would like me to research?'

'It's here on this button.' Will showed him the small silver button.

Ashmole peered at it. 'Is this it? You don't have anything else?'

Will shook his head.

'I suppose it will have to serve. At least the device is clear. I do hope this isn't a Scottish device because if it is, I can't help you. They're held in Edinburgh. Nothing to do with us.' He looked at it once again. 'Hmmm, looks English.'

He turned and reached up to the top shelf of the bookcase behind him. With difficulty, he pulled down a leather-bound book and heaved it on his desk. The book landed with a resounding thud. A small breath of dust rose into the air before slowly settling on all the surrounding papers.

‘This is the latest edition in our archives.’ He picked up a set of lenses from his desk and peered at the button through them. 'Now, you have to remember that each device is created for a person, not for a name. This one has the cross gules and escallops and a fess between three Cinquefoils Argent. Hmm, not so common.'

He opened the book. It's binding creaked as he did so. Will moved to look over his shoulder. Each page was painted in vivid blues, reds, whites, golds, silvers and greens, the devices of the Lords of England. He turned a page, scanning the devices as he did so, occasionally stopping to look at the button through his set of lenses.

After he had turned six pages, he stopped. 'Not here.' I'll try another, more recent volume. He stretched up again and pulled another large book down from the shelf.

He repeated the same process once again, going through more than twenty pages of devices this time. 'It doesn't seem to be here, young man. Could be very new. The button looks fresh.' He held up the button to the light. 'Quite recently made, as you can see. Not one of the old lords.'

'So you can't find it?'

Ashmole slammed the volume closed. Dust rose like a cloud and the motes danced in the light from the candle. 'No, sorry. Can't help you.'

'Is that it?'

'That's it. Unless you have more buttons for me?' said Ashmole.

Will shook his head.

'Well, if you don't mind, I'll return to my History of the Garter. I'm just dealing with Richard III. Not the easiest of characters as you'll appreciate.' With that, he opened his door and indicated that Will should leave.

Will found himself on the stairs before he could thank Mr Ashmole. He thought better of knocking on the door again. He returned the button to his purse. Their one clue seemed to be a dead end. Now, he would have to try Dryden and hope his luck was better with the poet.

Chapter 25

The rest of the day passed as Pepys had expected. The Commissioner filling his hours with manifests of cargoes, indents for muskets, receipts for corn, turnips, tallow, turpentine and treacle, and lists, endless lists of comestibles for the dockyard. And always, tables of choice meats and wines waiting for him should he get bored.

It was a very competent performance for somebody who was trying to hide the obvious by filling the space with the noise of facts. A performance that both disgusted and impressed Pepys in equal measures. But to such an experienced administrator as Pepys, the Commissioner could not hide the absence of workers and the lack of meaningful activity in the yard. Something was wrong and he was determined to get to the bottom of it.

It was only as they reached a small building at the end of the tour that the Commissioner became excited. He rushed forward pulling out a large set of keys from a bag carried by his valet.

'Let me show you my pride and joy, Mr Pepys.' The Commissioner inserted a large key into the door and turned the lock. The door swung open silently. Well-oiled thought Pepys. In the centre of the room was a raised dais with a large, black wooden box. On the front were four metal latches, each fastened by a small hasp. In the centre, was a keyhole and baseplate, again made of black metal.

'The Chatham Chest.'

'I am so glad you know of it, Mr Pepys.'

'It gave me much trouble in '67 when the previous Commissioner ran out of money for the seamen's pensions. We had to send a sizeable sum from the Treasury to ensure the men were paid.'

'A black day for Chatham, Mr Pepys. But since then, through judicious financial management by myself and Mr Fridley,' the man mentioned smiled wanly and took as small, humble bow, 'we have returned the Chest to solvency.'

'And how did you do that?'

Fridley stepped forward. 'We disposed of some assets, increased the levies from the seamen when they were paid off and lessened the number of pensioners on the rolls by offering a small payment.'

'The men took jam today rather than the possibility of no jam tomorrow.'

'Precisely, Mr Pepys. The English sailor is famous for his desire to live for the day and tomorrow will take care of itself.'

While Fridley had been speaking, the Commissioner had brought out a series of keys from his bag to unlock the four hasps. Finally, he produced a shiny, intricately fashioned key, inserted it into the central lock and stood back. 'If you would care to do the honours, Mr Pepys.'

Pepys stepped forward and turned the key. He felt the metal strike the tumblers of the lock.

'Please turn it once more, Mr Pepys, it's rather intricate,' said Fridley.

Pepys turned the key once more. There was a loud click, followed by the sound of metal on metal.

'You may lift the lid now, Mr Pepys,' said the Commissioner enthusiastically.

Pepys did as he was asked. Inside were countless bags of coin, nearly filling the Chest.

The Commissioner jumped forward. 'Almost 20,000 pounds at the moment. It always thrills me to see so much money in one place.'

He lifted up one of the bags and gave it to Pepys, whose hand immediately sank towards the floor with the weight.

'Each bag contains one hundred pounds. The weight is impressive, is it not, Mr Pepys? Worth a person's weight in gold. Even one as large as me.' He patted his stomach gleefully.

'Why is there so much?'

'We have been husbanding our resources, Mr Pepys. The men will be paid in July now,' said Fridley joining the two men at the chest.

'Not June as usual.'

'Not this year. We thought it prudent to move the dispensation of the money until July.'

'Won't that cause difficulties in the town amongst the sailors?'

'The men will only drink it if we pay out their pensions now. Better to encourage them to seek work. Let the resources of the Chest grow so that we can better manage the financial terms.' Fridley closed the lid.

'I thought we would save the best for last, Mr Pepys. I was certain you would be happy to see that the Chest was so replete with cash.'

'The Chest may be doing well, but I fear the sailors and their families are not.'

'You worry too much, Mr Pepys. We will take care of them in July, mark my words. One more month will make no difference. And now, may I tempt you to a glass of wine. You must be thirsty after your endeavours this afternoon.'

Pepys decided that he had seen enough for that day. 'Fridley, I'm still waiting for the complement of the dockyard.'

'And I'm still waiting for the Heads to compile it, Mr Pepys. As soon as I receive it, rest assured it will be delivered to you.'

'Good. Then lead the way, Commissioner, a glass of wine would relax eyes startled by the glitter of so much money.'

'And I have just the wine for your eyes, Mr Pepys. A Hock from Germany came in last week. It's done wonders for my eyes and for my gout.'

'Lead the way, Commissioner.'

*

Back at Hill House, Pepys dressed for the evening meal, putting on a fresh shirt and sponging his coat. The Commissioner had wanted to carry on drinking and eating, of course, but Pepys had made his apologies and escaped. The man could eat for Kent.

He needed time to think. The events in the foundry that morning troubled him. Had an attempt been made on his life? Or was it just another accident as everybody else seemed to believe? He had seen nobody up in the gallery. And if Master Daly meant to kill him, why go to all the bother of saving his life? In fact, why bother to kill him at all? The report to the King and his ministers was just the first step. Getting rid of him would simply mean that another man would comc to take his place. Unless...unless, it wasn't the report itself that was important, but the timing.

The words from Arlington came back to him. The Twelfth of June was the suspected date of the mutiny and the arrival of the Dutch. Just nine days away.

Perhaps that was the key.

There was a light tap on the door to Pepys' room. A sheepish-looking Balty entered, he still stank of drink.

'I'm sorry about last night, rather the worse for wear.'

'I asked you to collect information, not a hangover.'

'I know, I am sorry. It's just...well the night was young and the ale was flowing.'

'I'm sure the barmaids were flowing too.'

An expression of outraged innocence appeared on Balty's face, 'Not at all, Samuel. I swear it on my life.'

'Don't swear so easily, Balty, it's a life that has been full of barmaids, so I recall.' Balty's head went down. 'Enough of that, what did you find out? Or shall I rephrase that, what do you remember you found out?'

'You were right, Sam, something is happening in the town. Everyone seems to be on edge. It took more than a few tankards of ale to loosen their tongues.'

'And what did you discover?'

'There seems to be a Preacher holding meetings and spreading disaffection. I was invited to one, I think. Tonight at eight, sign of the Feather on Rotten Row.'

'Another sect?'

'I don't think so. I had the impression this Preacher seems more interested in the condition of the soul in this life rather than its presence in the next.'

'Did you get his name?'

'No, not yet. As soon as I started asking about the Preacher, people clammed up tighter than a duck's arse on Shrove Tuesday. And by the time...' He looked down at his feet again.

'By the time, the arses began to open, you were as drunk as a frog in a lake of wine.'

Balty's head came up. 'I said I was sorry.'

'No matter. You need to go to the meeting this evening. Be careful, though.' Pepys recounted the events of the day, particularly the 'accident' in the Foundry.

'Too much coincidence for an accident.'

'That's what I thought.'

'Looks like they meant to scare you, not kill you.'

'Scare me?'

'Sending you running back to London with your tail between your legs.'

'That's not going to happen.'

'Ah, but they don't know you, Sam Pepys, do they?'

'No, I knew the former Commissioner, Peter Pett. He was as venal as all of them, but at least he was efficiently venal. The King's dockyard was well run and the ships well built.'

'I wish it were ever so.'

'As do I. The inefficiencies of the Kings treasury makes us all dependent on our wits to supplement our earnings. But, the needs of the King and his Navy must be satisfied too. If people make a little extra on the side, so to speak, I see nothing amiss with that. Enough prattle.' He put on his coat. 'I am to dine this evening on the Sovereign. The boat will be waiting.'

'And I will go to my meeting after I've had the suet pudding your man has made. Suet pudding lines the stomach wonderfully. Gives the beer something to sit on.'

'Be careful, Balty, and be sober. I have a feeling that there is much more happening in this dockyard than meets the eye.'

'If my soul is saved tonight, be sure to tell the barmaids I miss them.'

Chapter 26

Will arrived at the theatre just in time for the start of the performance. But, with nobody guarding his seat, he was forced to find a place on a bench at the rear. He shuffled along and squeezed in between two large women, one of which was eating a plate of eels soaked in vinegar.

The play began almost immediately and Will leaned forward to hear the actors. Despite the distance from the stage and the occasional slurp from the woman as she inhaled another sliver of eel, Will could hear most of the words. The audience was strangely respectful tonight, he thought, as if the word had disseminated that here was a play that was worth listening too, despite what Sam had said.

At the end of the first act he stood up and, pretending to stretch his legs, took the opportunity to look down towards the front of the pit and up towards the boxes. Dryden was nowhere to be seen. If he was going to talk to him, the theatre was as good a place as any. He was sure Sam was wrong though. Which author changes his hard won words simply to suit a patron or send a message? Once again, Sam's pride had won over common sense. He was imagining it all, Will was sure.

The first four acts passed as before. Will was thinking of some oranges but decided to avoid the seller that had accosted Sam. He couldn't afford another scene like that. The woman sitting next to him was much quieter now, having finished her eels and moved onto a plate of small dainties, each of which she was depositing whole into her mouth. For a moment, Will switched his gaze from the stage to her face. The jaws working continuously in the flesh of the cheeks. The quick swallow, a little cough as a crumb caught in the throat, the mechanical grab of the hand and another cake popped into the vast maw of the mouth. A wonderful example of perpetual motion. Mr Fludd and his machine could learn from this woman.

He switched his eyes back to the stage. The deaths were coming quick and fast now, as they had done two nights ago. Nell Gwynn was enjoying her death scene, he could see it in her eyes. Will still preferred her in comedy though, particularly when she dressed as a man. How she strutted and preened around the stage, and when she grabbed her imaginary balls, well, he had never laughed so much in his life.

The play's last lines where being spoken, Nell lay lifeless on the stage. As before, two attendants walked out to place her on a bier and carry her off. And, as before, she popped up like a jack-in-the-box and said her lines;

'Hold; are you mad?
You damn'd confounded dog!
I am to rise, and speak the epilogue.'

Once again, the audience howled with laughter. Nell milked it for all it was worth with a couple of winks and a quick adjustment of her dress to show the top of her breast. Then she carried on as before, making fun of herself and the poet. Will listened for the part about the phallus, the part Sam believed that was written about him. But Nell never spoke the lines. Instead she said;

'To excuse his godly out-of-fashion play;
A play, which, if you dare but twice sit out,
You will all be slandered.

And be thought devout.

As the audience clapped and cheered, and the cast assembled on the stage for their curtain call, Will wondered if Sam was right. The words to the play had been changed. The ending was different. Perhaps though, Nell just made it up each night. Or Dryden himself had decided to amend it. The only way to find out was to ask him.

Will stood up, knocking over the lady's plate with its single remaining dainty. The woman looked at him as if he had just fondled her breast with his hand, and his hands had been cold.

He mumbled a quick, 'Excuse me,' and brushed past her. Dryden must be around somewhere. He scanned the departing audience. Rochester and his friends were leaving. He heard a smatter of their conversation.

'I much preferred it the other night, when Nell ended with a phallus.'

'You always prefer ending the night with a phallus, my dear.'

He pushed past them and down to the front where the apron intruded into the pit. He turned and looked backwards towards the emptying theatre. There was Dryden, just leaving from the middle box on the left. He recognised the long ginger periwig that cascaded over his shoulders like an orange waterfall.

Will bustled his way through the audience, once again bumping into the fat woman who had sat next to him. Once again, he was forced to mumble another apology. Out the doors at the end, and up the stairs, rising against the flow of people coming down. He pushed against one man, who pushed him back, sending him falling to his knees. A pair of shiny silver buckles were close to his eyes. He looked up past a white stocking and at the bright green leg of a pair of breeches.

'You see the man bows down before your poetic genius, Dryden.'

'I wish they all would. I might afford to buy the child some more milk.'

Will heard laughter from above. A pair of hands reached down and helped him to his feet.

'It always helps to understand the play if you actually look at the actors.' This was spoken by a man Will recognised. Thomas Betterton of Duke's.

'Really, Thomas, I always find it so much more revealing if I actually close my eyes and listen to the poetry of the words rather than be distracted by the overblown actions of a mere actor.'

'Well, you would, wouldn't you, Dryden? But nobody comes to listen to your words. They come to see us.'

'And if you didn't have my words to speak, what would you do on the stage, Mr Betterton? Ponce and preen, no doubt.'

'He does that with no help from your words, Dryden,' said a voice from the back. There was another round of laughter.

Will had recovered himself by now. 'Mr Dryden, I wish to talk to you about your play,' he stammered.

'Another fanatic,' said Betterton.

'Perhaps, another critic,' said the same voice from the back.

'Everyone's a critic, these days.' Betterton replied.

'I'm sorry. Mr…?'

'Mr Hewer, of the Naval Office.'

'Well, Mr Hewer of the Naval Office, I never talk about

my work. I let my words do the talking for me.'

'But I...'

'If you'll excuse me, Mr Hewer, I have a supper to attend. If I don't feed these actors, they will start to eat my words.'

'Aye, we will, Dryden. But your words don't give much sustenance.'

'See what I mean? A very greedy lot, actors, always wanting more lines than they need. I'll give you good night, Mr Hewer.'

With that, Dryden brushed past him, followed by his troupe of actors.

Will thought quickly, 'It's about a commission.'

Dryden stopped and turned. 'A commission? Why didn't you say? Come and see me in the Rose at eleven tomorrow. We'll breakfast together.'

Chapter 27

The barge rowed out smoothly to the Sovereign. With each stroke of the oars, the ship loomed larger and larger, until nothing remained of the shore, and all was wood and gold and rope. The immense stern soared above him, its golden walls and gilded windows topped by seven round lanterns. The largest, in the centre, but higher than the rest, capable of holding six people standing upright. Looking up at it Pepys had no doubt it was true.

The roar of a cannon deafened him. Were they being attacked? Had the Dutch arrived so soon? Then there was the boom of another cannon, followed by another and then another. Pepys counted to nine.

The rowers shipped their oars, holding them upright like so many soldiers standing to attention. The barge nestled into the side of the old ship. Pepys knew the vessel well, but it was the first time he was actually going to step aboard her. It had been built by the King's father over thirty years ago. These days, it didn't move far from its moorings. Despite its size and firepower, it had played no part in the war against the Dutch. The simple task of getting it underway proved far too dangerous and uncertain, while its size made it unwieldy and a slow sailor, retarding any fleet it accompanied.

Another expensive folly that the Navy Board had to find the money to maintain. But staring up at its vast wooden side, Pepys admired the magnificent grandeur of its size. Useless in war, it may be, but as the symbol of a powerful nation, it had no equal.

The scaly hand of a sailor reached out and grabbed his arm, helping him onto the rear gangway. He climbed the steps and waited a moment before stepping onto the deck. After all these years, boarding a ship always gave him a perverse thrill. He had helped build and maintain these vast machines of war. He had fought for them as they were made to fight for the King. He had struggled with the inefficiency and chaos of the Naval Office to keep them afloat. And now, here he was, being welcomed as an honoured guest and greeted by a nine gun salute. If only his mother, god bless her soul, could see him now.

He stepped on to the deck and felt the solidity of the oak beneath his feet. An officer, face weathered by years at sea, stood to one side. 'Mr Pepys, sir, it's a pleasure to welcome you aboard the Sovereign. The Captain is waiting with the other guests in the dining room.'

'Could I trouble you to see the ship before we descend?'

'Of course, Mr Pepys.'

Pepys walked towards the gangway that led to the Stern past a small group of sailors. Each of them eyed him suspiciously, before raising a scarred knuckle to their foreheads. These are not happy men, he thought, resentful and surly seemed to be a better description of their behaviour.

He climbed the ladder up to the quarter deck and strolled across to the aft rail. There, he leaned over and looked down at the water below, lapping softly against the hard wooden sides of the ship.

'She's near 120 yards in length, 106 cannon and a complement of 1000 men. The largest ship in the Navy.'

Pepys could hear the pride in the officer's voice. 'I believe she didn't see action in '67?'

'I'm afraid not, sir. She wasn't ready to sail. Short of crew, short of shot, short of everything. The Dutch didn't come this far down the Medway, otherwise, she would have been taken like the Charles.'

'I thank you for your honesty, Mr…?'

'Lieutenant Horn, sir, at your service.' The Lieutenant gave a little bow, which was returned by Pepys. 'Now if you would be so kind, I don't want to keep the Captain waiting. He has a short fuse...'

'Useful, when firing a cannon, Lieutenant Horn.'

'But not if it's aimed at a junior Lieutenant, Mr Pepys.'

They descended down into the depths of the ship. On every ceiling the lavish gilding that had been installed when the ship was built glittered and shone. Here and there gaps in the gold paint revealed where the ship had been damaged in action. The repairs had not nearly been as lavish as the original build.

They turned a narrow corridor and stood before a large double door. The Lieutenant knocked softly and entered. Light streamed from the room. Pepys blinked.

Horn quickly stepped in front of him. 'May I present Captain Smollett, Mr Pepys?

'Welcome, Pepys, you have finally arrived.'

The voice came from a small round man with a black wig and a tiny pointed goatee. His face and nose were a bright red, only surpassed by the crimson of the cheeks.

Pepys blinked again. The other guests came into focus.

'Let me introduce your companions for dinner. This is our ship's surgeon, Doctor Little. Can take a man's leg off in 23 seconds.'

'Don't forget, Captain, that includes removing his breeches. I'll get faster.'

Pepys bowed.

The Captain moved on. 'This is my second-in-command, Mr Quilt.'

An austere man bowed his head quickly. Pepys noticed

that his eyes had a curious lack of life, as if they had been taken from a dead man.

'It's a pleasure to meet you, Mr Quilt.'

The man didn't reply. The Captain continued as if nothing had happened. 'The Commissioner and his wife. You are well acquainted with him, I believe.'

'I hope you have recovered from your inspection of the dockyard, Mr Pepys. Such a warm day for tiring work,' said the Commissioner's wife. 'My husband tells me there was an accident.'

'It was nothing, Madam, an unfortunate slip by one of the men in the foundry.'

'I often tell my husband not to wander around the dockyard, don't I dear? A dangerous place to go wandering around, I say.'

'A dangerous place indeed, Madam.'

'And may I finally present Mrs Aphra Behn and Mr Thomas Cheney.'

Pepys bowed low. In front of him stood a small woman, not very pretty but with a twinkle in her eyes and a tilt of the head that suggested she was curious about the man standing in front of her.

'My pleasure, Madam.'

'Oh, it will be, I'm sure, Mr Pepys. I will see to that.'

Pepys was lost for words. Was the woman flirting with him? No doubt over the course of the evening, he would find out. He looked across at her companion. A tall, thin man with a weak chin, that suggested all the spine and depth of character of a jellyfish.

'I thought Mr Daly was to join us?'

'I'm afraid he has been unavoidably detained.' The Commissioner's double chin wobbled with the news. 'Pressure of work, I believe.'

‘I’ve always told Daly he works too hard. Just like you, my dear. Hard work is all well and good in its place, but I always say a dockyard is no place for it.’ The Commissioner’s wife patted the arm of her husband.

‘I do believe the Dutch might agree with you, Madam.’ Before Pepys could say more, Lt. Horn stepped forward and raised his glass.

'Ladies and gentlemen, let us drink the health of the King.' A glass of wine was placed in Pepys' hand by a bare-footed waiter. The assembled guests raised their glasses and poured the amber liquid down their throats. All except Mr Quilt who merely placed his lips on the rim of the glass.

'You're not drinking, Mr Quilt,' said Pepys.

'My second-in-command never drinks, do you Quilt?' The Captain patted the shoulder of his subordinate.

'Harsh spirits are the consort of the devil, Mr Pepys. I never allow them to pass my lips.'

'Did not the Lord turn the water into wine at the feast of Canaan, Mr Quilt?’ said Pepys.

'And was not wine drunk at the Last Supper, the Lord himself calling for a toast,' added Mrs Behn with a twinkle in her eyes.

'That's as maybe, but spirits cause confusion in the minds of men and we forget the existence of God.'

'Oh come, Mr Quilt, it is but a glass of wine.'

'It is a temptation of the devil, Mr Pepys.'

'I suppose you don't drink a dish of coffee or tea either.'

'No, Madam, I do not.'

'Life must be terribly dull for you, Mr Quilt.' She put her fan up to her face and peered over the top of it. 'I suppose you indulge in all manner of excitements, Mr Pepys, living in London as you do. One hears the court is quite the most exciting place to be these days.'

'The court does have its passions, Mrs Behn. I, unfortunately, am not part of them, being merely a humble servant of the crown at the Naval Office.'

Her eyes glittered over the top of her fan. 'What a shame, Mr Pepys. What a shame.'

'May I ask you to take your seats? The first course is ready to be served.' Once again, it was Lieutenant Horn who came to Pepys's rescue.

They sat down around the Dining Room table, which almost filled the small cabin. The courses, the conversation and the wine flowed smoothly. The Captain seemed a good sort, if a little forgetful. Mr Quilt remained as austere as ever, picking at his food like a blackbird searching for tender morsels in the soil. The Commissioner and his wife laughed heartily at other people's jokes without ever making any of their own. Mrs Behn was the heart and soul of the party with her stories of the strange beliefs of the natives of Surinam and the even stranger practices of their colonial masters.

Over a dessert of syllabub, the doctor was recounting his experiences of life as a surgeon.

'I have been under the knife too, you know,' offered Pepys.

'Really? And you lived to tell the tale?' said Mrs Behn.

Pepys hand went to his wrist and found his pulse. 'Yes, it's still there, beating at a rate. It must be your close proximity that has it so excited, Mrs Behn.'

'You were telling us of your experience under the knife.' The doctor leaned forward for the first time that night. Apparently, medical matters interested him far more than the head hunters of Surinam.

'It was back in '58. I had been suffering excruciating

pain for a long time. And, I ask for the forgiveness of the ladies present, if I describe the pain as being one that only a man can experience.'

'You had a stone?' said the doctor.

'Indeed, I did, Surgeon Little.'

'Men who have not suffered the pain of childbirth cannot begin to understand pain, Mr Pepys.'

'I do agree, Mrs Behn, however this pain led me to give birth to a child of one pound ten ounces. With the help of the surgeon, of course.'

'By whom where you treated, Mr Pepys?'

'By Surgeon Thomas Hollier of St Thomas and Barts on the morning of March 26, 1658. The day is etched in my memory, Doctor Little.'

'Pray, do tell us the details, Mr Pepys.'

'I'm afraid they are rather gory for such fair company, Mrs Behn.'

'Once again, may I remind you, the fair company that you so wish to protect,' here she pointed at herself and at the Commissioners wife, 'have both suffered the distress, and the elation, of childbirth. Nothing can surprise us after that, can it, Lady Turton?'

'Not at all, Mrs Behn. I have had seven children myself. Each one hard work, I can tell you.'

'No wonder they call it 'going into labour',' said Mrs Behn.

'You are a wit, Mrs Behn, you should write for the theatre,' chuckled the Commissioner.

'I intend to, Commissioner, just as soon as my business in Kent is settled.'

'How were you treated, Mr Pepys?' It was the doctor again, eager to learn more.

Pepys took a sip of wine and let his audience wait for

a moment. He had told the story often and knew that a few pregnant pauses increased the joy in the telling. 'As I was saying, it was on the morning of the 26 March, in '58, a Friday, I believe. The surgeons gave me a few glasses of brandy. Luckily, I was the first patient that morning otherwise the pain of waiting would have caused me more anguish than the operation itself.'

There were anticipatory chuckles around the table. Pepys took another sip of wine. The doctor leaned in closer.

'My clothes were stripped from me and I was tied to a chair, with my feet placed in stirrups on either side and my knees up around my ears. Four strong fellows pushed down on my shoulders to keep me still. I saw the surgeon preparing his knives. I believe I'll always remember the sound of the knife on the strap as long as I live.'

He took another sip of wine. 'I'm afraid the rest of the story is far too gory for mixed company.'

There were disappointed groans from around the room. Mrs Behn's voice rang out. 'Come now, Mr Pepys, that will not do. You cannot leave us hanging on the details. How will the good doctor ever be able to perform his duties on another patient should the occasion arise? And as for myself and Lady Turton, I would hazard we have seen, heard and experienced far more than any male around this table. All women, the fair sex, as you put it, have.'

Pepys took another sip of wine. 'As you wish, Mrs Behn, I will continue. I was strapped into the chair with four burly men pressing down upon my shoulders. I saw the surgeon approach with a knife. He made a cut around my private parts and then took what appeared to be an immense pair of tongs. As you can imagine, at this moment the pain was frightful and I was struggling with all my might against the four men who held me down. Then I saw him approach with the tongs and I...'

'What did you do?' said the Captain.

'I'm afraid to say that I passed out. The shock and the pain, you know. When I woke up, I was still in my chair, still being held down by the men, but the surgeon was holding up a bloodied round ball, like a small cannonball, in the tongs. He had a broad smile on his face and as he spoke, I passed out again.'

'What did he say?'

'One less bollock to worry about.'

The whole audience collapsed with laughter and the Commissioner blurted out a mouthful of wine. A small smile even crossed the lips of Mr Quilt.

'But you survived the ordeal.'

'I was lucky enough that the wound healed well and I was nursed back to health. Four weeks I spent in my bed though. It was touch and go at one point.' The table fell silent. 'It helped me understand the importance of life. That it is to be lived and enjoyed to the fullest, without fear of favour or punishment. To love life in all its glory and sadness, triumphs and disappointments.' He pinched his bottom lips between his thumb and index finger. 'I even began to write a diary about my life, chronicling what happened to me and my world.'

'I've heard about such diaries. You should write one, dear, you live such an exciting life,' said the Commissioner's wife.

Pepys looked around the table, seeing if his words had produced any reaction. Only Quilt seemed to be affected, coughing and bringing a glass up to his lips before pausing to inhale the wine rather than drink it.

‘You said it was touch and go at one point?’ asked the doctor.

Pepys took a long draught of his wine. ‘The wound wasn't healing properly. I think I would not have survived without the tender ministrations of Surgeon Hollier.'

'He bled you often?'

'No, he never bled me. Didn't believe in it. He said it weakened the patient.'

'How strange,' said the Commissioner, ' I always believe a good bleeding helps a man. Gets rid of the bad humours that invest our blood. Have myself bled once a week, whether I need it or not.'

'Interesting', said the doctor, ‘no bleeding. Perhaps, I will try that on one of my amputations and see if it helps.'

'Here's to your continued good health, Mr Pepys.' The Captain raised his glass and finished it off. He was joined by the rest of the dinner party. 'Now, I believe that you have an early start tomorrow on your visit to the new installations at Gillingham and Sheerness.'

'I believe I am to visit the new forts, yes.'

'Fridley has arranged a cutter for seven in the morning. I'm afraid the tides may be against you, but the weather looks like it is holding fair.'

'I should so like to join you, Mr Pepys. I have never seen the new forts from the sea,' said Mrs Behn.

‘I think that should be possible Mrs Behn. If you could be at the dock by seven 'o clock, I would be happy for you to accompany me.’

'Thank you, I will see you then.'

'You are welcome to join me too, Mr Cheney.'

'Unfortunately, I have business in Rochester tomorrow.' Mr Cheney spoke for the first time that night. As the man did so, Pepys could see the bright eyes of Mrs

Behn looking at him over the top of her fan.

'Good, that is arranged then,' said the Captain, 'Lieutenant Horn, please arrange for my guests to be taken back to shore. Do be careful, Ladies, as you descend to the barge. I do believe the wind has picked up over the course, and courses, of our meal.'

'I always take care, Captain, even when I am at my most daring.' As she spoke the words, Pepys noticed that she wasn't looking at the Captain but staring straight at him.

*

Back at Hill House, Pepys enjoyed a nightcap of the Commissioner's wine before removing his coat and breeches. The evening had gone splendidly. His story of being cut for the stone had been appreciated by everyone. Whilst the memory of being toasted for his good health at the end of it gave him a feeling of intense satisfaction. How good it was to be appreciated in polite company. And tomorrow, he would be visiting the new forts in the company of Mrs Behn. A prospect that gave him even more delight.

The rest of the day had been less successful. What was going on in the dockyard? It was obvious that all was not well. The men were listless and lazy. The docks were undermanned and inefficient. The stores woefully lacking. The Commissioner was either a fool or corrupt, or both. Only two areas seemed to be running smoothly: the magazine he had not been able to examine, and the foundry under the management of Master Daly. And why had the man not appeared at dinner?

As he removed his stockings, he thought back to his visit to the foundry. Had the accident really been an accident? He wasn't sure. One minute he had been examining the work of the men, the next he was on the floor, scrabbling around in the dirt with lumps of wood from a block strewn across his body and the heavy links of an iron chain lying perilously close to his head. Master Daly had saved his life he was certain. But why do that if he was the one who had arranged the accident in the first place?

And if it wasn't an accident, who was it who was trying to have him killed? The Commissioner? Mr Fridley? Person or Persons Unknown? And why try to have him killed anyway?

The question buzzed around Pepys' brain like an angry bee. He hoped Will was having more success with his inquiries at the College of Heralds and his interviews with Dryden and the lovely Nell Gwynn.

He put on his nightshirt. Perhaps Balty would have some answers after his visit to the Preacher's meeting this evening. Where was the man?

'Balty,' he called out. There was no answer. 'Balty,' he shouted, louder and more forcefully this time. Pepys hoped that he wasn't drunk again, fallen into another stupor in some wretched place in the docks.

He walked out of his room, down the corridor to Balty's door. The house was quiet, the servants having retired for the night. The only sound was the ticking of an admiralty clock in the drawing room.

He listened at the door. Was that the sound of snoring? He knocked softly on it, not wanting to wake the servants. 'Balty, it's me, Sam Pepys. Open up.'

He pushed the door. It slowly swung open. The full moon shone through the window, casting deep black shadows across the room.

He stepped inside. The sound he thought was snoring was simply the wind rustling through an ill-fitting window.

The covers were drawn over Balty's bed, the sheets and pillows undisturbed. The rest of the room had that particular stillness that the lack of something always produces. The lack, in this case, being the person of Balty.

Where was the man? If he was out drinking, eating and wenching again, this would be the last time Pepys would ever help that useless, insolent oaf of a brother-in-law. Elizabeth could plead till she was blue in the face, but his heart would be stone. He would do nothing more to assist the man.

He left the room, closed the door behind him, and stomped back to his bedroom.

What had he bothered to trust his fool of a brother-in-law in the first place? Would he never learn? The only person he could trust was himself. And maybe Will.

He wondered what Will had discovered in London? Had he found the diary? Or at least who had stolen it?

He hoped so.

He desperately hoped so.

Chapter 28

The morning sun broke through a gap in the night curtains thrusting an intense beam of light across the floor of his bedroom. Pepys awoke and, in the strange fog between waking and sleeping, thought he saw Balty standing before his bed.

'Where have you been?'

There was no answer.

Pepys repeat his question. 'Where did you go last night?'

The figure of Balty began to fade and dissolve in front of Pepys' eyes. He shook his head.

The light streamed in through the gap in the curtains but nobody was there.

He jumped up out of bed and rushed down the corridor. The door to Balty's room was still as closed as he had left it the night before.

He knocked and called. 'Balty, come out this minute.'

There was no answer. He knocked again. Still no answer.

He pushed the door open and stepped cautiously into the room. Sunlight streamed through the windows. The curtains remained tied to the wall. The bed lay empty, undisturbed and unused.

For a moment, Pepys stood in the room, staring at the undisturbed covers on the bed. Something was wrong. Something was definitely wrong.

Still in his nightshirt, he ran towards the servant's quarters. The valet was setting the table for his breakfast.

'Have you seen Balty? I mean Mr St Michel?'

'No sir, not since last night. Before you went to dine on

the Sovereign, he had four bowls of suet pudding and a bottle of sack. I supposed he was going out on the town, sir, as he had done the previous night.'

'You didn't see or hear him come back?'

'No sir. Shall I keep his setting for breakfast?'

But Pepys had already left the room. Where was Balty? What had happened to him? Pepys felt angry with himself for his ungracious assessment of Balty's character the night before. Even if the man had got drunk after the meeting, he would have come back last night. People like Balty always made it home, eventually. No matter how drunk they became or the quality of the company.

Pepys put on his shirt and breeches. There was a knock on the door. Balty had returned.

He opened it and Fridley stood there. 'Good morning, Mr Pepys, I hope you slept well.'

'Thank you, I did.'

'The Commissioner has graciously provided the King's yacht to take you to the new forts today. Would you prefer to breakfast on board or here at Hill House?'

'I would have thought that it was His Majesty's prerogative to provide his yacht for my use, not the Commissioners.'

Fridley didn't reply, merely bowing his head and rubbing his hands together.

'No matter. I will have coffee here, dining later with Mrs Behn,'

'Yes, sir. I will inform the valet.' He turned to go.

'Oh, Fridley,' Pepys talked as if it were an afterthought of no consequence. 'Have you seen Mr St Michel this morning?'

'No sir, not since we left Hill House last night. I believe the valet told me he went out.'

'Thank you, Fridley. I will join you in a moment.'

Fridley bowed and closed the door. Pepys returned to his dressing table and put on his linen vest. What he saw in the mirror pleased him. Already thirty-six years old but still a fine figure of a man. He turned to regard himself from the side. A stomach developing but the ladies liked a bit of a stomach. He remembered the words of the waitress at the Swan, 'I always likes a pot belly, bit of cushioning never did a girl any harm.'

A smile crossed his face at the memory. How he missed those easier, more joyous times.

He returned to the problem of his brother-in-law. Balty was missing and nobody had seen him. Should he get them to mount a search or was he panicking too much? Perhaps Balty had simply found the delights of one of the local barmaids too much to resist. If he called out a search and Balty was found with his breeches around his ankles, in the arms of one of Kent's finest ladies of the night, Pepys would look a fool. Worse, his reputation in the area would be destroyed. He would wait until he returned this evening.

He put on his breeches, followed by a coat and surcoat, it was bound to be cold in the mouth of the Medway. Finally, he picked up his best black periwig from the mannequin and placed it carefully on his head so that it rested evenly on his shoulders. A last check in the mirror. Now he was ready to face the world and Mrs Behn in particular.

He walked out of his bed room. Fridley was loitering outside. 'Let's get started, Fridley. The weather looks perfect.'

'A slight breeze off shore, Mr Pepys. It will mean the Captain will have to tack against the wind and the tide. It could be slow going today, I believe.'

'No matter. I have to inspect the forts for my report. Let's be going.'

'Mrs Behn is already on board, sir. She arrived earlier this morning.'

'Why didn't you say, man? No time for coffee, now.'

Pepys bustled out of Hill House with Fridley in tow. He hurried down the path that lead to the wharf. The yacht was a fine vessel; built two years ago by Castle at Rotherhithe. It was a greyhound of the seas, tied up at the wharf like a dog straining at the leash.

Already the jacks were hurrying up the masts, unfurling the sails and preparing for cast off. Mrs Behn stood at the stern watching all the activity around her. Pepys hurried on board, to be greeted by the Captain.

'Good morning, sir. Welcome aboard. We will be ready to sail in a few moments.' Pepys could see Mrs Behn walking towards him. She took him by the hand and led him below.

As they left the Captain and Fridley behind, she whispered in his ears. 'Finally, I have you alone.'

Chapter 29

Will had arrived at exactly nine a.m. He was greeted by William Unwin, the landlord of the Rose, and immediately shown to a table. The room was buzzing with gossip.

As he sipped his coffee, waiting for the arrival of Dryden, he couldn't help but hear the conversations going on around him.

'...Precious. Amber, you know, from the Baltic. Davies says it is going to be the next big thing in jewellery. You shouldn't miss out. If you want I can save you....'

This was from two gentlemen on his left. One was trying to sell a share of some cargo to the other. Will wanted to lean over and box the man's ears telling him, don’t listen to them, they just want your money. But, he didn't. Not the thing to do in the Rose. If a man was stupid enough to invest with a trickster, that was his problem.

He took another sip of his coffee. Hot, rich, fragrant and bitter, just as he liked it. Mr Unwin had said they had received a fresh shipment of beans from Turkey that very morning.

He listened to the conversation on his right. The man was leaning in very close to his companion. Will had to strain to hear the words.

‘Duke of York…have you heard the latest?… conversion...Catholic.'

'It's where I get all my ideas from too.'

For a moment, Will was startled. He turned his head and looked up. Dryden was standing in front of him, his long ginger periwig framing his sharp face.

'I...' was all that Will could stammer.

'If you don't mind, I prefer to sit out on the balcony in summer. Mr Unwin always keeps me a place.'

He strode off towards the balcony, nodding a greeting to the customers he knew as he passed them. He seemed to know many of them. Or they appeared to know him.

Will got up and followed him. He stopped, returned and finished his coffee in one gulp. It burnt his mouth, but it would be a shame to waste good coffee. He hurried after Dryden out into the fresh air, or what passed for fresh air in London.

Dryden had taken his place at the table and was already being served his morning cup. Will sat down, expecting another to be placed in front of him. It never came.

Dryden finished his first swallow. 'Ah coffee, the nectar of the gods. How did the muse visit scribes in ancient times without this ambrosia?'

Will wondered if Dryden talked like this all the time or was he merely putting on a performance? The answer came very quickly.

'Well, Mr Hewer, to business. You have a commission for me, I believe?'

Will was momentarily startled by the change in tone. Dryden seemed to have this effect on him. 'I...,' he stammered once again before his words formed in his mouth. 'I was wondering if your plays ever change as they are being performed.'

'All the time. Actors you know, not the most reliable of people, forget the words. Oh, we do have a prompter reminding them from the side of the stage but half of them are deaf, and the other half think they are better writers than me anyway.'

'No, I meant whether you changed your plays as they

were being performed.'

Dryden paused for a moment. 'Sometimes, when the act is flowing badly and I know I have lost the audience. Then I relook at it and write a new draft for the actors. Not common, though. Plays run for such a short time, it's hardly worth my effort or my consideration.' He took another sip of his coffee, noticed that Will was without a cup and snapped his fingers. Instantly, a waiter appeared at his shoulder. 'A cup for my friend.'

'Certainly, Mr Dryden.'

Will wished he could get such attentive service but he knew if he snapped his fingers in a place such as this, he would soon find them broken.

Dryden sniffed and sipped his coffee again. 'Why do you ask?'

'It's just...it's just that the other night, in the epilogue spoken by Nell Gwynn...'

'Ah, the lovely Nell, my beautiful Valeria.' He leant forward. 'Not a very good actress and a terrible wanton. Mother was a brothel keeper. Nell has had her share of ups and downs, if you take my meaning.' He leant back and winked at Will. 'But you didn't hear that from me.'

'She has the ear of the King, I believe.'

'And that's not all.'

Will needed to get the conversation away from Nell Gwynn's adventures. 'As I was saying, the other night, during the epilogue, Nell spoke your words. They were written by you?'

'They usually are. I am the playwright after all.'

'But last night the words were different. The epilogue wasn't the same as before.'

Dryden sniffed again and took another sip of his coffee. 'You are observant, aren't you?' He placed the cup back on the table and pointed to a man leading a donkey in the street below. 'See that man.'

Will looked over the rail.

'He spends his life leading a donkey around the streets of London. If you give him fourpence, he will place a stool by the side of the donkey and reach underneath it to stroke its teats until it produces enough milk to fill a small pail. A mother, or a nursemaid, then takes the pail and gives it to her children.'

'A milk seller. Thousands of them in London. One on every street.'

'Well, we writers are no better. Somebody comes along and gives us a few pence. We sit down and milk the years of our learning and give them back a pail of words, which they then feed to their colleagues, friends, children and enemies. They're just words after all. And a week from now, nobody will remember any of them.'

Will tried to understand what he was saying. 'You mean...'

'I mean exactly what I mean to mean, Mr Hewer, no more, no less. Now if you do not have a commission for me, I would prefer to enjoy my breakfast alone.'

Will thought about asking him more questions but, from the look on Dryden's face, he thought than this would not be good idea. 'I'm sorry for taking up so much of your time, Mr Dryden. Thank you for the coffee.' Will drained his cup and stood up.

'A word, Mr Hewer.' Dryden beckoned him forward with his index finger. Will leant closer.

'Don't follow those words to the end of their sentence. You are dealing with a particularly nasty man. A man I would not cross if I were you.'

'And which man is that?'

But Dryden had pulled out a London Gazetteer and was already reading it. Will stood there for a moment before realising that he looked like a fool. 'Thank you once again for your time, Mr Dryden.' He bowed and walked through the Rose and out into the street.

Will looked up over his shoulder at the balcony. Dryden was still sitting there, reading his newspaper.

‘Fancy a drop? Goes down well after coffee? Pulled it myself a minute ago.’

The old man held a pail of creamy milk in front of Will’s face. The donkey brayed its agreement with his master.

‘No, thank you. I fear I am not the only one to have been milked this morning.’

Chapter 30

As they sat down at the back of the yacht, Mrs Behn pulled Pepys closer to her.

'Show it to me?'

'Show it to you?' Pepys was surprised at the forward nature of her character. He was used to being in charge when it came to women. This woman and her very manly approach made him feel uncomfortable.

'Out with it, we don't have much time. Fridley will return soon.' She moved closer to him.

'Madam, I fear your intentions are mistaken. Much as I find you attractive, I have made a promise to my wife.

Mrs Behn moved away from him. 'I think you misunderstand me, sir.'

'I understand too well, Mrs Behn, a year ago I would have been more than willing to indulge in a little divertissement with you, but now I'm afraid my promise…' He shrugged his shoulders.

Mrs Behn raised her voice, a tone of exasperation creeping in. 'I think you misunderstand me, sir, I merely wanted to see your commission from the King.'

Pepys scratched his wig. Why were women always so difficult? Why were relations between the sexes so fraught with problems and miscommunication? Dealing with the legions of Beelzebub would be easier than the emotions of a woman.

He pulled out the letter from his pocket. She snatched at it and scanned down the page. 'Tell me everything?'

'Everything, Madam?' he answered feebly.

'Everything. I need to know your intelligence.'

And then he understood. 'You're Arlington's agent?'

'Of course, what else would I be?'

'I thought that...'

She pulled away from him and stared down with those sharp eyes. 'Oh sir, you flatter yourself, that I...with you?'

'Madam, I don't know what you mean. I thought that it would be somebody else, not you.'

'Well, it is me. I was born in Kent and still have ties to this area. It was natural for Lord Arlington to send me here to investigate the threat to His Majesty, the King.'

'You say that with a certain reverence, Madam.'

'There is nobody whom I admire more.' She looked at Fridley and the sailors as they prepared the yacht to make way. 'The rest of humanity pales in comparison to him.'

'Ah, I see. You were not of the Commonwealth then.'

'Never. Cromwell's head deserves its position above Traitor's Gate. I only wish that it had been done when he was still alive. Enough of this. What have you found out?'

'Let us eat as I tell you. I suddenly find that this breakfast holds a definite attraction for me.'

'It is the only thing at this table that holds any for me, sir.'

Pepys ignored the remark and poured the coffee for both of them. The table groaned with food. The Commissioner did enjoy the benefits of his position and he seemed determined that his visitors should benefit from them too. He took a piece of bread and spread it with a Seville orange marmalade he found in a pot.

Mrs Behn was looking at him, not eating. 'I'm waiting, sir.'

'And my stomach is waiting, Madam. At the moment, its needs shout out to me more.'

The yacht had now got underway, pulling slowly away

from the wharf.

‘And if I am not mistaken, we will be together on this yacht for the next six hours. Whatever I divulge, you will be unable to act on until we reach the dockyard. I suggest, in the meantime, we enjoy our breakfast and discuss the matter slowly and at length, sharing our intelligence. Does that plan suit?’

Mrs Behn merely grunted. But she reached for one of the cakes that were piled high on a tray to her left. She bit into it with a force that made Pepys wince.

When he had finished his marmalade, enjoyed three quinces and finished two cups of the excellent coffee, he began to speak. 'I have been here less than two days. In that time, it has become clear to me the dockyard is poorly managed, the people sullen and aggressive, the Commissioner inattentive at best. I have nearly been killed and my assistant, Balthazar Le Michel, has gone missing. But, other than that, it has been a rather pleasant trip to this part of Kent. Let me give you the details.'

'I wish you would.'

He leant back and looked over the Medway. The yacht was heading upstream past Upnor to the new forts at Gillingham and Sheerness. Above him, clouds scudded across the light blue sky, interrupted only by the flapping of the sails as they caught the breeze. It was time to tell this woman what he knew. He wished it were more substantial.

'My assistant went to a meeting last night. As of this morning, he has still not returned.'

'Which meeting?'

'That of a Preacher. I don't know the name.'

'My sources tell me he is called Lawson. He has spent the last six months organising the sailors and the dockyard workers.'

'I fear they have much to complain about.'

'No pay for those who work. No work for those who pay. And no work or pay for those with families to feed.'

'Fertile ground for any fomenter of trouble. Do we know anything about this Preacher, Lawson?' asked Pepys.

'Not much. He arrived in Chatham six months ago, from who knows where. He quickly built up a following in the dockyard and aboard the ships.'

'What sect is he?'

'I believe he is a fifth monarchy man.'

'I thought they had all been banished or executed?'

'A few remain preaching their seditious threats to the King. They dream of the coming of King Jesus, with the only person standing in the way of that arrival being His Majesty. This man, Lawson, has added his own little twist to those beliefs.'

'And that is?'

'The Dutch are the midwives of the second coming. Through them, the King will be removed and a new heaven on earth will be created.'

'I didn't know the Dutch had such a close relationship with God.'

'According to Lawson they do. And if your stomach is empty and your family starving, your head is more likely to believe anything.'

'You have reported all this to Arlington and Sir Joseph.'

'Of course.'

'Why don't they arrest the man? Throw him in the Tower and throw away the key.'

'I do not know. I thought perhaps you would be able to tell me.'

'It's far too early for me to tell you anything, Madam. I

had hoped that Balty, Mr Le Michel, would be able to tell me more when he returned from his meeting with the Preacher. Alas, he had not come back by the time I left this morning.'

'I have two men inside the church. I will ask them to look for your assistant.'

'Thank you, Madam, that would put my mind at ease.'

They heard a cough from across the deck. 'Begging your pardon, sir, but we are approaching Fort Gillingham as we speak. Would you like to come to the gang rail to look?'

Pepys left the table and walked to the port side of the ship. In front of him, a bluff rose from the Medway to overlook the river, an ideal site for a fort to prevent enemy ships from penetrating further up the waterway.

But of the new construction itself, he could see little. The earthworks had been constructed, however there was little activity in the new fort itself.

'We are going to land, aren't we, Fridley?'

'I'm afraid that's impossible, sir, the tides you see.'

Pepys looked at the fort once again. 'I can see very little work going on, Mr Fridley.'

Fridley looked down at his feet. 'We have run out of money, sir.'

'Run out of money?'

'Yes, sir.'

'But the King has expressly ordered that the forts be built.'

'I know sir, but without money how are we to build them?'

'The money has been voted for in Parliament and assigned by the Naval Board. Where has it gone, Fridley?'

'I do not know, sir. We thought about using some of

the finances in the Chatham Chest, but that's reserved for the seamen, sir.' A smug smile crossed the man's face and he began to rub his hands as if he were coating them with cream

Pepys realised that he was not going to get any more out of the man. 'And what about the complement of the dockyard, have you compiled the figures yet?'

'It is being done as we speak, sir. It should be ready for you when we return to the dockyard.'

Pepys grunted and looked again at the empty embankments of the fort. If the Dutch attacked now, Chatham and the Naval dockyards were virtually defenceless, in a worse position than they were two years ago. Did nobody know this was happening? And what of the Commissioner? He must be involved in all of this. He must know how unprepared he was for my inspection, yet he does nothing save ply me with fruits and fruitcake.

Another cough from Fridley. 'Do you still want to sail to Sheerness, sir?'

'Of course, Fridley. How am I to complete my report if I do not see everything?'

'The last person sent down by the Navy Board didn't bother himself, sir.'

'And who was that, Fridley?'

'Sir William Penn, sir, he came two months ago. I believe he reported back that everything was in ship-shape order in the dockyard.'

Penn, that fool, thought Pepys. But even Penn could not have been so stupid as to have seen a half-built fort and thought it finished.

'Let us sail to Sheerness, Fridley. I wish to see progress at the entrance to the Medway.'

'As you wish, sir. I will inform the Captain.'

Pepys returned to his seat next to Mrs Behn. He sat there in silence for a long time. The dockyard and the forts on the Medway were in deep trouble, but nobody was doing anything. Why?

Mrs Behn interrupted his thoughts. 'The Fort is half-finished.'

'You know?'

'Everybody knows, even the Dutch.'

'The King does not know.'

'Everybody else does.'

'Why keep the information from him?'

'My work has so far taught me one thing. There are some things we know, and some things we don't know. And there are others, we know we don't know. The importance of the work that we perform,' she pointed to herself and Pepys, 'is to lessen the latter and increase the former.'

'A friend of mine believes knowledge is power.'

'No. Power is power. Lack of knowledge is weakness.'

'Madam, you display a talent for the dramatic, you should be on the stage.'

'I would prefer to be writing for it.'

'Let us spend the next couple of hours before we reach Sheerness planning our next moves. I have but one more day after today before I must return to London and report to the King. By then, we must have completed our intelligence. The only way to protect the King is to provide him with the information he needs to act.'

Mrs Behn poured them both a glass of wine. She raised her glass. 'To power.'

Pepys raised his in turn. 'To knowledge.'

Chapter 31

Will had spent the rest of the day thinking about the warning from Dryden. He had decided he must continue with his investigations come what may. Sam was obviously in far more trouble than even he knew. The missing diary was just the tip of the iceberg. Something deeper and far more mysterious was happening.

Will did not consider himself a brave man. After all, he was only a clerk at the Navy Board, but he did know that he was a loyal man. A man who would stand by his friend, Pepys, just as Sam had stood by him in the past.

He remembered back in '64 when Earl Sandwich had wanted to have him removed from his position, it was Sam who had supported him, refusing to let him go. It was about time he returned the favour. And now was the time that he could do so. Loyalty demanded that he do it despite the danger. Friendship demanded that he do it willingly.

But the problem remained, how to get to see Nell Gwynn. He had decided on the direct approach and now stood outside the stage door of the King's Theatre with a bouquet of flowers in his hand.

'You can't come in here.' An attendant with a nose like a scarred beetroot stood in his way.

'I would like to present my compliments to Nell Gwynn.'

'Nell ain't receiving visitors no more. She is otherwise hengaged.'

'It would just be for a moment. To present these to her.' Will held up the bouquet of flowers. He had bought it that morning from a shop near the Exchange. At the time, they had seemed frightfully expensive. As he saw them now, in his hands, they simply looked frightful.

'Don't ye understand the King's English? Nell is otherwise hengaged. Her hasn't been receiving visitors for the last two month or more. 'Cept for one of course, an we all know who he is.' The attendant tapped his bulbous nose with one long and filthy index finger.

'Now listen, here...'

'Don't ye listen here to me. There's nothing wrong wiv me hearing. It's me smelling that's the problem. This here nose, gave up smelling years ago.'

'No, I meant listen to me. I need to go to see Miss Gwynn. I am her long lost cousin...from Wales, boyo.' Will had added the last sentence in what he hoped sounded like a Welsh accent.

'But Nell was born in Wappin'. Her never said nothing about being Welsh.'

'I'm her mother's cousin's aunt's boy, look you, boyo.' Will continued with his attempt at a Welsh accent. Not that the attendant would know a Welsh accent from a kick between the legs. He might even think a Welsh accent was a kick between the legs.

'I dunno...her is spoken for. More an my job's worth to let anybody through the door.' The man held out his hand.

Will produced a shilling and held it an inch from to the man's nose. He could see the reflection of the coin in the shiny red skin. 'Would this help in case there is any trouble?'

As quick as a coffee house owner, the man had snatched the coin and put it down the front of his breeches. 'Just five minutes, mind. Tell Nell I sent you.' Looking over his shoulder, he hustled Will through the door and down some steps. 'Second door on the right. Be quick about it. Nell's not one for hanging round. Likes 'em in and out right sharpish, she does.'

Will was about to thank the man but he had already gone up the stairs, preventing anybody else from entering. Will held out his bouquet of flowers in front of him, marched to the second door on the right, and knocked.

There was no answer.

He heard the rustling of clothes and a loud bump as something soft hit something hard. Suddenly, the door swung open and a man stood in the way. Even without the heavy stage make-up, Will recognised him as Maximin, or at least the actor who had played him in Dryden's play.

'Nell, you have a visitor.'

'Another. I told the old codger on the door not to let anyone else in. I'm tired for gawd's sake.'

'Well, he's here.' The actor stared at Will's bouquet. 'With flowers, I think.'

'Well, you better let him in then. Can't 'ave 'em standing in the street.'

The actor performed a full bow and waved his arm. 'You may enter, sir. Don't be long. Miss Gwynn has a play to perform.'

Will nodded. The actor pushed past him, carefully avoiding the bouquet of flowers. Will stepped over the threshold and into a small room. Nell Gwynn was standing in front of him.

'Flowers, for me, you are kind, sir. It's not often I get flowers.'

Will looked around the room. Every spare inch seemed to have a vase with flowers in it; roses, sage, and daisies were in abundance but forget-me-nots seemed to be the most common. He placed the bouquet down on the only free place in the room. A wooden chair with her costume thrown casually over the back.

'I hope you don't mind, Mr...?

'It's Hewer, Mistress Gwynn. Will Hewer.'

'I hope you don't mind.' She gestured at her make-up and at the mirror. 'I have to work at my face as you work at your coal face.'

He noticed that her voice had changed. Now it seemed far more actorly, as if she were on stage, rather than the broad London of just a moment ago. 'I'm not that sort of Hewer, Mistress Gwynn, but perhaps in the past, one of my ancestors may have hewed for a living.'

She gave a little laugh, 'I think mine *owed* for a living.' She started applying the white paint to her face. Immediately, her lips and eyes began to stand out like coloured flowers against snow. Elfin eyes, he thought, with joy and sparkle in them.

'What can I do you for, Mr Will Hewer? If you're looking for companionship, I'm afraid I'm off limits at the moment. But I can direct you to some of the other girls in the play.'

'No, no, thank you,' Will stammered, 'I have a confession to make, Mistress Gwynn.'

She stopped putting on her make-up for a moment and looked at his reflection in the mirror. He saw himself standing there, his suit too big for him and his wig awry, looking all dressed up with nowhere to go.

'Confess away, Mr Hewer, let me be your priest for a few moments, and our little room can be the confessional, But if you are here to confess your love for me, I fear you are in the wrong place, I am already spoken for. In fact, I am already shouted for, such is the pedigree of my present...,' she paused for a moment searching for the right word, finally settling on, '...companion.'

'No, no, Perish the thought,' he stammered again. He caught her staring at him in the mirror. 'Don't mean that. I did not come here with a desire to confess my love for you, but...'

'You are not the first to end such a sentence with 'but' Mr Hewer. In fact, I had Lord Abingdon in here just a week ago. Or at least, his but was in here.'

'I do not intend to be the butt of your jokes in the future, Mistress Gwynn. I merely want to confess that I used a subterfuge to gain entry.'

'So you admit you used subterfuge to gain entry to a woman's private chamber, Mr Hewer.'

Will could see that she was enjoying his discomfort, toying with him. Time to get to the point. 'I told the gatekeeper I was your long lost cousin from Wales.'

'But I have no long lost cousin in Wales, Mr Hewer. I was born and bred in London. And the only thing that has been long lost is my virginity. It doesn't survive long on the stage, you know.'

'It was my subterfuge to gain entry.' She arched her eyebrow. He carried on speaking before she could ask him more. 'I need to ask you a question.'

'Ask away, Mr Hewer, but if you produce a gold ring and get down on your knees, I will keep the ring but you will still not enjoy my favours.' She opened a drawer in her commode. Inside, were a dozen small ring boxes, all from the most fashionable jewellers.

'That is not my intention, Madam. I wish to ask you about your acting the other night.'

She relaxed, turned back to the mirror and continued to apply her make-up. 'I will tell you as I tell them all. Learn your lines and don't bump into the furniture. That's all there is to acting. And if you can't learn your lines, distract the audience with a flutter of the eyelashes and a heave of the breast. It is amazing how quickly a man's eyes move from a woman's mouth to her breasts. Even ones as insignificant as these.' She indicated the small lumps beneath her white linen shift. Will could see the outline of a pink nipple hard against the fabric, its round protuberance desiring to force its way through the restraining cloth. He was brought back to her mouth when she spoke. 'Does that answer your question, Mr Hewer?'

'I'm afraid it does not, Mistress Gwynn. My question is much more pointed than that.'

'More pointed than my breasts? Then please, ask away, Will Hewer.

He could feel her teasing him but he decided to plunge ahead anyway. 'The other night, you spoke a different set of lines in the epilogue compared with last night. Why was that?'

'You are a devout theatre-goer, Mr Hewer. The owner, Mr Killigrew, would like far more patrons like you. Two consecutive nights to see the same play, he will be pleased. Were you in the pit or the boxes?

'The pit, I'm afraid.'

'No matter, he will be pleased with the money. And when he is happy, I am happy.' She turned back to the mirror and applied kohl around her eyes.

She hadn't answered him. He decided to press on regardless. 'You did speak different lines. And you spoke them directly to my friend in the audience.'

She stopped applying her make-up. 'That man was your friend?'

'Mr Samuel Pepys.'

'I did not know his name.'

'But you did speak the lines to him didn't you?'

'Yes, I did. I was asked to direct my gaze to a man wearing a black periwig in the sixth row. It was not hard to find him sitting there.'

'Who asked you to do so?'

'The same man who wrote the lines, of course. Our playwright. Who else would ask me to speak lines?'

'Thank you, Mistress Gwynn.'

'And now if you have finished asking your questions, I need to finish applying my disguise for this evening. It is Valeria the audience must see, not Nell Gwynn.

'Until the epilogue.'

She looked at his reflection in the mirror again. 'Quite right, Mr Hewer, until the epilogue, when Nell Gwynn rises from the gates of death and speaks to her audience.'

For a moment, Will could see the sadness behind the eyes of the woman. Then, as quickly as it had be there, it was gone.

'So I must ask you to leave now, Mr Hewer, otherwise I will die a death before they have even murdered me.'

'Will there be a death knell?'

'You amuse me, Mr Hewer, but before you abuse me, I must ask you to leave. Nell must become Valeria. And a woman never changes herself in front of a man, only behind his back.'

'Thank you for your help. Mistress Gwynn, I'll bid you good night.' He bowed and opened the door.

'Good night, good knight,' she said before turning back to her mirror.

He closed the door and wished that he could have stayed longer with her. Just to enjoy her presence and her charm. What should he do now? Return to Dryden and ask him more questions? Why he had changed the lines and who had commanded the change?

Will was beginning to feel out of his depth. Sam would know what to do far better than him. Why wasn't he here, searching for his diary?

Chapter 32

After some obstruction from both the wind and the tides, the Royal yacht finally reached the new fort at Sheerness. Pepys was deep in discussion with Mrs Behn and it was only a loud cough from Fridley that dragged him away from their plans.

'We have reached the new fort, Mr Pepys.'

'I will be up in a minute, Fridley...' Pepys was interrupted by a loud gunshot from the fort.

'I think you had better come now, sir.'

Pepys grabbed his hat and rushed onto the deck. A cloud of white smoke came from one of the embankments in front of the fort, followed a second later by the sound of a cannon. Then another cloud of smoke and another boom of cannon.

He braced himself for the impact of the cannonballs into the ship, or the tell-tale eruptions of water as they landed in the sea. But there were neither. There were no holes in the rigging either.

'They are giving you a salute, Mr Pepys. Nine guns I believe.'

Again, his mind turned back, seeing his father, back arched like a branch of hawthorn as he sewed a garment in the light of a single candle in the shop at Salisbury Court. His mother, wearied by work and too much worry, waiting on another customer, on her knees in front of him, pinning back the flap of a coat. And he, looking at both of them, promising that he would never live like either.

The sound of another gun echoed across the water between the fort and their yacht. The smoke was a dense white, covering the shore. As it cleared, it became apparent that the cannon were not sited in the fort itself but on a low mound in front of it. The fort was still irregular and imperfect, with bastions of different sizes, all in the midst of construction. On top of one of the half-built bastions, a workman waved at Pepys, holding his hat in his hand.

'A shortage of money, Mr Fridley?'

'I'm afraid so, Mr Pepys. And a shortage of men, supplies, equipment, lime and mortar.'

'Is there anything which is not in shortage?'

Fridley pointed to the small mound. 'We have plenty of cannons, Mr Pepys. More than enough cannons.'

'But no protection for them. If the Dutch fleet arrived tomorrow, these cannons would be dispatched in minutes and the men killed.'

'I hardly think the Dutch will arrive tomorrow, sir.'

'When do you think they will come, Mr Fridley?'

'They will come when they come, sir.'

'And we will be just as unready as we were two years ago when they arrived off these shores and took the Royal Charles!' Pepys raised his voice. Fridley simply bowed his head.

The Captain and his crew watched from their positions on the deck and in the rigging.

Pepys was ready to explode. They had thought to deceive him with this display of flattery. Thought to trick him with a few cannonballs and clouds of smoke. Thought that he would be satisfied with the sound of the fort and not its substance. Controlling himself and his emotions, he said. 'This will not serve, Fridley. It will not serve, sir.'

He turned on his heels and descended to the state room. Mrs Behn was still sitting there, drinking a glass of wine. 'My intelligence tells me the fort is half-built and in no condition to repel an attack by the Dutch.'

'Your intelligence, once again, is correct, Madam.' ‘

More fuel for your report.'

'But nobody seems at all worried. I am seeing this lack of preparedness. It is almost as if they do not care I have seen it.'

'Perhaps they believe there is somebody who will protect them, come what may.'

'They may also have another stratagem.'

'Which is...?'

'I believe I will find out this evening when I dine with the Commissioner.'

‘And I will get my people to find your Balthasar for you. Luckily, Chatham is a small town with many wagging tongues. A few coins will loosen their lips.’

'I thank you, Mrs Behn, it would be a care off my mind.'

Pepys was tempted to tell her of the missing diary too. He had never met a woman like this. Soft and gentle on the one hand, almost a template of her gender, yet hard, unforgiving and fierce on the other. Like a man wearing a woman's clothes, acting like a woman. She could be playful and witty one moment, and sharp and cutting the next. She could be coy and innocent in one sentence, and forthright and amoral in the next.

He would never understand women. They were a foreign country to him

But he was thankful she was on his side. He feared she would make a formidable enemy if she were not.

'A penny for them, Mr Pepys.'

'I fear they are not worth even a penny, Mrs Behn. A farthing of thought on far things. Let us return to our plans. With the tide and wind to help us, I think we will make fair passage to Chatham. We have not time to waste, Mrs Behn.'

'For I have wasted time, and now doth time waste me.'

'It wastes us all, Mrs Behn. It wastes us all.'

Chapter 33

Will didn't see or hear the men as they crept up behind him. Nor did he have time to raise his arms. He didn't even manage to shout out before a rough hand covered his mouth and held him tightly.

He had been walking past the Exchange and turned left onto Finch Lane, thinking what to do next. Should he go to see Dryden again? Or wait and report back to Sam when they met?

The men grabbed him in the middle of the street. A hood came over his head and the world around him went dark.

A voice came from next to his right ear. 'Call out, say one word, and you're a dead man. You mark my words now, Mr Hewer.' Will was transported to a few days ago, a pain in his chest, and a man looming over him.

He heard a pair of horses clatter past him and the trundle of wheels, then the sound stopped. Rough hands pushed him upwards. He banged his knee on something hard and an involuntary shout came from his throat. In an instant, the voice was back at his ear.

'What did I say about calling out, Mr Hewer?'

Will expected to feel the sharp strike of a knife in his chest or the edge of a blade across his throat. He sucked in his final breath of air and held it.

No blow came.

Instead, he was pushed forward onto a wooden floor. He felt the floor rock gently and he heard springs squeal. There was the sound of a lash of a whip, and the floor rattled beneath him. He must have been bundled into the cab of a carriage. Where were they taking him? Somewhere quiet to slit his throat? He hoped not. He preferred his throat as it was without the addition of an extra slit.

He felt something hard press into the side of his head. He could smell the leather of its sole. Fresh, new leather. But there was no softness of a foot inside the leather. Just the solidity of wood.

The carriage began to pick up speed, the sound of the horses hooves loud against the cobbles of the street. Will felt his body being squashed into the side of a bench. The edge of the wood bit into his shoulder.

A voice came from above him. A different, more cultured, educated voice. 'I could kill you right now, Mr Hewer. All I would have to do was say the word to my men. One word. A little word. In a trice, you would either be knocking on the pearly gates of heaven or being welcomed into the warm embrace of hell. What do you say to that, Mr Hewer?'

Will tried to speak but the foot had pushed his head into the floor and the wool of the hood had blocked his mouth.

'Nothing? Good, I like silence in a man. It's a good sound, the sound of silence. It betokens acquiescence, acceptance and submission. Do you understand, Mr Hewer? Nod your head if you understand.'

Will felt the foot jab him in the back of his head. He nodded.

'Good. I believe we are going to get on like the Great Fire, Mr Hewer. I will talk and you will listen. The sign of a perfect friendship. Nod your head if you agree.'

The foot struck the back of his head again. Will was tempted to push back and try to sit upright, but the pressure of the foot pushed him further down into the floor.

He nodded his head.

'See we are getting on like a house on fire, if you will forgive the cliché, but one I do find so apt as we traverse London. What was I chatting to you about? Ah yes, silence. Such a lovely sound. A sound we require from you, Mr Hewer. Unfortunately, it has not been what we have been hearing of late.'

The coach jolted as it hit a hole in the street. Will's arm banged into the wooden leg of the bench again. He cried out in pain.

'I could ask Mr Blake here to show you one of his party tricks if you make another noise. Why don't we do that? Get the unpleasantness over and done with.'

There was a pause and then suddenly a sharp stabbing pain seared through Will's calf, up through his body and shot through his brain. He bit down on his tongue to stop himself crying out, tasting the acrid bitterness of iron in his mouth.

A polite round of applause echoed above his head. 'Well done, Mr Hewer. I do like a silent man. It would have given me much pain to ask Mr Blake to perform one of his party tricks again. But I fear it would have given you far more. Such is life. One man's word is another's pain. Was it not ever so.'

The coach lurched again. The pain was still in Will's head, torturing his mind. He had never known pain like it as it seemed to grow and expand in intensity rather than lessen.

'Where was I? Ah yes, silence. Now that we have achieved that wondrous state, let us deliver our little warning. You have been asking too many questions, Mr Hewer. Desist. There, as plain as I could make it. Do nod your head if you understand.'

The foot pressed into the back of Will's head. He nodded

and his forehead hit the leg of the bench.

'Good, I am glad to see we have finally achieved an agreement. I think it is time for you to leave us, Mr Hewer. But a word of warning before you do. Next time, Blake will not be so gentle. Will you, Blake?'

A grunt and then, 'No, my lord. I won't be so gentle with the little dandycock next time.'

The voice. It was the man's voice. The one he had chased through the streets of London. The one who had taken Elizabeth's locket.

He shifted his body trying to find out where the voice was coming from.

'See, Blake is a man I wouldn't like to meet in a quiet alley on a dark night, Mr Hewer. And, let me assure you, you would like to meet him even less.'

'Thank you, sir.'

'I think we have finished with you, Mr Hewer. I'm glad we had our little chat.'

The foot moved from the back of Will's head. He was finally able to lift his head from the floor of the coach.

'I hope that we can meet in more pleasant circumstances next time. Until then, I bid you a fond adieu.'

Rough hands grabbed Will beneath the arms. He heard the door open and felt the sudden inrush of air. The coach was making a fast pace over the cobbles of the street.

One moment he was gripped by strong hands, the next he was free from them and from any restraints.

For a second, he was flying through the air and then the ground hit him, knocking the air out of his lungs and chest.

The wheels of the coach continued their rattling on the cobbles of the street.

Will pulled the hood from his head. It was pulling

away, turning the corner into another street. But he could just make out a device on the cabin at the back.

The same device as on the button.

The device that didn't exist.

Chapter 34

Pepys sat on the edge of his bed, waiting for Fridley to arrive and escort him to dinner with the Commissioner.

He had discovered the third message placed casually on his desk when he had returned. The servants knew nothing about it of course. Nobody had entered Hill House since he had left that morning.

He read it through once more.

'I enjoyed your writing,
It was so enlightening;
The king and his mistress,
Causing so much distress.
The barons, dukes and earls
You think are such churls.
The love affairs of your life,
Would make light reading for your wife.
Now, you will do as you are told,
Or your world will grow cold.

What was he supposed to do? It was obvious the thief had read the diaries; these threats made it clear. But still there was no indication of what he was to do. It was as if the thief were building up to the order, making it stronger and more imperative with the threats.

Pepys examined the letter carefully. It was finely made, off white with a touch of yellow perhaps. He walked over to the window and examined it under the early evening sunlight. Yes, a creamy white paper with dark vermillion ink. An unusual colour. Not bought from the street sellers but from a more sophisticated supplier.

Given a week or so, he was sure he could find the man who made it. But he didn't have a week.

He brought the paper closer to his face. The writing was in an elegant, tutored hand. A hand used to writing clearly. A hand used to giving instructions. The hand of a soldier? Or a politician? Or a king? There was a hint of something there, something he vaguely recognised. What was it?

He walked back to the bed, picked up his coat and placed the note in the pocket. He had set the wheels in motion now, nothing could hold them back. Tomorrow, he would know if the joy of success was waiting for him, or the ignominy of failure.

But that was life. You assessed the risks and rolled the dice. Doing something was far better than doing nothing. In this case, he knew the risks were high, the loss of his position. His name dragged through the mud. Or worse. A visit to the Tower. Exile? Or execution? For a moment, Pepys imagined his head sitting on the entrance to London Bridge, the vacant eyes staring down at all those who entered the city. His wife, Elizabeth, on her knees, crying and praying for what remained of his body to be given to her. His friend, Will, comforting her in her madness.

Pepys shook his head. I must not think like that. The next day would require careful and diligent work. I must not think of the consequences. All had been organised as it could be organised. All that remained was the execution. Not his execution, he hoped. The trip back from the fort at Sheerness to Chatham had gone smoother than he expected. The winds and tides favoured them. He hoped they remained that way for the rest of his time in this god-forsaken town.

On their way down the river, they had passed the dry dock where the new ship, Royal Charles, was being constructed. A few men were working on the ribs of the ship but that was all. There was no urgency in the construction, no desire to finish the vessel and make it ready for sea. Fridley had appeared at his elbow when he was looking at the Royal Charles.

'She's going to be a beautiful ship when she's finished, Mr Pepys.'

'I'm sure she is, Fridley, when she is finished.'

'Sir William Penn thought the construction was moving along swimmingly.'

'He would. Sir William has the same knowledge of the construction of His Majesty's ships as he does of His Majesty's forts.'

'I think you do Sir William a great disservice, sir.'

'No, Fridley, he gives the King no service. His reports have mentioned nothing about the lack of progress.'

'I'm sure Sir William wrote what he thought was right, Mr Pepys.'

'And I will report what I think is right, Fridley.'

Fridley looked at him out of the corner of his eye. A smile flickered at the corners of his mouth. 'Of course, Mr Pepys, we would have it no other way.'

Pepys had wondered at the time who the 'we' was. Now, as he sat on his bed, he thought about it even more.

A knock came at the door. It opened and as if he knew that Pepys was thinking about him, Fridley appeared.

'I will escort you to the garden, Mr Pepys. The Commissioner thought, on such a beautiful June evening, a short promenade around it would stimulate the appetite.'

'Thank you, Fridley, I am ready.' Pepys put his periwig on his head and adjusted the locks so that they fell around his shoulders correctly. 'How does this look?'

'Excellent, Mr Pepys. Like one of the King's ministers.' Fridley placed his fingers in front of his mouth and appeared to blow on them. 'There is one other thing, Mr Pepys.'

'What is that?'

'I've have finally been able to complete the manning figures that you asked for. I've included all sections of the dockyard as you requested.' He produced a sheaf of papers from behind his back. 'They would be cumbersome to take to your supper with the Commissioner. I'll place them here on the dresser. You can peruse them on your return.'

'Thank you, Fridley.'

The man slithered forward and put the sheaf of papers down. Pepys noticed how Fridley never stood upright. He always was bent over, rubbing his hands. Cold clammy hands, strangely lifeless like the ends of two damp cloths, sticking out from the branches of a tree.

'After you, Fridley.'

'No after you, Mr Pepys.' Fridley separated his hands reluctantly and bowed down even further.

Pepys walked past him, out through the doors where they were joined by two guards. He continued to walk down the path to the Commissioner's house and the garden beside it. Fridley was just behind him with the two guards flanking on either side. It was a strange feeling as if he was being escorted to the scaffold not to supper. He glanced over his shoulder. The guard on the left was eyeing him strangely, his hand on the pommel of his sword, as if ready to spring into action at any moment.

They reached the bower that led to the garden, where another guard saluted them. So many guards just for dinner, thought Pepys.

'Welcome, welcome.' The portly body of the Commissioner waddled over to greet him. 'Finally, I have you all to myself, Mr Pepys.'

Pepys looked over his shoulder. The guards had stopped at the bower, blocking the exit.

'A glass of sack, perhaps, to soothe the throat. You must be parched from your long day in the Medway.' He offered Pepys a glass of wine.

'Thank you, Commissioner.' Pepys looked out over the perfection that met his eye. The clipped hedges, precisely manicured lawns and straight-edged paths stood in remarkable contrast to the chaos and untidiness of the rest of the shipyard. 'You have a beautiful garden,' was all he could say.

'In the Italian style, built by one of my predecessors, Pett, I think it was. I find it is an excellent retreat after the rigours of a trying day.'

'The gardens must use a lot of men to keep them in such a pristine condition.'

The Commissioner nodded, his jowls continuing to move long after his head had stopped. 'Quite a few, I must admit, but you can't put a price on peace and tranquillity, can you?'

Pepys took a sip of his wine, It was very fine, like a liquid peach with a touch of honey at the end. 'It is one of life's axioms, Commissioner, peace and tranquillity always come at a price, do they not?'

'I couldn't agree more, Mr Pepys.' The Commissioner smiled the broadest smile that Pepys had ever seen. The tips of his lips almost touched his ears. 'Shall we take a turn around the garden? I would talk with you and hear your thoughts.'

'Certainly, Commissioner.'

They walked down the steps that led to a sunken garden. Fridley following after them, still rubbing his hands.

'I don't believe there is any need for Fridley to join us.'

'Fridley knows everything regarding the business of Chatham and of the docks. He is like my right arm. Without him, I would be lost.'

The Commissioner patted Fridley on the shoulder.

'You are too kind, Commissioner, Fridley is merely here to serve.'

They stopped in front of a small fountain in the centre. The fountain was in the shape of a cherub holding a bow, ready to fire an arrow.

'I brought the statue from Italy. Another one of the perks of having so many ships arriving at the dockyard. I believe it was made by a man called Bellini. Damn fine sculptors these Italians. Runs in the blood, you know.'

'It is a fine piece.'

'I could get one for you, Mr Pepys, if you so desired.'

'Thank you, Commissioner, but I would have nowhere to put it, not living in such a house as this.'

'I'm sure that could be changed, Mr Pepys.'

'How so, Commissioner, I am but a poor clerk in the Navy Board. I live in a small house, adjoining my office, on Seething Lane.'

'I know it well, Mr Pepys. I have visited there very often on my trips to London.'

'I didn't know you came up to town, Commissioner.'

'At least once a month, Mr Pepys. People to see and places to visit. I think that, occasionally, one needs the delights of London to refresh one's body and soul after the arduous toil of managing the dockyard.'

'I couldn't agree more, Commissioner, but it is an expensive city in which to live.'

'And I suppose your salary arrives like an old man's piss; in dribbles.'

'You know the workings of the Navy Board so well, Commissioner.'

The Commissioner seemed to think for a moment. He glanced at Fridley, standing at the side like a hovering undertaker waiting for someone to die. Then he seemed to reach a decision.

'I do understand the expense of living in the city and, how shall we call it...,' his cheeks puffed out and he gave a little laugh, 'maintaining one's standards.' He took Pepys' arm just above the elbow and they walked towards the next section of the garden. Fridley following in their wake. 'For myself, it has not been easy, there is so little support from London.'

'You seem to manage quite well.'

'Indeed, I do. But my management of the dockyard would be severely affected by an unfavourable report.'

'I must tell the King what I see.'

The Commissioner threw up his hands in surprise. 'Of course, you must.' Then he leaned forward and lowered his voice. 'But there is many an obstacle between the eyes and the mouth.'

Pepys was confused. 'I don't understand, Commissioner.'

'What I mean is, what one sees and what one says may not necessarily be the same.' Pepys thought for a moment, 'You are asking me to lie in my report.'

Again the arms came up in mock horror, 'Of course not, Mr Pepys, perish the thought. I meant that you should merely comment in your report on that which has pleased you on this visit.'

'Avoiding that which has not, like the preparedness of the forts, the lack of workers in the yards and the slowness of construction of the Royal Charles...'

'I would argue that the forts are proceeding as planned, if a little slowly, that there are more than enough workers in the yards given our budget constraints, and that the progress on the construction of the Royal Charles has been hindered by changes in the design of the ship. As you can see, Mr Pepys, it is all a matter of perception and interpretation.'

'Perception and interpretation?'

'Indeed. The previous visitors to the dockyard have interpreted their perceptions in the manner in which I have described. Their reports to the King have been sent to me.'

'You have seen the reports?'

'Of course, my patron always lets me know what is happening in London.'

'Who is your patron?'

The man laughed, his jowls continuing to move long after the sound of laughter had ceased. 'Mr Pepys, if I told you that I would have to kill you.'

The threat lay between them like a dog turd on a banquet table. Pepys glanced at the soldiers guarding the entrance to the garden. All three of them were standing there, hands resting on their swords.

'I believe I have a solution that would suit all of us.'

'And what is that?'

'As you know, I am in charge of the Chatham Chest. Perhaps a small loan could be arranged from the Chest for the use of your good self.'

'But I thought the Chest was only to be used to help seamen in need.'

'Ah, the definition of what is a seaman and what is need remains with me.'

'An arduous judgement to make, Commissioner.'

'There you have it. You understand my position, Mr Pepys.' The Commissioner glanced at Fridley once more. Placing his large arm across Pepys' shoulders, he leant closer.

Pepys could smell the honeyed wine on his breath, tinged with something sweeter; the tang of violets.

'It seems to me, Mr Pepys, you find yourself in the most desperate need at the moment, to maintain your lifestyle in London in the face of rising costs and lowering incomes.'

'That is indeed true, Commissioner.'

'And you are a seaman, are you not?'

'Employed by the Navy Board, these last twelve years, Commissioner.'

'See. We have a need and we have a seaman. I'm sure the Chest could see its way to making a small loan to tide you over your difficulties.'

'How much would this loan be?'

The Commissioner glanced across at Fridley now standing behind Pepys. 'I think a loan of 2,000 pounds could be arranged quite easily. Of course, repayment would be on your own terms. When you felt you had enough money to repay the Chest. And, in the unfortunate event that you would be unable to repay the loan, it would, of course, be written off. These things happen, you know.' Once again, a broad smile that stretched from ear to ear spread across the Commissioner's face.

Pepys thought for a moment. 'That is indeed

generous, Commissioner. But my expenses are large at the moment. London is a very expensive place to live and my wife is unusually fond of jewellery.'

'Women usually are, Mr Pepys. How much of a loan would you need?'

'5,000 pounds would suffice, I believe.'

‘But, that's too much,' interrupted Fridley.

'Then, I'm afraid my perceptions of the affairs of the dockyard must remain as they are at the moment.'

'That is blackmail, you....'

'Gentlemen, gentlemen, let us not argue over a mere trifle. Mr Pepys, I know you to be a reasonable man, I suggest a loan of 3,500 pounds. How does that suit?' Once again, he looked across at Fridley.

Out of the corner of his eye, Pepys saw the man nod in agreement. 'What say you to that, Mr Pepys?'

'I would say it was a very generous loan from a very well-run dockyard, Commissioner.'

'Good, I knew that you would be able to perceive what we are attempting to do here. I look forward to reading your report to the King. Now, let us retire to my house. The chef is from France and he has brought in some new dishes for us to enjoy, accompanied by some fine wines from my own cellar.'

'Lead the way, Commissioner. My stomach is all yours this evening.'

'As are your eyes, Mr Pepys.'

They both laughed. Pepys could see the soldiers visibly relaxing, taking their hands off their swords and leaning against the wall of the garden.

Chapter 35

Will sat in the kitchen as Elizabeth placed a cold poultice on the bruise on his forehead. 'You say you bumped into a door jamb. It must have been a small door, Will.'

'It was Elizabeth. I should have been looking where I was walking.'

'Your mind was distracted?'

Will always loved the sound of Elizabeth's voice. That sweet lilt with the hint of French accent in each inflection.

'I was thinking of Sam.'

'Samuel will be fine. He is just visiting Chatham for a few days. Why do you worry so?'

It was obvious that Sam had told her nothing of the theft of the diary, nor of his mission for the King.

She tutted beneath her breath as she dabbed at the bruise with the poultice. Each time she touched the bruise a bolt of pain shot through Will's head, but he didn't flinch. He didn't want to show Elizabeth how badly he was hurt in both body and spirit.

'There, at least it is clean now. Let me see your leg.'

Will hesitated, 'But...'

'Don't worry,' she laughed, 'Jane will be our chaperone. Sam will not be jealous of you. You are not a dancing master.' She giggled and looked at Jane. The maid returned her smile and continued to wash the floor.

Will removed his shoes. He felt a squelching as he did so. The blood had run down his calf and pooled in his boots.

'How did you get this wound?'

'I can't remember. A spike I think.'

Elizabeth looked at him sceptically. 'Probably from the same door where you hit your head.' She rolled up his breeches until they were at his knee. 'This looks more like a stab wound. See.' She pointed to an incision about half way up the calf.

The cut was no more than half an inch across but the pain it gave Will was intense. Blood still oozed out from it.

'It's only a small cut but deep.' She turned to Jane. 'Can you cut up a piece of linen? We need to bandage this leg, otherwise he will continue to bleed.'

'Yes, ma'am.'

Elizabeth dipped her cloth into the bowl of warm, salty water. 'This is going to hurt, Will.'

She pressed the cloth against the cut and once again, a searing pain shot up Will's leg and into his head, fighting with the throb from the bruise. 'You were right, it hurts,' he said through clenched teeth.

Jane returned with a sheet that she had cut into strips. Elizabeth finished cleaning the wound and placed a small roll of spider's web directly onto his leg, binding it with the linen bandage.

'There, that should keep it dry. My mother swears by spider's web for treating wounds. You will have to stay here tonight, Will. You can't walk on that leg.'

'But...'

'But me no buts, Will Hewer. If Sam were here, he would insist as well. In his absence, I am the mistress of this house and you will do as I say. Jane, please prepare the day bed in the dining room.'

'Yes, ma'am.'

'Later, we must help Master Hewer up the stairs.'

'I'll be fine. No need to trouble yourselves.' Will tried to get to his feet but immediately he put weight on the damaged leg, it collapsed under him and he fell to the floor.

'See? Will Hewer, for once in your life listen to a woman. You will stay here tonight and rest your leg.'

Jane returned from upstairs. 'The day bed is ready, ma'am.'

'Good. Take this arm and I will lift the other.' Together they helped Will to his feet. In the time he had lain on the kitchen floor, the leg had stiffened and the throb in his head had become much worse. As he got to his feet, he almost fainted. He fell against Jane.

'I'm sorry, Jane,' he mumbled.

'No matter, Master Hewer.' Together they put his arms around their shoulders and helped him hop up the stairs.

'I wish Sam could see me now, with two women as my crutches.'

'Women are always men's crutches, Will, it's just that we are not so obvious as we are now,' said Elizabeth.

They reached the top of the stairs where they laid Will down on the day bed. Within minutes, he had fallen into a deep sleep, a gentle snoring coming from his open mouth.

'I don't believe that he hit his head on a door, do you, Jane.'

'No, ma'am, Master Hewer is always so careful.'

'Something is happening, Jane, and I believe Sam is at the centre of it.'

Chapter 36

Just a solitary candle flickered in Hill House as Pepys walked down the pathway. He expected to be greeted by the servants but none came out to meet him.

He opened the door and the flame of the candle fluttered in the breeze. Outside an owl hooted, twice. Pepys hoped the mouse had been warned but he doubted the animal had listened. The owl would feast tonight.

He had eaten a lot but drank little, despite the attempts of the Commissioner to ply him with wines from Spain and France and Germany. As he sat round the table with the Commissioner and his wife, he realised they lived in their own little cocoon of luxury, isolated from the strife and starvation of the world outside by Fridley's constant care and attention. The Commissioner no more knew of what was going on in the dockyard than the mice were aware of the preying owl waiting to devour them.

He picked up the candle holder and walked towards his bedroom. The shadows of his body and his outstretched arm played on the wall. A deep sense of unease slowly crept over him. Where were the servants? Why hadn't they come out to welcome him home?

He punched open the bedroom door but didn't step inside. He listened and waited. It seemed empty, but the servants hadn't left a candle burning for him. They always left at least one candle.

He stepped into the room. The light from the candle on his hand flowed with him, throwing the room into a series of warm yellow spots and deep black shadows.

On the table lay a sheet of paper, its cream colour

enhanced by the candle light.

Again, the vermilion ink stood out sharp against the white background.

He rushed across to pick it up. The words were coarser now. The teasing, playing and rhyming couplets no longer there;

Here are your orders:
Tell the King everything.

That was all? He looked on the other side of the paper to see if anything was written there.

Nothing.

The meaning was clear and yet it wasn't clear. Why did the thief want him tell the King everything? And what was everything? About the dockyard? About the forts? About his diary?

The curtain flickered. He was certain the curtain flickered.

There it was again.

It moved.

He marched over and pulled it aside.

Nothing. Except his reflection in the glass of the window. A face half hidden in shadow with a periwig slightly askew and a candle flickering in the draught from the door.

'You should be more careful, Mr Pepys.'

Pepys whirled round, the candle going out as he moved too quickly.

'See what I mean.' There was the sound of a match striking the edge of a tinder. A brief rush of flame and a face appeared for a second in the harsh light, before softening as the candle in Pepys' hand was lit again.

'Mrs Behn. I expected you to be waiting. Where are the servants?'

'I paid them off. Told them we wanted to be together, alone. They understood.'

For a moment, Pepys' mind flashed back to the morning and the promise it once held before Mrs Behn had left him in no doubt that their relationship was to be purely professional. Shame. He would have enjoyed discovering what lay beneath that manly exterior. Perhaps, the opportunity would yet arise…

'Mr Pepys, I said shall we depart?'

'Good. Are you ready?' was all he managed to stammer.

She showed him two pistols. 'As ready as we will ever be. The Preacher is in the middle of yet another meeting. The man loves to hear the sound of his own voice.'

'At the moment, unfortunately, so does half the dockyard.'

'We will have to stop him tonight. Two men are inside the meeting. More are waiting in the alley behind the inn. He is preaching in the room above.'

'And Balty?'

'Your assistant is being kept in the cellars beneath the inn.'

'He should be right at home there. No harm has come to him?'

'Not that I know. They are waiting for instructions from London.'

'You are sure they are waiting for orders?'

'That's what my men tell me. The Preacher is not sure what to do. He has sent a man to London.'

'It's the second time tonight that somebody has mentioned a person in London.'

'How much did they offer you?'

'Not they, just Fridley. He seems to be the man pulling the strings in the dockyard.'

'The Commissioner is his puppet?'

'It seems so.'

'But Fridley? Such a spineless specimen of a human being.'

'But a specimen saturated with a spirit of ambition like a sponge soaked with water.'

'You haven't said how much they offered you?'

'3,500 pounds from the Chatham Chest.'

'So that's how they are funding everything.'

'A man could live well on 3,500 pounds,' said Pepys wistfully.

'A woman could live better.'

She gave one of the pistols to Pepys. It was heavy, an unusual weight sitting there in his hand. 'I'm not really a man used to bearing arms.'

'Luckily, I am a woman who's more used to bearing them than bearing children. Come, we must go. The meeting will end soon.'

*

A crowd of people streamed out of the back door of the Inn, chatting to each other. One seemed to be more agitated than the rest. 'It's not right, we must act now.'

Someone grabbed his arm. 'Shush, Richard, now is not the time.'

'When is the time? When we're all dead, facing the Lord and explaining to him why we did not act against the evil that sullies his name?'

'Now is not the time, Richard. Soon, we will move and you can be in the forefront of our charge.' This voice was older, calmer, more controlled. He hustled Richard away down towards the houses that lined the river.

Across the narrow road, Pepys, Mrs Behn and her men lay in wait.

'We should trap the Preacher in his den, before any of these people return,' she whispered.

Pepys nodded. He stood up and marched quickly across to the back door, followed by Mrs Behn and her soldiers. She had a sword in one hand and a pistol in the other.

'Shouldn't we rescue Balty first?' he asked.

'No, we should neutralise the Preacher. We don't want him raising a hue and cry. And with him dead or captured, his flock will be as sheep.'

'By God woman, I hope you scare the Preacher, because as sure as God, you scare me.'

'Let us ascend, Mr Pepys.' She pushed him forward onto the stairs. Up above, he could hear someone walking on the wooden floorboards. Then, a bump as something large was dropped onto the floor. Pepys stopped and listened. The walking continued again. A single man walking up and down, as if deep in thought.

Pepys took one last look back at Mrs Behn and burst through the door. The Preacher was just placing some bibles down on a desk at the front of the room, talking to three men who sat on chairs facing him.

'Good evening, Mr Pepys, I was wondering when you would arrive,' said the Preacher, his voice ringing out in its lowland Scots accent.

'You're the Preacher? I saw you before on Tower Hill, walking with Debs.'

'Miss Willett? She is my betrothed, Mr Pepys.'

This wasn't going according to plan, why was the

man so relaxed and confident? 'Where is my brother-in-law? Why have you kept him locked up?'

The man's face displayed a smug air of innocence. 'Your brother-in-law is in the cellar, Mr Pepys. He will remain there until we receive instructions on his disposal. And, now that you are here, you may join him.'

Pepys looked over his shoulder. Mrs Behn's pistol no longer pointed at the Preacher but at him, the end of its black barrel a dark round void bristling with threat.

'I'm sorry, Mr Pepys, but they do pay well. Unlike the king.' The pistol jerked to the left and Pepys stepped backwards against the wall.

''You disappoint me, Mrs Behn.'

'I will survive your disappointment, sir, and enjoy a wealthy old age.'

'These men are plotting treason, Madam, and now you are their accomplice.'

The three men got up from their chairs and turned toward Pepys. Fridley's back was no longer bent, his hands no longer curling over each other like nesting slugs. Next to him was the Iron Master, Mr Daly, still as bulky as ever, a scowl plastered on his face. Quilt, his face pale and drawn, was the third.

'We are merely going to remove from the throne someone who has betrayed his country and his religion,' said Fridley. The man stood upright to his full height, commanding all those around him.

'Have you not heard, Mr Pepys, the Duke of York has become a catholic? All devout protestants have a duty to prevent the return of Romanism to these green and pleasant lands.' It was the Preacher who spoke. His voice had a mellifluous, soothing quality. Pepys understood why so many of the local sailors and dockyard workers had fallen under his spell.

'But it will only be green and pleasant again when the false king, that Satan and his hordes of depraved sinners at court, have been deposed. Then, and only then, will the Kingdom of Heaven be found on earth again. Then and only then, will men have food aplenty to feed their families and fill their stomachs. Then, and only then, will there be justice here on earth as there is in heaven. When King Jesus is on the throne, ruling with righteousness, stern and unforgiving.' The Preacher was back in the pulpit again. His voice losing its soothing quality, replaced by a more strident, harsher, commanding tone.

'Do not waste your rhetoric on me, Preacher…?'

The Preacher stepped into the full light of the candle. 'The name is Lawson, Mr Pepys. I can see that you remember me now, Mr Pepys. Miss Willetts sends her regards.' He paused for a moment and stepped closer to Pepys, leaning in to whisper close to his head. 'You used my fiancée appallingly. She forgives you but I do not.'

'Doesn't the bible say forgive those that trespass against you?'

'It also says that you must take an eye for an eye. Scripture will reveal anything to anyone. It all depends how one interprets it.' Fridley had spoken again.

'You have a very flexible and convenient view of Scripture, Mr Fridley.'

'No, I have an accurate view of Scripture.'

Pepys turned back towards the Preacher. 'You have made your bed with a very strange bedfellow, Mr Lawson.'

'I much prefer the title, Preacher. And strange times make for strange bedfellows. One day, I will convert Mr Fridley to a more accurate perception of the Lord's teachings.'

'Until then, money will do your conversion for you.'

'When money speaks, men, and women, tend to listen.' He nodded in the direction of Mrs Behn. 'As you have found out to your cost.'

The pistol in Mrs Behn's hand still pointed unwaveringly at Pepys. 'So easily bought, Mrs Behn.'

'Woman have always been bought and sold, Mr Pepys. I simply raised my price to receive what I was worth and not settle for the usual pittance.'

'And how many pieces of gold did you sell me for?'

'Enough so I will not be dependent on men like you for a long time to come. A woman's independence has always come at a cost, Mr Pepys.'

'Your independence though, came at my cost.'

'A small price to pay.'

'Not for me.'

There was the rasp of a blade as it left a scabbard. Daly moved towards Pepys, a shining, sharp dagger in his hand. 'Enough of this prattling. Shall I cut out his eyes, Preacher?'

Pepys was pushed down into a chair. The knife swung above his head and plunged towards his face. Pepys closed his eyes, feeling the sharpness of the steel an inch away from his eyeball.

'Just say the word, Preacher, and I'll take his eye out as quickly as Marlowe. An eye for an eye, as Mr Fridley said. Then I'll cut out his tongue, it's a sharp as this dagger.'

Pepys could smell Daly's breath bearing down on him. He opened his eyes. The knife was still there, its point hovering, ready to stab down, blinding him forever.

'Hold, please, Mr Daly, we await orders from London. They will arrive shortly.' The Preacher's voice rang out in his Scottish accent. 'You may do what you will with him then.'

The iron founder stepped back, slowly sheathing the knife back inside its scabbard. 'Should have finished him in the Foundry. The pretence of me saving his life was a waste of time.'

'It was a shame you didn't take the warning seriously, Mr Pepys. It would have saved us all a lot of unpleasantness if you had.'

Fridley brushed the fringe off his forehead. Was he the true leader of the revolt? Or was it the Preacher?

'We have work to do. Our orders are very clear.'

He spoke directly to one of the men who had come with Mrs Behn. 'Take Mr Pepys to join his brother-in-law in the cellar. We will decide what to do with them when we receive instructions from London.'

The man seized Pepys' arm roughly.

'Perhaps, an accident on the Medway will suffice for both of them, Mr Daly, rather than the removal of their eyes. They would make fine fish food, I think.'

'Mrs Behn! Your ardour overwhelms you. We must wait for instructions from London.' Fridley waved his hand.

Pepys was jerked up from his chair and pushed down the stairs.

At the bottom, the man unbolted an old ramshackle door on the right. It creaked open and Pepys was shoved inside, the door slammed behind him, the bolt rattling into position once again.

The cellar was dark. Pepys squinted his eyes down the stone stairs that stretched before him. In the corner, a single candle burned. Beneath the candle, sitting on the floor surrounded by a pile of empty wine bottles, lay Balty.

'Hello, brother.' He feebly waved his arm in welcome.

'Hello, Balty. I see you have made yourself at home.'

'I have indeed. The claret is over in that corner. The Sack is where I'm sitting and there is a very pleasant Madeira on top of the barrel. Could do with some food, though. A roast pig would go wonderfully with the Madeira.'

Pepys looked around the cellar. His eyes had adjusted to the dark now. It was large, stretching off into the distance, separated into three sections by the pillars of the Inn above. Balty was sat in the first section.

'I presume you searched the cellar, Balty.'

'Of course, Sam, first thing I did. No way out. As snug as a bug in a rug, we are.'

For the first time, Pepys felt immensely tired. He sank down to his haunches and leant his back against the wall. What was he to do?

The plotters were nearly ready to launch their attack on the throne, and he was stuck in this cellar with his drunken brother-in-law. Even worse, any minute they might come down and kill them both.

Another immense wave of exhaustion passed over him. He would just close his eyes for a few moments. Perhaps, an answer would come when he was better rested.

He let his body curl into a ball at the bottom of the stairs. He was so tired, just a minute's rest would ease his mind, take away the fog that surrounded it like a mist off Dogger Bank. As soon as his head hit the hard stone of the floor, Pepys was asleep.

'Strange man, said Balty, 'I thought he would have least had a drink with me before retiring for the night. Never fun drinking alone.'

Pepys didn't hear a word.

Chapter 37

Will had been dreaming.

Elizabeth was standing over him, dressed in her linen nightgown, a wry smile on her lips. She had bent her body from the waist, placed a kiss on his forehead and another on his mouth.

He sat upright.

The dining room was empty, with just a solitary candle illuminating the place where they had spent many happy hours together. He shook his head, opening and closing his eyes, trying to stretch them into wakefulness.

There was no Elizabeth and there had never been the velvet touch of a kiss. Will had known he had loved her since they day they had met. He had never once let his feelings be known and she had never treated him as other than a great friend of Sam's. But in his dreams, revealed to nobody, there was an understanding between them, that he would serve her in any way she had wanted.

Only once had he overstepped the boundaries of friendship, when he had given her the locket. Sam had found out and instantly ordered it to be returned. She had disobeyed him then, keeping the locket for herself in her jewellery box. It was strange how it was the one thing stolen by the unfortunate Jack Turner.

Who had stolen it from him? He was sure it was the same man who had stabbed him in the carriage. What was his name? Blake? How could he find him in the crowded streets in London?

He lay back in the day bed. The old house creaked around him. A mouse scurried behind the wainscotting, it's tiny feet scratching at the oak of the floor. Thousands of mice must have hidden behind there over the years, thought Will, each one hidden from his world, believing their world to be the only one that existed or mattered. Perhaps we men were the same. Only concerned with our own tiny worries, our own petty existence, when something bigger, more substantial, existed outside. But that was all we had, he thought, our own lives, our own worries. All we could do was look after ourselves and be loyal to our friends. Protect those who mattered to us. Like Sam and Elizabeth.

Will realised at that moment, he had let Sam down. He had not discovered who had stolen the diary. He had not found out who the device belonged to. He had not even managed to get Nell Gwynn to tell him everything she knew. The one woman in London who always spoke her mind, had closed it to him.

What a fool Sam was to trust him with these simple tasks. He had let his best friend down. He was no closer to finding the diary now than when it was stolen three days ago. Since then, a man had been murdered, Will had been beaten and abused, and Sam, well he didn't know what was happening to Sam. He could be lying dead at this moment.

Will sat up in his day bed. His head immediately began to throb and his leg joined in. No matter, he thought. I must find out more, even if it means that I get another beating. What do a few bruises matter when Sam's life is at stake?

He kicked off the clothes that had covered him. Why had Ashmole not been able to find the device in his books? If it was on the back of a coach travelling through the streets of London, it must be in current use.

Will's hand banged his forehead and immediately the

bump on his head throbbed with renewed vigour. He must have lied to me, he thought, but why? How had anybody known that he was going to visit the College of Heralds?

Then he thought back to his arrival at Scotland Yard. Meeting the man at the entrance of the College who had directed him up the stairs to meet Ashmole. It was almost as if he had been waiting for him. Waiting for him and sending him to the one man who would not help.

Will's head throbbed, the leg hurt even more. Should he return to the College now or wait until morning? He stood up and immediately fell on the floor as his leg refused to support his weight. Tomorrow morning it is, he thought, can't manage it today.

He levered himself up from the floor onto the day bed, struggling to lift his body without using his damaged leg. He lay there breathing heavily, staring up at the ceiling, hoping his body would heal by the morning. If it did not, he wasn't sure what he was going to do.

'I must go back,' he said out loud.

The only answer was the scurry of the mouse behind the skirting board.

Chapter 38

Pepys' eyes sprang open.

'Don't worry, it's only the rats. They get a bit noisy at this time.'

'How long have I been asleep?'

'About two and half candles, I think. Did you know a man dreams more than he eats? Fact that. Waste of time if you ask me.'

Pepys shook his head, trying to loosen the ropes of sleep that bound it.

'But if you are asking about the number of hours that you were transported to the Land of Nod, the answer is… I don't know. I would guess dawn has already passed though. The sun has risen on another beautiful June day.'

'Balty, we're in a cellar, beneath the ground. The quality of the day does not matter to us.'

Balty handed a half-empty bottle to Pepys. 'No water, I'm afraid, only wine.'

Pepys looked at the mound of bottles surrounding Balty. 'How many have you drank whilst I slept?'

'Oh, I don't know…,' he counted the empties by his side. 'At least seven, not counting those over there.' He pointed to another mound in the far corner. 'For some reason, I felt like moving, a change of view perhaps. Plus you were snoring quite loudly.'

Pepys held his head in his hands, 'Balty, why did you let me sleep so long?'

'You looked so peaceful and untroubled. Shame to wake you. You know, there was a time when I would have dreamed of an occasion like this.'

'Like what?'

'Being locked in a cellar, with nothing to drink but fine wine. But, strange to say, I'm not as happy as I thought I would be. My contrariness of nature never ceases to amaze me.'

'It amazes us all, Balty. I presume you searched here when they brought you down.'

'First thing I did, Sam. The only entrance is up there.' He pointed to the door where Pepys had come in. 'While you were asleep, the guards left me some bread and cheese.'

'Where is it?'

'Eaten. It went rather well with a bottle of the claret.' Balty scratched his large nose. 'Why are they keeping us here, Sam?'

'They are waiting for a message from London. Then they will act?'

'Act?'

'Decide what they are going to do with us. I'll not lie to you, Balty, it doesn't look good.'

Balty looked around the cellar. 'But what a way to go, hey.'

'I don't think they mean to allow us to drink ourselves to death, Balty.'

'Shame. At least, I would have enjoyed myself.' Balty scratched his nose once again.

'What do they mean to do with us?'

'I don't know. They won't stab or shoot us.'

'That's a relief.'

'Too obvious. Instead, we will meet with an unfortunate accident. On the Medway, perhaps, our boat capsizing. Can you swim, Balty?'

'No.'

'Neither can I.'

'We're done for then.' He reached up to take another bottle from the shelf. 'At least, I can meet my maker with a smile on my lips.'

'And breath stinking of wine?'

'Aye, that too. I'm sure the Lord will forgive me. This bottle is particularly delightful.' He smashed the neck against the large beer barrel on his right. The wine spilled all over his arm and down his clothes. 'Would you like some?' he offered the broken neck of the bottle to Pepys.

'No, thank you, Balty.' Pepys stared at the four foot high barrel on which Balty had smashed his wine. It was an excellent example of the cooper's art. French oak without a doubt and full of wine. It must weigh at least four hundred pounds.

'Balty, that barrel of wine.'

Balty stopped drinking out of the bottle. He wiped his mouth with the back of his hand. A red smear dribbled down his chin and onto the now off-white ruff of his shirt.

'Looks good, doesn't it? From Bordeaux, I think. Haven't been able to get inside it though. The bastards didn't leave me anything to smash it open. A small axe would have been perfect.'

'No. The barrel. How did they get it down here?' He pointed at the stairs. 'It's too big and too heavy to carry down. So how did they get it down here?'

Balty looked from the barrel to the stairs and back again. 'Beats me. I just drink the stuff, I don't worry about how it gets down my throat.'

Pepys stood up. 'There must be another entrance. A way for getting the barrels in here.' He thought for a moment. 'Where did you say the rats came from?'

'I didn't.' He pointed with the jagged end of the wine bottle. 'But in the early morning, they seem to have a little party over in that corner.'

Pepys rushed over. He started to move empty crates out of the way. A rat, disturbed by his noise, hissed and scurried for cover, followed by two others.

Pepys ran back to Balty and took the candle from its place on top of the barrel. He went over to the corner again and held the candle up. It flickered slightly in a draught. Then, he moved it down to the side of a barrel of ale.

It fluttered wildly, nearly extinguishing itself.

'Hey, be careful, without the light I won't be able to open the wine.'

Pepys knelt down and felt at the side of the barrel. There was a small gap between it and the wall. Pepys could feel the draught on the ends of his fingers, as soft as touching a piece of the finest silk.

'Come and help me move this, Balty.' He leant into the barrel but it would not move.

Balty stood beside him. A huge hand appeared on Pepys shoulder. 'Here, this is man's work.'

Pepys stood aside. Balty braced his feet on the floor and thrust his shoulder against the barrel. It shuddered slightly but did not move.

'This is going to take more effort than I thought.' Balty spat on his hands, adjusted his feet so that they pushed against the wall, and bent down. Thrusting with his legs, he wrapped his arms around the barrel and pushed.

Nothing happened,

Balty was going redder and redder but still he pushed. The barrel gave an inch, then an inch more. With a jerk, it began to slide across the floor of the cellar, emitting a loud groan as it did so.

Balty collapsed on the floor, gasping for air.

Pepys knelt down and looked behind the barrel, There

was a square hole cut into the wall. Inside, all was dark and musty, with the acid tang of old vinegar.

Balty still lay panting on the floor.

Pepys stuck his head in the hole. Immediately, he jerked it backwards and pulled away the cobwebs that covered his face and periwig. He took the wig off and placed it on top of the barrel. It was his best wig, no sense in dirtying it too much.

He put his head back in the hole again, more cautiously this time. The sour stench of vinegar assaulted his nostrils again. 'Balty, pass me the candle.'

Light appeared to the left of him. He took the candle and thrust into the hole. It flickered for a moment but then burned brightly, feasting on the draught.

The hole was a corridor, about four feet square, heading up to the ceiling at an angle of 45 degrees. Pepys squeezed himself into the hole and began to work his way up the narrow corridor. The floor was lined with wood. He pushed with his feet and knees crawling upwards like a child just learning to walk. As he neared the top, the draught became stronger and the candle fluttered wildly.

He could see a thin strip of white light around the top of the hole, with an even thinner white line running down the middle. The candle flickered even more as he got closer to the top. If he wasn't careful, it would go out. He let himself slide down and, at the bottom, passed it to Balty.

'What can you see?'

'Nothing so far.'

He climbed up the incline once more, using his knees and elbows to lever himself upwards. The fabric of his new suit began to tear at the elbows. Well, if he got out of this, he would treat himself to ten, no twenty, new suits from the tailor at the New Exchange. Hang the cost.

He reached the top of the corridor. The end was blocked by a sheet of metal, divided into two. The white line he had seen was where the two sheets met. Unfortunately for him, the workmanship was excellent. Better than he had seen in the dockyard. He placed his eye against the thin white line of light. The draught made his eye sting but he kept it there. He could see very little, just light and what seemed to be a grey wall about ten feet away. He pushed against the steel sheet but it stood firm. He tried again but it didn't budge.

Then there was an urgent whisper from Balty, 'Someone's coming.'

Pepys let himself slide down the chute. He heard a loud ripping sound as his breeches caught on something sharp. At the bottom, he leapt to his feet and ran across to the barrel where they had been sitting. Balty joined him with the candle.

The door above opened slowly. 'Gentlemen, we got some food. Dun want ye to starve. Not yet, anyhow.' The guard stood at the door, looking down into the cellar. Pepys and Balty were stretched out on the floor, bottles scattered around them, the light of the candle reflecting green through the glass of the bottle.

'Good to see you be enjoyin' yoursel'

He placed a lump of cheese and a hunk of brown bread on the dirty wooden floor of the stairs. 'Now, don't ye be eatin' this here food all at once. There'll be no more today. Town ain't floating in bread and cheese, ye know.'

With one last look around the cellar, he closed the door.

Pepys sprung to his feet. 'The door is shut at the top. See if you can move the barrel.'

'I need to eat first, Can't move doors on an empty stomach, it's bad enough moving barrels.' Balty climbed the stairs to retrieve the bread and cheese. 'Want some?' He offered Pepys a hunk of bread.

'No, you eat it. We need your strength.'

Balty didn't wait. He wolfed down a lump of bread and a larger lump of cheese, washing it down with a large swallow from one of the wine bottles on the floor. 'There. Always makes a man feel better does a spot of bread. Must be the French side of me.'

'Let's get moving, they may return.'

Balty squeezed himself into the hole. It was a tight fit. Pepys saw him stretch and began to worm himself upwards towards the thin line of light. He got to the top and pushed on the metal sheet. He pushed harder and then began banging on it with his bare fists. The metal didn't move.

'It's not going to open. I'll shout for help.'

'Don't,' said Pepys, 'you'll just attract the guards. Come back down. We'll have to think our way out of this.'

Balty slid down the chute, his body running into Pepys at the bottom. The two of them collapsed in a heap on the floor.

After he had extricated himself from under his brother-in-law, Pepys sat down beside the barrel. Balty sat next to him, an empty wine bottle nestling in his enormous hands.

'Couldn't move it. Always managed to get out of taverns before. I remember one time in Deptford…'

'Balty, if you don't mind, I'm trying to think.'

'Sorry, Sam, I'll just open another bottle.'

Pepys walked over to the large beer barrel. There must be a way of getting out of here. If they didn't manage to escape soon, the message from London would arrive. He heard the smash of the neck of a bottle against the barrel, followed by the glug as the contents began to empty into Balty's throat.

The plotters were not going to risk anything so close to June 12th. So much easier for him to have an accident. By the time anybody realised the truth, the Dutch would be in the Medway, the King would be off the throne and there would be a new ruler in England. Who could that be? Ever since the diary had been stolen, he had felt he was always one step behind. The messages seemed to know where he was and what he was doing. It must be somebody close to the King. Somebody who knew everything but who was playing a very dangerous game.

For now though, the identity of the leader of the conspiracy was the least of the worries. All that mattered now was getting out of this cellar.

Alive.

Chapter 39

Will swung his leg off the day bed. The early morning sun was shining through the drapes, its light diffused by the eternal coal smoke that cloaked London. He rested his foot tentatively on the floor.

Well, here goes, he thought. He levered himself up on his good right leg and gradually let the damaged one take more and more weight. Felt good. Not bad at all. He put all his weight on the bad leg and a searing pain shot through his knee and up to his hips. He sat back down on his day bed.

Have to take it slowly, young Will, don't put too much pressure on it. Let it recover for a few minutes.

He looked out through the gap in the drapes. London was out there. Perhaps the man who had done this to him was waiting, ready to pounce once again. He didn't think he was, but he was sure there would be people following him. How else had they known where he had been? He would have to lose them if he was to continue his investigations.

He had lain awake all night thinking. Should he continue asking questions? Should he take the risk? The threats of the man with the device had been clear.

And frightening.

And painful.

He increased the pressure on his leg as it rested on the floor, waiting for the surge of pain to shoot up his leg. It hadn't come yet.

But he owed everything to Sam. He had promised that he would find out about the device, Dryden, and Nell Gwynn, while Sam was in Chatham. So far, he had failed his best friend in everything he had done. The woman and the playwright were now off limits but the man in the coach had said nothing about going back to the College of Heralds. Perhaps he thought Will would never go back there. It was the one place that he had a valuable clue. What's more, he had seen the same device on the back of the man's coach.

He would go back. See Ashmole again and ask the same questions. But this time, he wouldn't accept any lies.

He stood up once more and increased the pressure on his leg, waiting for the sharp kick of pain.

This time, it didn't come. He tried a few tentative steps across the dining room. Still no pain. He walked up and down the stairs. His leg was stiff but there were no sudden surges of hurt. Now, he was ready to go out.

He crept up to the window and peeped through a gap in the drapes. The man standing outside the Inn across the way seemed to be watching the door of the house. He certainly wasn't drinking or waiting for anybody.

He needed to check the rear. He climbed the stairs to Sam's bedroom on the second floor. The room was still painted in its vivid shade of purple, the books arrayed like soldiers in long ranks behind their glass. The drapes were open. He sidled up to the side of the window and looked over the balcony. Another man was standing there too, smoking a pipe. Once again, he was doing nothing, occasionally taking furtive glances at Sam's house.

Will was now certain the house was being watched. Before going to the College of Heralds, he had to work out how to get out of Seething Lane without being seen.

Chapter 40

Pepys sat with his back to the barrel of wine. Next to him, Balty was finishing off the bread and cheese.

'Nothing like food to get a man ready to face the day. Always eat a breakfast, that's what I say. Sets you up right, even when you have nothing to do. Gets the bowels working, got to have working bowels, otherwise you get all clogged up. And a man who's full of shit, can't enjoy his food.' He ripped into the bread with his teeth and took another long glug of the wine. 'Have you worked out how we're going to get out of here, Sam?'

'I think so, but it has an element of danger.'

Balty's lips fluttered as he blew a raspberry. 'Walking down any of London's streets after six o'clock at night is dangerous. Breathing is dangerous. Being married is dangerous,' he thought for a moment, 'being married to my sister is even more dangerous.'

'And staying here, waiting for somebody to decide our fate seems more dangerous to me that anything we could do to escape.'

'You too speak the truth, Sam. So what are we going to do?'

Pepys leapt to his feet. 'Balty, gather the straw packing from that wine case and put it near the door.'

Balty did as he was instructed. Pepys had broken one of the wine cases into kindling and laid it over the straw.

'Oh, I see. You are going to burn the door down. Won't you burn us to death too? I never saw myself suffering the fate of a witch. I thought that was reserved for my wife.'

'No, I want to create the illusion of fire.' He looked around the cellar. In one corner, a pile of dry vine leaves spilled out from a box. He grabbed a large armful, dampened them with some wine from Balty's bottle and laid it over the top of the straw and kindling.

‘Take it easy with the wine, Sam. Shouldn’t waste wine. It deserves a throat, not to be poured on the floor. And that throat should preferably be mine.’

'Give me your handkerchief.'

Balty reached into his pocket and produced an old, yellowed piece of cloth, crusted solid.

'Sorry, not many clean handkerchiefs down a cellar.'

Pepys took out his own and poured the last of the wine over both of them.

'What a waste of good wine.'

'I'll treat you to a bottle when we get back to London. A good bottle.' Pepys stood back and looked at the neat stack against the door.

'All we need now is an effigy of the Pope like Gunpowder Treason Day. Shame, it's June and not November.'

'Balty, can you push the barrel back against the hole in the wall?'

'Of course, why?'

'Push it back but leave a small gap for us to squeeze through after we light the fire.'

'But the iron door at the end of the chute is bolted shut. You said yourself we can't get out that way.'

'We're not going to get out that way. Hurry, push the barrel against the hole.'

Balty went through his stretching routines, leant into the barrel, slowly easing it back towards the hole.

'Leave a gap for us to squeeze through. And put that rope on top of the barrel.'

Balty ran to the corner to pick it up. 'This one.'

'That will do.'

He ran back to the barrel, stretched again, cracking his arms and knuckles and pushed the barrel into place. 'It's done.'

'Right, here we go.' Pepys hoped to God and all the angels in the firmament this was going to work. On the downside, they could be burnt like two blackbirds in an oven or choked by the all-consuming smoke. On the upside, they may be able to get out of this black hole of a cellar. Sitting and doing nothing, waiting for the order for their execution, was not an option. He was never very good at doing nothing. Even as a child, he always wanted to be in the thick of things, involved up to his armpits.

He took the candle and placed the flame onto the dry packing. Instantly, the fire took hold and began to spread up the kindling to the damp hay. He threw the stump of the candle into the pile of packing and shouted, 'Fire! Fire!'

He ran to the barrel, now partially covering the hole, and pushed Balty inside. For a moment, Balty's stomach caught on the edge of the barrel.

'I shouldn't have eaten the bread and cheese.'

'You shouldn't have eaten anything for the last six years.'

Pepys pushed down on his large stomach with both hands, forcing the flesh to squeeze through the gap into the hole. Luckily, the fat was easy to move from Balty's waist to up near his armpits.

Pepys looked back at the flames that now crept up the door. Acrid brown smoke billowed out from the damp hay, crawling across the ceiling. Pepys could already smell the pungent, burnt earth aroma. He was taken back to his youth in the fens of Cambridgeshire, helping burn the stubble in the fields after the crop of winter wheat had been gathered in. The warmth of the flames in the fields, the cold draught of cider going down his throat, the laughter of the children as they danced away from the spreading fire.

He felt a tug on his coat from Balty. The flames in the cellar had now reached the ceiling. He shouted, 'Fire, Fire,' louder now and with more urgency.

This time he heard muffled shouts from behind the door. The guard had finally woken up and was spreading the alarm.

He looped the rope around the barrel, passing both ends to Balty in the hole. He squeezed through the gap, forcing his brother-in-law to one side and sitting next him in the chute.

They each took an end of the rope and pulled. The barrel didn't move.

'Put your back into it, Balty.'

'Give me your end of the rope.'

Pepys slid to the side, or as far to the side as he could, in a chute that was only four feet wide. Balty wrapped both ends of the rope around his powerful arms, leaned back like the last man in a tug of war and pulled with all his might. The barrel wobbled for a few moments like a drunken skittle and then settled back once again into position.

He tugged again on the rope.

And again, leaning back with all his weight into the floor of the chute, groaning like a constipated man who hadn’t shat for a week or more.

The barrel wobbled on its rim, then slid backwards, closing the gap between the wall and the hole, sealing out the glow of the flames.

Inside, all was dark and silent, save for Balty's rasping breaths. A wisp of smoke slid in through the gap.

‘Used to cook pigeons like this when I was a child.

Bury them in the ground, cover with earth and straw and then light it. Two hours later, the softest, most succulent birds you could imagine. Cooked to perfection.'

Pepys heard he smacking of lips as Balty relived the food of his youth. 'I don't think this is the right time to be thinking of roasting pigeons, Balty.'

'There's always time to think of food, Sam. Without food, there is no life.'

'Then maybe you could remember a style of cooking that is less similar to our present situation.'

'I see where you're going with this. Like a picnic. I remember one time on the hills above Taunton…'

'Shush.'

Outside they could hear voices shouting. The smoke was still seeping through the narrow gap where the barrel joined the wall. The smell of burning leaves and straw was getting stronger and stronger, beginning to choke.

'I hope they see the fire and smoke soon,' said Balty, covering his mouth with his arm.

'So do I. Here, wrap this around your mouth.' He handed Balty his wet handkerchief.

'I always knew wine would save my life.'

'Climb to the top of the chute and place your mouth over the gap in the metal. Breathe through the crack if the smoke gets too bad.'

'You've thought of everything.'

'Somebody has to.'

Pepys placed his ear close to the gap, shutting his mouth and forcing himself to hold his breath.

Outside in the cellar, he could hear more voices now and the sounds of frenzied activity; footsteps on the stairs, shouted orders, the tramp of feet, the splash of water and the hiss of fires being doused.

The smoke was increasing in the hole. He put his own wine-soaked handkerchief around his own mouth. 'Come on, come on,' he whispered.

Then he heard a loud shout. 'The prisoners, where are they?'

'Dunno sir, they must have run when I went to get help.'

This was followed by a loud slap across someone's face and the sound of feet running up the cellar steps.

More shouted orders, but unclear this time. Pepys could hear the urgency in the voice even if he couldn't hear the words.

The smoke coming into the chute was lessening now. Balty was above him, still breathing through the gap in the metal sheet.

Pepys lay in the chute for a few minutes, making as little sound as possible. Then he sat up, leant forward and listened.

No sound.

Quiet as a merchant's charity.

He tugged Balty's leg. Reluctantly, the big man slid down beside him. Pepys couldn't see his face in the dark but he knew that there was a big smile on it.

'What now?' Balty asked.

'We get out.'

'How?'

'We use number eleven's pony.'

'What?'

'Our legs.'

They sat side by side, their backs pressed against the chute. They pushed with all the strength in their legs. The barrel moved easily this time, sliding along the cellar floor on the water used to put out the fire.

Pepys cautiously popped his head out of the hole.

The cellar was in chaos. Broken wine bottles lay everywhere. Along the floor, the spent lumps of hay still smouldered. While a dark streak of soot stained the lime wash of the bricks. Everything stank of that pungent post-fire smell. A bitter, acrid smell that stung Pepys' nostrils.

He popped his head out even further. Nobody was there. The cellar door was open.

He pulled himself out and then helped Balty to squeeze past the barrel once more.

Balty took a look around the once pristine cellar. 'What a waste.'

'We have to move quickly.'

'Where to?'

'The river.'

He picked up his wig from on top of the barrel and placed it back on his head, adjusting it so that the two wings fell correctly on either side of his shoulders. There was no point in looking slovenly.

They climbed to the top of the stairs, past the fire scarred door and peeped out.

The corridor was empty.

Pepys pressed his finger across his lips and signalled for Balty to follow him. Slowly, he inched out, keeping his back to the wall and placing his feet silently on the flagstones.

From above, there was the sound of clapping, a slow sarcastic clapping.

'Well done, Mr Pepys. Well done, indeed.'

Mrs Behn appeared from around the corner, dressed like a man in leather doublet and trousers, her hair hidden beneath a close-fitting hat.

'I don't believe I could have done it better myself.'

Chapter 41

‘You weren’t fooled, Mrs Behn?’

She advanced towards them, pulling her sword out from its scabbard. Balty stepped in front of Pepys. 'You'll have to take me first.'

Pepys placed his hand on Balty's shoulder. 'I don't believe that will be necessary, Balty, but I do applaud the sentiment and the intent.'

Mrs Behn reversed the sword and presented the hilt to Pepys. 'You may have need of this.'

'Not me, I think that is more Balty's line of work.'

The big man took the sword and swished it twice to get the feel of its weight. 'Not bad, but could do with a little more weight in the hilt.'

'It's a ladies blade,' said Mrs Behn.

'Ladies blade or not. It still kills, I presume,’ said Balty practising his lunges and parries.

'Oh, it still kills, just a little more stylishly.'

'All the same to me, as long as they be dead.’

‘Mr Pepys, I thought I would never see you again.’ She curtsied, remembered she was dressed as a man, and changed it into a bow.

Pepys returned the bow. ‘Mrs Behn. I'm happy to see you again. You had even me fooled for a moment. The jibe about the accident on the Medway was a little too close to home.'

‘The truth is never comfortable for any man, Mr Pepys. And it is good to see you alive. Even if you are a little blackened by the experience.’ She reached up and wiped Pepys' forehead with her handkerchief. ‘As you can see,’ she pointed to the men behind her, ‘we were all ready to rescue you when we saw the fire. You were in there for a long time.'

'How long?'

'It is now the morning of the 8th of June, Mr Pepys.'

'What? I was in the dungeon for more than a day?'

'You did have a long sleep, Sam, and I was reluctant to wake you. You looked so peaceful,' muttered Balty.

"I need to be in London to report to the King by tomorrow.'

'Let us move. Quietly, gentlemen, the Preacher's agents are everywhere in the town.'

They crept down the alley, stopping at the entrance to check that the road was clear.

Pepys stood next to Mrs Behn, while they waited for the horses. 'Did you find out the identity of the leader of this gang of madmen?'

'Not yet, but I did see the orders that came from London. You were not to be killed but let go, Mr Pepys.'

'Released? Why would they want to release me? I thought I was sure to die.'

'So did they. The order caused much argument and discussion amongst the Preacher, Quilt, Daly and Fridley. You'll be pleased to hear that they decided to ignore it and kill you anyway.'

'I'm afraid the news does not please me, Mrs Behn.'

She wiped his face again with her handkerchief. 'I stole the letter.' She opened her leather doublet and passed the paper to him.

He could still feel the warmth of her body on the letter. The message came on headed notepaper. 'It's the same shield as on the silver button. But why would he want to release me?'

'We can worry about that another time.' She pushed

him and Balty across the road to another alley on the other side.

As he ran, Pepys folded the letter and put it inside his coat. It would have to wait till later.

'We need to get out of here. The Preacher has his men everywhere looking for you.'

'The river?'

'I think not. They will expect you to go there. We must ride much further, gentlemen.'

'Not again,' said Balty. 'Does anybody happen to have any syllabub?'

Chapter 42

The wicker basket clattered and groaned around him

'Bloody heavy this week, Jane. What you got in 'ere, a dead body?'

'You should be so lucky, Tom Drayton, what you got is a ton of work for your laundry, that's what you got.'

'A ton of work for my back is what it is missus. How'm I gonna get this 'ere load on my cart?'

Will heard the soft pad of Jane's footsteps as she came down the steps. 'Lord a mercy, Tom Drayton, if you ain't the weakest sniveler this side of Wapping. Them be just a few drapes and sheets.'

The basket seemed to strain around Will, and he felt himself being lifted into the air and dumped unceremoniously in the back of a cart.

'See, didn't take more than a second.'

'You should come and help me on my rounds, Mistress Jane, I'd be getting a lot more done with 'e.'

Will felt the cart rock from side to side.

'You'd be getting nothing done and 'e knows it. Just you keeps your eye on the street.'

'I'd much prefer to keeps my eye on 'e.'

'I'm sure you would, Tom Drayton. But it's what I keeps me eye on what matters, ain't it?'

Will heard a loud slap, a donkey brayed, and the cart jerked forward.

'Today's the seventh. I'll bring the laundry back on Wednesday, Mistress, perhaps 'e can keeps your eye on me then,' the driver shouted over the rattle of the wheels on the cobbles. He couldn't make out Jane's reply but the driver's loud laughter told him it was probably bawdy.

Will shifted his position in the laundry basket. The drapes lay beneath him whilst the sheets covered his head. It was stifling and hot inside, his throat was already parched and dry, his tongue sticking to the roof of his mouth. He hoped the driver was near to the end of his round, otherwise he would die of thirst.

That would be an interesting article in the London Gazette. Navy Board man found dead in laundry basket. He laughed at himself. You do have a penchant for looking on the dark side of life, Will Hewer.

The cart rumbled on through the streets of London. Will heard and felt it stopping twice to pick up more laundry, each time the driver spent his time chatting with the maid.

'For God's sake, man, get a move on. I'm going to die in here,' he said under his breath.

The second time, another basket was thrown on top of his, the new weight producing a loud creak and an alarming slant in the basket, pushing his head closer to his knees. For a moment, he thought he was going to be crushed beneath the weight of sheets.

Once again, he wrote another article detailing his death for the London Gazette.

Eventually, the cart stopped. He smelt the odour of rough tobacco as someone lit a pipe and smoked it.

Then two people were speaking. 'Bout time you came, Tom Drayton. I been waitin' 'ere for a while, I been.'

'You been enjoying your pipe, Jamie Finn, not waitin' for me. Gives the donkey a rest anyways.'

'Bloody things always resting.'

Will heard the sound of a kick on soft flesh, followed by the loud, indignant bray of a donkey.

'Let's be havin' a spot of tucker before us move all

this lot. That wench up on Seething Lane cleanin' out the whole 'ouse by 'e weight of it.'

'That be Jane, bain't it.'

'Aye, well stacked she be. Like two ripe stocks of corn. I'll be givin' 'er a seein' to on Seething Lane, you mark my words.'

'The only thing you be givin' a seein' to is a pot of ale.'

Will heard the men's laughter and their steps as they walked away. Now was as good a time as any to get out of this wretched basket. He tried to push open the top but it wouldn't move. He tried again, pushing with all his strength, but still it wouldn't budge. The basket on top must be weighing down upon the lid.

This time, he shifted his position, so that he squatted on his legs. He pulled as many of the sheets as he could away from his head and hunched his shoulders against the wicker lid. He took three deep breaths and thrust upwards with his legs. The wicker lid creaked with the strain. He thrust harder. The lid flew open. He stood upright and took the last remaining sheet off his head.

Two old women were walking past the cart on their way back from the market. They let out a shriek of fright.

'Don't worry,' said Will quickly, 'I'm just practising my Jack-in-the-box.' He squatted down into the basket and jumped up again. 'Ta-da'.

The woman looked at him and then at the donkey. Then they took up their skirts and began running down the alley.

The donkey brayed.

Time to get out of here. He stepped out of the cart and jumped down onto the road. Once more, a dagger of pain shot up his leg. He leant against the cart, breathing heavily. Got to be more careful, Will Hewer, you're not as young as you used to be.

The donkey brayed in agreement.

Will let go of the cart, said goodbye to the donkey and limped down the alley in the opposite direction from the women. Now he had to get to the river and the College of Heralds. After that, a boat to Greenwich to meet Sam. He wasn't going to let him down this time.

Chapter 43

They ran down the alley and across to a stable where Mrs Behn had four horses waiting.

'Up you get, Mr Pepys, we must ride quickly before they decide to return to the cellar.' She formed a cradle with her hands to help him get aboard the horse.

He ignored the proffered help. 'We need to move quickly, Mrs Behn. My report to the King is due tomorrow.' He grunted as he swung his leg up to the stirrups and levered himself clumsily over the nag.

'We will not dawdle, Mr Pepys.'

Balty had already hoisted himself aboard another horse. They were joined by one of Mrs Behn's men.

'We won't have much of a lead. The Preacher will no doubt hear about four people on horses riding out of town.'

'Ladies first, Madam.'

'Always the gentleman, Mr Pepys.'

'One does try, Madam. Sometimes though ones efforts are entirely wasted.'

'Not wasted, sir, simply misplaced.'

'The story of my life, Mrs Behn.'

'I'm sure your wife wouldn't agree, sir.'

'I'm equally sure she would, madam.'

'When are we going to stop to eat? I'm feeling a little peckish.'

'Later, Balty, when we have put miles between ourselves and this accused town.'

The man kicked his horse into motion. He was followed by Mrs Behn, Pepys and Balty. They avoided the High Street but trotted down a series of alleys, emerging onto a huge open park above Chatham.

It stretched out before them, a vast grassland dotted with stout trees.

'What a beautiful place.' At any other time, Pepys would have loved to have walked among the ancient oaks and elms, picnicking with Elizabeth, or, if he were lucky, with another lady.

Mrs Behn looked over her shoulder at the town where hung the shore of the Medway. She could hear shouts and noise coming from near the docks. 'Another time, I fear, Mr Pepys. It seems our escape has been discovered.'

They raced across the parkland, Balty bouncing in the seat of his saddle like an apple bobbing in a barrel. Pepys hung on to his horses neck with both hands. Only Mrs Behn seemed to be enjoying herself, her hair flowing behind her, caressed by the wind.

They emerged onto a wide track rutted by the wheels of dozens of carts and drays. Pepys looked up into the sky. The sun was on his right hand side, beating hotly against his face. He pushed his nag harder to join Mrs Behn.

'We're heading east, madam, we're going the wrong way.'

'I know, sir, this is the Canterbury Road. The Preacher and his men will be either out on the river or guarding the Rochester Road, they will not expect us to come this way.' There was a long pause, 'I hope.'

'You hope, madam. And will hope get me to my meeting with the King in time for the 9th?'

'No, sir, it will not. But your nag will. And not being captured by the Preacher will. So I suggest that you concentrate on riding, and let myself and my man concentrate on getting you there.'

'But how will that happen if we are going the wrong

way?'

'Because sir, we will turn off this road just before Sittingbourne, then we will take the road to Maidstone, and from there the London Road to Greenwich. Remember I was born and raised in these parts, sir, I know the roads like the back of my hand.'

'I will leave myself in your capable hands, Madam. We must get to London before the 9th. Maybe, I know now who the traitor is.'

'You do, Mr Pepys?'

'Yes, madam, I do. All we have to do is discover what Will has found out to see if my theory is correct.'

Mrs Behn looked at the rutted track in front of her. 'Well, if you do, sir, we had better ride mighty fast if we are to reach London in time.' She kicked her horse into a canter. Pepys and the man followed suit.

Balty was left behind. 'Wait for me,' he cried, trying to spur his horse to go faster. The horse ignored him, carrying on at its gentle trot.

Chapter 44

Will took a public wherry down to Whitehall Palace. There were seven other people on board and four chickens. He stared out at the river, avoiding all eye contact with his fellow passengers. For the first time, he noticed how busy the river was. Boats of all shapes and sizes rushed up and down and across, shouting and bellowing to clear the way or simply claim a right of way, nearly striking each other as they jostled for their own particular stretch of water.

Somehow, Will did not know how, the Wherrymen avoided each other.

The river itself was full of floating trees, lumps of wood, a few dead pigs, a dead dog, and a few things that Will couldn't recognise but imagined could once have been human beings.

He made the mistake of looking inwards and a fellow passenger caught his eye.

'Going for a new job, me.'

'Really?' said Will trying to turn back to look at the river.

The man continued anyway. 'In the palace as a night-soil collector. Me uncle got it for me. Only cost me five quid. Had to borrow that, but can't get nuffin these days wivout a bit of an investment.'

'Is that right?' Will tried again to look away.

'That it is. Bit of a cushy number. Empty the piss pots in the morning and make sure they're under the bed in't evenin'. Can't say fairer then that, can a body?'

'No, I don't suppose you can.' The man had obviously not heard of the unwritten rule that nobody spoke to a fellow passenger on board a wherry. In Will's circles it was considered the height of rudeness. However, Will had not met many night soil collectors before.

The man continued despite Will continuing to stare out at the river. 'Going up in the world, I am. Used to be a dog-skinner. Not much call for the trade these days. What wiv them new furs from the Americas. Well, we all hafter change, don't we?'

Will grunted.

'I'll be on the lookout for hopportunity in't palace. Gots to keep the eyes open for hopportunity. Never knows when it knocks, does you?'

Luckily, the ferryman called out Will's pier at that moment. 'I have to alight here. Enjoy the new job.'

'Thanks, I will.' The man stuck out his hand. Will looked at it and, for a moment, thought of the number of chamber pots that the hand may have handled. He shook it anyway.

'Good luck.'

'*Bon chance*, as they say in Italian. Learnt it at the Palace, I did. Speaks a foreign language now. Me ma, bless her soul, would be chuffed. Strange thing is…'

The man was still speaking when Will leapt off the boat and onto the pier. He retraced his steps from his first visit. Down past the chapel and the Great Hall, and across Scotland Yard.

This time, there was nobody waiting to direct him up the stairs to Master Ashmole's rooms. He went up anyway and knocked on the door.

He heard a chair scraping back, a few shuffling steps , the door cracked open and a head peered out. 'Who is it?'

'It's me, Will Hewer.'

'You brought my breakfast?'

'No, Master Ashmole, I came earlier.'

Ashmole was wearing exactly the same clothes as on Will's last visit, the room looked exactly the same, even the candle seemed to be the same height. Only the motes floating in the air had changed.

'I remember you. The man with the button.' Ashmole attempted to close the door.

Will put his foot in the gap. 'Master Ashmole, you told me the device on the button didn't exist.'

The door tried to close again. ‘No, I didn't.'

Will shoved the door with his shoulder. It flew open and Master Ashmole staggered back into his room. 'What do you mean?'

'I didn't tell you it didn't exist. I said I couldn't find it. There is a difference, young man, listen to the English language.'

'You quibble with words when my friend’s life is at stake.' Will took two steps into the room. His arms came up as if to strike the herald. Ashmole raised his own arms to protect himself and blurted out. 'I'll show you the device.'

Will flexed his muscles. It was unbelievable what the mere threat of violence could achieve. No wonder that Blake and his kind thrived in the world. He took another step towards Ashmole.

The man scurried away to a bookshelf at the far end of the room. He reached up high and pulled down an ancient volume, its cover thick with dust. He ran to his desk, thumping the volume down on top of the books that lay there. 'Here it is. I'll show you. Do you have the button?'

Will reached into his purse and pulled out the silver button once again. He thought it strange that this piece of silver had once lain in a dying man's hands and now was going to protect the living. Such is life. And death.

Ashmole took the button and peered at it through his lenses. 'Yes, quite distinct. See. Argent on a cross gules with five escallops and supporters of a dapple-grey horse proper on the dexter, and a stag argent on the sinister. A better design than the recent ones. We've had to design so many since His Majesty returned to the throne. Such a lot of new nobility after Cromwell's time. Not much call for heraldry then.'

He turned over the pages of the book. Once again, Will could see the gaily painted devices, symbols and escutcheons. Perhaps, he should get a device made for himself? He wondered how much it would cost.

Ashmole stopped turning the pages and peered through his lenses at one particular device, comparing it with the image on the button. 'Yes, that's it,' he said finally.

He tapped one picture about half way down the left hand page.

Will stepped forward to look at the image and the family name written beneath it. Him? So he was the one who had killed Jack Turner. And the one who had tortured him in the carriage. Why? Why had he done it when he already had so much power and wealth? Sam would be surprised, and a little scared.

The man they were looking for was one of the most powerful in the land, and the King's closest friend.

The Duke of Buckingham was not a man to be crossed.

Chapter 45

They rode most of the rest of that day, stopping only to water and feed the horses at a stream. The old pilgrim's route to Canterbury was quiet.

'Not many pilgrims anymore,' said Pepys.

'Not any. All the old saints fingertips, toenails and foreskins were thrown away by Henry. He kept the jewelled boxes, though. A clever man.' Mrs Behn stroked the muzzle of her horse.

'Shame. Chaucer wrote about the pilgrims.'

'Who?'

'Geoffrey Chaucer. The Canterbury Tales.'

Mrs Behn shrugged her shoulders.

'Your education is wanting, Mrs Behn, if you haven't read Mr Chaucer's work. I think you would like the Wife of Bath. A woman after your own heart.'

'A man writing about women?' She laughed. 'No man knows the depths of a woman's heart.'

'What about Master Shakespeare or even our poet laureate, John Dryden?'

'Shakespeare comes close. I do like his Lady Macbeth. But Dryden…the man's a ninny with the wit of a flea on the arse of a donkey.'

'Madam, I think...'

As Pepys was speaking, there was a puff of smoke followed by a flash and a loud bang. The man riding in front of them put his hand to his chest and slowly began to fall off his horse.

Two other flashes followed in quick succession. Pepys heard the sound of a mosquito buzzing past his ear.

'Quick, this way,' shouted Mrs Behn.

Pepys dug his heels into the side of his horse. Another bullet whizzed past his head. The horse, sensing the danger to its rider, leapt into action, galloping down the track after Mrs Behn.

Pepys looked over his shoulder. Balty was following him, his head next to that of his horse, holding on for dear life.

Two men had emerged from the undergrowth in front of them. They carried what looked like long sticks. Slowly, they put them to their shoulders and pointed them at Pepys.

Mrs Behn let out an immense roar, charging the man on the left.

The other man was levelling his rifle now, taking careful aim, pointing directly at Pepys. He could see the dull gleam of the barrel and a head lowering to sight along it. There was a large feather in the man's hat. So large it looked like it was growing out the man's head. Strange the things one notices when one's life is in danger.

The man's finger reached around for the trigger. Pepys pulled his horse's reins, kicked the nag on either side of the stomach, and followed Mrs Behn's lead in roaring at the top of his voice. What came out of his mouth, though, was the high pitched scream of an opera singer rather than the snarl of a highly trained killer.

The effect was just the same. The horse charged right at the musketeer with Pepys holding on for dear life. The man's eyes opened wide in terror. His head and the feather jerked away from the barrel of the rifle.

The horse hit him full in the chest, knocking him over like a rag doll. Pepys heard a soft, shallow thump as the man went down and the hooves of the horse thundered over him.

He looked back. Mrs Behn’s charge had forced her man to run back into the cover of the undergrowth, where he had turned and was lowering his rifle once more.

Balty was racing past him. Pepys saw the man's musket come to the horizontal and his finger curl around the trigger. A cloud of smoke came from the pan, followed by a smaller puff from the end of the barrel.

Balty stopped for a brief moment as if checking that the bullet had missed, and then continued riding.

'This way,' shouted Mrs Behn.

'But, Balty...'

Another bullet whizzed between them, thudding into a tree on their left. Pepys could see the trail it had cut into the moist air.

'Quickly.' They rode toward the right, cutting through a thin orchard of apple trees. Pepys looked back once again. Balty was following but slowly.

'I must go back for him.' Pepys turned his horse around and galloped back to Balty.

His brother-in-law was holding his arm. A round, red patch was growing steadily larger on the sleeve of his coat.

‘My arm, Sam. I do believe the man shot me.’

Pepys grabbed the reins. Balty slumped forward in his saddle, holding onto the horse's neck with both arms.

Another bullet whizzed past Pepys’ head. He kicked his horse and it started forward.

They galloped back to where Mrs Behn was waiting for them in the orchard.

'We must ride for the Maidstone Road.’ She grabbed Balty's reins and kicked her horse into a gallop. Pepys followed her as quickly as he could, holding onto the neck of his horse as it danced between the apple, quince and medlar trees.

After a couple of miles, she stopped beneath a grove of young oaks. Pepys jumped down and rushed around to Balty. The man was still holding onto his horse's neck for dear life.

'Balty...' said Pepys.

Balty sat up in his saddle. 'That was a damn close thing. Don't want to do that again. Anybody got a drink?'

'Your arm.' Pepys pointed to Balty's left sleeve. A large red blotch stood out against the rough cloth.

Balty stared down at the arm, noticing for the first time how much blood he had lost. He fell from his horse. Pepys caught him and lowered him to the ground.

'We should take his coat off,' said Mrs Behn. 'But we can't stay here long. They could be following.'

They removed Balty's coat. As Mrs Behn examined the sleeve, he began to come round. Balty looked at the red blood against the white sleeve of his shirt and fainted again. 'Can you save the arm?' he groaned.

'Just a scratch,' she pronounced, 'I've seen worse cuts from the prick of a sewing needle.'

'But the blood...' said Pepys.

'He bleeds like a stuck pig, but he'll survive. She pulled the shirttail out of Balty's breeches and tore strips from the fabric.

'My shirt,' he pleaded. Then he noticed the round stain on the material of his coat,

'My jacket…?'

'A man and his clothes.' Mrs Behn snorted as she wrapped the cloth around Balty's arm.

'We'll get new ones when we get back to London. My tailor will look after you.'

Mrs Behn stood up. 'When you two men have stopped discussing your attire and your tailors, I suggest we get moving again.'

'Are you fit to ride?'

Balty nodded.

'Good man.' Pepys helped him back on his horse and then climbed aboard his own.

'My jacket,' said Balty pointing down to the wrinkled blood, sweat and wine-stained material.

'For God's sake...' said Mrs Behn and kicked her horse into a gallop.

Chapter 46

Will was sure Ashmole would report his visit and his threats. If his time in the coach was anything to go by, he was a marked man. He liked his body and didn't want any more marks on it.

He limped across Scotland Yard toward the pier. Mr Blake was obviously an expert at torture. The sort of man that all good households could not do without. Particularly, if they were engaged in treachery and treason.

Where to now? He couldn't go back to see Dryden or Nell Gwynn. He was sure that they were being watched in case he did. Sam had said to meet him at the Swan in Greenwich on his way back from Chatham. He wouldn't arrive until this evening at the earliest, but at least Will would be safe there.

A pair of guards walked past him. They stared as they did so, one of them forcing him to move out the way. Will kept his eyes to the ground. Now was not a time to antagonise anybody.

He reached the pier. As he walked down it, he felt as though all eyes were on him. The hawkers looked up from their wares set out on the wooden decking. Passengers waiting for the next ferry to cross the river eyed him up and down. One man even spat on the floor as he walked past. Was he imagining all of this? Was fear playing tricks with his mind?

He didn't know and didn't care. He just wanted to get out of London as quickly as he could. At least, in Greenwich he could relax and wait for Sam.

He hailed a wherry to come to the pier. 'Where you wanna go, squire?'

'To Greenwich.' Will mumbled under his breath, trying not to let the other passengers hear his destination.

'Whazzat?'

‘Greenwich,' he said a little louder.

'Greenwich?' the ferryman shouted back. 'I dunno baht Greenwich. A long way is Greenwich. Quite a pull for my boy and me.'

'I'll give you one pound.' Will spoke out of the side of his mouth.

'Whazzat? You'll have to speak lahder. Me is a bit mutt and jeff cos of me piles. Fects the ears summit rotten, they do. I got the piles from sittin' here on this boat. But I’m a wherryman, where else would I sit?'

'I said I will give you a pound to take me to Greenwich.' Will spoke loudly and slowly, giving up the pretence of trying to hide his destination.

'Nah need to shaht, I ate deff just got piles. A pound it is. Right generous, sir.' He held out his hand for Will to step aboard.

'Make it as quick as you can.'

'In a hurry are we, sir? As quick as a bishop wiv an altar boy. That's what we be. You just sit in the back and let me and me boy hurry you dahn to Greenwich.'

The boy took the oars and started to skull into the middle of the river, working with the tide. From the back of the boat, Will saw two men rush down to the end of the pier, knocking over three passengers and kicking the hawker's wares into the river.

He hunkered down beneath the gunwale of the boat. The men stood on the end of the pier, scanning the river.

'Dun worry baht them, sir. We is just like any other boat on this here river.' He spat in the water. ‘Used to be a sodger. Was at St.George’s Hill with Winstanley when

Fairfax sold us dahn the river. That's why I became a boatman. Just me, the boy, the boat and the river. They don't betray ye.' He spat once again.

Will hunkered down even further. He couldn't wait to get to Greenwich. At least there, he would feel safer.

Chapter 47

They skirted around the outskirts of Maidstone, hiding in the trees at the side of the track whenever they spotted anybody coming towards them.

'We'll never make it in time at the rate we're going,' said Pepys.

'I think we'll go faster once we hit the London Road,' replied Mrs Behn.

'But won't they expect us to use it?'

'I don't think so. They ambushed us on the road to Canterbury and the coast. They won't expect us to double back.'

'You didn't expect them to find us on the Canterbury Road.'

'The Preacher is cleverer than I thought. And he has more men.'

They stopped for a moment, allowing Balty to catch up.

'When are we going to eat? And my arm hurts,' he moaned.

'There's an inn a few miles up the London Road. We can rest the horses and get something there.'

'We're going to stop?'

'We have to stop, Mr Pepys. The horses need hay and water. Or would you have them collapse beneath us?'

'I need to be in Greenwich this evening.'

'We'll make it, providing we meet no more problems.' She kicked her horse into a trot. 'Come on, Mr Balty. The best steak pie in Kent is just two miles away.'

The prospect seemed to please Balty. He raised his head and kicked his horse with his heels to join Mrs Behn in her trot. The horse paid no attention, carrying on at the same pace.

They reached the Inn twenty minutes later. Balty once again bringing up the rear. Mrs Behn stopped outside.

'It's very quiet. Usually, it's packed with travellers.'

A man came out to greet them. 'Hullo there, come far have ye? Good day for it.'

'You're not busy today.'

'Aye, that's true. Trouble in Maidstone, they say. Men on the streets. Though what they been doing in the streets of Maidstone, Lord only knows. Nothing in Maidstone for anybody to be on the streets for.'

Mrs Behn dismounted from her horse. 'Can we get fresh horses?'

'I got three nags in there just right for you. Going to London, are we?'

'Could be.' Mrs Behn answered.

'I only ask cos if you are, you can leave 'em at my brother-in-law's place. The Mitre in Southwark. Will cost you, though. These nags are my best uns. Been with me for years, they be. Quiet as spring lambs but good riders.'

'Get them ready. Plus we'll have some food while we're waiting..'

'A steak pie?' asked Balty.

'Sorry, sir, no steak today on accounts of the trouble in Maidstone. I got a luvverly bit of mutton, though. Roasted by the missus it was on Tuesday. No, I tell a lie. Today's Friday so it must have been Monday.'

'Mutton will be fine,' said Pepys getting off his horse.

'Should be fish seein' as it's Friday but don't 'ave any fish 'cos...'

'Because of the trouble in Maidstone, we know. Can you hurry up, landlord? We need to move on.'

'Right, it is, sir. Three horses and three muttons.

Coming right up. Not on the same plate, though. Just my little joke, sir. I likes a joke with me guests.'

The three of them walked into the Inn leaving the Landlord to stable the horses and prepare fresh ones. Balty ordered a pint of ale and proceeded to drink it down in one go.

Pepys and Mrs Behn looked at him.

'What? I was thirsty and since there's no pie, I may as well have pint or two.' He patted his arm. 'Kills the pain.'

Mrs Behn snorted. ‘It's a scratch man. I've seen worse cuts in a child's playground.'

Balty ordered another pint of ale from the landlord's wife. 'Still hurts.'

'How far is it to London?'

'Not far, about six hours steady riding,' said Mrs Behn. 'And Greenwich?'

'Closer. Around four I think. You are thinking of stopping in Greenwich?'

'I have to meet someone there.' Pepys stopped talking as the Landlady put three steaming plates of mutton stew in front of them.

Balty began to attack the food with the energy of a man who had been fasting for forty days. Pepys and Mrs Behn picked at their plates.

'You have an idea who is behind all this?'

'I do. But I'll know for certain once we meet Will in Greenwich. I hope he can provide some answers to a few questions that have been troubling me.'

'Questions?

'Too many questions, Mrs Behn. I think I know who is behind all of this but why? And why now?' Pepys shook his head. 'I need to find the answers before the Privy Council meeting tomorrow.'

'And if you don't?'

'Well, I think you will be visiting me in the Tower, Mrs Behn.'

'I'll bring you something warm to wear.'

'I think I would prefer something metal to wear, around my neck.'

'You shouldn't think in those terms, Mr Pepys.'

'I have to, Mrs Behn. Many men would come to see me dance at Tyburn.'

'Are you going to finish that?' Balty pointed to Pepys's plate. Pepys shook his head.

Within seconds, Balty was wolfing down another plate of stew. 'It's good,' he muttered between mouthfuls.

'We'll cross that river when we come to it, Mr Pepys.'

'Our Rubicon will be the Thames at Greenwich. I only hope that Will can make it.'

'Your nags are ready, sirs and madam.'

'Come let us go, We'll only know when we reach Greenwich.' She stood up.

'True. No point in worrying now before the cat has even eaten the cream.'

She looked at him quizzically.

'A phrase from my youth in Cambridge. It means...'

'I know what it means. Sometimes, you surprise me, Mr Pepys.'

'Coming from you, Mrs Behn, that can only be a compliment.' They both left the Inn.

Balty finished a last spoonful of mutton stew and stuffed three slices of bread from the trencher in his pocket. 'Wait for me,' he shouted.

Chapter 48

Up ahead, four soldiers were stopping all boats going down the river.

'Quick, take your wig, coat and shoes off and put on this hat and apron. Just nod whatever I say.' The wherryman tossed him the clothes. He quickly threw his periwig into the bottom of the boat where it floated on a lake of dirty Thames water like some drowned rat.

More expense.

He put on the hat and apron. They both stank of fish, the hat worse than the apron.

The soldiers were talking to the Wherry in front of them, questioning the passengers. After they had been released, one of the soldiers gestured for their boat to come alongside.

With two strokes, the young boy coaxed it next to the soldier's boat.

'You carrying passengers?'

The wherryman looked at his boat and then back at the soldiers. 'Does it look like it?'

The soldier ignored the insolence of the Ferryman's answer. 'Where you going to?'

'Up river.'

'Up river, where?

'Wherever there's work for him.' He pointed to the boy at the oars. 'And fish for him'

He pointed to Will.

'You a fisherman?' he asked Will.

Will was about to answer when the Wherryman interrupted. 'You won't get anyfing from him. Deaf and dumb since birth, that one. A bit simple, too if you gets my drift. A good fisherman, though.'

'The simple ones usually are. He stinks of fish, right enough,' said one of the soldiers.

'Probably washes with 'em.' The two soldiers fell about laughing at their joke.

'What you looking' for?'

'A man, name of Hewer. Stole from the Palace at Whitehall.'

'What did he nick? One of the King's whores?'

'Nah, they're two a penny. Dunno what he nicked, just been told to nick him.'

'When we rowed past that wherry over there...' he pointed to another green boat far downstream, 'they were talkin' and laughing' about the Palace. Were very happy with themselves, if you catches my drift.'

The soldier peered downstream at the green boat coming towards them with the two men sitting in the back. 'We catches your drift. Thanks for the tip, friend. Not many these days that helps a soldier.'

'Just doin' me bit. Can I go now? Fish don't catch 'emselves.'

The soldier waved him on, turning his attention to the green boat coming towards him. The boy pulled the wherry away and down the river.

'I can't thank enough for your help,' said Will.

'Keep ye thanks.' He spat in the river. 'Told ye, I can't stand sodgers. You'd better keep the hat and apron on. Could be more of the bastards on the river.' He spat once more.

Will watched as the globule of spit was swallowed by the lapping waters of the Thames. He had to get to Greenwich now and warn Sam. Whoever it was that was after them, had enough power to stop every ship on the river. Who could be able to do that?

*

He was still thinking about his problem as they approached the pier in Greenwich. 'Thank you once again, Mr...?'

'The name be Pettifer. John Pettifer. And this be James, my son.' He pointed to the young boy who had done all the rowing. 'He don't speak much but he thinks a lot.'

'Thinking's good for you.' James spoke for the first time in the journey. 'Too much noise in the world.' With those few words, James shipped the oars and the boat coasted to the Pier.

Will hopped off the wherry. He tried to say thank you once more, but John Pettifer was having nothing of it. Before he had even started to speak, the small boat was already pulling away.

'Look after yourself, Mr Hewer, there's some evil men in this world.' With a last wave, John Pettifer turned away and faced upstream, not looking back.

Will was sorry to see both of them go. In their boat he had felt safe for a short while. Now, he was alone again and exposed. 'I need to get away from here,' he said to himself.

He was supposed to meet Sam this evening at six o'clock in the Swan Inn. He looked up in the sky. By the sun, he thought it was just after one. Five hours to wait. On the streets, he would be exposed. He didn't want to meet any more soldiers and, without the cover of the boat, they would surely arrest and detain him. A night in the Tower held no joy for Will.

He looked around the pier. A few old buildings

hovered over the water to his left. The last remnants of good King Henry's foundries. Now disused, they looked forlorn and unhappy. In front of him, Greenwich Hill stretched to its old Roman ruin on the top. To the right, the town of Greenwich itself.

He decided to walk into town. Perhaps, he would rent a room at the Inn and wait for Sam there. A lot safer than walking the streets. He checked his purse. One pound, seven shillings and fourpence. A fortune by the standards of the Wherryman but Will was acutely aware he was running out of money. Being Sam's friend was an expensive proposition.

Nevertheless, there was enough here for one of the smaller rooms at the Inn. He walked up the steps from the pier and on towards the town.

He didn't notice the two men following him.

Chapter 49

The rest of their ride to Greenwich passed uneventfully. Even Balty managed to keep up with Pepys and Mrs Behn as they raced their horses along the empty road.

'It's too quiet,' said Mrs Behn, 'almost as if the road had been closed.'

'I think we have outrun our pursuers, Mrs Behn. You are too suspicious.'

'A woman is always suspicious. Men's motives are often suspect, are they not? From an early age, we learn to look for the hidden reason, the cause that lies beneath the surface.'

'I think you think too much, Mrs Behn. If Man is as duplicitous as you seem to suggest, how is it that woman can fall in love?'

'It is interesting, Mr Pepys, that the phrase is always 'fall in love'. Like tripping or stumbling. Or falling from grace. Or leaving the paradise of Eden to face the uncertainty of life outside heaven. Women always 'fall', Mr Pepys. They descend from a lofty state to fall into the abyss that is love.'

'For a woman, Mrs Behn, you do have a most cynical turn of mind.'

'Not cynical, just realistic. Years of acquaintance with the male character has left me bruised and battered by its inability to accept me on my own terms.'

'A woman, independent?'

'Just so, Mr Pepys. A woman who does not 'fall' and certainly does not 'depend.'

'And one who does not love either?

‘I did not say that, Mr Pepys. I believe each moment of a happy love is worth an age of a dull and ordinary life. If life is it be lived, life is to be loved.’

‘A passionate speech, Mrs Behn.’

‘I am a passionate woman, Mr Pepys.’

‘I wish I had discovered the source of your passion much earlier.’

'Greenwich up ahead.' Balty interrupted their conversation by pointing at the town with a piece of bread in his hand.

'We need to head for the Swan. I arranged to meet Will there. I fear we are late.’

'Be careful, Mr Pepys. The Preacher may have sent word ahead.'

Pepys scanned the town. 'I suggest we approach from that direction.' He pointed to the London side of the river. 'If anything, they will expect us to come from Kent, not from London.'

'You are learning some tradecraft, Mr Pepys.'

'I was taught by a Master. Or should I say a Mistress?'

Chapter 50

He didn't know how long the feeling had been growing in him. He had walked into Greenwich Town, stopping just once to buy a few marlars from one of the hawkers that lined the street.

It was while he was giving the man his threepence that Will caught a movement out of the corner of his eye. He immediately turned his head but saw nothing unusual. A group of maids were shopping in the market. A paper seller was displaying his wares. An old man, back bent like a branch of hawthorn and head sticking forward, was creeping down the street with all the determination of a tortoise after a piece of lettuce.

He shook his head. You're nerves are getting the better of you.

'Whassat? More marlars?'

'No thank you, these two are enough.'

'Suits yourself. Best Marlars in Kent these are. Come off me dad's tree, they did. Can't beat a marlar when you've got a cough.'

Will edged away from the hawker down London Road. Maybe I should visit the church? A good long sermon will help pass the time. He could even have a nap if the vicar droned on too long. He remembered that Pepys occasionally visited St Alpheges, complimenting the fine quality of the sermons and the even finer quality of the female parishioners. But that was Sam, ever one for the ladies. Will could never understand why Pepys philandered so. If he had Elizabeth as a wife, well…

At the next corner, three narrow streets converged with an elegant church the centre, St. Alpheges. A long stream of male and females, old and not so old, were going through the doors. Will hurried after them, entering the cool white interior, lit by a few candles in plain iron holders. Will immediately approved. Here was a church after his own heart, plain without being austere, godly without being sanctimonious.

He took a seat at a pew in the middle, waiting for the service to start. On the white walls, three brass plaques commemorated notable worthies of the town who were buried in the church. Will noted with pleasure that one of the names was Thomas Tallis. He enjoyed the Lamentations when Sam and Elizabeth held their musical evenings in Seething Lane. If only life would return to those happier times, rather than running around London fearing for his life.

He read the memorial to the composer. The last lines intrigued him;

'As he dyd lyve, so also did he dy,
In myld and quyet sort (O happy man!)
To God ful oft for mercy did he cry,
Wherefore he lyves, let deth do what he can.'

Not a bad epitaph. One that would suit his own life and character too. The church was filling nicely now. Will glanced back towards the door. Two burly men were entering and taking off their hats. They stopped at the font and stared over the congregation. Will was sure that one of them nodded to the other when he spotted Will.

He was now sure he was being followed. What should he do? He sat facing forward, crouching lower in the pew. They had seen him. He was sure they had seen him.

The vicar was mounting the pulpit, ready to begin the service. The congregation naturally began to quieten. Will could hear the two men taking their seats at the back of the church.

The vicar stood at the pulpit resting his arms on the wooden stand. He opened his mouth and began to speak. A wonderfully sonorous drone that echoed like chamber music off the white-painted walls, soaring into the rafters. The text of his sermon was Proverbs but Will was not listening, conscious that the two men were sitting directly behind him. Could he look around?

The vicar was reciting a passage from the bible. 'A friend loveth at all times, and a brother is born for adversity,' the voice rising and lowering with the import of his words.

It was as if the sermon were made for him. He loved Sam, even though he was a difficult man to love. And he was certainly facing adversity. The two men behind him were evidence of that.

He dropped his hymnal on the floor, taking the opportunity to glance over his shoulder before he leant forward to pick it up.

The two men were still there. And they were staring straight at him.

Will crouched even lower in his pew, brushing against an old woman sitting next to him. He received a glare that could have sunk a thousand ships.

What was he going to do? The men were waiting at the back. There was no way he could escape from them.

The vicar continued to drone on, reading further from the excerpt from Proverbs, explaining the beauty of loyalty and brotherhood.

Will didn't hear the words and didn't care. He sat

there, beads of sweat running down his brow even though it was cool inside the stone larder of the church. Should he check again?

He turned around quickly, bumping once more into the woman sitting next to him.

'Sorry, sorry,' he said.

All he received in reply was a loud, 'Shush.'

The men were still there and they were still staring straight at him.

The Vicar seemed to be building towards a climax now. His voice was rising, the words soaring to the rafters.

And then there was silence, followed by that peculiar noise of people coughing, shuffling in their seats and coughing once more. Why did people always do that?

The vicar was descending from the pulpit, walking down the aisle towards the door. The woman next to him stood up, followed by the rest of the people in the row. They all began to file out towards the exit.

The service was over. He would be left alone with the two men in the church. His mind raced.

Will shoved past the old woman, stepping on her foot as he did so. 'Sorry, sorry,' he said over his shoulder.

He brushed past two rather pretty young women and stood in the aisle. The vicar was coming straight towards him.

'I was wondering, Reverend, what you meant when you spoke about non-trinitarianism in your speech.'

The vicar smiled. 'That's a fascinating theological point, young man, at the heart of all modern beliefs. But as you can see, I must say goodbye to my parishioners as they leave. Perhaps you would care to visit me in the rectory and we could discuss it then?'

The vicar carried on walking past Will towards the

door. The other parishioners were starting to leave the pews, following their vicar.

'Ah, but, if what you said is true, then surely, God is one being.' He ran after the vicar, knocking several young women out of the way. 'It strikes me that if one accepts that idea, then Jesus cannot be a God, too.'

That is indeed true, but Jesus is the son of God, and through him, accepts deity even though he is not a deity himself.'

Out of the corner of his eye, Will caught the two men standing on either side of the aisle. He nodded his head, encouraging the Vicar to continue.

'This really is an interesting theological debate. You must let me tell you about my ideas later in the rectory.'

Will put his arm around the Vicar's shoulders. 'I'm fascinated by the subject, Reverend. I wonder if Jesus accepts deity without being a deity himself, where does that leave Mary? Is she a deity, too?'

'Ah, there you are beginning to swim in the dangerous waters of Catholicism and its worship of the Virgin…'

They walked past the two burly men, Will holding the Vicar close to him. Both men continued to stare at him.

The vicar was talking as they walked to the door but Will couldn't hear what he was saying. They reached the exit and Will ran out into the street.

'Do come for tea, this evening.' The vicar shouted after him as Will turned right and headed down Stockwell Street. Where was he going to go? It was nearly six. Time to head towards the Swan. He hoped that Sam would be there waiting for him.

As he ran away, he heard a commotion from the church and the sound of hob-nailed boots on the street behind him.

He quickened his pace, banging into a barrow full

of apples being pushed into position by a hawker.

'You oughta watch where you is going, you does.'

'Sorry, sorry,' said Will, pushing the man out of the way. His barrow fell over to one side and apples tumbled out from it onto the hay strewn cobbles.

'Oi, what's the bloomin' rush fer?' shouted the man.

An apple flew past Will's head and smashed into the wall. He ran even faster, past more hawkers and their customers.

He heard shouts from behind him. 'Stop, stop.' He thought they were saying. But there was no likelihood of him stopping at that moment, the memory of the knife stuck deep inside his calf and the excruciating pain that followed was too fresh.

The shouts were getting nearer and louder now. The men were gaining on him. Will ran round a corner and crashed into a man selling brushes and brooms. Will felt a surge of pain though his left knee as he fell on top of the man.

He had to get up before they got here.

'Mr Hewer.'

Will looked up into the sharp mouse-like face of one of the men. He was joined on his right by the bigger, bulkier thug who was already panting from exertion. Will could see the muscles that lay beneath the bulk of the bigger man but, strangely, it was the little one who scared him more. The keen eyes beneath two caterpillars of eyebrows looked down on him.

'Mr Hewer, you have led us a merry chase.'

Will reached out with his hand and felt it close around the handle of one of the brooms. He grabbed it and stood up, swinging the end around in a wide arc. The little man ducked and the broom crashed into the skull of the bigger thug. Surprisingly, he collapsed to the ground like a sack of winter wheat.

Will raised the broom above his head, ready to bring it down once more.

'Will,' he heard a shout behind him, 'whatever are you doing, striking Mr Jones with a broom?'

Will turned slowly around. There was Sam and Balty astride horses behind him, next to a man he did not know.

'Mr Jones?'

'Mr Jones, from the docks in Deptford.'

'That's what I was trying to tell you, we're here to help,' said the sharp-nosed man.

A moan came from the brush seller as he regained consciousness, followed by another louder groan from the big man lying sprawled in the gutter.

'Help?'

'We was asked by Mistress Jane to keep a watch on you, case you got in trouble.'

'These men work for me in the dock at Deptford. Mr Jones is one of my best carpenters.'

'Thank you kindly, Mr Pepys sir, I does my best to be of service.'

The big man sat up, nursing his head.

'Deptford? Docks?' Will looked from Pepys to Mr Jones and down to the big man sitting on the cobbled street.

'This is Mr Beeble. I always uses him when there may be a bit of trouble.' Mr Jones pointed down to the big man who was now shaking his head vigorously, trying to force some sense into it. 'But given your agility with a broom, I might ask you next time, Mr Hewer.' A smile spread across Mr Jones' face.

'I am sorry, I hope he's not hurt too badly.'

'Don't worry about Mr Beeble, his head's thicker than the walls of the Tower.' Another groan came from the big man. 'Might have a bit of a sore head for a couple of days though.'

'Let us repair to the Swan, Will. We have much to talk about. It seems that you have a lot to tell me, and I have even more to tell you.'

Pepys turned his horse down the lane on the right, which Balty was already half way down. The sign of the Swan was just visible at the end.

'Stand up there, Mr Beeble. You need a few draughts of ale to clear your senses and maybe a poultice for that head.' Mr Jones helped the big man to his feet and staggered down the lane.

Will shook his own head, took one last look at the groaning Mr Beeble, and followed them both.

Chapter 51

Over a few bottles of wine, Will explained to Pepys what had happened in London.

'You were lucky to escape with a warning, Will.'

'A painful warning, Sam. I have a feeling it will be even more painful next time.'

'Hence, the unfortunate attack on poor Mr Beeble?'

On hearing his name, Mr Beeble raised his tankard from the next table. His head was bound in the best linen but it had not affected his ability to imbibe copious amounts of strong beer.

Will raised his mug in return, looking rather sheepish as he did so. 'It wasn't my best moment, Sam.'

'I rather think it was,' said Mrs Behn, with a twinkle in her eye.

'So, let me understand this correctly, after a little pressure from you, Ashmole identified the device we found in Jack's hand.'

'It was the Duke of Buckingham's crest.'

'And you say, you saw the same one on the back of the carriage?'

Will nodded.

'What do you think, Mrs Behn?'

'I don't know what to think, Mr Pepys. All the clues seem to point to him but…'

'But?'

'He's a drunkard, a liar, a thief and a libertine. All the attributes of a good politician. But a traitor too? It just doesn't make sense.'

Pepys squeezed his bottom lip between his index and forefingers. 'I'm with you, Madam. It all seems too neat, too packaged. As if someone were saying, 'Here is the thief. Here is the traitor. Can't you see it?'

'Exactly, Mr Pepys. I am glad we are of the same mind.'

'But...but...it's not the Duke of Buckingham?'

'It may well be, Will, but what's his motive?'

'Power? Money?'

'Not him? He's not interested in power and he has far too much money as it is. No, our Buckingham is motivated by just one thing, Will.'

'And that is?'

'His own pleasure. Whether it be in the company of women, the fools of the court or the misfortunes of others.' Once again, the fingers squeezed Pepys' bottom lip. 'There is a far more devious mind at work here, not the addled wits of a devout libertine.'

'Do you know who it is?'

'I have an idea. Let me see the letter again Mrs Behn, if you would be so kind.'

She produced the letter that she had stolen from the Preacher. At the top lay Buckingham's crest and, on the bottom, his florid signature. Pepys brought the paper up close to his face and examined it carefully. 'Yes, I am beginning to get some idea who is behind this. The cleverest men sometimes make the most obvious errors. Perhaps, their intelligence blinds them to what has been staring them in the face.'

'You are talking of our thief and murderer?'

'No, Mrs Behn, I am talking of myself.'

'What are we going to do?'

'We must get into London and meet with Dryden once more.'

'And Balty?'

The large man lifted his head from a plate of pie at the

sound of his name.

‘Staying here. He’s had enough adventure for this week.’

‘Food’s good,’ said Balty, through a mouthful of pie, ‘ale’s even better. Can’t beat good ale for healing gunshot wounds. Well known fact that.’

‘How are we going to get to London? The place is surrounded by soldiers intent on keeping us out.’

‘Mr Behn has a plan, Will. One which I think you will heartily approve.’

Chapter 52

'Is this really necessary? I don't like it all.'

'Are you complaining about the colour or the fit?'

Will adjusted his bodice once more, trying to stop it digging into his chest. 'All of it. I don't like it.'

He was wearing a maid's costume Mrs Behn had borrowed from one of the girls at the Inn. Under a blue bodice he wore a cream woollen shirt with matching cream dress. The whole costume was rounded off by a fetching baby blue bonnet that was tied tightly under his freshly shaven jaw.

'It's too tight.'

'I think you look rather fetching, Will, in a strange sort of way.'

'Sam, please don't joke at a time like this.'

They were on the road to London, aboard a small cart filled to the brim with turnips, taking the roundabout route to enter the city through London Bridge. Pepys was holding the reins and gentling coaxing their pony to keep moving.

'I assure you, Will, this is no laughing matter.'

'I'm dressed as a maid, and you look like some country farmer's wife. We'll be a laughing stock when people see us in London.'

'But at least we will be in London, Will. Once there, we can change our clothes and vanish into the maw of the city.' Pepys tugged at his blue pinafore. 'I rather like this. The pocket in the front is useful, and the skirt is certainly more airy than a pair of tight breeches.'

Will shook his head and sighed. 'Did you really have to wear make-up, too?'

'I think it suits me. The combination of arsenic and talcum makes my skin look very pale. And I do like the wigs Mrs Behn found for us. So much more comfortable than my periwig.'

'Where is Mrs Behn?'

'She's gone ahead and will wait for us over London Bridge.'

'Do you trust her?'

Pepys thought for a moment. 'I did wonder for a while back in Chatham, but there is nobody else we can trust. Later today, I need to present my findings to the King and the council. After that, I will be either a hero or in the Tower.'

'If we survive that long…'

'All we have to do is get into London, Will. Once there, I have to question one man and I will be sure.'

'Who's that?'

'Dryden. Somebody paid him to write those verses about me.'

'He wouldn't tell me.'

'I went to University with him, Will. I think he will talk to me. And don't forget, I do have this.' Pepys produced the King's warrant from the pocket of his pinafore.

'Good luck to you.'

'Good luck to us, Will. And it looks like we will need it now.'

Up ahead, a company of soldiers was guarding the entrance to London Bridge, stopping and searching every cart that was crossing over the Thames.

'Let me do the talking, Will.'

'Don't worry, I won't say a word.'

The cart in front of them stopped. A farmer jumped

down and peeled off the cloth covering his goods. A load of hops, redolent of summer meadows.

Will started coughing immediately, attracting the attention of one of the soldiers. He looked them up and down, and sauntered over, his helmet and breast plate gleaming against the deep scarlet of his shirt.

'Good morning, Madam, visiting London, are we?'

'Just bringing' our wurzels up to market.' Pepys replied in the high falsetto with a touch of country burr that he had been practising all last night with the help of Mrs Behn.

Another soldier joined them on the opposite side. 'Come here often do you?'

Pepys affected modesty and fluttered his eyes. 'London. London, baint be a good place for a God fearing mistress like me.'

The first soldier put his hand on Will's leg. 'And what about you? Is London a good place for you?'

Pepys' voice went up higher. 'My maid, Wilhelmina, was struck dumb years ago but she be God fearing too.'

The soldier on Pepys side shouted across to his mate. ' Sounds like the perfect woman, Robert. Can't nag but can wash and clean.'

'Aye, she does that.' The first soldier moved his hand higher. 'Good and healthy. Bet you could give man a real struggle in bed.'

Pepys could see that Will was about to kick the grinning soldier in the face. 'I wouldn't do that if I were you.'

The soldier moved his hand up to Will's thigh. 'Why not? Looks like she's enjoying it?'

'Well, she would, wouldn't she?'

'Why's that?'

'None of the men in the village will go anywhere near her. She got Turkish Delight, ain't she?'

'Turkish Delight?'

'Caught it off one of them foreigners, didn't she? Last man that lain with her, well it don't bear telling what happened to him.'

'What happened?' asked the bearded soldier closest to Pepys.

He gestured for the man to come closer and bent down to whisper in his ear. 'Dropped off after five days, didn't it? Nobody will go near her after that. Well, no man wants his thing falling off in the middle of the street, do they?'

The soldiers both stepped back from the cart. The bearded man began to laugh. 'What a load of codswallop. Heard better stories on me old ma's knee. Search them and the cart,' he shouted.

'Hold there!' An officer stepped forward, out of the shadows beneath the arches.

His men immediately stopped clambering on board the cart.

He checked a sheet of paper in his hand. Looking from it to Pepys and Will. 'These aren't the ones we're looking for.' He waved the cart forward with a sharp, 'Get a move on, don't hang about here.'

Pepys clicked the pony forward onto the crowded thoroughfare in the middle of the bridge.

'Turkish Delight?' whispered Will between gritted teeth.

'Just keep smiling.'

On either side, the soldiers stepped back quickly as the cart passed them and edged its way through the crowds.

'We're home again, Will. I don't think I've ever been more pleased to see the noise, dirt, shit and smoke of the city. Breathe it all in and smell the beauty of London.'

Will did as he was told and immediately began to cough.

'Now, we must find Mrs Behn, go home, talk with Dryden, and report to the King at noon.'

'Is that all?'

'Ah, there is Mrs Behn.' Pepys pulled the reins to the side of the road where Mrs Behn sat upon her horse.

'No problems crossing the bridge, ladies?'

'None. Except for Will's extraordinary ability to attract soldiers.'

'I can understand. He does have a rather comely shape in a dress. Variety is the soul of pleasure.'

Will pulled at his bodice. 'Can I take this off now.'

'Not quite yet, Will, we need to make sure we are not followed. Home first, I think, to change into something more fitting.'

Mrs Behn looked at Will sitting next to Pepys at the head of the cart. 'I don't think we'll find clothes more fitting than the ones you are wearing, Mr Hewer. You make a damn fine woman, even if I do say so myself.'

Chapter 53

'Samuel Pepys, what is going on?' Elizabeth stood in the hallway of Seething Street, her hands on her hips. Jane came out from the kitchen and gave a small screech of delight.

'No time to explain now, Elizabeth.' Pepys tried to brush past her to climb the stairs.

All five feet of her stood its ground. 'Is that you, Will? You're wearing a skirt? And rouge?

Will reached up and began to frantically rub away the red powder on his cheeks.

Jane touched the fabric of his skirt. 'Good material, could last a girl a long while this 'un. Can I have it when you've finished with it, Mr Hewer?'

'I...well...it's only...' Will mumbled his reply to the carpet on the floor.

Pepys tried once more to edge around his wife. She stood her ground, arms firmly placed across the banister.

'Well, Samuel Pepys. You owe me an explanation.'

'It was the only way we could enter the city safely.' Mrs Behn stepped into the hallway and took off her hat, bowing like a man from the waist.

'And you are, sir?'

'This is Mrs Behn, dear.'

'Mrs Behn? Has the world turned upside down? My husband and his best friend are dressed as women. And I've just been introduced to a man called Mrs Behn. Samuel Pepys, what is going on?'

Another high pitched squeal erupted from Jane. Elizabeth stared at her with eyes as hot as pokers. 'Don't you have work to do, Jane?'

'Beggin' your pardon, ma'am. I'd like to know too.'

'It's a long story, dear.'

'I have plenty of time.'

'Unfortunately, we don't. I promise I will explain everything this evening, Elizabeth.'

She turned to face Will and here voice softened. 'Please tell me what is going on, Will.'

Will attempted to brush past her and go upstairs. Once again, she refused to move.

'Elizabeth, we are to see the King in three hours. If we do not resolve our business before that meeting, it is probable both myself and your husband will spend this evening in the Tower.'

Her body softened, the small shoulders slumped forward and the arm dropped from its sentry post guarding the stairs. 'Promise me one thing, Will.'

'Anything, Elizabeth.'

'This has nothing to do with that wanton, Deborah Willetts?'

Will glanced across at Pepys who had already began to climb the stairs. 'I promise it has nothing to do with her, Elizabeth.'

There was a loud creak as Pepys stepped on the third stair from the top.

Elizabeth whirled round, 'Samuel Pepys, if you don't explain everything to me this evening, I will leave you. Is that clear?'

'Yes, my dear. I promise everything will be explained on my return.' He nodded once and began to climb again.

'And where is my locket? The one Will gave to me?'

'It's still being polished, Elizabeth. I will pick it up after my meeting with his Majesty.' He turned to Will. 'I'm afraid it's time to stop being a woman, much as you enjoyed the experience. If you would be so kind as to wait for us, Mrs Behn, we will endeavour to become real men again.'

'I have no hesitation in waiting, Mr Pepys. Waiting for a real man is something women do all their lives.'

There was another high pitched squeak from the maid.

'Fetch Mrs Behn some tea, Jane. I don't suppose you want to change too, Mrs Behn?'

'No madam, I'm quite comfortable as I am.'

'Why does that not surprise me?'

*

'These are a little too big.' Will pulled up the sleeves of the brown suit, but they immediately fell down over his wrists to hang loose, covering his hands.

'It's my fourth best suit, Will, have a care with it.'

'Fourth best? I suppose I should be honoured.'

'If we come out of this with our skins intact, I promise you will have a new suit from my own tailor in the New Exchange.'

Will held up two fingers. 'Two suits. You still have to replace the one that was damaged on Jack Turner's roof.'

'Two it is, Will, but now to business. I see the house is being watched again. No doubt they already know that we are inside.

'How will we get out without being seen, Mr Pepys?'

'We won't, Mrs Behn. I want them to know exactly where we are and what we are doing.'

'Why, sir?'

'It's time we brought everything out into the open. All the players need to be on the stage now. Nobody should be left hiding in the wings.'

'Where to now?' said Will, once more pulling up the sleeves of his suit.

'I think we will visit Mr Dryden at his coffee shop. He should have taken his seat by now.'

'Do we have time, Mr Pepys? Your report to the King is due at noon.'

'He who would search for pearls must dive below.'

'I hope this doesn't end like one of Dryden's plays.'

'And how is that, Mr Hewer?'

'With everybody lying dead and Nell Gwynn speaking a funny monologue over our bodies.'

Pepys opened the door of Seething Lane and stepped out. Immediately a Hackney cab pulled up in front of them. 'I took the trouble of asking Mr Foster to transport us around town. I thought it would save time.'

'Good mornin', gents. I suppose I can't interest you in goin' to see an hangin' at Tyburn. It's a triple bill today. A murderer and two sheep thieves.'

'I suppose your brother has saved us ringside seats?'

'No, I'm afraid not, Mr Hewer. He doesn't have the franchise for Tyburn. My cousin has though. He always has the best seats in the house does cousin Harry.'

'I'm afraid the hanging will have to wait for another day, Mr Foster. Take us to the Rose in Covent Garden.'

'Rights you are, Mr Pepys. We can goes to the hangin' later. They won't even have finished puttin' up the scaffold yet. Always a bit slow at Tyburn. Lazy sods, they be. Giddy up there Horace, or else I'll sell pots of you to the booksellers.' He jerked the reins across the horse's back, and the coach surged forward.

Three men put down their drinks at the Inn opposite and immediately began to run after the coach, slipping in the mud and slime of the street.

Chapter 54

'Good morning, Dryden, it gives me pleasure to see you again.'

The playwright jumped at the sound of Pepys' voice, spitting out his hot coffee across the latest issue of the London Register.

Pepys took a napkin and wiped the liquid from the front page of the paper, staining it like old parchment. 'I see Rochester has been up to his old tricks again,' he said, squinting down at one of the columns. 'How tiresome. Won't you ask myself and my companions to join you?' He indicated Will and Mrs Behn standing beside him.

'Good morning to you, Mr Hewer and Mr…?'

'May I introduce Mrs Behn?'

'You dress rather sharply for a woman, Mrs Behn.'

She tapped the sword that hung from her waist. 'I do like to make a point of impressing people, Mr Dryden.'

'It seems your tongue is sharper than your clothes or your sword, Mrs Behn, but won't you join me anyway?'

He indicated a seat next to him at the table. Mrs Behn sat down, joined by Pepys and Will.

'Now, how can I help you? I'm afraid I don't have much time. The small matter of a successful play, don't you know.'

'I will come straight to the point, Dryden. Who asked you to write the words that Nell Gwynn spoke to me from the stage?'

'That is direct, Pepys. I remember even at Cambridge you were a terribly direct young man.'

'And I remember that you were a terrible failure. Couldn't even pass the tripos.'

'The academic life wasn't for me. Too many wrens soaring on the backs of eagles. That's rather good. I must use that again.'

Pepys brought his fist down onto the table, causing the cups and cutlery to rattle and jump. The other guests on the balcony all stopped what they were doing and turned to stare at their table.

'A disagreement about the stage. Happens all the time,' said Will to nobody in particular.

'Who asked you to write the words?'

'Nobody asked me to write them. They emerge from here and from here,' he tapped his head followed by his heart, 'as a butterfly emerges from imprisonment in its shell.'

'Then why did Nell speak a different speech on the night following? And why did she stare straight at me?'

Dryden smiled to himself. 'Perhaps, she was enamoured of you, Pepys. You may be invited to join her and the King in their chamber. It is rumoured that he enjoys sharing his affections.'

'You haven't answered my question. Why did Nell speak two different speeches on two separate evenings?'

'A poet and playwright often changes his mind from one minute to the next. An evening is a long time in literature.'

Pepys sat back in his chair. He gripped his bottom lip between his thumb and index finger, squeezed and let them stroke his chin. 'Let me tell you something about Mr Dryden, a man who changes his opinions as often as a tailor changes his thread. I remember a young man fresh from Cambridge who was employed by Cromwell's head of spies, John Thurloe. Heaven knows what he did, but nothing good ever came from Thurloe's office. So enamoured of the Lord Protector was our good friend, Dryden, he even wrote a eulogy to the man on his death, titling it *Heroic Stanzas*. Yet two years later, our Mr Dryden had the gall to publish *Astrae Redux*, a poem lauding the return of his Majesty to England, followed soon after by *To His Sacred Majesty: A Panegyric on his Coronation*. Did the world ever see such a turncoat?

'A man cuts his coat according to the cloth.'

'But there is more that people do not know, isn't there, Dryden?'

Beads of sweat appeared on Dryden's brow. 'I don't know what you mean, Pepys.'

'I remember a young Puritan at Trinity who was in such thrall to his tutor, Thomas Hill, he would do anything to please him.'

'I have come a long way since those days.'

'The higher one climbs, the further one has to fall.'

Dryden lifted up his coffee cup, staring at Pepys over the rim. 'Am I to fall from grace then, like the Archangel Gabriel?'

'I always find it amusing when you compare yourself to an angel, Dryden. But your fall will be much more prosaic, I believe. More like Icarus whose wings melted in the power of the Sun.'

'And which Sun will melt my wings? You, Pepys? I think not.' Dryden took another sip of coffee and smiled.

Pepys reached into his pocket and produced a sheaf of paper which he unfolded and placed in front of Dryden. 'You might want to read this.'

Dryden glanced down at the paper, quickly scanning the words written there and recognising the florid signature of the King at the end. He snorted, 'This is a letter empowering you to investigate the affairs at Chatham dockyard. Nothing to do with me, Pepys.'

'You haven't read the paper correctly, Dryden. As in Cambridge, you haven't the patience to actually read and understand. Your knowledge is superficial.'

Dryden looked at the paper again. 'It's still just a warrant empowering you to investigate Chatham and report back to the king on what you find there.'

Pepys smiled. 'Good, you finally read it accurately. Will, when do we meet the King?'

'In one hour and 53 minutes if the clock on the wall over there is any guide.'

'Thank you.' Again, Pepys pinched his bottom lip. 'When I meet him and make my report, I will be extremely distressed to point out the involvement of the King's subjects in treasonable activity against his Majesty.'

'What's that got to do with me?'

'One of those subjects will be the poet laureate.'

For the second time that morning, Dryden spat out his coffee. 'Me..? I…you can't..'

'After they imprison you in the Tower and investigate for two or three months, you may be found not guilty and return to normal life as Milord Coventry has just done. But…'

'But what?'

Pepys smiled. 'One can never underestimate the caprices of Monarchs. One just has to look at the revenge the King meted out on the dead body of the Lord Protector to see that one should not trifle with him.'

Will held up the London Register. 'I read the King often attends the questioning of suspects. Apparently, he is well versed in the use of the Rack and the Judas Chair. Not to mention the Pear of Anguish.'

'Thank you, Will, we mustn't forget the pain of that particular iron fruit.'

Dryden's body sagged as if all the air had been let out of it like a pig's bladder. He stared down at his coffee cup, his shoulders sagged and he spoke in a whisper. 'You don't know who you're dealing with, Pepys. If I tell you, it could cost me my life.'

Mrs Behn placed her hand on the knife in her belt, pulling out an inch to show the shine of the blade. 'If you don't tell him, it *will* cost you your life. You could become the second Kit Marlowe.'

Instinctively, Dryden's hand went to his eye.

'I'm sure Dryden could become a much better writer than Marlowe,' said Pepys.

'That would be true, Mr Pepys, if he managed to live longer and drink more coffee.'

Dryden held up his hands. 'I'll tell you, I'll tell you, just spare my eyes. A poet without eyes may as well spend his life in the graveyard.'

'And write on tombstones.' said Pepys, raising his arm to wave at the waiter.

The man rushed across with a new pot of coffee.

'And bring us a plate of your French pastries, Mr Dryden is feeling peckish. Talking does that to a body.'

'Certainly, sir. Anything else?'

'A dish of sweetmeats for me,' said Will.

'Of course, sir.' He left the jug on the table.

Pepys picked it up, pouring coffee for himself, Mrs Behn and Will. 'Now, Dryden, I believe you had a story you were going to tell us.'

Dryden adjusted his orange wig, taking his time. Mrs Behn's hand went to the hilt of her knife.

‘I didn’t know who was behind the speech.’

Pepys’ fist crashed to the table once again. Dryden jumped. The hubbub in the cafe continued on as if nothing had happened.

Dryden lowered his head and whispered. ‘I’m telling the truth, on my honour as the Poet Laureate.’

‘You lost your honour a long time ago, Mr Dryden, but there is still time to re-discover your honesty,’ said Mrs Behn.

Dryden took a deep breath. Pepys took another sip of coffee.

‘I was visited by a one-legged man, he gave me the words and made it plain that they were to be spoken by Nell that evening.’

‘Anybody can come in to give you words for your play? I should give you some myself.’ Pepys stared at Dryden.

‘He made it plain the fortune of my family was dependent upon my acquiescence.’

‘And how did he make it plain?’

‘He stabbed me in the leg with a knife.’ Dryden rolled up his stockings to reveal a small wound on the calf that was in the process of healing. ‘He said the next blow would fall on my manhood.’

Mrs Behn laughed. ‘I doubt he would be able to find it.’

Pepys touched her gently on the arm. She stopped speaking. ‘And what else did he give you?’

Dryden’s head went down. ‘Ten pounds. A poet’s life is a perilous one and writing is not as lucrative as people think.’

‘It’s still a handsome sum for just a few words. What did he tell you to do?’

‘He said Nell was to say these words to you, Pepys,

instead of her usual soliloquy.'

'He mentioned me by name?'

'Yes. I arranged for you to sit in the sixth row so poor Nell would know where to look. She's a clever girl but not terribly bright, if you know what I mean.'

'Indeed, I do, Dryden.' Pepys pinched his lower lip between his fingers. 'And this man, what did he look like?'

'Not so tall, about your height.' He pointed at Will. 'One-legged but with a boot covering his wooden leg. His stump made a peculiar sound as it thumped across my rooms. A sound I will never forget as long as I live.' He stared into mid-air for a moment, 'could be an excellent theatrical device.'

Pepys shook his head. 'What did he look like?'

'Dressed in black from head to toe. Old-fashioned clothes, the sort ex-soldiers wear. Grey hair. A voice that had a twinge of Oxford in the voice. The county, not the University.

'Oxford, you say. That's interesting.'

'A self-educated voice, I would say, but one that still betrayed its roots in the 'o' and the 'u' sounds.'

'You said you didn't know who was behind the speech. Which suggests to me that you weren't aware then, but you do know now.'

Once again, Dryden's shoulders sagged. 'I had the man followed. He went to a tavern, The Bell on the Strand. A man was waiting for him there.'

'Who was waiting?' Will had leaned forward and stuck his face close to Dryden.

Dryden lent across to Pepys and whispered in his ear. 'Buckingham.'

'Another lie, Dryden, even now you tell me lies?'

Dryden jerked back as if struck across the face, 'I…I…'

'It makes no odds. I think I already know who was waiting in the Tavern. It all makes sense now.'

Will tapped his fingers on the table. 'Are you going to let us in on the secret too?'

'Not yet, Will. Not yet. We have a few things we must do first.'

'And they are?'

'I must write a letter. And we must visit this tavern.'

'That's it? You're not going to do anything to me?' I will not be part of your report to the King?' said Dryden.

'Not today. You have done enough to yourself. Words should never be bought or sold, Dryden, just enjoyed, appreciated and worshipped,' said Pepys.

'Easy for you to say. You don't have to make your living from them.'

'We need to leave now if we are to meet the King at noon. He will be late, but that is a King's prerogative. Mrs Behn, I need to trouble you to take a letter to someone immediately.'

'I'm at your service, Mr Pepys.'

'I would that to be true.'

'For a letter it is. May I have it?'

'What?'

'The letter.'

'I'll write it now. Landlord!' Pepys waved his hand in the air. A bald-headed man with a harried look on his face rushed over.

'Yes, sir, Mr Pepys.'

'Paper and ink, if you please.'

'Mr Dryden is going to be doing more of his writing, is he?'

'No, it's my turn. The stage is set and now I must assemble the players.'

‘That’s a shame. I like Mr Dryden’s plays. Proper English they is. None of your foreign muck. English as, as English is.’

‘So they spoke English in ancient Rome, did they?’ asked Will.

‘Well, I wouldn’t know nothing about them Romans, being as I was born in Wappin’ and am a Landlord of this here establishment. But, I know this, you can’t beat a good bit of English to stir the heart. Even if it is spoken by one of them Roman foreigners.’

‘Thank you, Mr Unwin, the pen and ink?’

‘Coming right up, sir. Any more coffee to help you with the words?’

‘Another pot would serve, Mr Unwin. And another plate of your French pastries, I seem to have finished these.’

‘Helps with the words they does. A bit of French pastry adds sweetness to the tongue and the brain my mother used to say.’ Another waiter approached. ‘Here is your pen and ink, Mr Pepys. Write something nice will you. Something like that Marlowe chap. He was good, he was, until they took his eye out at an Inn.’

Dryden flinched once again.

‘What do you expect if a writer visits an Inn? Shouldn’t be allowed. I’ll get you the coffee and the pastries.’ He bowed and edged away, continuing to tut and shake his head as he dodged between the crowded tables.

Pepys had already finished writing his note and sealed the letter by the time the Landlord returned.

‘Finished already, Mr Pepys? That was a short play.’

He handed the letter to Mrs Behn and stood up. ‘Will, you must come with me to meet the King.’

Will hoisted up the sleeves of his coat. ‘I’m not dressed

for it.'

'Nobody will notice,' Pepys said over his shoulder as he was leaving the coffee shop, 'they only see themselves at court. But first, we must go to the Bell Inn. I think we should see if our one-legged man is there.'

Chapter 55

Pepys and Will left the Rose through the door on Russell Street. As soon as they did so, two burly men stepped out from an alley on the left, followed by two more from the right. In their hands, Pepys could see the gleam of blades reflected in the morning smog.

Mrs Behn came up behind him. 'What's going on, Pepys?'

He heard a slow handclap from in front of him. The one-legged man came out from the shadows and limped slowly towards them. 'Good morning, Mr Pepys and Mr Hewer.' He made a lavish bow, his wooden leg and its leather boot sticking out stiffly in front of him. 'It is good to make your acquaintance again, Mr Hewer. Alas, the circumstances could be happier.'

Pepys looked across at Will. 'It seems we will be spared the trip to the Bell. Our quarry has come to us.'

'I see you have another companion. The other young gentlemen is…?'

Pepys glanced down at the thugs. They had formed a line on the street in front of the entrance, blocking his escape. The street itself was empty. The usual hustle and bustle of London replaced by an eerie quiet as if the plague had suddenly struck. Behind him he heard the slam of the coffee shop's door and the metallic sound of locks being slid into place.

'My name is Aphra Behn. Mrs Aphra Behn'

The one-legged man laughed. 'I'm delighted to make your acquaintance Mrs Behn. I must say I approve of your attire. Leather suits you. I have no quarrel with you, madam. If you would like to leave now, my men will not stop you.'

'If it's all the same to you, sir, I prefer to stay with my friends.' She pulled her sword from its scabbard and tossed her knife to Will.

'That is your choice, Madam. We all must choose our path in life.'

Pepys noticed the pronunciation of 'choose' and 'life'. Dryden was correct, the man was from Oxford. 'I see you have blocked mine, sir. I didn't catch your name?'

'That's because I didn't give it, sir. But you may call me Mr Blake. As for you, Mr Hewer, I did warn you not to go bothering Mr Dryden. You were given fair warning.'

Pepys lifted his head. 'Dryden told us everything. He had followed back to the tavern and saw who you met. He told us who your master is.'

'I thought he would. Did he believe I was so stupid I wouldn't notice? I've been playing this role for a long time.'

'Since Naseby, I would guess.'

The man whistled. 'You know me well, Mr Pepys. Since Naseby, it is true. So you also know who my Master is?'

Pepys looked at the thugs in front of him. They were shifting their weight from one foot to the other, impatiently waiting for the order from their leader.

'I do know, sir. And I must say, at first it surprised me, but the more I thought on it, the more it made sense. I presume he has my diary too.'

'That he has, Mr Pepys. Well hidden it is.'

'He's read all its secrets?'

'Pretty reading they made too, Mr Pepys. He particularly liked the lines about the King.'

'I thought he would.'

'Thinking is bad for a body, Mr Pepys. Knowledge is even worse. It can lead to accidents. Unfortunate accidents, like what happened to poor Jack Turner. He knew too much as well. Had an accident with a knife. Cut his throat. But what am I telling you for, you already know.'

Before Pepys could answer, there was a loud scream from the left. A blur of dark brown and two of the thugs in front of Pepys vanished beneath a scythe of legs and spinning wheels. The two others jumped to their right to avoid the coach as it careered down the street, Mr Foster standing up from his seat, reins in hand.

He pulled back hard and the horses slid to a stop, bringing up a cloud of dust and filth.

'Thought you might need an 'and, gentlemen. Or one of these.' He tossed a cudgel to Pepys.

'Thank you, Mr Foster, I was hoping you would arrive.'

'Saw 'em waiting for somebody and guessed it was for you and Mr Hewer.'

'I thank you once again.'

The two thugs had picked themselves of the ground and now were advancing on Pepys. Mrs Behn knocked him out of the way, rushed down the stairs and lunged with her sword, piercing the first thug through the heart.

The man was surprised by the speed of the attack. He slowly looked down at the metal sticking out of his doublet. The knife dropped from his hand. He reached up to pull the sword from his body, grasping the blade with both hands, before his eyes closed and his body collapsed forwards.

Mr Foster jumped down from his coach, a stout cudgel studded with iron nails in his hand. The second man looked at the cudgel, and at Mrs Behn coming towards him from the other side, threw the knife into the gutter and turned on his heels, running down to the Strand..

'Remind me never to cross you, Mrs Behn.' said Pepys

'I'm surprised you need a reminder, Mr Pepys. I thought you would remember our encounter on the yacht.' She went back to the thug and pulled out her sword from his chest. 'I do hope he hasn't bent it. A good sword is hard to find these days.'

A dog barked at the end of the street. They saw the black tail of a cloak as it vanished into an alley at the end of Bow Street.

'He's mine.' Will let out a scream and chased after the fleeing man.

People began to appear out of nowhere, standing in their doorways and staring at the three bodies that now lay in the street. From the balcony above their heads, a spontaneous round of applause erupted with shouts of 'Well done, that man.'

Pepys took a deep bow, milking the applause for all it was worth.

He was tapped on the shoulder by Mrs Behn. 'I believe your friend may require some assistance.'

Will was just disappearing around the corner. 'I believe you are correct, Mrs Behn. Please deliver the letter to this address as quickly as you can.'

'You don't require my assistance?'

'I think we will be able to manage quite well, thank you. The letter is more important.'

'Good luck, Mr Pepys.'

'Luck has nothing to do with it, Madame. Let's go after him, Mr Foster, I fear Will may do himself more damage than he does that man.'

'It'll be my pleasure, Mr Pepys,' he threw the cudgel

into the bottom of the cab and jumped up to grab the reins. 'The one thing I enjoy more than a good hangin' is a good scrap. I likes the feel of a cudgel hittin' an 'ead. That's a proper sound, that is.'

He lashed the reins down on the horse's back and the hackney jerked forward, throwing Pepys back into the horsehair seat.

'Have a care, Mr Foster, I would prefer to arrive alive.'

'Hold on tight, Mr Pepys. Hoss, do your business.'

The hackney jerked forward once more, picking up speed as it raced down the street, swinging around the narrow corner with Pepys hanging onto the leather strap with all his strength.

'There's Mr Hewer,' shouted the cabby, 'race on hoss.'

Pepys heard the loud rattle of the wheels on the cobble stones and the beat of the horse's hooves as the carriage picked up even more speed down Russell Street.

Mr Blake was the one person who knew where the diary was hidden. He mustn't be allowed to escape again.

Chapter 56

Will felt a sharp pain in his leg as he raced after Blake. A slick of blood stained his stockings at the top of the calf. The wound had re-opened.

Perhaps this wasn't such a good idea after all.

He slowed as he turned the corner onto Drury Lane. He wasn't going to fall for the same trick again. Being felled by a wooden leg once was bad enough.

Drury Lane was lined with hawkers selling their goods. Where was Blake? Will looked to the left.

No sign of him.

He looked to his left, down towards the Strand.

There he was, just limping past the man with the hung geese. Not far ahead now.

Mustn't let him get away.

The man was moving quickly for a cripple, his stiff leg swinging him forward in a hop and a skip. Will raced down the street, bumping into a startled vicar and his maid.

'Sorry, you honour.'

'Young people today, no sense of propriety,' the vicar shouted at the back of the rapidly disappearing Will.

Blake limped on in his peculiar gait, turning the bend into Wych Street, avoiding the shoppers and merchants that crowded the corner.

Will was gaining on him, slowly but surely he was getting closer. His breath was flowing evenly, the pain in his leg forgotten. All he saw was the black cloak of the man as it weaved between the stalls.

For a one legged man, he moves well, thought Will, the stiff legged gait almost as fast as me with my two legs.

Blake was opposite the New Inn now. For a moment,

Will lost sight of him in the crowds that surrounded the front of the tavern.

Where was he? Had he gone into the Inn? Or was he still running?

Will stepped onto a mounting stone at the side of the street. He was above the crowd now, staring across a sea of faces.

There was a flash of black against the white of an ink stall, the sheaves of parchment and paper twisting slowly in the breeze. It was him. Still ahead. Still running.

Will jumped down from the mounting stone and a sharp lance of pain shot up through his calf.

Got to keep going.

Mustn't let him get away.

Will limped after him, elbowing his way through the crowd of drinkers that flowed out into the street.

Mustn't let him get away.

The man was running past St Clements and into Butchers Row. He was moving much slower now. Will could see that his leg was dragging, no longer pushing him forward as it had before.

The bells of St Clements rang above his head. What time was it? Already eleven? Pepys would be late for his meeting with the King.

The words of Lord Arlington formed in his head. 'The late Mr Pepys'. Can't let that happen.

The man's black cloak was rushing through the meat stalls on either side of Butcher's Row. Hanging sides of beef, dead rabbits, pig's heads and long ropes of entrails formed the backdrop to the man's flowing cloak.

Will slipped on a slick of pig's blood. His legs went from under him and he was thrown onto his backside. The man wasn't far ahead, just merging with the rush of people in the Strand.

Can't lose him now. Not now.

Will picked himself up and ran after the man. He could catch him here. The man was slowing, fighting his way through the crowds that jostled their way under Temple Bar.

This was his chance. One final effort.

His feet raced over the cobbles and shit of the Strand. The man was under Temple Bar now, a flock of sheep forcing him to one side, pushed against the wall. His hands were on his knees, his chest sucking in air in huge gasps.

Will had him now. He looked into the man's eyes and saw exhaustion.

'Give yourself up. Nowhere to run now.' He shouted over the backs of the flock.

The man smiled.

Just then, the shepherd beat the backside of a ram and it reared up, pushing the rest of the herd forward.

The man's path was free. He began to run again, his wooden leg still dragging being him.

Will tried to move forward but his legs were encased in wool. A plaintive baaing echoed off the painted ceiling of Temple Bar.

Will edged his way through the flock, feeling the rough wool and warm bodies, stepping on cloven hooves and hearing screaming baas of complaint.

Then he was through. Free to run. Free to catch the man.

Blake was only thirty yards ahead now, moving slowly, the dead wooden leg dragging like an anchor.

He had him.

Will slowed to a walk. 'You can't get away. Not this time.' he shouted.

A few people turned to the raised voice, wondering

what was happening. Most minded their own business.

But Blake kept moving forward, dragging his wooden leg behind him.

Will looked to where he was heading. A Hackney, waiting beside the road, at the end of Chancery Lane.

Will began to run forward. But the man was already opening the door of the carriage and hopping in.

Will shouted. 'Stop. Stop.'

But the cabby either didn't hear or simply ignored him, happy to have found a customer after waiting for an hour.

Will ran as hard as he could, reaching out to grab the back of the cab. He felt the rough wood of the back panel. A leather strap was dangling down. If he could only grab that and heave himself up.

The cab was picking up speed, the wheels rattling loudly either side of his body.

He reached up and touched the leather. The end of his fingers were so close. Just reach a little more.

The cab hit a bump and the leather strap jumped out from his fingers. Will stumbled forward, the momentum of his legs taking him into a full length dive into the road.

He looked up.

Blake was leaning out of the window, smiling. As the cab pulled away, he put the two fingers of his right hand against his forehead.

An ironic salute or a wave goodbye?

Will watched as the cab moved further down the Strand and on to Fleet Street.

He had let Pepys down again. The man had escaped, taking with him any chance they had of proving who was behind the murder and the theft of the diary. Will buried his head in his hands. How could he have been so stupid?

'Are you going to be sitting there for a long time, Will? Because if you are, I'll arrange for some refreshments to be sent to you from the Angel.'

Pepys was leaning out of a cab, his head towering over Will.

'Have an hurry, if you please, Mr Hewer, we needs to catch up wiv the 'ackney.'

Will saw the even higher face of Mr Foster looking down on him.

'Please do as Mr Foster says, Will. I don't want Blake to escape yet again.'

Will stood up, dusted down his stockings, removing a dark lump of sheep shit that had become stuck to his ankle, and stepped up into the cab.

Pepys clapped him on the back. 'Well done, my little dandycock.' As he spoke, Pepys stopped for a moment and stared in to mid-air.

'He won't escape, Mr Pepys. I knows London like a Baptist knows the bible.'

The sound of leather reins on a horse's back rang through the cab and Pepys was thrown hard against the seat once more.

'Hold on tight, Will,' was all he managed to shout as the vehicle picked up speed, racing down Fleet Street.

Chapter 57

Above them, Mr Foster was shouting encouragement to the horse and lashing the reins across its back. 'Race on, hoss, race on.'

The horse seemed to hear the excitement in his master's voice. The carriage wheels bounced against the cobbled stones of Fleet Street. The newly built houses on either side flashed past in a blur of red brick, white walls and fresh paint.

Pepys leaned out of the window. The other Hackney was racing too. Blake was leaning out of the cab, the smile no longer fixed to his face. Pepys saw him shout something at the cabby but couldn't hear what it was.

The pedestrians; shoppers, merchants, hawkers, visitors or just people out for a morning stroll, heard the noise of the rattling wheels, the shouts of the cabbies and the beat of the horses hooves. They pressed themselves into the side of the road, jumping away from the racing carriages.

Pepys saw a few raised fists that blurred past.

'We is gaining on him, Mr Pepys. The hoss has got his racing shoes on.' Mr Foster let out a scream of delight and the carriage surged forward once more.

They were getting closer. Will pushed his head out of the window next to Pepys. The carriage was just twenty feet ahead now. Blake was shouting up at his cabby again. The man was looking over his shoulder at Mr Foster, wondering what kind of devil was after him.

Pepys looked ahead. They were getting near to the new Fleet Bridge and beyond that Ludgate Hill. A large cart overloaded with wooden planks was filling the centre of the bridge, creeping slowly forward as the carter manoeuvred his overladen cart on the narrow roadway.

They were abreast of Blake's carriage now. The cabbie was looking across at Mr Foster, and lashing his horse into even greater efforts.

A knife embedded itself in the wood an inch above Pepys' head. He saw Blake raise his arm to throw another. A malevolent smile etched into his face as he took aim.

'Whoa, whoa.' shouted Mr Foster urgently.

The carriage stopped racing forward, the wheels sliding and skidding across the dirt of the road, the end of the carriage shaking like the tail of a fish.

Pepys was thrown against Will, his head banging on the wooden side of the window.

He looked out to see the other cabby leaning back with all his might, trying to physically pull his horse to a stop. But they were already on the bridge.

The carter's eyes were open in disbelief, his hands limp at the reins. Blake's carriage fishtailed as the horse pulled left to avoid a crash.

The wheel caught the edge of the balustrade that bordered the bridge and shattered. The carriage rose in the air, turned sideways and toppled slowly into the Fleet, snapping the drive shaft as it fell.

The cabby was thrown up and out, his body rising to its apex and then falling back to the ground with a soft thud. Lying there motionless, his hat still on his head.

Pepys opened the door and rushed down to the bridge. The horse had stopped in front of the cart, its eyes wild with fear and excitement.

The Hackney was sinking gradually into the dark sludge that had once been a river called the Fleet, swallowed like a black snake devouring its prey. Only the bottom of the wheels now remained above the stinking mud.

People were gathering to watch the vanishing carriage. Someone had seized the reins of the horse and was gentling it to quietness. The carter was saying 'Nothing to do with me. Nothing to do with me,' over and over again.

He felt Will's presence at his side.

And then he saw it.

On the left bank was a body, strangely twisted, one leg missing.

Pepys jumped down to the bank, kneeling beside the man. Blake raised his right hand and whispered something.

Pepys lent in close, placing his ear next to the man's mouth.

'Naseby.'

That was what the man had said. Naseby.

The arm dropped down to the ground and the man's head twisted to the side. A small trickle of something black and evil ran from his lips and congealed on his beard.

'He's dead,' said Will.

'You do have an ability to state the obvious, Will.' Pepys patted down Blake's pockets, reached into the inside of his coat and pulled out a diamond locket. 'I believe this belongs to Elizabeth.' He passed it to Will. 'You will have the pleasure of returning it to her. I would give it a quick wipe, though. It was supposed to have been cleaned.'

Pepys reached into another pocket and pulled out a sheaf of papers. At the top of each sheet, Buckinghams's crest was crisply printed. At the bottom, his signature was scrawled in black ink, ending with a deliberately egotistical flourish. In between, the rest of the space was blank.

'That proves it,' said Will, 'he was working for Buckingham.'

'Actually, it proves exactly the opposite, Will.' Pepys stood up. 'We must leave, the King is waiting.'

'What about him?' Will pointed to the bent and twisted body of Mr Blake.

'As you so cogently put it, he's dead.'

Chapter 58

Samuel Pepys adjusted his periwig one last time, ensuring it fell across his shoulders in the manner proscribed by the latest fashion. 'Whatever happens, Will, I thank you for your friendship.'

'Don't talk like that, Sam, you have faced worse before.'

'When, pray?'

Will thought for a moment, 'The Commons debate on the Navy in '67.'

'A walk in Regent's Park compared to this, Will.'

'You do have a flair for the dramatic, Sam.'

'Because all the world's a stage, Will and we are just players on it.'

There was a hustle and bustle at the end of the corridor. The King appeared from nowhere followed by the Duke of York and an army of courtiers.

'It looks like the bell has rung for your performance,' whispered Will.

The King strolled towards them, chatting to the Duke. Sam and Will bowed low. He appeared not to have noticed them until as he was about to enter the chamber, he turned. 'Mr Pepys, you are about to report on your investigations in Chatham, are you not?'

'I am your Majesty.'

'I hope it is both brief and accurate. I can count on you?'

'As you would count on an abacus, your Majesty.'

There was a high-pitched giggle from the middle of the assembled courtiers.

'Was that a pleasantry, Mr Pepys? I hope your report is

as brief and as pleasant.'

'I will be no more than seven minutes, your Majesty.'

'So accurate, Mr Pepys. Well, I will time you, do not disappoint me.'

'I will not, your Majesty.'

'And good afternoon to you too, Mr…?'

'Hewer, your Majesty. Will Hewer.'

'Ah yes, the maker of things. Well, the one request that I have today, Mr Hewer, is that you make me happy.'

'I will try my best, your Majesty.'

'I can ask for no more. We will call for you when we are ready. My council, the Cabal, I think the people have taken to calling it, must be fed and watered first, lest they take bites out of each other.' The courtiers all tittered as expected.

A courtier opened the double doors to the Chamber. The King and the Duke of York strolled in, leaving the court to kick its heels in the corridor outside with Pepys and Will Hewer.

'He remembered me, Sam. The king remembered me.'

'Not your name, Will.'

'And he asked me to make him happy. We are going to make him happy, aren't we Sam?'

'That really depends how one defines happiness, Will.'

Their conversation was interrupted by a shout from the end of the corridor. Sir William Coventry was pushing his way through the courtiers to get to Pepys' side.

'I got your message, Mr Pepys.'

'Thank you, Sir William, I didn't think you were going to make it. I will need your help in there.' Pepys gestured towards the chamber.

'I don't know how welcome I will be. The King says he has forgiven me but one can never tell the capricious nature of monarchs.'

'But still you came?'

'I wouldn't miss it for the world. It's about time Buckingham received his just desserts.'

'I will call upon you, if I may. It will be clear when I would like you to speak.'

'Call away. I will be ready.'

The doors opened and the hubbub from the courtiers died down. All eyes turned to the servant dressed in blue brocade who stood in the middle of the open door. 'Mr Pepys. The King will see you now.'

Chapter 59

Pepys adjusted his periwig once more and strode through the door into a long corridor which opened out at the end to reveal a large chamber. He kept his head upright and his step firm and precise as he strode down the corridor, his feet echoing on the black and white checked marble floor. The footsteps of Will and Coventry made a counterpoint to his own, the sound repeating but out of step.

He turned the corner into the chamber at the end. Light streamed in through the large picture windows behind the King, circling and shading his head like a halo. In such a light, one could almost believe in the divine right of kings, he thought.

In front of him, the Cabal sat on the table with the King at its head, glasses of wine glinting like rubies on the table. Clifford, the Treasurer of the Household was closest to him, sitting next to Sir Joseph Williamson. Lord Arlington was next to the King, the black plaster across the top of his nose solid against the white skin. On the right, Lauderdale from Scotland was at the end, with the ginger wig of Cooper glinting like a copper nest in the sunlight, next to him. At the far end, closest to the King, Milord Buckingham sat still and unmoving.

Pepys bowed low, conscious that both Will and Sir William were also bowing just behind him.

'I don't believe I requested your presence, Sir William.' The King's eyes suddenly went from boredom to fire.

'I asked Sir William to come, your Majesty. He has aided me greatly in my investigations and his presence will help resolve the mystery surrounding this report.'

Pepys unwound from his bow and stood upright. The King was still sitting against the light, his face and expression hidden. A servant was pouring wine from a jug into the King's glass. He reached forward and lifted it as if in a toast. 'I do hope the unpleasantry between yourself and milord Buckingham has abated?'

'Myself and Lord Buckingham are fully at peace with each other, your Majesty. A storm in a wine glass that has now blown over.'

Buckingham raised his glass. 'Your Majesty, myself and Sir William are fully reconciled. We may never be friends but we certainly are not enemies.'

'Good. I don't expect my counsellors to love each other or love me, I have my mistresses for that.' The voice became harder, more commanding. 'But I do expect them to work together for the greater good of the Kingdom.' He took a long draught of wine from his glass. 'There. Enough speechifying from me. It is time to hear from Mr Pepys. I believe he was to report on the state of the dockyard and forts in Chatham and the south coast.'

'That is correct, your Majesty,' nodded Arlington.

'Time to begin, Mr Pepys.' Charles glanced at the clock standing against the wall. 'You said you would complete your report in seven minutes?'

'I did, your Majesty.'

'Well, the time starts now, Mr Pepys.'

'Thank you, your Majesty.' Pepys moved out of the light and into the shaded areas on the left behind Clifford and Sir Joseph. He noticed the Duke of York for the first time, leaning casually against the fireplace. He bowed deeply in his direction.

At last, he could now see everybody and judge their reactions. It would be important to see their faces as he delivered his report. He knew his fate was in their hands. They had to believe him or this evening he would either be in the Tower or dead. Elizabeth's face flashed in front of his eyes. He had treated her badly, wronged her. If he got out of this alive, he would keep his promise and take her to Paris to revisit the places she had so enjoyed in her youth. It would be his way of thanking her for her beauty and her fidelity. It was a shame that they didn't have children together, but it was God's wish that they did not.

'We are waiting, Mr Pepys, your time is wasting.'

Pepys lifted his head and spoke. 'Your Majesty and the Kingdom are in great danger. As we speak, forces are assembling intent on dethroning your Majesty and replacing him with another Lord Protector.'

'You exaggerate, Mr Pepys,' said Buckingham shaking his head and smiling smugly at the King.

'I fear I do not, Milord.'

'And who is this man who would be King?'

Pepys' eyes swept across the room, taking in all the seated counsellors and the Duke of York leaning against the fireplace. 'He is here in this room amongst us. He is one of us.'

Chapter 60

The room erupted as everybody started speaking at once. Only the King remained quiet, twirling his moustache with the ends of his fingers dipped in wine. Eventually, even he grew tired of the noise.

'Mr Pepys.'

'Yes, your Majesty.'

'May I remind you that you have just six minutes and fifteen seconds left.'

'I am aware, your Majesty,' said Pepys bowing from the waist.

'May I also remind you that accusing his Majesty's ministers of treason is a capital offence.'

'I am also aware that I am risking my head, your Majesty.'

'Do not risk it too much. It sits rather prettily beneath your periwig at the moment. It wouldn't look so good sitting beneath the arch of London Bridge.'

'May I explain myself, your Majesty?'

'Please proceed, you have but six minutes left to save your neck. I would talk quickly if I were you.'

'I will take your advice, your Majesty.' Pepys bowed once more. He stood up and walked behind Lord Arlington, facing Buckingham. 'The good Lord here and Sir Joseph Williamson,' he placed his hands on the chair backs of both men, 'asked me to look into the affairs of Chatham Dockyard in secret.

Unfortunately, my mission was known to everyone before I had even begun. You, Mr Cooper,' he pointed at the ginger wig facing him, 'made it very clear that I should report back that the Catholics were involved in stirring up trouble. I am sorry to tell you that I found no such Catholic ferment. In fact, the religion involved is a sworn enemy of Catholicism.'

'How dare you?' shouted Cooper. 'I did not want you to present a prejudiced report, but merely to find out the truth as we have done regarding the recent Great Fire. The Catholics and their acolytes most certainly started it.'

'I don't think they did, Mr Cooper.'

The face beneath the ginger wig smiled, showing some ugly teeth, stained as ginger as the wig. 'The Lord Mayor and the people of London beg to differ, Mr Pepys.'

'I regret to say I do not agree with them, Mr Cooper.' The man opposite was about to interrupt again but Pepys moved to stand behind the King and carry on speaking. 'As for Sir Joseph and Lord Arlington, they see plots everywhere, committed by everybody.'

'That's because there are plots everywhere, Mr Pepys.' Sir Joseph spoke in his usual unhurried drawl.

'In this case, you were both correct. There was a plot to kill the King and seize the throne.'

Again the room dissolved into a storm of accusations and shouts coming from every member. The King raised his arm once again and it gradually subsided. 'You have made that accusation before Mr Pepys, but have yet to put any evidence forward to support it. May I remind you that you have now less than five minutes left?'

Pepys bowed. 'I will endeavour to speak more quickly, your Majesty.'

'I would if I were you. Long windedness bores me and I am not a pleasant person when I am bored.'

'I will continue, your Majesty. Only you, Milord Buckingham, did not tell me how to write my report. I fear it was beneath you to do so. However, you have often accused the Dutch of seeking to undermine the crown, wanting to repeat their successes of two years ago.' He pinched his bottom lip between his index finger and thumb. 'I am sorry to report my Lord, that I found no such involvement. They may be waiting for England to fall into chaos and anarchy but they are not actively encouraging the dethronement of his Majesty.'

'So you didn't find anything, Mr Pepys?' said Buckingham.

'On the contrary, My Lord, I found a dockyard rife with corruption and malfeasance, encouraged by the Commissioner and his assistant, Fridley . A Preacher creating an army to replace your Majesty on the throne by King Jesus.'

'I thought we had rid the Nation of these Fifth Monarchists, Sir Joseph?'

'Apparently not, your Majesty. There are plots everywhere.'

'So you keep telling me. Pray continue, Mr Pepys. But let me warn you, your time is running out.'

Pepys cleared his throat. 'An armoury whose weaponry had been seized by an insurrectionist band of disaffected soldiers and sailors, led by Quilt and Daly. They are, as we speak, preparing to march on London to dethrone his Majesty. This band has been financed and led by one of the men in this room.' Pepys thrust out his arm and pointed at each of the men in turn.

The King slammed his fist down on the table, shaking the glasses and the carafe. 'That is the last time you will make that accusation without proof, do I make myself clear?'

'You do, your Majesty. I will now provide the proof.'

'Good, you have less than four minutes to convince

me and I am not a man that is easily convinced of anything.'

'What your Majesty does not know is that the day before I was sent on my mission to Chatham, a diary was stolen from my closet in Seething Lane. A diary containing some unfortunate injudicious comments regarding certain personages here present.'

The King smiled.

Pepys moved quickly on. 'The thief has been threatening me with publication of those comments.'

'Given your presence, it seems that you are to appear in the broadsheets, Mr Pepys.' said Buckingham

'That's the point, Milord. He wants me to report everything to the King.'

'I don't understand, Mr Pepys.'

'Neither did I, Milord, until recently. Let me explain.'

'I wish you would, Pepys.' The King yawned and signalled for another glass of wine.

He reached into a pocket in his waistcoat and produced a silver button. 'Do you recognise this?' He passed it over to Buckingham who glanced at it quickly.

'My crest. My servants all wear clothes with buttons like these.' He turned towards the King. 'A mere affectation, your Majesty. It amuses me to advertise the ownership of my servants.'

'The button you are holding was found in the hand of a dead man. The man who had stolen my diary.'

'Really Pepys, you should take better care of your books,' said Arlington.

The men seated around the table laughed.

'But that's not all. The same evening I went to the Theatre to see Dryden's new play, Tyrannic Love.'

'I've heard Nell is quite good in it,' said the King to

Buckingham.

'She is, Charles, I've seen her myself.'

'Not as much as his Majesty has seen of her, I'll wager,' said the Duke of York laughing and coughing at the same time.

'At the end of the play, she spoke some lines about me. Dryden indicated he was paid by you, Milord, to write the lines.'

Buckingham slammed his glass down on the table. 'That is a damned lie. I will not be spoken to like this by a pipsqueak of a clerk from the Navy Board.'

Out of the corner of his eye Pepys saw Sir William walk slowly to the fireplace and join the Duke of York there.

'There is more, my Lord. My assistant, Mr Hewer, was abducted and stabbed. After being thrown from a coach into the street, he had the presence of mind to look back at it and saw a device painted on the rear. The same device as appears on the button. Your device, my Lord.'

'For a man who has been abducted and stabbed, you look remarkably well, Mr Hewer.'

Will bowed low. 'Thank you, your Majesty. I was merely stabbed in the leg.'

'Are you accusing me of abducting and stabbing your servant, Mr Pepys?'

'I'm his assistant, not his servant.'

Buckingham stared at Will Hewer as if he were something that was stuck to his shoe and did not smell very pleasant.

'Finally, my Lord, this letter was procured by one of Sir Joseph's agents, from the leader of the Fifth Monarchists. It contains details for an insurrection in Chatham followed by a march on London and an opening of the Medway for Dutch ships.'

'Treason.'

'Yes, your Majesty. The letter is written on my Lord Buckingham's notepaper.'

'I know nothing of this, your Majesty, it's a forgery.'

For the first time, a bead of sweat appeared on Buckingham's forehead. He leant forward as if to beseech the King.

'Taken individually this proof may not be substantial, but taken together, it does provide condemning evidence, does it not?'

'It's all lies, your Majesty. I know nothing of these letters. They are all forgeries.'

'But you do have experience writing plays, do you not, Buckingham?' Sir William had spoken from the fireplace.

All the other members of the council were staring at Buckingham. The King spoke first. 'Do you have anything to say, my Lord?'

'Your Majesty, I…these are all forgeries. Believe me, when I say I had nothing to do with them.'

The King looked down his long aquiline nose at the abject figure of his childhood friend.

There was a sudden shift of mood in the room. Pepys could see the other members of the Cabal lean away from Buckingham. It was as if the man was alone in his small pocket of space, isolated from anybody else.

Pepys walked over to stand behind Lord Arlington, staring across the table at Buckingham. 'I believe you, my lord.'

'But…but, you've just said that I was guilty.'

'What game are you playing, Pepys?'

Chapter 61

'Your Majesty, I simply said that all this evidence pointed in the direction of my Lord Buckingham. But, it struck me that it was all a little too obvious. My Lord is a clever man, but to allow his servant to leave a button in the hand of somebody he had just murdered? I think not. And to send detailed instructions for an insurrection on headed notepaper? Even he would not be so stupid or so careless. As for my assistant, he saw the device on the back of the coach but it is a simple matter to paint a piece of wood, is it not? And then hang it on the back of any twopenny coach.'

'It's fourpence.' Lauderdale had spoken in his thick Scottish accent.

'What is, my Lord?'

'A coach.'

'Thank you, my Lord, I am corrected.' Pepys bowed low. 'A fourpenny coach.' He pinched his bottom lip once more and carried on speaking. 'Finally, the poet laureate may know his way around an iambic pentameter, but his knowledge of the truth is, how shall we say, a little more haphazard. His desperate need for money has probably bought his tongue.'

'Wrack him. He'll soon by speaking words full of truth. And he won't have to go on the stage to do it.'

'That will not be necessary, Lord Arlingtom. I have already ascertained who was behind all of this. You see it soon became apparent to myself and Mrs Behn…'

'Mrs Behn?'

'One of Sir Joseph's agents, your Majesty.'

'You employ women in your work, Sir Joseph?'

'They make by far the best agents, your Majesty. Many

a secret is spilled alongside the spilling of semen.'

'You have a very indelicate way of phrasing it, Sir Joseph, true though it may be. Pray continue with your tale, Mr Pepys,' he glanced at the clock, 'you have less than a minute left to convince me.'

'As I was saying, your Majesty, it soon became apparent that all these clues were a little too obvious in pointing directly at Lord Buckingham. It was almost as if his Lordship was being targeted. I asked myself who would benefit most from a report from me that he was involved in a plot against you? Of all the people here, only one hated him so much to frame him for murder and treason.

Pepys watched as Sir William slid his hand into his pocket. He decided to plunge on regardless. After all, he only had his head to lose.

'And that person is?'

'Sir William Coventry, your Majesty.'

They all turned to stare at Sir William. His face remained composed and calm.

'Samuel, after all I have done, you would slander me so?'

'You asked me to find the truth. 'To do my job' I think were your exact words. Well, I have done it.'

Sir William advanced towards the King with his arms held out to his sides. 'Your Majesty, I'm afraid Mr Pepys has overstepped himself, making accusations against myself and Lord Buckingham that he cannot substantiate.'

'Have you any proof, Mr Pepys?'

Pepys turned and spoke to Will. 'Please fetch Mr Blake, Will.'

Will stood there, his eyes blinking rapidly before he finally nodded his head and marched across the room, vanishing from sight down the corridor.

Pepys heard the door open. Then the soft slide following by a hollow thump as the footsteps of a one-legged man hit the marble floor. The sound became louder and louder, echoing across the room with every step.

Sir William took two steps closer to the King. 'Mr Blake is a disaffected servant. I released him three weeks ago because of his unsatisfactory performance. Of course, he will support Pepys' allegations.'

The sound was even louder now.

Slide and thump.

Slide and thump.

Slide and thump.

Then, just as it was about to enter the chamber, the sound stopped.

Pepys stepped forward. 'May I present, Mr Blake, your Majesty.'

Sir William reached into his pocket and pulled out a small bound volume. 'As for the character of my accuser, it can be seen plainly in his own words written in secret in his diary.' He held up the diary for everybody in the room to see.

'Is that your diary, Mr Pepys?'

'It is, your Majesty. Purloined from my closet by a thief called Jack Turner.'

Sir William opened the diary at a marked page and read from a paper inserted between the leaves. 'Here is what he says about your Majesty. '...everybody does nowadays reflect upon Oliver and commend him, so brave things did he make and commend him for them.' He lifted his head and sighed theatrically. 'He praises the late dictator in no uncertain fashion, your Majesty, and then goes on to compound his offence, '...that it is a miracle what way a man could devise to lose so much in so little time.' The man, in this case, being your Majesty.' Sir William flicked through the pages of the diary. 'There is more to read that will offend your Majesty's ears and the rest of this august assembly. This man,' he pointed at Pepys, 'is a traitor who practises horrible calumny on the reputation of his Majesty.'

A smile appeared on the King's face. 'He seems to have my character down to a T.'

'As for you my Lord Buckingham, he is even more cutting.' He looked down and found his translation of the text. 'This will make the world think that the King has good councillors about him, when the Duke of Buckingham, the greatest man about him, is a fellow of no more sobriety than to fight about a whore.'

'Are these your words, Mr Pepys?' asked Buckingham.

'I'm afraid they are, my Lord.'

The King coughed. A quiet cough, a subtle cough. 'And we have enjoyed them immensely. Sir Joseph was always efficient in providing me with copies of your previous writings, Mr Pepys, along with those of Mr Evelyn and various others, including you, Sir William.'

Pepys' jaw opened wide, dropping to rest on his chest.

Sir Joseph spoke up. 'It was hardly a secret, Mr Pepys. A Lieutenant in the Navy first reported it to us in '62. It has been relatively easy to obtain copies of it from your home and your office in the Navy Board since then. Normal practise, you understand. Monitoring people. Allows us to find out what people are really thinking. You were most correct in reporting your conversations, Mr Pepys. And as for your various marital indiscretions, well, I'm sure we are all grown men here.'

'I always enjoyed your adventures, Mr Pepys. Thought

about writing a diary myself for a long while, but Sir Joseph counselled against it. A king does not reveal his secrets even to himself.'

'I will take the diary, Sir William.' Lord Arlington held his hand out.

'But...but, that can't be true, I was the only one who knew about the diary. Pepys told me so.'

'You and half of fashionable London, I'm afraid.' Lord Arlington thrust his hand out and took the diary from Sir William's grasp.

'You all knew?'

'I'm afraid so, Mr Pepys. Sometimes, the protection of the State can interfere with the privacy of the individual. It is one of the conundrums of modern life. What is secret and what is not?'

'You can ask Mr Blake to come forward now, Mr Pepys.'

'I have a confession to make, your Majesty.'

'I thought as much.' The King raised his voice and shouted towards the corridor.

'Come forward, Mr Blake.'

A man stepped into the chamber. 'I thought you said I wasn't to enter, Mr Pepys?'

'Mr Betterton, not on the stage this evening?'

The actor bowed low. 'I am, your Majesty, Mr Pepys asked me to create a private performance at noon. However, I didn't know that you were to be in the audience.'

'Bravo, Mr Betterton,' the King clapped his hands, 'one of your better performances and without a word spoken.'

'Did I do it correctly, Mr Pepys? I thought of making the slide longer but one doesn't want to overplay it. Can't over-egg the pudding.'

'You were perfect, Mr Betterton. Thank you for your time.' He turned back to the King. 'I apologise for the subterfuge, your Majesty, but it was necessary for Sir William to reveal himself.'

'It wasn't Blake?' Coventry spluttered.

'No, Sir William, Mr Blake died this morning.'

'A wonderful piece of theatre, Mr Pepys, quite charming. Luckily, you were here to stage it.'

'I believe luck had nothing to do with it, your Majesty. Sir William wanted me to report to you today.'

'But the fight this morning, the soldiers on the bridge…' stammered Will.

'All as staged as our play, with Mr Betterton. It was all too easy; the escape from the cellar, the failed ambush, the soldiers allowing us to pass just as we were about to be discovered. Even I couldn't have such luck. We were always meant to escape. Sir William knew the more difficult he made it to report, the more I would ensure that I did.' He spoke to Coventry. 'The others were meant to die this morning, I was the only one who would escape, isn't that true, Sir William?'

'You were always a clever little tailor's son, Pepys. You should have kept to your sewing.'

'I have one question.' The King raised his hand. 'Why did Sir William go to all these lengths to ferment a rebellion and then want you to reveal it?'

'I think I can answer that, your Majesty. It troubled me for a long time. And then, Mr Hewer said something that helped me understand.'

'I did?'

'You did, Will. You said that, where Elizabeth was concerned, you always felt like a white knight coming to her rescue. It set me thinking. What if Sir William were positioning himself as a white knight, ready to come to the rescue of the throne? After all, you were faced with a rebellion by Lord Buckingham and by the inability of your closest advisors, Lord Arlington and Sir Joseph, to know what was going on. I think you may find the details of the plot in Sir William's pocket, waiting to be revealed.'

Coventry clamped his hand over the pocket of his coat 'Pepys, how could you betray me so?' He turned to the King and held his arms out. 'Your Majesty, I beseech you…'

'Search him, Sir Joseph.'

The head of the King's secret agents reached into Coventry's pocket and pulled out a large sheaf of papers. 'They seem to be details of the plot in Chatham and London, my Lord.'

'Your Majesty, I beg you…'

'Beseech all you will, Sir William, but this audience is over. Sir Joseph, kindly arrange for this man to spend a few days in one of the bedroom's in the palace whilst we decide his fate.'

'Of course, your Majesty.'

'As for you, Mr Pepys, I thank you for your report.' He turned towards Arlington. 'I believe you need to despatch troops to Chatham, Arlington, to arrest the Preacher and the Commissioner.'

'It will be done, your Majesty.'

'Do it quietly and with the minimum of force. I do not want the sheep who were led astray to be savaged by our wolves.'

'As you command, your Majesty.' Arlington bowed low.

'Good. I think we are adjourned. I believe I have a game of tennis that requires my attention.' He stood up and strolled out of the chamber. Just as he was about to enter the corridor, he turned and spoke directly to Pepys. 'Oh, one more thing. No more diaries. I wouldn't like your words to get you into trouble again.'

'As you command, your Majesty.'

The King strolled down the corridor to be greeted raucously by his courtiers as the door was opened for him.

The last words that Pepys heard were from his Majesty. 'That was a tedious meeting. Time for a little exercise. Do you have the balls, Rochester?'

He didn't hear the reply, just the laughter of the courtiers

.

Chapter 62

'You have done well, Mr Pepys.'

'Thank you, Sir Joseph. It wasn't a pleasant duty. I have long admired Sir William and his work.' Pepys stared across at Sir Joseph Williamson sitting opposite him. He was in the same room where, just one week before, he had been told to go to Chatham and report on the dockyard. It was still as bare as before with just the expansive wooden desk sitting in front of the large sash windows and two hard back chairs. So much had happened in one week, but still some things remained unclear. 'I have one question, Sir Joseph.'

'Ask away, I do believe I owe you that much.'

'You knew all about the rebellion in Chatham, didn't you?'

Sir Joseph Williamson smiled like a cat who had just seen a young sparrow hop in front of him. 'Of course, we knew. The one thing about the Fifth Monarchists is their inability to keep anything secret. They have the dubious desire to shout 'King Jesus' from every pulpit. It makes them very easy to spot even in a crowd of Presbyterians, Anabaptists, and assorted other sects and practises.'

'So if you knew all about them, why did you need me?'

'That's two questions, Mr Pepys.' Sir Joseph stroked his long nose and continued on in his lazy drawl. 'We didn't know who was funding them and how they were doing it. Mrs Behn had infiltrated their meetings but she had not been able to discover their leader.'

'The finger pointed straight at Lord Buckingham.'

'We would probably have taken that at face value. After Mrs Behn reported the discovery of the letter.'

Pepys coughed loudly.

'You are surprised that she reported everything to me? You forget sir, she was in my employ. After the discovery of the letter, we had Lord Buckingham followed but saw nothing out of the ordinary. Nonetheless, we would have arrested him if you hadn't pointed out the real culprit. How could you be so certain it was Sir William who was behind everything?'

'I wasn't certain, that was why I had to arrange the little play we enjoyed earlier. There were a few clues that pointed in his direction however.'

'And they were?'

'Firstly, Sir William was the only person I had confided in about the diary.'

'But we all knew about it. I'm afraid to say I have been reading and enjoying it for the last ten years.'

'That does distress me, that my secrets should be such common knowledge.'

'Nothing is truly secret, Mr Pepys.' Sir Joseph's voice had a harder edge to it. 'What else led you to suspect Sir William?'

'The letter.'

'The one to the Preacher from the leader of the plot?'

'Exactly. It had a peculiar smell to it. The aroma of lemon verbena. Very singular. The only person who used such a sweet smelling powder to dry his ink was Sir William. It was one of his affectations.'

'Is that all?'

'One more thing he said made me think. I told him about the death of Jack Turner…'

'The thief?'

'He mentioned that he had been stabbed, but I only told him that he was murdered.

Somebody else must have told him the details of the killing.'

'His servant, John Black.'

'Exactly. What will happen to Sir William?'

'The King has a soft spot for him, given his service with the King's father and his efforts during the restoration. He will be allowed to quietly spend the rest of his days on his country estates. As an MP, he will be permitted to speak in Parliament, but have no role in government. The King is firmly set against him ever returning.' Sir Joseph scratched his nose once again. 'A shame. A man of remarkable talents.'

'But what about the murder of Jack Turner?'

'What of it? A thief died and the man who killed him died, too. That was a master stroke of yours, asking your servant, Mr Hewer to fetch a man who was already dead.'

'We had to drive Sir William out into the open. There was no real evidence against him. '

'Except for the testimony of Blake?'

'Who unfortunately had already died and thus was unable to speak.'

'A fabulous deception, Mr Pepys. I must use it myself one day. I feel, and Mrs Behn agrees, that you have a predilection for our line of work.'

'I think not, Sir Joseph. I enjoyed the solving of the puzzle but I'm afraid duplicitousness does not come naturally to me. No offence meant.'

'And no offence taken, Mr Pepys. Needs must, as some poet or other once said.'

'Lydgate.'

'I'm sorry?'

'Jonathan Lydgate. 'He must needs go that the devil drives.'

'Quite so, Mr Pepys. And the devil in this case compels us to protect the King and his Kingdom whatever the consequences to ourselves. And speaking of consequences, you have made a few enemies, Mr Pepys.'

'Have I?'

'Mr Cooper is angry that you have managed to disrupt his plans to blame the Catholics for the troubles in Chatham. He is building a parliamentary base that needs something to hate and despise.'

'It is always easier to play on fears than to build hopes.'

'Quite so, Mr Pepys. I fear that you have destroyed his hopes and now he will play on your fears. You have made an enemy there. Mr Cooper is quick to blame and slow to forgive. In addition…'

'There's more.'

'My Lord Buckingham was made to look a fool.'

'But I stopped him from being arrested for treason.'

'Nobody enjoys being made to look a fool. Especially not when he has as high an opinion of himself as Lord Buckingham. And to appear so foolish in front of the King, well, you can understand why he might not smile kindly upon you.'

'But I saved his life…'

Sir Joseph shrugged his shoulders. 'The nobility places much store in their pride.'

'And to owe a favour to a commoner such as myself, a tailor's son, affronts that pride.'

'There, you have it in a nutshell, Mr Pepys. Two enemies that I would not like to have in London.'

'What do you suggest I do, Sir Joseph?'

'Well, you do hint in your diary that you have long planned a trip to France with your wife…'

'She has always wanted to revisit Paris.'

‘What better time to do so. It would take you out of the capital for three months and allow my noble Lords to quietly forget their anger and their embarrassment.’

‘But what of my post in the Navy Board?’

‘I’m sure a leave of absence could be arranged. Pressure of work, an ailing relative on your wife’s side. You know the sort of excuses that could be made. The post will be kept open for you when you return, the King would see to it.’

‘It does seem the right time to go and it would make Elizabeth so happy.’

‘There is one other matter that we need to resolve.’ He slowly reached down and opened a drawer. ‘I think this is yours.’ He handed across the diary.

‘Thank you, Sir Joseph, I thought I would never see it again.’

‘I particularly enjoyed my own appearances in the pages, Pepys. It gave me much hilarity to read about myself in such terms. ’

‘I do apologise. My pen runs away with me sometimes.’

‘Not at all, Mr Pepys, I think it is quite accurate and not a little flattering. But, no more diaries, don’t you agree? This one has done enough damage already.’

‘No more diaries, Sir Joseph. This is the last.’

*

Will was waiting for Pepys in a carriage outside the Palace. ‘Thank god, you are safe. I thought you were going to be arrested and thrown in the Tower.’

‘And why would Sir Joseph do that, Will? The matter has been resolved, the plotters arrested, and I even have my diary returned.’ He held up the book for Will to see. ‘All we have to do now is return the locket to Elizabeth's possession and the world will be returned back to its equilibrium.'

'I'd forgotten about the locket. You wife will be happy to see it again.'

'She will be delighted and I will give you the opportunity of returning it to her. After all, you did give it in the first place.'

'I couldn't do that, Sam.'

'You can and you will, Will. Let us speak no more on it. Mr Foster, Seething Lane, if you please.'

'You sure you don't wanna go to see an 'anging, sirs. If you don't wanna go to Tyburn, one of the other cabbies told me there's another on at the Tower. It's a special bill with the highlight being a woman. I always finks a woman dangles and dances right pretty on the gallows.'

'And I suppose your cousin has retained some seats for us?'

'No, sir. He's got the concession at Tyburn. It's my sister that runs the Tower.'

'You seem to have the hangings of London in your pocket, Mr Foster.'

'Nah, sir, but we is a sporting family. Loves a bit of entertainment, we does.'

'Unfortunately, we will have to forego the pleasure of seeing a woman hang. Seething Lane, if you please.'

Pepys pushed Will into the cabin. He heard the cabby's mouth click the horse away from its oats. The carriage rolled forward as the old horse clopped his way down the street. Above his head, he heard Mr Foster muttering away.

'Dunno what's wrong wiv people today. Don't wanna go to an 'anging. Well, I never heard the likes of it. A good ‘angings the best entertainment there is.’

‘We’ve disappointed him again.’

‘Such is life, Will.’

Chapter 63

Pepys walked into his purple closet and sat down at his desk. He took his diary out of his pocket and placed it in front of him.

The return to Seething Lane had gone well. Will had been his usual charming self, returning the locket to Elizabeth once more.

'But it looks just the same as before, Will.'

'It's supposed to look the same as before, Elizabeth. That's the whole point of having it polished.' Will had winked at him over Elizabeth's shoulder. He would have to watch Mr Hewer from now on, the man had become an accomplished teller of falsehoods. So different from the diffident friend who had started out on their adventure.

Elizabeth had been delighted when he told her they would be going to Paris as soon as the arrangements could be made. Prancing gaily around the room, practising her French and talking of learning new songs and dances from French men. He had become fiercely jealous when he heard her speak. A visit from that black cloud that sometimes troubled him. But her joy and enthusiasm had soon dissipated that dark mist. He would have to watch her carefully in Paris though. Far too much temptation in that city.

He picked up his quill and opened the diary to the entry for the 31 May 1669, flattening down the spine with his left hand.

What was he to write? Obviously, the truth was out of the question. Sir Joseph and his agents were sure to check.

Something anodyne, not too harsh and not to honest. Something he could read later and read between the lines.

His mind flashed back to the image of Daly holding the knife inches away from his eyes, its blade glinting in the candlelight of the church.

He began to write, using the same code that he had employed for the last ten years;

And thus ends all that I doubt I shall ever be able to do with my own eyes in the keeping of my journal, I being not able to do it any longer, having done now so long as to undo my eyes almost every time that I take a pen in my hand.

A smile crossed his lips. He would know what it meant, even if nobody else did.

He scattered a little talc across the page and sealed it with his blotter. He took one last look at the words written, and closed the book. That chapter of his life was now over. It was time to start a new, more adventurous career. One that suited his personality and his abilities far better.

It was time to become Samuel Pepys, Investigator.

If you enjoyed *Samuel Pepys and the Stolen Diary* check out Endeavour Press's other books here: http://endeavourpress.com/

For weekly updates on our free and discounted eBooks http://endeavourpress.com/

Follow us on *Twitter* @ endeavourpress
and *Goodreads* https://www.goodreads.com/user/show/19286592-endeavour-press.

Printed in Great Britain
by Amazon

44516153R00212